Jake hurried out the door into the sunlight—and into the outstretched arms of several members of the local militia.

"Jake Gibbs, I arrest you on charges of spying for His Majesty the King."

There was a note of reverence in the man's voice when he mentioned George III. Jake didn't have time to point out how unseemly that sounded coming from a patriot, however, for a soldier immediately flung a chain around his shoulders and tugged him to the ground. Jake tried to protest, but a thick fist slammed into the side of his head and knocked him unconscious . . .

Jake Gibbs, Patriot Spy:
from St. Martin's Paperbacks

BOOK I: THE SILVER BULLET
BOOK II: THE IRON CHAIN
(COMING IN NOVEMBER)

hope you
like it

can't to see

you!

THE SILVER BULLET

JIM DeFELICE

■ SMP ■
ST. MARTIN'S PAPERBACKS

THE SILVER BULLET

Copyright © 1995 by Jim DeFelice.

All rights reserved. No part of this book may be used or reproduced in any manner whatsoever without written permission except in the case of brief quotations embodied in critical articles or reviews. For information address St. Martin's Press, 175 Fifth Avenue, New York, N.Y. 10010.

ISBN: 0-312-95570-7

Printed in the United States of America

St. Martin's Paperbacks edition/July 1995

10 9 8 7 6 5 4 3 2 1

Introduction

Last summer my wife Debra and I visited my uncle George and aunt Vera, who live on the remains of a farm in the Hudson Valley. The property came into the Irish-American side of the family sometime just before the Revolutionary War. It's mostly a subdivision now, except for their early eighteenth-century house and a structure dug into the side of a hill that was once used as a root cellar.

We did the barbecue thing in the afternoon, cooking up hot dogs and debating whether Sam Adams qualifies as a microbrewer. Lunch over and the women talking about relatives' baby showers, my uncle winked and said he wanted to show me something.

Normally when he does that, it means he's managed to smuggle some single-malt Scotch into the root cellar, so I grabbed my beer and followed him there.

"Your aunt got out of control with the spring cleaning," he explained, "and threatened to throw out all my sports stuff."

By "sports stuff" my uncle was referring to one of the world's most enviable collections of memorabilia relating to the New York Yankees and football Giants. There is, for instance, a hot dog wrapper from Don Larsen's perfect World Series game in 1956, and a pool cue touched by Lawrence Taylor in a Tampa Bay sports bar the night before Super Bowl XXV. Priceless artifacts.

"It's all safe in here," he added quickly, "but look what I found." He reached down and pulled up first one stone and then another, piling the thin slate slabs neatly on the side to reveal a long-hidden trap door.

At the foot of the creaky, dilapidated stairs, a dirt-encrusted bottle with a cork stopper and metal cage on top was thrust into my hands. I looked at it doubtfully, and only reluctantly took the pliers my uncle handed me.

The cork flew off with a pop.

"Try it. Go on."

Dubious does not begin to describe my attitude. Yet with the first sip, I knew I was drinking some very, very special beer.

"It's two hundred years old if it's a day," he said. "There's a hundred bottles here at least, and they're older than the hills.

"That isn't the half of it," he added as I took another sip. "Look at these papers."

My uncle held the lantern up to reveal a cavernous underground room, filled with bundles and bundles of yellowing parchment. He reached to the nearest pile and handed me a packet that had already been opened.

And so began my acquaintanceship with Jake Gibbs, hero of the American Revolution.

I haven't had a chance to examine most of the manuscripts yet—the papers are very old and must be handled delicately—but each bundle appears to be a separate portion of Gibbs' history. By all appearances, the tales were written during the Revolution itself, though it's difficult to tell if they were intended as a true history or a somewhat fictionalized tale, as James Fenimore Cooper's *The Spy* is of Enoch Crosby's adventures. Jake Gibbs appears in no history or document of the Revolution that I could discover, but many of the other characters and certainly the locales do, and the general historical layout seems correct.

Thus far I have been unable to learn anything about the author. I'm tempted to make certain favorable parallels to the works of such later American writers as Washington Irving and Cooper, though I suppose I'll be accused of favoritism if he turns out to be an ancestor. On the other hand, the writer has an annoying habit of stopping the narrative in midstream while he delivers a lecture on the local politics or the superiority of rifled barrels over smoothbores.

Nonetheless, I found the story in that first manuscript, and in the others that I have examined, amusing, just the kind of tale to while away a summer afternoon or a winter evening. And so, with my uncle's encouragement and the help of my agent and editor, I am here presenting a much-trimmed, somewhat freely translated version of what we found. I've substituted modern names and language for some of the more quaint and obscure turns of phrase where it seemed appropriate, but otherwise tried to keep the tone of the original.

The events unfold during the spring of 1777—difficult months for the American Cause, as the author would style it. Washington had been chased from New York City the previous fall, and despite some celebrated but in truth limited victories, his army had spent a hard and destitute winter. In the North, the redcoats had kicked the Americans out of Canada and had been stopped from attacking Fort Ticonderoga only by the approach of winter. A strong push by General Howe in New York and Burgoyne in Canada—but I'll let you read the story for yourself.

Jim DeFelice
Chester, N.Y.

THE SILVER BULLET

THE
SILVER
BULLET

One

Wherein, the hero is quickly introduced, and just as quickly confronts dangers of miscellaneous nature.

Late May 1777

Jake Stewart Gibbs stepped through the finely carpentered doorway and was immediately hooked around the neck. With a sharp yank he was dragged inside the upstairs room of the small inn on the northern outskirts of Albany.

Taken by surprise but far from bested, Jake used only a portion of his strength as sham resistance until he could map a counterattack. It was soon done: Kicking the door closed to cut off any pursuers, he lunged forward. The momentum of his lean, six-foot-two frame pushed himself and his assailant face first onto the large feather bed, which after all wasn't that horrible a place to be.

"So I see you've missed me."

"You told me you'd be back in a week," answered his captor. "I've waited all this time."

"Two years?"

"Nearly."

"You never got my letters?"

"Not one," she said, a little too quickly to be believed.

"But I heard you were engaged." Jake paused to take advantage of his situation with a kiss. He'd spent the entire day riding from Kingston, hoping Sarah Thomas's lips were as full and warm as he remembered.

They were.

"Oh, that wasn't a real engagement," said Sarah. "He was a Tory. I accepted his proposal as a diversion. It was a plot."

"I see."

"I was trying on your profession," she said, reaching up to unbutton the top of Jake's waistcoat. The round disks were cut into twelve-pointed stars that caught slightly as she slipped them between the vest's felt-faced holes. The buttons were not merely fashionable; their design was a clandestine signal to a small coterie of patriots that the sharply dressed young man leaning on the bed was an officer of the special services—a spy, to use the vernacular, though the word covers but a tenth of the activities he pursued in the name of Liberty. Jake Gibbs's adventures in New York and the Jerseys this past month and a half alone were literally the equivalent and worth of three brigades: the first had been saved because his intelligence helped it avoid an ambush, the second was not needed for his single-handed capture of a high-ranking British officer traveling behind the lines to Philadelphia, and the third had been freed from prison through his planning and leadership of a daring midnight raid on a small town near Brunswick.

Jake Gibbs's service to Major General Nathanael Greene, and through Greene to General Washington himself, had covered a wide swath of territory and circumstance since he joined the Rhode Islander after the disastrous 1775 winter campaign in Canada. But the only territory he was interested in exploring right now sat immediately in front of him.

"You know I could never marry a Loyalist," said Sarah, pouting as she looked into Jake's deeply blue eyes to see if he had taken her seriously. "He was a traitor, and I helped the Committee arrest him. Johnny would have been proud."

Her light spirits dipped ever so slightly. Sarah, barely twenty, was already a widow; her young husband John Thomas had been left for dead on the Canadian battlefield. The rout was so complete his burial had to be left to the enemy.

Jake had not only been at that battle; he had watched Captain Thomas go down. An agent and scout for General Montgomery, he was wounded himself trying to reach him. Evacuated to Albany following the fiasco,

Jake had been nursed back to health by Sarah. Afterward, they had provided each other with some solace.

"You've grown more beautiful than my imagination allowed," said Jake, brushing her cheek gently. She smiled and kissed him, her breasts overflowing the loosely strung bodice of her nightshirt as she leaned forward on the bed.

Jake rose and pulled off his coat and vest, carefully folding them on the small chest. Sarah kneeled on the bed and put her arms on his back, helping him loosen his shirt.

"When I saw you come into the tavern and talk to Father," she whispered, twirling a lock of his blond ponytail around her finger, "I knew you would come upstairs to look for me. I took off my clothes and waited."

"And what will we do if your father comes up the stairs?"

"You'll have to marry me, I suppose."

Jake had meant the question to be entirely rhetorical, and dodged her very specific answer by turning and kissing her firmly. Then he sat and started to pull off his boots. Sarah slid to the floor to assist. His cares flew off with his socks as she rubbed the muscles of his thigh and calf. He leaned back, inviting her to loosen the belt of his britches.

But as always for Jake Gibbs, trouble was lurking outside the door. In this instance, at least, it was polite enough to knock.

"Oh no, my father," yelped Sarah, grabbing for a blanket to pull over herself as she ducked behind a nearby wardrobe.

"Who is it?" Jake asked calmly. He was answered by the smack of the thick door swinging back against the wall. Two young men dressed in hunting clothes stood on the threshold, long rifles in their arms.

"Jake Gibbs?" demanded the one in front, a boy of sixteen or seventeen.

"Perhaps," Jake replied, leaning back on the bed with a slightly bemused expression.

"Let's go," said the second soldier, hiking his pants as

well as his voice. If he was older than his companion, it wasn't by more than a week.

"I'd suggest you both tell me what you want," said Jake. He braced his legs and pulled them apart, making it more obvious that he had a pistol half cocked in his hand between them. This was no small pocket pistol, but a full-bore English officer's gun, custom-made by Styan in Manchester, England, a few years before. Not for Jake, of course, but its original owner was no longer in need of such weaponry, making do quite nicely with pitchfork and tail.

"I rather doubt you'd be able to aim your rifles before my pistol decorates your chest," Jake said lightly.

"Why would you shoot us?" said the first soldier, the boldness flown from his tongue. "We're on your side."

"Which side is that?"

"Colonel Flanagan wants to see you," said the second. The soldiers' plain hunting dress—common to many in the Continental Army and state militia—bore no military markings, let alone insignias of rank. Jake assumed they were privates from the fact that they practically genuflected when they mentioned their commander.

And they must be Americans—even the lowest redcoat conscripts would have been trained to separate when faced with a gun barrel; one shot could take the pair through both hearts.

Sighing, Jake propped himself up on the bed to get a better look at his fellows in arms. Presumably they made up in enthusiasm what they lacked in drilling.

"You are good shots with those rifles, I hope."

"They're not loaded, sir," said the soldier in front.

"Not loaded!" Jake jumped from the bed in a huff. "Trust me; the next time you burst into someone's room in the middle of the night, have your gun loaded, or at least have a bayonet handy. You'll be in for a nasty surprise if you don't."

"Our rifles don't take bayonets, sir."

Jake smirked, suddenly feeling like these boys' uncle. In truth, he was no more than six or seven years older, though his experiences sometimes made him feel a grizzled old man. He touched their rifles—handcrafted Penn-

sylvanians, at least—patted them each on the shoulder
and set his pistol on the dresser. He winked in Sarah's
direction, but she was too shy, and too concerned about
her father, to let herself be seen.

"So who is this Captain Flanagan?" Jake asked.

"Colonel Flanagan, sir," said the first man. "He is
General Schuyler's aide."

"Schuyler's with Congress in Philadelphia."

"He's on his way back. Colonel Flanagan has orders
from him, sir, pertaining to you. He requested your presence in the name of the general."

Jake sat on the edge of the bed and contemplated the
situation. Major General Philip Schuyler was technically
in command of the Northern Department of the army,
which included Albany as well as most of northern New
York and New England. But Congress had superseded
his control a few months before by placing Horatio Gates
in charge of the troops at Ticonderoga and northward.
The political row was quite notorious; you couldn't get
within a hundred yards of General Washington's headquarters, let alone Philadelphia, without hearing some
rumor of its latest development.

Jake had a low opinion of Schuyler and a somewhat
worse appreciation of Gates. Still, he was not in a position to disobey a summons from a major general, or even
one of his aides. Most likely, the colonel was only looking
for information—call it gossip—about his commander's
situation.

But how had Flanagan learned of his arrival? Jake was
supposed to be on leave; the only person in Albany who
knew he was here was Sarah, starting to shiver despite
the blanket.

"Tell you what, friends," said Jake, taking a stagy
glance toward the wardrobe. "It's worth half a crown if
you find me in, say, half an hour."

To their credit and his frustration, the patriots couldn't
be bought. The best he could do was make them wait
outside for a minute, during which he kissed Sarah and
promised to return as soon as he told Schuyler's ape to
fly off. Jake and his horse were soon trotting behind as

the men double-timed to Schuyler's mansion on the
banks of the Hudson.

He didn't need them to lead him through the streets
and then the half mile or so south of town; he was familiar enough with the Pastures, having gone there some
years before while traveling with his father as assistant
and secretary. He especially loathed its overwrought
Chippendale roof railing, which crowned a pretentious
and yet somehow frumpy Georgian-style house. To Jake,
who had been in Britain but four years before, the Pastures was at best a third-rate copy of a third-rate English
country home, hardly worthy of a true democrat. Especially if the democrat was of Dutch extraction.

But then Jake was always finding the Dutch a confused
and confusing race.

"Lieutenant Colonel Gibbs."

Jake extended his hand to meet Flanagan's as the
officer walked across the large study where he'd been
waiting. The colonel, in his mid-fifties, was dressed in a
well-tailored blue and white uniform, with officer's silver
epaulettes. Stocky and several inches shorter than Jake,
he wore a powdered bag wig, which had gone more or
less out of fashion even in the provincial cities with the
onset of war. But then Jake didn't think he'd been asked
here to comment on Flanagan's coiffure. He stood stiffly
in front of the proffered chair and asked why he had
been sent for.

"Relax a moment," replied Flanagan. "Would you like
a drink? I'm sure the general would insist."

Schuyler's taste in Madeira was legendary, but Jake
declined. Sarah was waiting. Flanagan went to the sideboard and poured himself a half glass.

"You've heard, of course, that General Schuyler has
countered the New Englanders and their slander," Flanagan said as he carefully measured his drink. "There are a
few *i*'s to be dotted, but Gates is out and the old man is
back. You can count on that. General Washington himself is lobbying on his behalf."

Flanagan's comment about the New Englanders,
though true enough, was a bit of a faux pas—born in
Philadelphia, Jake had spent much time in Massachusetts

and had originally been enlisted as an officer in a Massachusetts regiment. No matter where his superiors lined up politically, he felt close to the New Englanders whose spirit had first imbued him with a lust for freedom. But he said nothing.

"He's standing for state governor as well, you know," added Flanagan, whether to try and awe him or make idle conversation, Jake couldn't be sure. "He'll win that battle, too."

"No doubt. So why precisely am I here, Colonel?"

Until now, Flanagan's manner had been anything but impressive; Jake theorized he was merely trying to draw out the latest command gossip. But as Flanagan turned to answer Jake's question, he seemed to grow several inches. His face, which had appeared a bit flaccid and tired, now suddenly looked vigorous and determined. Jake had seen this in many officers promoted from the working classes because of merit in the field—they were awkward in the drawing rooms, but sharp swords in battle.

"The Northern Department has need of the Revolution's finest spy," said Flanagan. "General Washington directed General Greene to find you. He in turn sent word that you would be here—a most fortunate coincidence."

"With all due respect, Colonel," said Jake, "I'm not in the habit of spending my time on local conspiracies. I do not want to sound like I have an inflated head, but surely there are other men available for your local problems."

"This is not a local problem." Flanagan's voice had the measured cadence of a man used to giving orders. "The Revolution is at stake."

Jake wasn't swayed at all. Inevitably, when someone used such inflated terms, the job turned out to be the simple apprehension of a merchant who sold a few grains of contraband tea on the side. "Well, if it's only that," he said sarcastically.

But Flanagan's voice, instead of cracking with fury at being found out, dropped to a bare whisper. "Burgoyne is planning an invasion down the Hudson. We don't know

when; we don't know by what route. If we cannot stop
him, the continent will be split in two."

A bucket of snow could not have sobered Jake's disposition more effectively. As he waited for Flanagan to continue, he felt his heart start to pump. A certain itch
developed in his thigh muscles, and his senses sharpened
so acutely that a piece of dust could not fall in the room
without his being aware of it. For if certain physiques are
made by nature for certain tasks, Jake's was tuned for
facing danger.

"We need intelligence on the British plans," said
Flanagan. "We need it as soon as possible—it already
may be too late. Our forces are too small to be spread
out across the entire state. If we do not know the proper
route, and when to expect them, we will surely be beaten.
Ticonderoga will fall, then Saratoga—and the British will
stand at the head of the Hudson. All will be threatened,
including Albany."

Jake folded his arms across his chest as he considered
the difficulties of a mission north. "There must be a
dozen men under your command who are more familiar
with the territory between here and Canada," he said.
"And if time is of the essence—"

"I'm not trying to flatter you, but given the critical
nature, we must have someone whose success is guaranteed. I'm not," Flanagan added in a softer, very measured voice, "asking you to volunteer. Your command
arrangements have already been changed."

He reached inside his brocaded vest and pulled out
several folded sheets of paper. "You have been assigned
special duty under General Schuyler and are to act exclusively as his agent until further notice from the commander-in-chief."

Jake took the papers and saw immediately that the first
was written in General Greene's neat if flowery hand.
The opening sentence set it out as authentic: "Considering the happy consequences of such an important and
critical operation and the great need for thoughtful but
timely accommodation : . ." The overwrought tone was
unmistakable; General Greene couldn't write a requisi-
tion without referring to the glorious potential of the

American future, and throwing in a few references to Swift and Locke on the side.

The second sheet was an adjunct's note approving the temporary posting in the Northern Department; the third a paymaster's notation for funds that would be available for the mission. But the clincher was a letter from Joseph Reed, which would have been dictated by General Washington himself. The sum of this bundle of papers was that Jake had been assigned to the Northern Department "indefinitely" for "special and diverse missions, as it shall please the commander of said department."

What the hell, had he been lost in some dice game?

Jake handed the papers back. "This isn't merely a matter of politics with Gates, is it?"

"I'm not a political man, Colonel," said Flanagan, making a face as if he'd just eaten a peach out of season. "I was a farmer before the war, and I share your displeasure for backroom maneuverings. But I assure you that General Schuyler would not have gone to the lengths he did to obtain your services if they were not critical."

Nor would General Washington or General Greene have agreed, Jake realized. There was no arguing the strategic importance of defeating a British attack before it reached Albany. Indeed, if Burgoyne were to succeed and, at the same time, General Howe were to attack northward from New York, all the land along the river would have to be abandoned. The Revolution would be strangled in the middle states, and possibly throughout America. With the British controlling the Atlantic and blocking the Hudson, there would be no way for the South to communicate with New England—Liberty would die a slow, withering death.

But Canada—good God!

"Colonel, Governor Carleton put a hundred crowns on my head," said Jake. "I'll be shot as soon as I reach Montreal. It's not that I'm afraid; it's just that I'm liable to be found out before I gather the intelligence and can return; the mission will fail."

Well all right, he admitted to himself—he was a *little* afraid. But that never stopped him.

"You've faced these sorts of difficulties before," said

Flanagan. "I understand that you snuck into Quebec and returned with a lock of Carleton's hair, stolen from his bedchamber."

"A distortion," said Jake, who despite the seriousness of the moment suppressed a smile at the memory. He'd actually taken the governor's wig, using it as part of a disguise to leave the enemy city in broad daylight.

"There are signs that the invasion will be launched within a week or ten days," said Flanagan. "If we don't know the route by then, we're lost. Even now, I have doubts about getting our forces in place."

"He has to come down the lakes. It's the only way he can move a large army."

"But which side?" asked Flanagan. "And when does he leave? With how many men, and what will be their organization? And who—"

"It's quite all right," said Jake. "I know what you need. But I worry that you may be depending too much on one man, and perhaps the wrong one at that."

"Nonsense. If you can't pull this off, no one can. I have a fresh horse waiting out front. You'll find some money, papers, and a map in the saddlebags. Anything else you need will be readily provided."

Jake Stewart Gibbs stayed silent for a minute, his eyes fixed on the hands of the study's ornate grandfather clock. It was just about to strike midnight. Neither he nor the colonel spoke as the last seconds clicked off and the room shook with the deep, sonorous tones.

A condemned man sticking his tongue out at the executioner would find more mercy than Jake if he were captured in Canada. Even disguised, he could not count on passing unrecognized in Montreal or Quebec, as he so often did in New York City; not only would many of the local inhabitants remember him, but his profile was all too familiar to the governor himself.

Undoubtedly, General Washington had weighed these dangers and decided to risk sending him nonetheless. The war stood at its most critical juncture. Trenton notwithstanding, the winter had been a difficult one. To lose Ticonderoga—let alone Albany—would be a crushing blow.

"I hope this is a good horse you've gotten me," said Jake when the chimes came to an end. "The last time I went to Canada I ended up traveling half the way on foot."

TWO

Wherein, the journey begins, with sad leave-taking of the widow Sarah and a misplaced confidence in the state of local security.

*F*lanagan didn't expect Jake to leave until morning, but the agent was one of that small class of men who can go for days with only a few winks of sleep. He did not intend to delay his start with anything approaching a full night's rest, and therefore launched his mission the second he left the Pastures, setting out on the best road north.

Which, not coincidentally, was the same road he had traveled to meet the colonel and which, not surprisingly, led him straight through Albany to Sarah's father's inn, the Golden Peacock.

Someday, Jake thought as he got off his horse, he must ask Mr. Roberts what the point of a golden but nonetheless monochromatic peacock would be, since the bird's whole reason for existence was the rainbow of colors at its tail. He hoped tonight, however, to avoid the opportunity to raise the question. Mr. Roberts was a powerfully long-winded speaker, and the explanation for the tavern's name would undoubtedly fill the sails of a fleet's worth of frigates. It would also make it difficult to sneak upstairs and take proper leave of Sarah, as he was honor bound to do.

Jake was in luck, in a way—the front door was bolted, with a long board across it to prevent entry. This meant that all inside had gone to sleep, the Albany innkeeper taking precautions that once would have been shown only on the frontier.

The building was simple if sturdy, constructed of two stories; the room where Sarah would be waiting was in the rear. This could be easily reached from the back of Jake's new horse, a fine, athletic, and, more importantly, very tall beast. There were but two complications: First, the glass window at the outside and then the secured shutter inside would have to be opened as quietly as possible. Second, and the reason stealth was required, Sarah's two sisters would be sleeping with her, and might cry out in alarm—or perhaps jealousy—if woken.

The horse Flanagan had provided was undoubtedly fleet of foot, but it turned out to be a less than ideal ladder. Though hitched to a nearby post, the animal shifted uneasily as Jake rose on its back. He cursed silently as he tried to steady himself against the side of the building with one hand and pry open the window with the other.

Fortunately, the laws of physics regarding levers and pulleys were working in his favor. Jake's long hunting knife made as handy and efficient a siege machine as any the Romans had ever used, and the ropes inside the window casement handled their job with equal vigor. The window flicked upward like a startled bird taking flight. Jake took this as a good sign—Sarah had no doubt greased the way for him.

With such optimistic portents, he did not fret when the horse darted to the side, leaving him hanging by his fingers on the sill. The animal was, after all, tied, and would be waiting when he returned.

The bricks in the building were smoothly laid, with mortar placed smartly and quite thickly; a toehold was impossible. No matter. Jake had entered many a window at a greater height under much more dire circumstances, without the promise of so great a reward—placing the knife between his teeth, he pushed with his arms and shoulders to snatch his knees up on the ledge, using such strength that a lesser house might have fallen to the ground. Kneeling inside the window on the casement, half inside the house, Jake found the shutters inexplicably fastened. This was but a minor annoyance; once more the knife did good service, slipping the wooden fastener with such ease that Jake, in a more leisurely moment, would have considered whether the deer-antler handle housed a beneficent spirit.

No time for that now. Desire beat a steady drum of advance in his chest as he peeked inside. The room was dark, and the light from outside dim, the moon obscured by clouds; Jake crouched in the window for a long minute before making out the outlines of the bed. Sure enough, there were three figures there, each shadow a barely distinguishable lump of covers and nightcaps.

One of the sisters was snoring almost as thickly as a man; the sound was fortunate, as it covered the soft creak in the floorboards when Jake snaked inside. But even with his eyes fully adjusted to the interior light, he couldn't distinguish one lump from the other—which was Sarah?

He was just about to prod the body closest to the window, figuring that his lover would have posted herself there so she could hear his approach, when he was interrupted by a loud hiss from behind. Spinning quickly, he dropped to his knees, afraid that he was about to have a long and not altogether comfortable interview with Sarah's mother.

A second hiss cured him of such misconceptions. It was the sound a snake would make, yet it was the tone of an angel.

"You almost woke my father," said Sarah when he joined her in the hallway.

"Your father?"

"He and my brothers always sleep together when there are many guests. Didn't you hear him snoring?"

Jake made his apology in kisses. They tiptoed downstairs to the large front room, snuggling in blankets before the fireplace. Their communication was wordless, their sentiments expressed solely in the soft, steady crush of two bodies falling together.

They were so absorbed in each other that they missed the stirring of a patron in a nearby chair. The man had found no room upstairs; whether he thought the figures before the fireplace were real or part of a pleasant dream, he said nothing more than a mumbled, "This is why we must be free," and dropped back off to sleep.

'At length, Jake prepared to take his leave. He watched as Sarah got up to poke the embers and throw another log on. The small flash of flames sent a red light into the room, illuminating her naked body with a fine glow. For a moment, and a long moment indeed, he regretted that he had been called to duty.

"I'll come with you," offered Sarah, so loudly that he had to put his finger to her lips.

"It's much too dangerous."

"It's dangerous for you," she said. "I will be able to breeze in and out like a bird."

"No. Carleton is sure to have troops haunting the woods. Besides, I may have to pretend to be a traitor to get into Canada, and I doubt that's a disguise you could stomach."

She continued to protest, but there was no question of Jake's taking her with him. The most he would promise was to return as quickly as possible.

"And in one piece," she instructed.

"And in one piece," he answered, kissing her.

"Without a cannonball in your side," she added, kissing back.

"Without a cannonball in my side." Another kiss.

"And don't disguise yourself as a Mohawk this time." A longer kiss.

"I can't make that promise." Two pecks. "I hate the Iroquois, but there are advantages to looking like one."

"You don't look like a savage." A long, deeply planted kiss.

"I can if I have to."

"No tattoo then," she said, surrendering.

Jake remembered the banter eight or nine hours later, well north of Albany and halfway to Saratoga, when he noticed small but distinct hatchet marks on some fir trees off the road. They were blazes such as those made by Indians traveling through unfamiliar territory. Leading well off into the woods along one of the few uncultivated areas near the road, they immediately struck him as suspicious. The cuts, which Jake got off his horse to examine, were not very fresh; the sap had stopped running.

But neither were they so old that they could be attributed to last year's campaigns, and it seemed exceedingly unlikely that they would have been made during the winter, when the terrain was so much more obvious.

There were, of course, many Indians in the area, and some were friendly to the patriot side. Schuyler's ability at managing relations with the local tribes was undebatable; he had kept many Indians neutral, or at least nominally neutral. Still, the British had alliances with many natives, especially the fierce Iroquois tribes. The services the king expected of his allies included scouting behind enemy lines; this might be evidence of a recent foray.

Even if the danger was not immediate, the blazes were a bad omen. Jake's journey would take him through country where the patriots were not nearly so populous nor well-established; if Indians were active here, they might be on the warpath farther north.

Natives were only one worry. Flanagan had provided Jake with the official papers needed to pass through the American lines, as well as forged ones for Canada. But this was not to say his passage would be easy; strange travelers were always regarded with suspicion no matter what authority they cited, especially as one neared the battle lines. Worse, Jake's most promising cover once he reached British territory would be as a deserter to the patriot cause; in order to propagate it convincingly, it was best to at least hint at it south of the border, in hopes any local spies would carry the news northward.

While local Tory sympathizers might be accepted with nothing more than threats and a few rocks through their windows, patriot wrath was readily unleashed on those with unfamiliar faces. Jake felt confident he could work the game successfully; he had done so often in the hellish no man's land of Westchester, known euphemistically as the "Neutral Ground." But his situation would be considerably improved if he could find a merchant authorized to travel between the two sides; he knew from his experience in New York and the Jerseys that such persons had various ways around meddlesome authorities. Finding them was not necessarily easy, however, nor was it without its own dangers, since many of these entrepreneurs turned out to spend the better part of their days working as robbers and cutthroats.

Except for his notation of the marks along the trees, Jake's ride to Saratoga was uneventful, the various fords passed with nary a trifle and the mid-spring day turning positively pleasant. The horse Flanagan had provided proved a more than suitable mount, and brought him northward at a good pace, never seeming to tire and needing only an occasional drink of water to sustain its strength.

Had Jake been a tourist and his pace more leisurely, he might have stopped and stared a good long while at Cohoes Falls, where the water was gushing with a force that would have surprised Noah himself. The cataract spanned twelve hundred feet, a whale's mouth multiplied by ten. The roiling water made the sound of a brigade's worth of artillery stemming a redcoat charge.

The ferry above the falls was a very small boat that accommodated only Jake and his horse. The ferryman asked no questions of him once the six shilling fare was presented. The horse made the only comment—a low neigh of appreciation that he was avoiding the chilly water and its stiff current.

The land around Saratoga was rich farmland, well-cultivated. General Schuyler had a large tract there inherited from his father. Tenant farmers leased farms from him, paying for the privilege of sweat with a quarter or so of their yearly produce. The practice was widespread in New York, inherited from the Dutch domination; Schuyler was but a small player in it. Still, Jake thought it unseemly for a patriot to act as a medieval lord. Neither New England nor Philadelphia had any similar institution, and the patriot spy felt his revulsion of Schuyler returning as he rode.

Jake skirted Saratoga, moving gradually westward as he rode north. Experience told him he could make better and safer time on the secondary routes, even though they were neither as good nor quite as direct as the roads along the river. With little traffic and less people to raise questions, he was freer to let his horse find its speed. Occasionally he would leave the road and proceed over open fields, the horse seeming to know by instinct the best route.

There is an undeniable law of nature that opposites attract. And so it was in this case—the very pleasantness of the day, the light, summerlike breeze, and the fresh, green spring scents around him conjured up not easy thoughts but hard memories of the last time Jake had traveled to Canada, by a much different route but with roughly the same destination. Then the surrounding fields and woods had seemed dark and foreboding, the cries of the birds—above all, the owls—trying to warn the patriot army to turn back.

The plan to take Canada had been ill-conceived. It was not so much the idea but the timing; they came too late in the year. The failure of the French Canadians to rally against the British and join them in the great experiment of Freedom was bad enough, but the coming on of winter, the approaching new year—and the mandatory end of most of the army's enlistments—combined for certain destruction.

General Montgomery had not seen it. Such a great leader, such a powerfully insightful man in every other respect, and yet he had not seen the guarantee of failure.

Or had he? Did he decide to gamble nonetheless, roll the dice in hopes of winning a wild victory that would surely have ended the war?

There was an even more weighty question, at least as far as Jake personally was concerned: Why had he not succeeded when he tried to talk the general out of the assault? Clearly, Montgomery had trusted his assessments and advice during the campaign, and yet he rejected them at the moment when they were most critical. Had he simply failed to make his points clearly enough? Jake asked himself now as he recalled the disaster. Was he somehow responsible for the defeat?

The moody recriminations clouded Jake's vision, and blinded him for a long while to the curl of smoke that rose around the farm in the distance, an ugly black vine tangling upward, not from a hearth but from staved-in roof beams crying with the unstanchable sorrow of death, unjustly delivered.

By the time Jake realized what it was, he had already unconsciously turned toward the farm and urged the horse to a gallop, though even the animal must have known it was too late.

Three

*T*he Indians who lived in this area were predominantly of the Iroquois confederation and had long had contact, for better or worse, with the white man. The confederation's main tribe near Albany was called by the English "Mohawks," a name that also applied to the river and the valley ending at the falls Jake had so recently admired.

"Mohawk" was a somewhat unfortunate though accurate appellation, applied not by the tribe itself but by Algonquin peoples nearby with whom they had warred for many years. Loosely translated, it meant "man eaters." The term was literal, and while it failed to capture nuances of the religious ceremonies that involved the act, it was nonetheless an appropriate indication of the ferocity of the Mohawk world. Their universe was different than the whites'; dreams and nightmares were still literally true, and the dead stepped seamlessly from one life to another, status in the next determined largely by bravery and stoic fortitude in this one.

Jake was looking at one of their nightmares now. A small farmstead, set in a small hollow amid no more than twenty cleared acres a good mile from the main road, had been ambushed and set ablaze by raiders within the past day. Little more than a cottage, the house had only one hearth and chimney; its stones towered now above the caved-in roof timbers. The front and far side wall were both tumbled down and burnt. A jagged edge of the back wall remained, three-quarters the height it had stood until yesterday. A quilt still hung at one end, and next to it, a sideboard with a set of earthen dishes untouched by the flames. A broom was propped on one side, its straw head barely singed, as if waiting for the owner to set about the daily chores.

This had been a very poor farm, with no outbuildings to speak of, a lean-to a few yards from the house apparently serving as the barn. That, too, had been destroyed, pulled down and flattened by fire. The settlers' well stood between the two structures. Jake eased his horse gently toward it, knowing what he would find there.

The hole was narrow, with an irregular wooden wall at the top. An arm of the dead man's body had caught on a sideboard, hanging the corpse in a pose that made it seem as if he were trying to climb up. His face gazed toward heaven, frozen in the shape of his dying thought: Why?

Jake led his horse back to the house and dismounted, tying it to a board. The beast protested loudly and shook its head, as if warning Jake away from the ghosts that surely inhabited the site. Its cries were so adamant he feared it would harm itself; Jake undid the rein and brought it over to the remains of the lean-to, where the animal consented to wait more calmly, commenting on the scene with sad, soft nickers.

The dead man was not quite middle-aged. He had been robbed of his shoes, but otherwise his clothing was so poor and tattered that it had obviously been left by the raiders as worthless. Nor had he been well-fed—Jake had no trouble lifting him and carrying him to the front of the house.

Several large stains of blood marked his chest. He had been scalped; a piece of skin flapped back on his skull as he was set down. Jake had to tilt the head to get the skin to stay in place. He closed the man's eyes and said a short, simple prayer he'd been taught as a youngster.

Prudence dictated that he leave the house immediately, since it was possible whoever had attacked was watching still. But Jake wasn't listening to prudence at the moment. Though grimly alert, he was concerned with giving the dead man a decent burial. He was also aware, as he scanned the remains of the homestead, that the man had had a wife—a soiled bonnet was among the ruins.

He found her three or four yards into the woods, the back of her simple dress decorated with large blood-stains. Jake was surprised to see her long black hair still intact; he would have thought it quite a prize.

He was even more surprised to see the body move.

At first it seemed an optical illusion. Jake looked quickly around the field, half expecting a trap, as if the warriors had some way of poking the body from afar to distract him.

Seeing nobody, he looked back down. The body moved again, ever so slightly. The woman was alive.

He turned her over gently. A gurgle of blood passed from her lips. Jake gently brushed the caked dirt and mud away from her face. The skin was soft but brittle, death already stealing in. There could be no hope for her.

Looking more carefully at the woods around her, he realized that she had crawled here from several yards away, apparently having hid after she was shot. But her survival meant only that she had delayed death by an hour or two.

"Who did this?" he asked.

To his great surprise, she murmured something in response. Jake pulled her up closer to hear. The light, undernourished body belonged more to the next life than this; he felt as if he were intruding in heaven.

"Can you tell me who attacked you? Were they Mohawks?"

But the dying woman had other priorities. "My baby," she said, "in the cellar."

The effort to voice these small words wore on her severely; she slumped in his arms. Jake realized she didn't have enough strength even to be moved; she might last another minute or two at most. Gently, he picked her head off his lap and, with his coat as a pillow, placed it on the ground.

He ran to the cabin quickly, resolved to show her lingering soul that her baby was still alive. All other thoughts temporarily abandoned, he flew to the ruins like a mythological bird of prey, possessed by an unworldly power. Though the embers were still hot, he tossed them aside, feeling nothing.

It was not easy to find the opening, especially with the ruins of the house on top of it. Jake pulled and poked at the floorboards, trying a good three-quarters of them before finally discovering the one that led to the subterranean chamber.

Or hole. The space below was barely the size of a chest, which explained, perhaps, why the woman had not tried to hide there herself.

It was empty, except for a small, soiled blanket where the baby had lain.

Technically speaking, Lieutenant Colonel Gibbs was guilty of a great dereliction of duty. Considering the weight Schuyler, through his deputy Colonel Flanagan, had placed on the mission to Canada, Jake's decision to pursue the child's abductors was nearly a direct betrayal of his oath as an officer.

From the point of prudence, it was lunacy. Assuming he was correct and the raiders were a Mohawk scouting party headed or motivated by British troops, they would be well-armed and would outnumber him at least six or eight to one. Even if he could somehow overwhelm them, little of military value would be gained; complete and utter victory would only delay him from his more important goal.

Yet Jake could not help himself. As a professional spy and soldier, he was not supposed to be motivated by anger. Indeed, if you had stopped him now, as he pushed his horse ever deeper through the woods after burying the husband and wife in a shallow grave, he could have cited many instances when he had postponed revenge for the good of the Cause, when he had let slights and injustices, cold murder among them, pass so that Freedom might be achieved in the end.

But had you been able to stop him—had you been able to draw near enough to see his face—you would have realized here was a man possessed. Here was a man who wanted nothing except the return of that small baby, and would not be stopped, not even by the direct command of George Washington himself, until he rescued it.

The path the raiders had taken was obvious enough, if you knew what to look for. A trail jutted out of the woods at the west end of the clearing; Jake noticed some gunpowder among the broken branches. A few yards deep into the forest he came upon some loose dirt and footprints which the murderers had not bothered to erase.

Though Jake had many talents, he was not in the true sense a woodsman. Had he been, he would have read volumes from this sign of prints, for a pure Mohawk war party would never have been so careless. The Indians who were along on the raid did, indeed, include Iroquois speakers, but they were a collection of individual and vastly different warriors under the direction of white men. This could have been read in the tracks themselves, from the shoe and moccasin markings. But it would have made small difference in any event.

The trail crossed a small brook and then opened up, becoming a highway in comparison to its start by the cabin; Jake galloped along for nearly three miles until a sixth sense told him to slow down. The sun was already sliding low toward the treetops; something tickled his nose and he flew off his horse, pistol in hand.

The scent was another fire, but this was fresher, and more carefully planned—the raiding party must be making camp nearby. Jake proceeded up the trail a ways farther, walking his horse slowly and as stealthily as possible.

He'd gone only a few hundred yards when he heard voices in heated exchange ahead. Quickly and as silently as possible he retreated, looking for a place where he could secure his horse. The nearest spot, a small copse thirty yards from the path, was back two twists along the trail; Jake tied the horse and took his guns from the saddle holsters. Each was primed and half cocked, ready to be fired, as was the Segallas pocket pistol in his jacket.

The ground rose slightly, and Jake walked in a semicircle toward the crown, realizing this would be a perfect vantage to post a guard.

He did not see the man until he was almost upon him.

Fortunately for Jake, the guard's attention was directed wholly toward the trail below. The man crouched forward, one hand against a tree, a musket wedged in the fold between his stomach and thigh. His head was shaven Indian style, with a shock of black hair feathered up in the middle of the scalp, but from twenty yards Jake could not quite tell if he was truly an Indian or a white man made up as one.

The problem was the same no matter his ancestry: the sentry must be taken down silently, before he could alert whomever he was protecting. Jake had a potion secreted in a pouch in his belt designed for just such a job—its main ingredient was distilled from scorpion poison, and it could silently paralyze a man with one breath.

But the guard knew his business. Dry leaves had been gathered in shallow piles to make a stealthy approach difficult. He couldn't count on sneaking close enough to use the powder, which would have to be clamped over the man's nose from behind.

Jake put two of his guns on the ground, where they would be safe, then drew his long knife and held it in his right hand. He kept his best flintlock pistol, the Styan, in his other hand, to be used if the man turned around before he was close enough for the knife.

Two steps, three; Jake sucked his breath into his chest, moving cautiously between the shrubs and leaf piles until a mere ten feet separated them. The brook he had crossed closer to the house flowed several hundred feet away, but it wasn't quite loud enough to cover a last dash. He stopped and stood like a statue, debating what to do.

Shoot, and the whole company would descend. Remain stationary, and sooner or later the guard would turn around.

Providence weighed the odds and decided to nudge its brother Wind, which in turn rustled the leaves. Jake launched himself, hitting the lookout even as he started to turn. He held his knife extended in front of him like the prow of a Viking ship battering an enemy vessel. They rolled together briefly, the Indian's gun flying aside as Jake drove the knife home. Surprise kept the man from yelling out, that and the barrel of Jake's gun, slammed severely and repeatedly against his chin. The knife finished the job with a quiet but deep slice upward that dissected the sentry's heart.

He was truly an Indian, though he did not wear the typical Mohawk markings on his face. Jake pulled him down the hill some distance and wedged his body in a rocky crevice, covering it with leaves. He quickly wiped the blood from his hand as if it were poison, and went to look for the camp.

There were about a dozen Indians, including a few women. Two white men dressed in rough clothes were among them. These two seemed to be in charge, or at least thought they were; a rebellion was obviously afoot.

Stepping forward to listen, Jake's boot caught against something. At first he thought it was a log, but realized as he brought his leg back that though solid, it was soft, not hard. Looking down, he saw a dull yellow piece of cloth on the ground.

A child's rag doll.

He leaned down to pick it up, some vague hope of using it to calm the child on the ride to safety forming in a corner of his brain. In the next moment that hope was shattered into revulsion and horror, and he felt a sharp spear of pain in his chest—he was holding not a doll, but a dead child in his hand.

One of the white men, a tall, skinny man with a pock-marked face, had ordered it killed. That was what the argument was about, Jake realized as he held the baby's still-warm body to his chest.

There was a certain quality his brain had, when nearly overwhelmed with danger, to proceed to some higher plane and make ready, preparing to strike with the calm detachment of a rattlesnake. His mind was there now, observing, mapping strategy. Not even his mentor General Greene could have sized up an enemy with such placid intelligence, while every muscle in his body boiled with anger.

The man directing the Indians yelled in resentment that they could all leave and go to hell as far as he was concerned. The other white stood silently and with bent shoulders. Jake guessed he was a British officer; had he cared to make further surmises, he might have hypothesized from the man's pallid manner that he was appalled by what he had just witnessed.

Such theories would have been correct, but they were irrelevant as far as Jake was concerned. More to the point was his theory, gathered from the different gestures and the Englishman's words, that the Indians had not wanted the baby killed. Indeed, though Jake's scant ability with the Iroquoian tongue prevented him from knowing this, the boy had been intended for one of the women now standing in dismay at the edge of the group. It was to have been a surrogate for one she had lost this past winter.

It seemed he stood there listening forever, the poor child's body growing ever colder. Finally the argument ended and the group cleaved in two, Indians and whites, the latter joined by a single native.

Jake, figuring he would trail the whites until they were far enough from the others to strike, began to move silently back toward his horse. The patriot quickened his pace when he heard one of the Indians heading in the same direction, calling to the lookout he had earlier relieved of his duties on a permanent basis.

But when Jake arrived at his horse with the dead child, the animal wanted no part of it, rearing and whining as soon as he brought the dead body near. Jake had to leave either the child or the horse; the decision was unfortunate but obvious.

He ran a few feet into the woods, back toward the stream. With his boot he rolled a log to the side, then took a long, thick stick and dug quickly into the sandy dirt. Covering the poor child's body, he pulled the log back on top, marking a grave that even in his haste he realized would provide small comfort for the baby's soul. But there was little else he could do; the Indian was now shouting for the slain lookout and running directly toward him in the woods.

Jake slid down behind a tree and surprised the man as he ran past. The branch he had just used as a burial shovel was now changed to a death lance. Jake caught the

Indian just below the waist. The man's momentum carried him nearly to Jake's fist, the stick plunging deep into his abdomen. In a quick, unconscious rage Jake finished him off, crushing his skull savagely with the butt end of his pistol before the man could utter even a syllable of surprise.

He left the body where it fell and ran to his horse.

It is barely believable, but Jake's fury increased with every yard covered. He mounted the horse, intending to circle around and head off the whites if possible. Urging the beast through the thick bramble, over fallen trees and past the shallow creek, he had no care for the noise he made. For a long while Jake had no care for himself, only for revenge.

But they had too good a lead on him. When he finally reached the main trail again with no trace, his horse slowed practically to a walk; its deep pants warned Jake not to push it faster.

The trail soon took him across a main road. One way was west, quite probably the way the men had gone. The other was northeastward, most likely back toward the river.

Back toward his mission.

Jake paused there, listening, but all he could hear was the faint rush of the water slipping through the rocks in the nearby creek.

His anger had delayed his mission several hours, perhaps half a day—precious time that could help save many lives, and perhaps the entire war. He'd have to make up for this by riding through the night, pushing himself still further. Revenge was a luxury that he could not indulge in.

There had been many such deaths in the war; every loss was a tragedy to someone, every death senseless until the final goal of Freedom was achieved. That was the only way of revenge; individual retribution was but pyrrhic pleasure.

Sadly, but with a firm resolve, Jake turned the horse's head up the road and placed his boots against its sides. The animal caught its second wind and seemed relieved to run once more.

Four

Wherein, the Honorable Claus van Clynne, Esquire, is pleased to make his acquaintance with the narrative's hero, and vice versa.

The knife blade slit the air in front of the portly Dutchman's chest with a suddenness that caused him to catch his breath and contemplate his future in the afterlife.

The picture was not altogether pleasing, consisting primarily of large flames and a satanic figure who looked suspiciously British. Sobered by the image, with no desire to end his career so suddenly, especially at such a small inn in a tiny hamlet in country barely tamed and shamefully less than consistently Dutch, Claus van Clynne, Esquire, decided to take a pacific tack. He put up his hands and puffed his cheeks in a pose he believed both angelic and compliant. After a second he ventured a grin, fluttered his fingers and cleared his throat.

"Well, well, my friend, I never thought it would come to this," huffed van Clynne. "A Dutchman pulling a knife on another Dutchman. What poor manners the English have led us to, eh?"

Van Clynne frowned ever so gently at the man holding the knife, Pieter Gerk, and then gave a knowing wink to William Pohl, Gerk's partner. Pohl, a timid and eminently reasonable man in van Clynne's opinion, had turned whiter than a flake of fresh snow. Most of the rest of the inn's patrons had moved toward the door, ready to make their escape. The tavern was twenty miles north and a trifle west of Fort George, a good distance from the lake itself; disputes here had a nasty way of proving deadly, and not just to the combatants.

"You are a liar and a cheat, Claus van Clynne," said Gerk, punctuating his statement with a flare of the knife.

"Everyone is entitled to his opinion," said van Clynne contritely. The squire was, after all, a gracious man who could make allowances in such cases. Gerk had lived in the woods for many years, trading furs with the Indians. Plus he had often had contact with the British, a factor that undoubtedly accounted for his behavior.

Van Clynne turned his attention to Pohl, as if the speechless man had argued for recklessness. "No, no, I say. Everyone can speak his mind. We are in America, are we not? Now, in respect to the asking price for the furs, if you won't take wampum, then a sum of fifty continentals, it seems to me—"

"You will pay in crowns," demanded Gerk. "Not worthless Congress money."

"Careful," said van Clynne in a stage whisper meant to be overheard, "let us not bandy politics about."

"I want real money, backed with gold."

"Guilders, then. I suppose I can make the adjustment. Let us see, at six guilders per skin—"

"I want British crowns."

The word "British" excited a reaction in van Clynne's face akin to a bee sting. His cheeks pinched hollow, his nose twisted around, both eyes became slits, and the whole package went beet red.

"Now listen to me, Pieter," blustered van Clynne. "I will be damned if I am going to start surrendering to these English imbeciles. First we use their money, then they will have us wearing their ridiculous pointed hats. Where will it end? I tell you, when I reach Canada I won't pay with British money, the government be damned. Guilders are a universal currency, and a man should be honored to receive them."

"Your guilders are often cut," said the man.

"Cut? Never. I assure you, whole Dutch currency is all I use."

"You paid for your dinner with English money, you lying dog."

Van Clynne sat back from the table and sighed outwardly, while smiling to himself. They had reached the point in the negotiations that he especially liked, where all the skins, as it were, were out on the table. All that remained was the downhill slide toward a handshake and rum all around. "I suppose that if you insist on payment in a debased currency, I can arrange it. When will delivery take place?"

"Not so fast," said Gerk. "We haven't set a price."

"That's right, Claus. We haven't agreed on a price yet," ventured Pohl.

"But we just agreed on the equivalent of six guilders. We started at dollars and translated that, and now I shall calculate it in pounds—I can add, say, one percent inflation if you like, but this late in the season I will have a difficult time selling the pelts myself."

"We agreed on nothing," said Gerk, once more brandishing his knife. "Six guilders is robbery. You are a liar and a thief and a cur, and I am going to kill you where you sit."

There was only so much van Clynne could take, even from a fellow countryman with a knife and an evil glint in his eye. To be called a liar and a thief and a cur in the same sentence called for immediate action.

After another sip of ale.

Van Clynne took up his tankard slowly, managed a strong if slow pull, and then splashed the remainder of its contents into Gerk's face. This distraction gave him the advantage he needed to upset the table with his prodigious waist. Gerk was taken by surprise and fell to the floor, where the sharp bounce of his head off the hard wooden plank immobilized him.

Pohl, meanwhile, jumped back out of the way. He was not so reasonable as van Clynne believed, however. In fact, as van Clynne leaned over Gerk's prostrate body to retrieve the knife, Pohl drew a pocket pistol from its hiding place at the back of his coat and aimed at van Clynne.

It was a small weapon twenty years old, in mediocre repair. The ball it held was no more than the size of a small bumblebee. Nonetheless, even a bee's sting, properly aimed, can be fatal, and van Clynne presented a large target of opportunity. An immense target, actually, and difficult to miss. But Pohl missed nonetheless, thanks to the timely intervention of a stranger, who had been sitting nearby with his lunch. He threw Pohl's arm upward and punched him in the side. The pistol flew into the air, where the stranger promptly snatched it.

"Nasty little thing," said the man, looking at the gun. "Shouldn't go waving these in public; they often misfire."

The stranger's quip as well as his exploits will readily identify him to all who have already made his acquaintance—the interloper was none other than Lieutenant Colonel Jake Stewart Gibbs, having stopped here for a bit of lunch after riding all morning and most of the previous night.

The proprietor of the inn appeared in the doorway, wearing the universal look of dread innkeepers all over the world put on when they ask the question: Who will pay for this mess?

Van Clynne went to the keeper and whispered an answer so eloquent that the man promptly escorted his two assailants to the door.

"I hate to resort to violence," complained van Clynne to the man who had saved his life. "But I will not be called a cur, even by a fellow countryman. It will cost me seventy skins, but—well, had they been any good, undoubtedly he would have sold them much earlier; the season in truth is gone. Frankly, I deal with him only because I've a soft spot for his wife and children. It's a disease, compassion; it robs a businessman of good sense."

"No doubt."

"Your name, sir?"

"Jake Gibbs. And yours?"

"Claus van Clynne," said the Dutchman with a flourish. "Pleased to make your acquaintance."

As Jake bowed his head in answer to van Clynne's gesture, the Dutchman fixed on Jake's tricornered hat and frowned. Such hats were common among English-bred colonists; surely their creases conformed to some irregularity within the skull. His opinion of the stranger dropped appreciably, though he was careful not to share it.

"Thank you, sir, for your assistance," said van Clynne gracefully. "I am obliged."

"No problem. Always pleased to help a fellow traveler."

"Yes, yes." Van Clynne harrumphed in the direction of the pocket pistol which Jake still held in his hand.

"I think not," he replied, understanding that van Clynne wanted it.

"Thieves come in all shapes and sizes these days," grumbled the Dutchman. "The whole world is going to hell."

"I didn't say I was keeping it. Just that I wouldn't give it to you." He carefully uncocked the miniature lock and unscrewed the barrel to remove the bullet. "Buy me a drink?"

"Buy you a drink?"

"I did save your life."

"Yes, well, perhaps he would have missed."

Jake tapped the belly in front of him but said nothing, motioning to the chair instead and calling over the innkeeper for two ales.

"On me," said Jake. "You're a trader?"

Van Clynne made a face immediately. "A trader, sir, is a man only shortly removed from the lowest form of life scuttling about the forest floor. I am a merchant, a free-lance proprietor, a good man of business and a man of standing in the world, I daresay."

"I see."

"I deal in commodities and services. At present, I am going north to arrange for the purchase of some good Canadian wood, as well as some other odds and ends. I have many interests. Upon occasion I even consent to handle a few odd furs, though as I have said, it is mostly a matter of charity, vainglorious charity."

"You're going to Canada?"

"I may." Van Clynne eyed his drink cautiously, but then lifted his tankard and drained off a good portion.

"You have the papers that will take you past the patrols?"

"I have the right to come and go as I please," said van

Clynne haughtily. "I am a businessman. I have rights of passage from both Carleton and Philip Schuyler."

"I'm going that way myself. Perhaps you can guide me."

"Guide? The road is well-marked."

"I've never been over it."

"Hmmph." Van Clynne finished off the rest of the ale, then pushed the tankard forward for a refill. "Twenty crowns," he said after the girl had taken it off to the kitchen.

"For?"

"Twenty crowns to take you across the British lines with me. That's what you want, isn't it?"

"Perhaps."

"Ha! You don't have the proper papers and are afraid of being apprehended—most likely by the patriots, who would tar and feather you for breakfast."

Van Clynne quieted as the girl approached with his refilled cup. He waited until she had left before speaking again.

"You're a Tory, aren't you?" said the Dutchman under his breath.

"Actually, I'm on a business trip, as you are," said Jake smoothly. "My family is in the apothecary trade, and we are looking to buy rattlesnake essence from the Indians to the north. I have the requisite papers."

"I quite mistook you, sir," said van Clynne, rolling his eyeball up and down like a periscope surveying the countryside from the safety of a fortress wall. "It will cost thirty crowns to take you north with a story like that. Plus expenses. No paper money, please."

"It's not such a bad story," said Jake.

"Ha!" Van Clynne's laugh momentarily filled the inn before he returned his voice to its strategic softness. "I should like to hear it told at Ticonderoga. The first thing I would do, if I were you, would be to lose that hat. Get something sensible like mine. Beavers are meant to be round."

"Ten crowns," said Jake.

"Thirty-five."

"You're moving in the wrong direction."

"I'm Dutch."

"I'll give you fifteen when we reach Montreal."

"Five now, and twenty at Crown Point."

The price for a canoe ride from Albany to Crown Point —before the war—was about five New York pounds, just a bit over what van Clynne was asking for a shorter journey that would not include the amenities or expenses of transportation. The reader may draw his or her own conclusion as to how hard a bargain the Dutchman was driving.

"Twenty in total," said Jake. "At Montreal. I have a friend there who will lend me the money. I've barely enough shillings now for the trip."

Van Clynne's eye once more slipped into periscope mode. A frown came to his face, and he stuck out his hand to seal the deal.

"I can spot them a mile away," he said after they had each had a sip of beer. "That's your black stallion with the fancy bags out there, isn't it? I saw it on the way in and said to myself, now there's a Tory."

Jake smiled but said nothing. The rattlesnake story— which had some vague elements of truth to it, since his family was in the apothecary business—was indeed pathetic, but it was supposed to be. This Dutchman was perfect, completely of a type most useful to a man in Jake's profession. The more you puffed up their egos and let them think they were brilliant, the more they played the cooperative fool. Van Clynne was just the person to help him avoid notice as he crossed the border.

"This beer—the brewer is not Dutch, I daresay," grumbled van Clynne. "There was a time when every wife knew how to make ale, and every wife's ale was a nectar to the angels. Now—pfffff. Taste this. Taste it."

"You finished your whole tankard already."

"Due to thirst only. I would not have another. No, no, under no circumstances, though my thirst does remain quite strong, sir, now that you mention it."

"I didn't mention it. And I'm not going to buy you one."

Van Clynne frowned, realizing there was more to this Mr. Gibbs than his silly hat or lame story foretold. Still, twenty crowns was twenty crowns, especially in British currency.

"I suppose your friends will be waiting for us outside," said Jake, draining his cup and rising to resume the journey. He was anxious to get moving.

"I doubt it," said van Clynne. "I know these fellows well. They're cowards. Must be in the next county by now."

But Jake proved to be the better judge of character. Pieter Gerk, armed with a fresh knife, accosted them halfway between the door and the paddock where the horses were tied. His sidekick Pohl was conspicuously absent—

Jake ducked just in time. Pohl missed and flew through the air spectacularly, though he was in no position to admire the trajectory. Jake reached up and knocked the man's foot as he passed, altering his path enough to change what would have been a four-point landing into a one-point crash, that point being his head.

But Pohl was a robust man, with an extremely thick skull. Somewhat to Jake's surprise, he managed not only to get up, but to punch him in the stomach when he approached. Jake fell back and pulled a small black pouch from under his belt where it had been secreted. As Pohl charged blindly toward him, he stepped aside and clamped his hand and the bag's contents on Pohl's nose.

The miscreant stood straight upright, temporarily paralyzed by scorpion powder. A flick of Jake's wrist sent him in a heap to the dust.

In the meantime, van Clynne had stirred himself, knocking Gerk back against a tree and once again separating him from his knife. If the Dutchman was portly, he was spry for his size; his frame held a good deal of muscle along with the fat.

Jake grabbed the knife from the ground and surveyed the situation. He was sorry to have used the last of his paralyzing powder, but it would have lost its potency soon anyway.

"I suppose we should give them their weapons back," he suggested.

"Give them back?"

"Yes," said Jake. "I wouldn't want to be called a thief."
He bent the polished but poorly tempered steel into a
curve with the flat of his palm. The display of arm
strength had the intended effect on Gerk—his shudders
made it clear he wouldn't bother following, though Jake
thought it prudent to toss the two halves of the pocket
pistol and some shillings in the dirt for their troubles, just
to show there were no hard feelings.

"Must be an English knife," said van Clynne as they
rode away. "They're making the damn things so cheap
these days."

"They certainly are," said Jake.

Two hours later Jake began to question whether he had
indeed chosen the right guide. He was by now well ahead
of schedule, thanks to the remarkable shortcuts van
Clynne was showing him. But this advantage in speed was
coming at a heavy price—the Dutchman had a penchant
for discourse.

Not discourse, precisely—complaint. His entire philosophy might be summarized thusly: The world had gone to
hell in the past fifty years.

Actually, there were hints that the decline extended to
the collapse of the tulip bulb market, but Jake didn't care
to interrupt the flow of words for an exact date. His companion was clearly a man who saw the tankard not only
half empty, but on the verge of rusting through. Every
portion of the world was in sorry shape—just now van
Clynne was complaining that the fir trees were not nearly
as green as they used to be.

His own thoughts wandering as a matter of self-preser-
vation, Jake nearly missed the import of van Clynne's
sudden harrumph.

He looked up to see three men on horseback blocking
their path. Adrenaline flushed into his body as he realized they were the same men—two whites and an Indian
—whom he had unsuccessfully followed yesterday evening. Providence had delivered them to him.

It had also placed rifles in their hands, aimed sharply
in his direction.

"Good sirs," said van Clynne lightly. "How can we be of assistance?"

"You can start by handing over your worldly possessions," said the pockmarked man—the same demon who had ordered the child's death. His deerskin hunting shirt, fringed collar and cuffs showed signs of many hard scrapes.

His white companion was similarly dressed, though his clothes were considerably newer and not so sorely tried. He wore the look of a man who disdained these transactions.

The reader will remember that the previous day Jake had guessed that this man was a British officer. Today, Jake was at leisure to construct an entire narrative for the trio: The pockmarked man was a Tory loyalist and criminal, who thought the entire adventure an excuse for robbery and murder. The second white was a British spy fresh from England, learning that the woods had their own cruel morality. The last of the group was an unattached Iroquois warrior, seeking glory but unsure of his course, let alone his companions.

While his eyes were glued to the trio, Jake's hands were slipping unseen behind his coat to grasp the Styan handgun secreted at the back of his saddle. His two other pistols were in plain view at the front; loaded as always, they would be useful in their turn.

"Now, now, gentlemen," said van Clynne, his voice three times as cheery as it had been at any moment since he had left the tavern. "We have a letter from General Schuyler himself, a good Dutchman, guaranteeing us free passage."

Van Clynne, noting the smile and disdainful frown, hastened to add, "And his worship, Governor Carleton, likewise has granted us permission to travel. So sirs, I beg you—"

"On your knees when you beg," said the pockmarked man.

"Claus van Clynne goes on his knees to no man!"

"On your knees you swine." The pockmarked man lifted his light cavalry musket toward van Clynne. His companions followed suit.

Frowning and grumbling heavily, van Clynne shifted on his horse, leaning over to comply.

"You, too." Pockmark gestured menacingly at Jake.

Jake nodded meekly, and leaned to the side of his horse as if dismounting. But as he did so, he swung his pistol up and got off a shot that added a fresh mark to the Tory's face, this one brighter red than the others, tinged around the sides a dark black. It was the devil's own sign, reserving the murderer for the special place in hell put aside for those who kill children.

As he dove to the ground, Jake pulled a fresh pistol from the saddle holster. He tumbled behind his horse, springing to his knees and pushing the gun forward as he pulled its trigger, throwing its bullet toward the disguised British officer.

In retrospect, Jake decided that it might have been better to miss, or merely wing the man, since he had already dropped his weapon in fright. The officer might have provided some information on British intentions and, at the very least, explained the details of his mission here. But there is no taking back vengeance once unleashed—the ball found its mark square in the man's chest.

Jake had no time to second-guess himself at the moment, for he was now on the opposite side of his horse from his remaining gun. More critically, he was directly in the aim of the Iroquois brave.

In the next second Jake heard a loud whizzing sound that he mistook for the approach of a bullet or maybe an angel, come to lead him to the river Styx.

But he was mistaken. Completely intact and no nearer his Maker than he had been for many months, Jake rolled over to see the Indian flat on his back, his weapon unfired and his skull punctuated by a large tomahawk.

A tomahawk? Where had that come from?

"This will cost you an extra five crowns," said van Clynne, walking over.

"What for?"

"Physical exertion." The Dutchman lowered himself with great difficulty and retrieved his hatchet from the man's skull. "And just after I've had it sharpened, too," he said, glancing at the blade as he wiped it clean on the dead man's leggings. "You know, there was a time when a blade stood up to usage. Now they are much too easily dulled."

Five

Wherein, the story proceeds northward, with various and sundry discussion of miscellaneous items, including the fine art of hatchet-throwing.

Jake was anxious to continue on his mission, but prudence as well as duty required him to give the men a decent burial, even if they would not have returned the favor. Before laying them in their graves, Jake rifled their clothes as discreetly as possible, looking for papers or anything else that might give him more information about the task they had been assigned, if any. The only thing interesting he found was a Hawkins and Wilson smoothbore flintlock pistol. The British-made gun was a handsome weapon—General Washington himself owned a pair.

It was much too useful to be buried with the dead men —Jake stuck it in his saddlebag.

The Dutchman said very little as they went about the grim task of burying the men. Jake wondered what van Clynne made of them and their identities, whether he considered them mere bandits or disguised rangers, as Jake did. But there was no way to ask without inviting suspicion about his own identity and purpose.

Besides, Jake was too busy digging to talk; van Clynne's contribution to the job became more and more theoretical as it proceeded.

The horses would fetch a decent price in Ticonderoga, but the Dutchman surprised Jake by letting them go free. Clearly this was a businessman who took only prudent risks. Allies or even enemies of this murderous trio might well recognize the horses, and pointed questions might not be as easily turned away as this late attack.

Frowning as deeply as ever, van Clynne mounted his horse and waited impatiently as Jake said a short prayer commending the men to their fate. As he was sure they were going straight to hell, it was more in the way of thanksgiving than mourning.

Back on the road, the Dutchman's tongue soon loosened. He began by complaining about the weather, which had turned very warm; he moved on to remarks about the thickness of the mosquitoes. In truth, the bugs were not thick at all, since it was still only May, but logic had no bearing on van Clynne's arguments, and if Jake had pointed this out, the Dutchman would instantly have found a dozen arguments to sustain his point. Jake kept his mouth shut, and presently, by some segue he couldn't track, van Clynne was giving him a lengthy dissertation on the state of Indian affairs.

"The fellow was an Iroquois from the Onondagas. A loner, but it is a bad sign nonetheless."

"He's not Mohawk?"

Van Clynne launched into the differences between the Maquas or Mohawks, who controlled the fur trade, and their Iroquois brothers to the west. The Mohawks called themselves "Ganiengehaga," meaning "the flint people" and referring to one of their stock trading items.

"Have the Iroquois joined the British?" Jake asked, hoping his companion might yield some tidbits useful for Schuyler's defense. If he was to be harangued all the way to Canada, he might as well try and make some use of it.

"Some yes, some no. There is a great debate among them even now. Schuyler has kept the tribes near him neutral so far, but there's blood between the Iroquois and the British, and with these people, blood will tell," said the Dutchman.

"What do you mean, blood?"

"Blood. One of their chiefs is related to the damn English. What's worse, one of the English took an Iroquois for a bride. You know what that means."

Jake shook his head.

"These people are ruled by their women. It's disgraceful. I am a great admirer of the Iroquois, except in this. They can't make a move without their squaws. Let me give you a piece of advice that will stand you in good stead for the rest of your days—any woman who rules you will ruin you. Why do you think the Indians are so given to drink?"

Jake gave a noncommittal grunt.

"Now in my day, a woman knew her place. Ensign Niessen at Wildwyck—there was a man who understood women. Had only to raise his eyebrow, and his supper was fetched. And the woman was a good brewer besides. Aye, an excellent wife. Not like today."

Wildwyck, as van Clynne eventually explained, was the true Dutch name for Kingston, changed from the even more appropriate Esopus by the admirable governor Peter Stuyvesant, who, though not without his faults, would tower over mankind like the Alps over Europe if he were alive today.

The name Wildwyck, as van Clynne did not explain, hadn't been used officially for perhaps a hundred years. As for Ensign Niessen, the man had lived a good century ago, something Jake knew because the house he stayed at near Kingston just a few days before had been built by Niessen's son, already a full generation gone.

Though he spoke of him as a cousin, van Clynne couldn't have known the ensign himself. His round face, obscured by a thick beard, was of indeterminate age, but Jake reckoned he wasn't past fifty. There was a certain youthfulness in his voice, too, despite its constant pessimistic tone; it was quite possible that the Dutchman was only in his early forties, or perhaps even his thirties. This was much older than Jake, of course, but not nearly ancient; Dr. Franklin and many other leaders of the Revolution had marked considerably more years off the calendar. But van Clynne seemed to have acquired old age in his youth, cultivating it rather than running from it as most men do. His clothes were old-fashioned, cut fuller and looser than Jake's, even taking his girth into account. His belt was cinched with a massive buckle, ornately decorated in silver. Large buckles held his shoes tight to his feet, and despite the dust of travel, it was obvious that they had been blackened this morning, a bit of fussiness one ordinarily wouldn't have associated with a country traveler. His stockings were a red russet—another obsolete mark, and an unusually colorful gesture for the otherwise cloudy Dutchman.

His breeches and coat were a dull brown. The sleeves were open peculiarly in a fashion worn almost exclusively in the Hudson Valley. Van Clynne's hat was a fine beaver, well-proportioned for his head. Though the style was still popular, this particular hat looked ancient. It wasn't that it was battered or worn; on the contrary. But the pelts themselves seemed somehow to have come from old beavers, with vague streaks of gray showing through in the light. The brim at the front was turned up slightly, affording a good line of sight to the burgher.

"I'm not a burgher," van Clynne said sharply.

"I meant no offense."

"Next you'll be calling me a patroon." The word spit from his mouth.

"I just meant to ask where you came from," said Jake contritely.

"I haven't asked you similar questions, have I? We have a business relationship, you and I; best to keep it that way."

"Fair enough."

"I retain the title Esquire from the British, since they are in possession of our country," said van Clynne. "Especially since they are in possession of my piece of it."

"The English took your land?"

To Jake's surprise, van Clynne didn't answer, changing the subject instead.

"It was a nice pistol."

"Which?"

"The pistol you took from our friend. British, yes?"

"I think so," said Jake.

"The flintlock is an intriguing invention. It was perfected by a Dutchman, you know."

"You're pulling my leg, right? The Dutch haven't invented anything in two hundred years."

Van Clynne shot him a nasty glance and continued with his dissertation. "The only truly great weapon, though, is a blunderbuss. The wheel lock—do you know how many families have been saved by its invention? Ask the river Indians what they think of it."

"Bit of a pain to twist the spring when you're under attack, isn't it?" said Jake.

Jake had no need for a course on ballistics and was not inclined to listen to van Clynne's discussion of the merits of smooth and rifled barrels. But his interest was piqued when suddenly the Dutchman began giving him an amazingly detailed description of a breech-loaded rifle.

Such a gun had been perfected only a few years before in England. Jake had seen one while he was there at school, and had not failed to be impressed by it. In fact, he harbored hopes of conducting a special mission to England to retrieve one as a model for manufacture in the near future.

The gun's key feature was a screw-threaded, ten-point plug in its breech at the top of the barrel. This allowed the ball or bullet to be placed there directly, rather than having to be rammed down the rifled barrel. Powder was wedged in behind it—you didn't have to worry about measuring, since only the right amount fit. Back comes the plug, lock cocked and—

"Boom!" said van Clynne.

"Boom," echoed Jake. "Tell me, squire, where did you get such a weapon?"

"Who said that I had one?"

"You talk as if you do."

"No, no," said van Clynne. "It is just an idea of mine. A fancy."

Jake doubted that strenuously, but kept his opinion to himself. Instead, he opened a line of inquiry into another area that had lately interested him.

"Where did you learn to throw a hatchet like that?"

"I will answer that question," replied van Clynne, "if you'll tell me where you got that potion that stood our friend up like a skittle pin."

"I told you I'm searching for cures," said Jake. He'd hoped the drug had escaped his companion's notice, but van Clynne was proving a wily type. "This was just a little concoction I came across in my travels."

"And would you have any more of it, by chance?"

"Afraid not," replied Jake, who would have answered the same even if he had. "It isn't easy to obtain."

"The wilden taught me how to throw the ax," said the Dutchman, paying off his end of the bargain. "Wilden" was the Dutch word for Indian or native. "Mohawks specifically. It's all a matter of balance. Would you like a demonstration?"

Jake soon found himself dismounted, standing next to van Clynne as he extolled the virtues of a straight handle and a true head.

"Your target must be an odd number of steps away, five, seven, or nine; farther than that and you add uncertainty," said van Clynne. "You grasp the butt end of the handle exactly in the middle of your palm." He demonstrated. "Note my legs, loose, evenly apart. My weight is on my right foot."

"I noticed the strain."

A brief frown passed over van Clynne's face. "Here, stand over there, before that tree."

"Why?"

"You want a demonstration, don't you?"

Against his better judgment, Jake walked to the front of the tree and turned to face van Clynne. He was rewarded by the swift whiz of an ax sailing head over heels in his direction.

First he ducked, barely in time. Then he flew at his assailant.

"Wait, wait," protested van Clynne. "I threw it to land exactly over your head. I never miss. Go and see. Go and see."

Jake loosened his grip on van Clynne's cravat. He turned toward the tree, where the head of the tomahawk was buried deep in the trunk. Sure enough, the handle rested a measured inch above his scalp.

"Now I'll give you a demonstration," said Jake, pushing van Clynne to the spot where he had stood.

"N-Not with an ax, I hope," stuttered the Dutchman.

Jake had already removed his four-shot Segallas pocket pistol from his vest pocket. It was a magnificent miniature gun with four tiny barrels, each with its own separate frizzen and flash pan, so he did not have to reprime after each shot. Nor did he have to reload, blasting one trigger, then the next, flipping the barrels with a quick twist and firing the third and then the fourth.

. Such a beautiful gun was a rarity in America, a fine and deadly specimen. Van Clynne did not remark on it, however. In fact, the Dutchman seemed quite speechless as Jake bounced the first two bullets off each side of the hatchet head, and then, feeling a bit peevish, buried the others next to the soles of van Clynne's shoes.

"As long as we understand each other," he said, nodding to van Clynne.

"We do, sir, we do," said the squire, brushing himself off as the color returned to his face. "You trust me, and I trust you. It is a good business arrangement."

Thousands of years before, upper New York had been covered with a massive glacier, a huge spit of ice that fitfully gave way to a puddle of cold water huge enough to be considered a sea. The remains of that Laurentide ocean stretched to Jake's right as dusk began to come on, visible through trees and the occasional meadow. He and van Clynne were approaching the fringes of patriot territory, and could feel the boundary in the growing chill as an evening wind began kicking up from Canada.

How much colder had it been ten thousand years before, when Mother Nature began blowing her warm breath on the ice, pushing back the invading ice so she could experiment anew with life in the valley? Her soft breath left behind huge deposits of scraped-white rock, booty and symbols of the struggle. Representatives of those rocks greeted them now, gleaming in the last red rays of the day—Fort Ticonderoga, the American stronghold and key to the defense of upper New York.

The patriot victory at the fort two years before was already celebrated in song and legend. A pair of American forces had combined in the capture—one under Benedict Arnold, the other under Ethan Allen. Taken together, they had not more than two hundred men under them, but the fiercest fighting was between themselves; the fifty or so defenders of the fort were mostly old pensioners put out to pasture with what was consid-

ered, until that moment, easy duty. The Americans'
booty was not merely the fort, which protected Albany
and the Hudson headwaters, but something on the order
of eighty bronze cannon. Those weapons had become the
backbone of the American artillery corps.

Jake and his guide were admiring the stone walls from
a distance because they had made a strategic decision to
avoid the fort and surrounding settlements. People there,
officers especially, had a tendency to ask questions and
look at papers, and even if these were—all in order—as
van Clynne assured Jake they were—still, such matters
were best not continually put to the test.

"Can we hire a boat north of here?" Jake asked as van
Clynne directed him to take a left at the next fork in the
road. Even though they'd made remarkable time, he
wanted to go faster still, and a boat would shorten the
journey.

Van Clynne held off answering as a wagon approached.
He nodded at the man driving it as if he knew him, and
continued on.

"We're not taking a boat," he said. "Too many war-
ships of both sides on the lake."

Last fall the British had come as far south as Crown
Point, about fifteen miles north on Lake Champlain.
They were halted by caution, the approaching winter, and
an American flotilla. Jake was unsure of the exact status
of hostilities on the water, but as his traveling companion
seemed extremely well-informed, he followed along without comment.

The Dutchman knew not only every highway and by-
way here, but also the deer paths and spring streams.
They splashed up one of the latter as night came on,
avoiding a small village whose population, according to
van Clynne, consisted entirely of very nosy housewives.
Their immediate destination was a house two miles farther on. It was owned by a Dutchman whose formula for
brown porter was unrivaled in the state, according to van
Clynne, who began proclaiming the virtues of its brewer
as they pushed through the dark woods.

As the lane narrowed, Jake's sixth sense of danger detection began to assert itself. He didn't fear a double-

cross from his companion riding ten yards behind him so much as another ambush, this one more easily accomplished in the blackness. Placing a pistol in his left hand, Jake reined his horse carefully with the other. His eyes scanned carefully for movement and his ears tuned to the specific frequency of human footfalls.

It was just such a sound thirty yards to his right that caught his attention. When he heard the second step he leaped off his horse and sped silently through the woods, gun in hand.

Van Clynne jabbered on, not even aware Jake had dismounted. His first notice of the ambush came with the loud crash and muffled moan the intruder emitted as Jake caught the man from behind, cupping his hand over his mouth to keep him from screaming out.

Pardon—her mouth. There was no mistaking that once he touched the soft smoothness of her face. Jake, seeing she was unarmed, turned her gently toward him with his left hand, which held the pistol. He was mildly surprised and somewhat pleased to see defiance, not fear, in her eyes.

When he let go, reaching down to pick up her fallen basket of early blueberries, she leveled a blow at his head.

He ducked and upended the girl, grabbing her around the middle.

"Let me down," she screamed, kicking and punching. "My father will shoot you if you hurt me."

"I meant no harm," said Jake, setting her down gingerly—her muscles were nearly as strong as her spirit. "I thought you were coming to attack us."

"Who are you, riding through the woods at night?" she demanded. "Another soldier from the fort, or some damn Tory?"

"Johanna, Johanna Blom," shouted van Clynne, arriving late to the commotion. He explained in a very excited Dutch that Jake was a friend and meant no harm.

Jake's passing knowledge of the language allowed him to add that, had he known their assailant was this pretty, he surely would have surrendered without a fight. That remark prompted Mistress Johanna to attempt another punch, though its intended victim noted that this one was grabbed more easily than the others.

Apologies offered if not wholly accepted, Jake and van Clynne were escorted to the Blom house. Fifty years before, the two-story clapboard affair—as van Clynne explained in his flourishing style—had been an estimable stopping point for travelers. New roads, more dependable boats along the lake, and the failure of the local beaver population had conspired to cause its decline, though Blom still let rooms from time to time, and his taproom remained popular with the male population of the small hamlet up the road a quarter of a mile, especially those seeking to avoid their wives.

Jake and his guide were soon sitting in front of the hearth, the fire stoked against the late spring chill, a mug of nut-brown porter in hand. The fire glowed and reflected off the hard-scrubbed floor, turning the whole room a bright yellow.

The porter was round and pleasing in the mouth, Jake had to admit. Even better was Mistress Johanna, who lost none of her spark indoors. As van Clynne and Blom fell into a long debate about the decline in the quality of ale yeasts—a crucial ingredient in the beer—she took up a station to Jake's left in front of the fireplace. Johanna propped a long iron poker across her lap, though the fire was not in need of much attention at the moment.

"That's quite a stick you have," joked Jake.

"In case you attack me again, I want to be prepared."

"I'm already in your power."

Johanna shot an embarrassed glance toward her father. He was deep in conversation—surely the decline in the yeasts went back fifty years, and had to do with the shift of the Atlantic currents.

Though pretty, Jake had already concluded she was too young for more than the mildest flirting, and he merely nodded and sipped his beer as the girl walked slowly back to the kitchen, hesitating enough to let him know she wouldn't mind being followed.

Meanwhile, van Clynne and Blom had changed not only their topic of conversation but their style of talking, low whispers replacing loud boasts.

"You've stopped by just in time, Claus," said Blom. "We have a little adventure planned this evening, around midnight."

"A party?"

"You might say, though the guests of honor won't take much pleasure in it. The Smiths have been hosting a British agent, who's trying to recruit the countryside to desert to the king."

"Found no takers, I hope."

"None. But we can't have that sort of thing going on in the neighborhood. We're going to tar and feather the devil tonight, and send him on his way. Myself and a few of the local Liberty boys." Blom glanced toward Jake, who pretended to be engrossed in watching Johanna leave the room. "Do you think your friend would come along?"

Van Clynne made a face. "I think not."

Jake slunk back in his spindled chair and waited for the Dutchman to give him away. He had resigned himself to admitting he was an American agent—and positioned his pocket pistol in case they weren't ready to believe him—when he heard van Clynne say that Jake was a Quaker and thus could not participate in any warfare.

"Best to leave him totally in the dark," added the Dutchman.

"Have you tested his loyalties?"

"Oh, I vouch for him," van Clynne bristled. "But let us not take unnecessary chances. The more people who know of an operation, the more chance for something to go wrong. Some people just can't keep their mouths shut."

Even disguised as a Tory deserter, Jake Gibbs couldn't pass up an opportunity to wreak a little havoc on the British cause, especially if all he was sacrificing were a few hours of sleep and the possibility of fending off the innkeeper's daughter. Besides, he wanted to make sure van Clynne survived to help him north in the morning.

Jake wasn't sure what to make of the Dutchman's lie about his being a Quaker. Perhaps he felt obligated by their business deal, or else his demonstration of prowess with the pocket pistol was still fresh in the squire's mind. In any event, van Clynne didn't mention his planned sojourn when they were packed off to the upstairs room to sleep.

Unlike many backwoods inns, there were separate beds. Jake didn't object when van Clynne took the one nearest the door, nor did he let on that he was still awake a half hour later when Blom knocked on the door and whispered that it was time to leave. The Dutchman had fallen asleep—his snores were akin to the doleful soundings of a beached whale—and Jake was treated to a few minutes' amusement as Blom tried to wake him. Finally, the innkeeper pulled the Dutchman's beard, and he bolted upright with a start and whispered curse.

Jake let the pair get a head start, then snuck out of the darkened house and trailed them up the road. Van Clynne's grumpy voice carried farther than the light of his torch. He spent much of the short walk complaining about the sudden chill of the night—in the old days, spring came on with reckless abandon, and there was never a need for as much as a jacket once the snow had gone.

Jake saw why Blom had been interested in recruiting him when the pair met four or five men gathered in front of the hamlet's small church. None of these Liberty boys was younger than sixty. The tiny community had sent all of its young men and a few of the older ones as well to the nearby fort; these old gentlemen were all that remained of the local male population.

They were a feisty lot nonetheless, and in the manner of Liberty men across the continent, had prepared a proper tar bath and an effigy to impress the British recruiter with. As they passed a bottle to rally their youth for the coming action, Jake slipped back in the woods, as much to stifle a laugh as anything else—these ancients sounded like a squad of nineteen-year-old privates, ready to take on the world. But there was no need to tell one versed in the apothecary sciences that age was largely a matter of the mind.

Just as he settled into the darkness, Jake heard someone else moving through the nearby woods. He stood deer-still and watched a small figure emerge from behind the trees, study the gathering, and then retreat. The patriot spy followed along as quickly as he dared, and as quietly as possible. The shadow—so short and thin he must be a boy of eight or nine—climbed over a rail fence into a cleared yard and began running; Jake had to let him get a very long lead before he decided it would be safe to pursue.

It was easy enough to see where he went. Well before Jake arrived at the back of the house, he realized the destination must be the Smith family homestead, and that the boy must be allied with the Tories.

"They're on their way, Father," said the lad to two taller figures in the road in front of the house. "They're in front of the church."

"Good, Jamie. Go inside with Mother and make sure the cannon is ready. Mr. Peters and I will be here awhile longer."

Peters—whose accent gave him away immediately as a British officer fresh from south Wales—was working on a vast ditch in the road in front of the house, filling it with water from a nearby well. "We're ready," he told Smith. "We've just got to cover the trench with the rushes and dirt. No one will see it in the dark."

"I don't want to hurt anyone," said Smith.

"They're coming to kill you, man," declared the British recruiter indignantly. "This is merely a small trick you're playing on them. No need to feel guilty."

"The swivel cannon, though."

"We'll fire it only if they attack the home. You've got to protect your family."

"What if it goes off by accident?"

"Buck up, Smith. These people are rebels."

Jake let the reluctant Tory continue his debate with the devil as he snuck to the back of the house, determined that there would be no such accident. In truth, most Loyalists did not feel the qualms Smith expressed, and Jake saw some hope for him—though not if the evening proceeded as planned.

A small lean-to was located at the back of the house, serving the family as a summer kitchen. The voices inside the building indicated that mother and son—and at least two other children—were working on the swivel gun in the front room. Jake could easily sneak in while their attentions were turned toward the cannon and the street.

He had brought two of his pistols with him, and he took one now from his belt. Already loaded, he wanted to use it to scare the family into submission—but only scare them, for he was loath to hurt women and children, no matter how misguided their loyalties. He therefore took the unusual expedient of removing the flint from the firing mechanism—the pistol was cocked, and except to a careful eye would seem ready to fire. Jake could even pull the trigger, though nothing would happen. The other gun remained ready at his waist.

Hearing noises in the distance up the road, Jake wedged his foot inside the door and eased it open, sneaking into the kitchen—and directly in front of the business end of a large, ancient, but very definitely loaded and simmering matchlock.

Six

Wherein, Jake finds that not all Whigs and Tories are ready enemies.

"*D*rop your weapon, sir, or you will find yourself singing in Gabriel's choir," said the gun's master, the same lad who had earlier acted as advance scout.

Jake couldn't help but admire the young man's spirit. He also couldn't help but hold his arms out at a fair length, then slowly bend his knees for the ground.

"I'll just set my pistol down here," he said, placing it on the long, woven carpet before him.

"Now take a step away. Smartly if you please," said the lad.

"As you wish," said Jake, who stepped with his right foot off the rug—and with his left foot pulled the cloth suddenly forward, judging that the boy was too light and the floor too polished to offer much resistance. He judged correctly—and caught the lad and his gun as they flew upward.

"Let go of me, or I'll tell Mother!"

"I'll tell her myself," said Jake, holding the squirming lad beneath his arm like a log as he fetched and extinguished the matchlock. "I admire your bravery, but you're expressing it on the wrong side of the fight."

"My father will have you hung."

"Your father will do well not to be hung himself," said Jake, carrying the boy forward into the front room where his mother was waiting.

"Put my son down, sir, or I'll shoot you through with this swivel cannon."

The woman had turned the gun, mounted on a thick

steel tripod in the middle of the front hall, to face him. She was holding a fuse stick in her hand. Jake could see from the flush in her throat that her heart was beating at close to its limit.

"Come now," said Jake, taking another step inside. "I have no desire to hurt you, and I know that you don't want to hurt your son."

"I warn you, sir, don't test me."

The swivel was a very light but also exceedingly deadly gun. A bit more than four feet long, it weighed near two hundred pounds, but was situated on a mount that made it relatively easy to maneuver, even for a woman. It could not be turned quickly, however, and Jake had only to take two quick side steps to get out of its line of fire. With his third he tossed the boy toward his mother. Instinctually, she put up her arms to catch the lad, and in so doing dropped the wooden switch she meant to use to fire the gun. Jake clamped down on it with his foot, dropped the matchlock and pulled his pistol out.

"Please, madam, step away. This gun is loaded, and I will feel very bad if I have to shoot you."

"Go ahead, rebel," said the woman. "I am ready."

It was terrible to see such bravery wasted in a Tory, and Jake shook his head. "I would not make your poor children orphans," he said. "Into the kitchen with you now."

Two little girls emerged from behind a chair and brought the standstill to an end. The woman gathered them to her quickly, and cursing Jake to hell, escorted her brood to the back.

Unfortunately, this was not the end of this family's bravery. For in his rush to press his advantage, Jake had left his deflinted pistol on the threshold. As the woman made a break with her children for the backyard and freedom, her son Jamie decided he had not yet surrendered—slipping from his mother's arm, he went back into the house and grabbed the gun, continuing inside to confront the intruder.

"Well you're just the type we need fighting on our side," said Jake as he looked up to see the boy before him. The lad's mother was just coming inside, and now Jake saw the brave look from before had been turned to one of deep worry. "I should like you to meet General Washington," he told the boy as he continued to work on the cannon, wadding a piece of the carpet in the mouth so it would misfire. "He has a gun just like that one."

"He's a rebel and a scoundrel," said the boy.

"No, no, the general is a brave man," said Jake, picking up the lit stick. "You would like him very much, and he would like you. He likes brave lads."

The boy steadied the gun in both hands. In truth, he might have had a good chance of hitting Jake had it been able to fire.

"Put down the gun, Jamie," said his mother behind him. "He said he wouldn't hurt us."

"You can't trust a rebel, Mum."

As Jake took a step forward, he realized Mrs. Smith's face might not only express concern for her son but for him as well. Perhaps they might find their way to the right side and do it good service.

They certainly had the raw materials of spunk and bravery—the boy leveled the pistol and pulled the trigger at point-blank range.

"The flint is in my pocket," said Jake as he took it from the bewildered boy. "But this other gun is well-loaded. Take the boy and the other children into the woods, madam. The cannon will make a dreadful mess when it explodes."

Outside, the festivities were just getting under way as the old Liberty boys marched up the road with much shouting and threats to the king's well-being. They had mounted their vat of tar on a small cart and pulled and pushed it along with such abandon that it slipped quite easily into the moat Smith and the British villain Peters had constructed.

"That's what you get, rebels," said Peters, emerging from a nearby bush and standing over the ditch.

"We'll run you out," promised one of the few men who had not fallen into the water-filled hole. "And you, Smith —we'd hoped for better from you."

Smith's response was cut short by a tremendous explosion from inside the house.

"My wife and children!" yelled the Tory, running for the building.

He was no doubt surprised to find his neighbors running right behind him, echoing his concerns. Jake certainly was, as watching from the shadows he saw the men help Smith put out the flames and call for his family in the shattered ruins. Suddenly politics had ceased to matter, and the Liberty boys even held off citing this catastrophe as an example of what came of associating with the British until Smith was tearfully reunited with his family.

The reader knows that most encounters between would-be Loyalist and ardent patriots have not ended with optimistic promises to help rebuild the former's damaged house as this one did, but Jake could not help but smile as he slipped toward the road, realizing that the British recruiter—now helping douse the flames—would find no further succor here, and would indeed end the night by being placed under arrest.

Jake could also not help but smile at the cries of the one man left in the muddy pit, Claus van Clynne.

"Help," called van Clynne, who could not get a good enough footing in the slippery mud to pull himself out of the waist-high water. "I can't swim. This water is deeper than the Atlantic. A rope or a hand before I drown would be greatly appreciated."

Not wanting to blow his cover unless absolutely necessary, Jake crept silently to the edge of the moat and made sure the Dutchman was in no immediate danger. He then trotted back toward Blom's house, so pleased by the events of the night that he found himself wishing Johanna were just a few years older.

Seven

Wherein, van Clynne's prowess as a lover is extolled, and the travelers reach British territory.

"So?"

Van Clynne shot Jake a puzzled glance from the back of his horse. "So what?"

"How'd it go?"

"How'd what go?"

"You left your bed in the middle of the night. I assume you had a midnight rendezvous in town."

"I told you, I spent the entire night sleeping outside the door to our room. Why did you bar it against me?"

"Oh, come on, Claus." Jake gave him a wink. "I've heard stories about you Dutchmen. It's not for nothing you wear your breeches loose, is it?"

"I wear my breeches in very proper fashion," protested van Clynne, stroking his beard for emphasis.

"When you wear them. What, do you expect me to believe you spent the night swimming in the ocean?"

"Well," said van Clynne, stifling a sniffle, "I did have things to attend to."

"You're a good man of business, squire," chuckled Jake.

As difficult as it is to imagine van Clynne's already rotund body puffing, it did seem to inflate under the stimulus of Jake's flattery. Of course, that did not stop him from continuing his complaint that he had not had much sleep.

The detour around Ticonderoga had taken them far to the west, and they were now traveling back toward Lake Champlain. Jake did not have a firm idea of where they were, surmising only that Crown Point—in British control—lay well to the southeast. Van Clynne evidently intended on bypassing the British frontier garrisons, much as he had tiptoed around the American stronghold at the foot of the lake. Not a horribly bad idea, all things considered.

As a precaution before leaving the Blom house this morning, Jake had burnt the papers from Schuyler allowing him to travel unmolested through patriot lines; if stopped by a British patrol, they would raise many embarrassing questions. His only documents now were a list of Indian goods he had supposedly been sent by his father in Philadelphia to search for, and a letter from Governor Guy Carleton's secretary vouching for his character. Both, of course, were forgeries, though Jake had some confidence no British soldier would realize he'd never quite mastered his father's habit of looping his *o*'s at the top.

Having set out when it was still dark, they breakfasted shortly after the sun rose, stopping on a hill that looked out toward the lake, still a good two miles distant. They split a venison pasty prepared by Johanna. It was not a fifty-fifty split—Jake felt he was doing well to get a quarter of it.

As his experience in the ditch last night hinted, van Clynne's reluctance to venture on the water was largely based on his fear of drowning. Nevertheless, it now appeared a wise decision, as Jake saw when he remounted his horse and looked toward Lake Champlain. A trio of gunboats were exchanging intermittent fire with two smaller craft. From this distance the battle appeared more in play than earnest. The geysers from the errant cannon fire looked like pimples suddenly erupting on the water's clear face.

No wonder Flanagan had asked him to complete the mission within a week, a time span that was so short as to be nearly ludicrous. The British were already testing the American defenses; the invasion might come at any moment. This might even be its vanguard.

The boats shifted about with neither side gaining an advantage. Jake and van Clynne watched silently from the distance as the drama played out. They were so absorbed in the battle that they did not hear the approaching riders until they were almost upon them. When they did, the Dutchman merely shrugged, continuing to watch the battle. No doubt this was part of a strategy of nonchalance; Jake told himself once more that he could not have chosen a better guide.

And so the moment of truth stole up quietly, trotting forward in the form of a British lieutenant and his sergeant, who shouted roughly at them but then likewise turned their attentions to the battle in the distance.

"Got the damn rebels on the run," said the sergeant when the two small fleets parted.

Jake grunted in assent. Van Clynne said nothing.

"You will honor me, gentlemen, with your papers," said the lieutenant.

"And what if I have no papers to treat you with?" said van Clynne hostilely. "What will you do then?"

"We'll take you back as prisoners and spies," answered the officer, drawing his sword from its scabbard.

A moment before, Jake could not have had a higher opinion of van Clynne, whose services as a guide had been invaluable. Now his estimation shifted one hundred and eighty degrees—the man was inviting not only suspicion, but death. Nonetheless, Jake remained outwardly calm. He could have his Styan in hand and fired before the officer had finished kicking his horse's flanks for the charge. Then he'd reach down and test his new Hawkins on the sergeant.

"In the days of Governor Stuyvesant, no traveler was ever ill-treated," said van Clynne, reaching into his vest for the papers. "Even an Indian would get proper respect. A man's word was his guarantee. Now, without a piece of foolscap signed by every monkey in the province, one can't even journey three leagues. Every sneeze is regulated."

The officer put his sword back in its sheath and nodded to the sergeant, who dismounted, snatched the wad of papers from van Clynne and handed them over. The lieutenant unfolded the several pages, paying careful consideration to the signatures if not the rest of the words, before handing them back.

"Who's he?" asked the officer.

"My son," said van Clynne.

At that, everyone raised an eyebrow, including Jake.

"He doesn't look Dutch," said the sergeant. "He's dressed like a macaroni." Macaroni was a derogatory term for a dandy, and though Jake would not have been taken for such in the city, out here the fine cut of his clothes tended to stand out.

"The ways of the young," said van Clynne, shaking his head. "I wish I could talk some sense into his head. Perhaps you can."

"Be happy to try," said the sergeant, reaching toward Jake's horse.

Jake pulled the reins around and answered him with a string of oaths in ill-formed pidgin Dutch. Though ruinous to van Clynne's ears, they were enough to convince the soldiers. The Dutchman grabbed his papers back and prodded his horse forward, setting off down the road. Jake followed quickly.

"Why did you give them a hard time?" he asked when they were out of earshot.

"They were British." To van Clynne it seemed a natural explanation. "I told you the hat would draw attention, didn't I?"

"Did you really think they'd believe I was your son?"

"What do I care?" said van Clynne. "You're a deserter, and they won't shoot you for that."

"What do you mean, I'm a deserter?"

"You are. You're a Loyalist who's had enough of the fight. I'd wager that your neighbors drove you from your home and sent you packing. Rattlesnake cure, indeed."

"I am an apothecary," said Jake, adding a slightly mournful note to his voice, as if all van Clynne had said were true.

"Yes, well, I'll take my twenty crowns now, if you please."

"We agreed on Montreal. I have a friend there who'll give me the money."

"Listen up, fellow. You have more than twenty crowns

in your purse, I dare say. I don't care to know your business, but my guess is that you want to get north as quickly as possible, to see your friend or family, whichever it may be. Now, I have business to transact in several houses near here, and I will be all day and possibly the next two or three about it. You may tag along if you wish, but we've gotten through the American lines, which was where the danger lay for you. Wasn't it? Well?"

Jake nodded solemnly. Van Clynne was quite pleased with himself.

"Cut through this field and take the road there," he said, pointing to his right. "You'll come upon the highway, and you can ride straight to Montreal. It's eighty miles at the most, no more."

"How do I know you're not sending me into a trap?" said Jake, caught up in his role as a Tory coward.

"If I were going to turn you in, I would have done so near Ticonderoga. Besides, there's no profit in it—unless, of course, you don't pay me now."

Jake reached inside his clothes to the money belt around his waist. He counted out four gold guineas and then two crowns. Together, the coins could have kept a Boston family in clothes and bread for more than a month.

Van Clynne examined them to see if they had been shaved, a common practice. Each was intact and practically new, an oddity he noted but did not remark on. Before finding their way to Jake's money belt they had been in the charge of a British paymaster, but the tale of that detour lies outside our immediate scope.

"Thank you, good sir," said the Dutchman, doffing his hat as he dropped the coins into a purse he kept on a long string around his neck. "And now, I bid you farewell."

"Good luck in your business," said Jake. "Until we meet again."

"I'd get rid of the hat if I were you," were van Clynne's parting words.

The city of Montreal lies at the foot of Mount Royal on a strategic island in the St. Lawrence. The great French explorer Jacques Cartier discovered it and claimed it for the greater glory and profit of the French kingdom in 1535, though it was not until 1642 that white men made a lasting settlement. The profit in question was largely spiritual, with the Association of Montreal formed by Sieur Paul de Chomedey de Maisonneuve aiming squarely at converting the heathen and adding their population to heaven.

The French, and their Jesuit priests especially, felt a special calling to promulgate the Word in the wilderness, baptizing freely and spreading the spirit of Christianity by whatever means necessary. Smallpox was not meant to be one of those means, but it was nonetheless distributed more quickly and efficiently than the scriptures.

Jeffrey Amherst took Montreal for the British in 1760. Robert Montgomery took it for the Americans in 1775. By the fall of 1776, General Benedict Arnold and his tattered band of disease-ravaged soldiers had given it back, abandoning it in disarray.

By that time Jake was already hard at work for General Greene in New York. After being wounded at Quebec in late December 1775, he'd been evacuated to a makeshift hospital. There he'd refused to let the surgeon take off his leg, preferring death to life as a cripple. His stubbornness had cost him great suffering, but Jake had gambled that he could survive the wound without infection or complication, and won. In truth, the decision had been made at least partly from the wild despair of having seen his friend Captain Thomas and then General Montgomery die but a few yards from him on the battlefield. For a dark moment Jake Stewart Gibbs had not truly cared whether he lived or died.

A great deal of time had passed since then. Jake shifted himself on his horse as he rode along the St. Lawrence, fighting off the sad memories as he steadied himself for the tasks ahead. He decided to promote himself from druggist to doctor—his new cover story would proclaim him a country physician heading to the big city for supplies. Jake, though not specifically trained as a doctor, knew a good portion of medicine from his family's trade and his studies of natural philosophy. He could not only fool any soldiers who questioned him; he could probably treat them better than the military quacks at their camps.

The only deficiency in his story was his dress. As the British sergeant had pointed out, he looked a bit too much the gentleman to be a rough traveler. He adjusted his appearance by loosening his shirt and removing the eagle feather stuck in his cap, but a wary mind at the city's fort could easily find questions for which vague answers would be his only reply.

Which was one reason he didn't intend on going straight in the front door, at least not tonight. Another was the fact that he was tired and hungry, and it was already quite late. The last, and most important, reason was that he was hoping to renew an old acquaintanceship.

*"Jesu—*back from the dead!" exclaimed Marie Sacré when she opened the door.

"Comment vas-tu?" he said in a bashful and rusty French.

"Très bien. But my God, I never expected to see you! *Zut!"*

"Can a poor traveler enter?"

"Of course!" Marie's hair was held back in a simple, almost frontier style, but the thick, smooth material of her mauve-colored dress hinted that she was not merely a plain farmer's wife. The smooth cotton flattered her shape and at the same time was warm and comforting.

"Comme les français sont amiables!" said Jake. The French are so easy.

"Don't get fresh," she said, pulling him along into the front room of the large, two-story brick building.

As Jake took a step onto the wide-beamed floor, a long narrative of his journey formed on his tongue. He was just able to cut it off when he saw the room was not empty.

Not at all. Its occupant rose from his chair, dressed in the bright red jacket favored by followers of His Royal Majesty, the King of England.

"Captain Clark, let me introduce you to my cousin, Jake Gibson," said Marie, putting her arm on his shoulder as she amended his name. "Jake is quite a traveler. He's just come from Quebec."

"Indirectly," said Jake, his only option to play along with what she said.

"Then you must have seen Burgoyne!" exclaimed the British captain, taking his hand and pumping it like a glassblower's bellows with a strong, crushing grip.

"I left before he arrived," said Jake, hoping that made sense—and that he wouldn't have to be more specific. "I had business with the savages."

"We don't call them savages anymore," said Marie in the light but firm voice one used to correct a child. "They are allies."

"What business are you in?" the captain asked.

"I am a doctor of sorts," said Jake, looking at Marie to make sure she heard—and agreed.

"Of sorts?"

"In the backwoods, one handles many things. One learns many things," said Jake, warming now to the task of fooling and then pumping this Captain Clark for information. "I have these past few months been contemplating the efficacy of a rattlesnake cure. I learned of it from a Jesuit, who told me the Huron swore by it as a cure for many diseases, including cancer and pox."

"Inoculation works against the pox," said the soldier.

"Not in all cases. The humors must be properly balanced."

Marie disappeared into the other room. Jake settled in a chair next to the fire, warming himself. His face and manner were nonchalant, but beneath the facade he was coiled and ready to strike. His pocket pistol was charged, though he wasn't sure even all four of its bullets could fell the large man across from him. Fortunately, the officer appeared unarmed, without even his sword. Obviously, he was on very friendly terms with the house's occupant—a fact which not only surprised but perturbed Jake. To find Marie cozying up to the other side wounded him more than the powerfully built redcoat ever could.

"I thought of studying medicine myself before joining the army," said Clark. "I still may, when I return home."

"Yes," said Jake. "How long since you left England?"

"Oh, I've been here for over a year. Came with Burgoyne to rout the rabble, as it were, but I was transferred to the governor's staff. The general, of course, spent the winter in England—jolly wish I could have."

Jake nodded. "But he's back now."

"He certainly is. Thank you, my dear," said the captain, rising as Marie returned with a tray of tea and cups, along with a dish of supper for Jake.

She placed the tray on a small settee; Jake noted that she didn't have to ask the British officer how much sugar he wanted when dropping in the lumps.

"It looks to me your cousin wants something stronger than tea," said the captain when Jake didn't take his cup.

"My system is allergic to tea," said Jake.

Marie turned the harsh undertone to his voice aside as lightly as a compliment. "Oh, I've forgotten, cousin, about your unbalanced humors. How silly of me. Would you like some coffee instead?"

"No."

"Good, because I haven't any." She laughed. "I'll get the rum."

"Allergic to tea?" said the officer. "You sound like a rebel."

He was joking, but Jake wasn't. "And what if I do?"

The man didn't take up the challenge, tut-tutting as he sipped from the delicate china cup. "Meant nothing by it, my friend. You'll have to forgive me; being a soldier one sometimes finds jokes at other people's expense too easily. My brother is allergic to cats, actually. Quite the thing —put one in a room with him and in two minutes he's sneezing a storm. The devil must spend the day outside his door to catch his soul at some unguarded moment."

Marie, standing at the door, shook her head sternly, warning Jake off. In any event, the captain proved unprovokable and skillfully evasive. An hour's worth of fishing failed to produce anything useful.

"You're still attending the ball tomorrow night, yes?" Clark said to Marie as he took his leave.

"Of course."

"Bring your cousin," he added. "He should meet Governor Carleton. And General Burgoyne. Doctors are in great demand."

"He'll be there, I'm sure," she said before pecking the captain on the cheek.

Eight

Wherein, Jake has a heart-to-heart discussion with his close friend and sometime cousin, Marie Sacré.

"*B*ut a British soldier, Marie."

"And what, I should have sat here alone like a nun waiting for some jackal of a farmer to appear on my doorstep? Thank you for your advice, Jake Gibbs, but I don't need it. I have fended for myself long before I met you, and will do so long after you are gone. Which, I assume, shall be shortly."

She pushed away from him on the bed, folding her arms across her breasts. Her stays and hoops, petticoat and dress, lay in a trail back across the room.

"You've always had a sharp tongue. Perhaps I should give you a good spanking," Jake teased.

"Try it," she said without humor, adding in French a phrase that translated roughly as, "And if you do, I shall make a puppet of your louie."

"You already have."

"Fiddle. No woman can tame you. She would be a fool to try."

"That's why I love you."

"And what is the reason you've come back?"

"You're not enough?"

"I know you, Jake Gibbs. You'd never risk your neck for me."

"I've risked it for much less."

She stepped off the bed and pulled a casual shift from the drawer of her bureau, then went downstairs for something to drink.

Marie Sacré was the descendant of the earliest settlers

of the area. Well-known in Montreal, which lay less than
five miles to the north, she was considered by half the
inhabitants a wild eccentric, a thirty-year-old woman who
had never condescended to marry. The other half regarded themselves in constant competition for her
charms, striving to break her vows against marriage and
win her large estate as their prize.

Or as an added prize, since her charms were of considerable value themselves.

Jake had met Marie during the summer of 1775. General Montgomery assigned then-Captain Gibbs to scout
Montreal and its environs in preparation for his invasion.
After mapping the defenses and delivering his recommendations, Jake returned and entered the city disguised
as a local trapper. His new assignment was to recruit
Canadians to the Cause, laying the seeds for a local revolt as the Americans approached.

While his French seemed masterful to American ears,
Jake quickly discovered that his accent not only gave him
away as a foreigner, but greatly undermined his standing
with his audience. A squad of redcoats ended his second
attempt at rallying support, and he was forced to flee the
market area about ten steps ahead of the bayonets. He
ran down an alley and met Marie, making a forcible impression by knocking her off her feet. Fortunately, he
caught her in midair and whisked her upright with the
sweep of a dance master. The soldiers closing in, he
bowed and dove behind a pile of boxes in a desperate
attempt to hide.

Something in her expression had told him she would
not give him away, but Marie went beyond his best expec-
tations. Jake listened as she assured the soldiers the alley
was empty, but a man had just run inside the leather shop
across the way. As the soldiers charged off, Marie hurried Jake to her carriage on the street. He threw off his
coat and his hat, assuming an ad hoc position as her
driver; they rode back down through the square he'd
been chased from, past the eyes of several of the soldiers
who'd done the chasing.

In the days that followed, Marie helped him
clandestinely meet with local opponents to the Crown.

The opposition network was one of the reasons—along with the critically weak defenses—that Carleton abandoned the city when Montgomery approached.

By that time Jake had given himself a new mission, having perpetrated one of his greatest hoaxes. He presented himself to his former employer, Carleton, saying he had fled rebel lines to join him. Completely taken in, the governor once again made him his secretary—a position the young patriot used to great and sundry advantage. Carleton did not begin to suspect him until they had retreated together to Quebec, and even then did not take the proper precautions until Jake had managed to do considerable damage to the British cause. Placed under house arrest, he managed the disguised daylight escape Colonel Flanagan had earlier alluded to—but as those exploits are to be recorded elsewhere, we dwell too much on the past to the expense of the present.

"I thought you had gone to find Clark and turn me in," said Jake when Marie returned to the room.

"Don't be ridiculous. I've brought some whiskey. You always liked it."

"I still do."

She made a face, setting down the flagon in front of him. "French wine is better," she said before sipping from her own glass of rum. "But it has been so long since I've had some here. All we seem able to get these days is Portuguese rot."

"Your grapes?"

"Last year's crop was burned on the vine."

"Maybe this year's."

"Yes. It seems more auspicious."

She settled into the wooden chair across from him, pulling it forward and hooking her sockless feet on the front rungs, her toes tickling the cross spindle. Her easy rock back and forth in the chair seemed gently seductive.

"Tell me about Burgoyne's army," he said.

"I don't know much. It's obvious that an invasion is planned soon. There were rumors of an attempt this past winter, but apparently the lakes were not sufficiently frozen. At least that was the excuse. It was a mild winter, I'll admit. The snow left in March, but much of the river was

still frozen until a few weeks ago. So perhaps they were
just scared."

"How many troops have come to Montreal?"

"You're the spy, not me. All I can tell you is that they
are as rude as any soldiers I've met. A whole troop of the
devils were caught last month stealing the hair from
cow's tails; apparently they fix them to their caps as an
insignia. There was a huge row over it. Do you remember
Pierre Jacques? Well, they were his cows and he took
offense. He went after the soldiers—twenty of them,
mind you—and speared one with his pitchfork. They
brought him up on charges and were going to hang him
before I intervened."

"You?"

"I went to Carleton himself."

"How is my friend the governor?"

She shrugged. Marie had always had a decent opinion
of Carleton, and as a large landowner, had stayed on
good terms. He did not suspect her connection with Jake.

"There is a large troop at Boucherville," she continued. "They would be the advance guard of an invasion. I
know this because I went with Tom on a visit there."

"Tom, is it?"

"There are rumors of boats being built. Many trees
have been taken from the forest."

"I saw some of the work on the way here," said Jake.
"The invasion must be planned very soon. Does Tom talk
about it?"

Marie ignored the sarcastic accent her interrogator put
on the British captain's first name. "He's very careful
about what he says, even with me. But everyone knows
General Burgoyne will replace the governor, and that he
is to attack quickly. Tom is hoping to be transferred to
the general's command once Carleton resigns, which may
be any day."

In Jake's view—perhaps prejudiced since he knew Burgoyne only by rumor—Carleton was a much better commander and governor; his resignation was a break for the
Americans. But perhaps it had come too late.

"General Burgoyne is quite a man of learning," remarked Marie. "They say he writes poetry and plays."

"I've heard he was a better poet than a general."

"If that is so, why did your army retreat to Ticonderoga?"

Jake had no answer for that. Burgoyne's reputation in Boston had been that of a dilettante whose major military achievement was staying behind the lines while others took a beating. But the facts were these: He was now in Canada, and the Americans were not.

"Carleton met Burgoyne in Quebec a few days ago," Marie continued. "The ball Tom mentioned is in honor of the general's arrival here tomorrow. The governor may be angry, but he keeps to the proper forms."

"One thing I always admired about him. I'll compliment him on it tomorrow night if we meet."

"You can't be serious about going to the ball."

"I wouldn't miss it," said Jake. He was indeed serious —it would give him a chance to chat with every field officer in Burgoyne's army. It would be an easy matter to obtain the invasion plans, at least in outline. With time running out on the Americans, Jake couldn't afford to spend several days scouting troops or planning a break-in at the British headquarters. He had to get back to Schuyler as quickly as possible—time was even shorter than Flanagan suspected.

"I'll have to buy a new suit of clothes and some face plasters. Since your good Captain Clark has already seen me, I don't want to arouse his suspicions with a different disguise," said Jake. "Perhaps you can help me pick out something dashing."

"But Jake, if Carleton sees you, he will certainly recognize you."

"I'll just have to take care that he doesn't, won't I?"

Nine

Wherein, Jake visits Montreal high society, and has a ball or two.

*F*or an eighteenth century man, Jake was rather eccentric about bathing. He tried to take a bath twice a week if possible, and occasionally more, even in the winter. This flew in the face of scientific thought, and was one of the few areas where Jake, who had made a strenuous study of the philosophic arts and endeavored to live by their principles, strayed from the reasoned path. He simply loved to bathe, and despite the weight of the mission ahead, rose early the next morning and headed out to the stream behind the house to indulge himself.

Marie's homemade soap was strong, pricking at his skin. The early spring air was quite cool yet, no more than forty degrees. Still, Jake let himself collapse back on a rock in the middle of a small pool of rushing water, watching as one of Marie's dogs chased after a pair of ducks by the stream bed.

His thoughts soon returned to matters of more significance. With the cover story of a physician already established, he could sound out the British soldiers at the ball about joining the expedition. Details of the coming attack would flow from their mouths like the silky water around him.

As long as they didn't remember him. Jake knew that the British Army had been greatly reinforced since his last sojourn, and that most of the old guard had been transferred, but there was at least one man guaranteed to know who he was—Carleton.

Even with his hair freshly curled and as many plasters

on his face as fashion allowed, it wouldn't be easy to fool the governor. But a more complete disguise would mean he couldn't go as Marie's cousin. Even if he found another way in, he'd be deprived of Captain Clark's very useful entrée.

All in all, his best course was simply to avoid Carleton. It couldn't be too difficult if the gathering was large. Undoubtedly the governor would be preoccupied, and besides, the last person he'd expect to see in Montreal again was his long-lost secretary.

Jake turned his concerns to his rusty dance steps as he walked back up the path to the house, trying to remember whether it was at beat six or eight that one dipped his knees in the minuet.

He had settled pretty firmly on six by the time he sat down to breakfast. He was mildly surprised and not a little pleased that the servant girl had cooked a full plate of wheat cakes for him on Marie's instructions. A pile of dried berries topped the plate and some fresh sausage held down the side; it was easily the best breakfast Jake had had in weeks.

"Perhaps after breakfast, you can give me a shave," said Jake as the girl returned to the fire.

"We'll have the barber do that in town, if you don't mind," said Marie, entering the room behind him.

Jake thought he detected a slight tone of jealousy in her voice. If so, he dispelled it with a slightly more than cousinly kiss on her cheek, then sat back down to work on his cakes.

"We'll have to buy you some fresh clothes, if you're to go to the ball," said Marie as she looked over her servant's work.

"Good. There's some business I want to attend to in town," said Jake.

Marie's expression warned him from saying anything more revealing in front of the girl, as if that were really a danger. He finished his meal, and within a half hour had hitched Marie's horse to her chaise, or *cariole*, as the French called it.

Marie's estate was located only a few miles from the bank of the St. Lawrence directly to the south of Mon-

treal, but to reach a place where they could board a ba-
teau they had to travel in a large circle to the east,
passing through three neighbors' holdings. Each of these
had been broken into smaller estates and farms; Marie
waved and greeted each person they passed by name.

Marie did not own a house in the city, but as the journey was somewhat lengthy, she planned to spend the afternoon and change for the ball in the apartments of a
friend.

After she got Jake outfitted, of course. She knew a
tailor who could be pressed into quick service for a few
extra coins. Jake could make due with his present
breeches, but a coat of powder blue—now that would be
just the thing to set off his shoulders, wouldn't it?

"And you'll have to get a new hat!" she exclaimed.

"But I like this hat. It's been with me since Boston."

"Exactly."

In the end, he did get a new hat, a large, round beaver
with an upturned brim and golden feathers that made
him look vaguely Spanish, or so said the tailor. The man
muttered considerably at the amount of work he was expected to do to prepare the coat—luckily ordered by a
customer who had the bad sense to die the day before he
was to pick it up.

The blue jacket threatened to clash with Jake's brown
breeches, but the addition of a yellow brocaded vest
turned the outfit into something quite modern, even racy,
for the colonies. Two watch chains signified the cutting
edge of fashion, with their charms, ribbons, and baubles
hanging off and making a pleasing clang when Jake
walked. The fact that their ends were fastened to pieces
of metal instead of watches was besides the point.

If there was a woman in Montreal who could have
resisted his charms when he arrived, she would be positively swooning now. A bit of lilac water, a good deal of
scalding to his hair, which was then powdered and tied in
a correct black bow beneath his hat—London itself
would have fallen at the feet of this young swain.

Which, Jake supposed, was a good enough cover for a
spy. For who would suspect the man who stood out from
the crowd and called attention to himself instead of lurk-

ing in the shadows? "Do I look like Jake Gibbs, the rebel agent provocateur?" he would say to anyone confronting him. "Well sir, I am not, though from what I have heard of the dog, I would be glad to meet him face-to-face, so that I could challenge him on the field of honor for insulting the king. Rumor has it he hung the rosary of potatoes around the king's effigy, and I would very much like to avenge that dishonor."

Hopefully, brave words would be enough. For Jake had come to town unarmed, except for his pocket pistol—a larger weapon would have drawn too much attention, most especially at the ball.

Jake tested his self-assurance as well as his disguise by striding through the Montreal marketplace not far from the wharf. The square teemed with soldiers, but they did not seem to pay him much mind; to them he was one more useless dandy.

Had they followed him, they might have changed their opinions. After making his parade—and adding several more plasters to his face to shore up his disguise—Jake walked to the printing shop of Fleury Mesplet. This was the same Mesplet who had come to Montreal with the Americans during the winter of 1775. A protégé of Franklin, he had stayed after his countrymen had fled. Though he had not completely given up his allegiances, he was not, strictly speaking, an American spy.

Nor was he particularly happy to see Jake, whom he had known as a boy growing up in Philadelphia.

"Not much of a disguise, then?"

"If you're trying to look like a man of fashion," said the printer, himself very much the opposite, "you've quite succeeded. But your chin gives you away. Everyone in town will know it's you. You're notorious."

"My chin's too square?" Jake playfully took it in his hand and tried to see its reflection in the window. The window not being of glass, he was unsuccessful. "Perhaps another strategically placed plaster."

"Leave by the back door," said Mesplet. "I don't want anyone to know you're here."

"Now, now, relax, Fleury. Dr. Franklin sends his regards."

Not even this piece of flattery—invented for the occasion—could calm Mesplet, who took the unusual expedient of removing his sign from the front of the small, wooden building and then barring his door, as if he'd gone home for the day.

"You're worried about nothing," said Jake. "Neither the barber nor the tailor made the slightest peep, and I stayed with them for hours. Then I went to the market, showing my face at every booth. I could have lunched with a troop of soldiers without worrying. I was only here for a few weeks—no one even remembers me. It's Quebec where I have to watch out."

"You won't be so smug when Carleton meets you."

"Do you think these plasters are too obvious? They itch, and I'd rather do without them, frankly."

"Jake, what do you want? Half the town already suspects me of being a rebel."

"Aren't you?"

"I can't help you."

"I don't want help," said Jake, picking up one of the handbills Mesplet had been working on and reading it. "'Fire-arms made to your specification.' Not bad. But you don't need this dash here in firearms; it's one word."

"What is it you want?"

"When is Burgoyne starting his invasion?"

"I haven't the slightest idea."

"Fleury." There was ever the slightest hint of physical injury in Jake's voice.

"Honestly, I don't," protested the printer, practically screaming. "Do you think I wouldn't tell you?"

"They haven't had you print amnesty proclamations or anything like that?"

"Would they trust that to someone they suspect of being a rebel?"

"Why did Carleton let you stay in Montreal?"

"They put me in jail after Arnold fled. I was in Quebec for months."

Jake, unsure whether or not that was true, nodded solemnly anyway, as if in apology.

"You should see Du Calvet," said Mesplet. He uttered the name so lowly Jake could barely hear it.

"So my old friend is still here then?"

Mesplet nodded. "He knows everything."

If the printer had been alarmed by Jake's visit, Du Calvet was infuriated. The risks involved in his coming north were incalculable, Du Calvet said; he endangered not merely himself, but many others in the town. For the tide had clearly turned here, due in no small part to the poor behavior of the American occupation force in the winter of 1775-76; the French were now at best neutral toward the rebels.

"Arnold was an ass," added Du Calvet.

"I quite agree," said Jake, who blamed the commander for his friend Captain Thomas's death. "But your spies have not done a good enough job informing General Schuyler. Otherwise I would not have had to come north."

"Perhaps the problem is that neither Schuyler nor Gates wants to believe what we tell them," answered Du Calvet. "And perhaps Congress would do better not to keep changing commanders every time the wind blows."

"Since you don't want me here, I assume you will help me leave."

"Gladly. I will have a wagon and papers waiting for you tonight."

"Tomorrow morning, on the Post Road south of Montreal. I am otherwise engaged this evening."

"Where?"

"At the ball."

"You're insane!"

"Frankly, I think I dance rather well," said Jake. "Have the wagon waiting."

"The British army would love to hang you," said Du Calvet solemnly. They were his parting words, except for curses when Jake promised to save him a dance.

Upon reflection, Jake might have admitted that he had gone about things a bit rashly. A more cautious spy would have snuck into town at night, waking Du Calvet or some other American sympathizer in bed, persuading him to gather information while he hid in the attic or cupboard. But Jake considered the words "cautious" and "spy" to be contradictions. Besides, he didn't particularly like attics and grew claustrophobic in cupboards.

In any event, any admonition toward caution was now beside the point: He was sitting in a room of the Governor General's Palace, enjoying the attentions of a small coterie of ladies, none of whom he recognized from his last sojourn in Montreal—and none of whom, he had reason to hope, would recognize him.

He'd breezed past the most difficult portion of the gauntlet nearly an hour before, clutching Marie's arm firmly as her captain took her forward and with great ceremony introduced them to Burgoyne.

It was not for nothing that Burgoyne was called Gentleman Johnny. The general was a handsome man, perfectly tailored—if Jake looked like a dandy, Burgoyne had him beat by three leagues and a half. The fifty-four-year-old general's jaw clenched and jutted as he threw a gratuitous bon mot in Marie's direction, showing off his Parisian French. She looked quite ravishing in her fine yellow dress, he said; she would fit in perfectly in Westminster.

Burgoyne then turned to Jake, who pretended to practically faint at the introduction. The general looked at him oddly for a moment, as if they had met. They hadn't, as far as Jake knew, though he proclaimed such had long been his ambition.

There was a vast line of guests, and the general's attention quickly turned to the woman behind Jake, whose breasts were bulging from the top of her stomacher. Just in time, too, for Carleton had entered the hall and was bearing down quickly on the general.

Jake's disguise now included a gold-embroidered eye patch as well as his strategically placed face plasters, along with a bit of rouge and some deft work on his eyebrows. Still, he could not trust any amount of makeup or patches to keep him safe from Carleton. He slipped quietly into the background. Leaving Marie to the greasy grasp of Captain Clark, he worked his way through the crowd, gathering female admirers as a protective screen.

The entire building was filled with talk about the coming offensive. Burgoyne told everyone—literally everyone

—that the whole thing had been his idea, how he'd written a book to impress the king with the grand plan to separate the rebellious colonies, etc., etc. The book, a few wags commented in the hallway, was nothing more than a hastily printed and error-strewn pamphlet, but with similar allowances for exaggeration, Jake had no trouble putting together the outlines of the campaign. Burgoyne would start out from Crown Point and take Ticonderoga, and then with the aid of a second prong sent through the Mohawk Valley, fall on Albany. He had thousands of men mustering to sail down Lake Champlain, and it seemed obvious from various hints that he would proceed along the east side of Lake George. Two things were critical to his grand design—a populace that would return to the British as the Canadians had, and an assault in force up the Hudson by Howe from New York City.

The northern drive would not only pacify the towns and villages along the river, but would threaten to surround the rebels' army of the Northern Department. Schuyler would find himself between Burgoyne's hammer and the anvil of General Howe in New York. Washington would either retreat to New Jersey as Howe advanced— Burgoyne apparently thought the American general was too cowardly to attack—or be crushed. Either way, the rebel army in the north would evaporate and the middle colonies would be secured.

Jake's own knowledge of the terrain from Ticonderoga south, vague as it was, supplied a second reason Burgoyne would attempt to get as far south as Albany as quickly as possible. Any large force would have trouble being supplied from Canada; its lines of communication would stretch thin and be an easy target for irregulars. By contrast, the river could move tons of food and supplies. Winter, too, would be easier in Albany than on the lakes.

Any man or woman in the hall could have told you the general's plan within a half hour of arriving. A woman with a stomach strong enough to stand the general's incessant preening—and breasts large enough to hold his attention—could even say which army units were heading south with him, inept subalterns or no.

But no one could say when the attack was due to be launched. Such information was now Jake's greatest desire, and it induced him to continue wandering through the party, chatting with everyone he met, always ready to gracefully retreat at the slightest sign of the governor. Fortunately for Jake, Carleton did not like Burgoyne, and kept his distance from the general. The spy could always escape his attention by heading toward Gentleman Johnny.

"There you are," said Marie, finding him as he prowled a corner of an elegantly appointed sitting room just off the ballroom. "What are you doing?"

"Admiring the drapes."

"She's cuckolded her husband twice in three years," hissed Marie, nodding at the neighbor who stood before the red velvet fabric.

"Is that a recommendation, cousin?"

Marie frowned heavily.

"Do you know when the invasion is to begin?" Jake whispered.

She shook her head. It seemed to be the one secret Burgoyne was intent on keeping.

There was a cry of violins from inside; the entertainment was about to begin.

"So would you like to dance?" Jake asked Marie.

"Must you tempt fate?"

"Oh come on," he said, adding, as if he missed her point, "my leg is perfectly healed."

Marie sighed and took his arm, letting him lead her to the dance floor, where they took up a place in the line of dancers. The first dance was a minuet, begun with its requisite bows and curtsies to the guests of honor. As Carleton's attention was drawn by a consultation with one of his aides at the other end of the room, Jake put himself quite into the dance. He kissed his hand with great flair as he offered it to Marie, bending his knees slightly and then stepping forward on his toes, forward and lower, moving to the left, facing his partner, flourishing, taking hands and whirling around, working through a set of four and ending back with his cousin.

The American hadn't danced in several years, and

leading through the ring of dancers, he realized he was starting to get just a tiny bit heady. That was quickly cured—Jake saw from the corner of his uncovered eye that Governor Carleton was heading down the row toward him.

But the dancer was caught by the beat of the music. Their turn had come to play second couple, and Jake and Marie stood idly, waiting as the first pair took up with the fourth.

Well, he thought to himself as the governor approached, this shall certainly make an interesting story for the crier to shout in the morning—notorious spy caught out of turn at the ball on the eve of the invasion.

Ten

Wherein, Jake makes certain discoveries of extreme interest to the Cause, and the British make discoveries of their own.

Governor Carleton was no more than ten feet away when Jake realized Marie was clearing her throat quite loudly. Did she expect him to run?

No, she expected him to step forward and take the hand of the lady across from him—they were, after all, dancing.

He bowed with perfect timing, if just a bit of unnatural flourish, as Carleton passed behind him in a fury. The governor was so focused on his business that he saw no one else in the room, not the American agent or even the aide scrambling behind him. And now Gentleman Johnny was excusing himself and coming in the same direction.

Curiosity is an extreme motivator for a man in the spying profession, where naturally the mind tweaks itself toward inquiry. True, such a trait has its drawbacks, but for an agent on special services it is the engine of innumerable achievements. So it should not be surprising that Jake, having escaped discovery by the narrowest of margins, instantly decided to double the odds by following the two British officials and seeing what they might be up to. He bowed to his dancing partners, all seven of them, and excused himself, holding his hand to his stomach as if overcome by a sudden ailment. Then he made for the door as if he had taken a double dose of cathartic.

His quick exit brought him nose-to-back with General Burgoyne, who had stopped to confer with some aides near the door. Jake slipped off to the side as the general first gently critized the men for interrupting, and then said, reluctantly, that he would go up with the governor and see what this new message was about.

The stairs were unguarded. Jake waited for the general and his minions to ascend and go down the hallway. He was after them in a flash, taking three steps at a time, checking for his pocket pistol as he climbed. Snug in his waistband, it was primed and ready; he had only to flick the safety and fire.

It was purely a weapon of last resort, since using it would draw immediate attention to himself. His weapon of first resort consisted of all his senses—hearing in particular, which led him down the hall to the secretary's room, just outside the governor's office. The interior chamber was closed, but even the thick door could not muffle Carleton's loud voice as he upbraided Burgoyne.

Not upbraided, exactly; more like complained against the general's libels and the willingness of Lord Germain to hear them.

"My resignation is on its way to that coward Germain as we speak," said Carleton.

"Intemperate words," said Gentleman Johnny. "Lord Germain enjoys the full confidence of the king."

"He has not changed his stripe."

The argument continued, but Jake's eavesdropping did not—someone was approaching down the hallway. Jake looked quickly for a hiding place, but found nothing more suitable than the underside of a large desk as an officer and a man dressed in civilian clothes entered.

"Wait while I get the governor," the officer told the man, going in the meantime to the window and pulling the drapes closed. The window was right next to the desk —Jake was close enough to smell the grease polish on the officer's boots.

"My orders are to give the letter to the general, not the governor."

"The governor is still in charge," said the officer testily. "He is waiting with the general." He turned sharply on his heel and knocked on the adjacent office door before entering.

Jake flattened himself beneath the desk while the messenger paced a few feet away. A canteen hung from a leather sling at his side; undoubtedly that contained whatever he'd come to deliver. But even as Jake considered the wild thought of snatching it and dashing for the patriot lines, the door to the office was reopened and the man summoned inside.

Jake got up and snuck next to the chamber to hear what was going on. Burgoyne apparently took the fact that the message was to be delivered to him personally as a veiled insult to his choice of staff officers. Carleton, for his part, was annoyed that Burgoyne and not he was the recipient. The general ripped open the letter and read it aloud, both as a feigned courtesy to Carleton and a dramatic display of his trust in his subordinates.

Burgoyne's voice betrayed some regret as he proceeded. Howe had made it clear he had no use for his plans to invade northern New York, and indicated that he would not bother to support the action with his troops.

Jake had little time to consider the strategic import of this happy news—Burgoyne exploded in fury and led the whole mess of them, governor, messenger, and assorted hangers-on, into the secretary's room, in search of something to write on. Jake nearly lost his eye patch to a splinter in the floorboard as he dove back beneath the desk.

"You will deliver my message to Howe himself," Burgoyne declared as he entered.

"Begging your pardon, General, but that is explicitly against protocol. We have an elaborate procedure. I've never met Sir William; I have a staff officer I deal with, who in turn deals with another officer."

"If I'm good enough to be met personally, Howe is no better," said Burgoyne. He reached over the top of the desk, hovering less than eighteen inches from Jake, and quickly wrote a note. "He's to carry on with the offensive the way I mapped it out. The orders from England are quite explicit, even if they are worded to avoid offending his delicate sensibilities."

"Sir, again I must protest. For matters of security, I should not know what the message contains. This way, I can dispose of it, and honestly answer—"

"What is your name and rank?"

"Captain William Herstraw, sir."

"Are you always in the habit of telling your superiors their business?"

"No, sir."

While Burgoyne was defending his bruised ego, the other officers were shifting nervously around the room. Jake's ribs did their own shifting, trying to stifle the outraged squeaks his lungs were emitting in protest of being contorted to fit his chest beneath the desk well.

Burgoyne finished his message and straightened. Jake, sensing the session would soon end and he could escape, began to feel relief—until the general sat on the edge of the desk. The wood groaned with the weight and pressed down into the spy's back.

"Now I will tell you a bit of your business," the general said to the messenger. "Any simpleton, even a rebel, will search your canteen for a message. You need something a bit more secretive, and easily disposed."

"I don't intend on being searched," replied Herstraw. "I travel among the rebels as a poor yeoman farmer and am never suspected."

"Our own messengers use silver bullets," said Carleton, with a note in his voice that meant he wanted this whole business concluded. "Captain Clark, can you prepare one for Captain Herstraw?"

Clark—the same Clark you're thinking of, if you're thinking he's Marie's—didn't answer. Instead he walked toward the desk.

The same desk you're thinking of, if you're thinking of Jake's. Jake pressed in deeper and tried to conjure some excuse, lame as it might be, as Clark approached.

Fortunately, Clark did not come around to the back of the desk, where he might have had occasion to glance down and see an unaccounted-for leg. Instead he reached over the side and pulled the drawer open—and in the process whacked Jake on the side of his skull.

Which would not have been so bad, had Jake's wig not gone flying with the friction of the drawer.

A popular manufacturer in France once sewed small strings on his wigs. These were meant to be tied to the collar or back of the neck, so the wig could be easily retrieved if knocked loose by the wind or some other force of nature. Surely such a device would have been a godsend for Jake at the moment. The wig was lying on the floor, positively due for discovery once the drawer was closed.

Jake strained his fingers from their sockets, grabbing at the ribbon that tied the ponytail. Meanwhile, Clark rummaged through the shallow drawer, looking for a sharp knife to open the silver ball with. He leaned harder and harder on the desk, pressing Jake's side.

"We use them to communicate with Sir Johnson and his Indians," Clark said. "I only need a thin blade."

Jake felt like volunteering his own pocketknife. Clark shook the drawer and tried opening it farther—scraping against Jake's skull.

"Damn drawer is always sticking. I have a penknife in here somewhere."

By some compression of the spine that would no doubt strike an anatomist as impossible, Jake managed to duck his head down as Clark struggled with the drawer. The same motion, fortunately, gave him a better grip on the wig's ribbon.

Which pulled loose from the hair as soon as he exerted pressure.

"Will my knife do?" volunteered one of Burgoyne's men.

"Yes, I think so," said Clark, slamming the drawer shut across the top of Jake's head.

Jake managed to whisk the wig up as the drawer closed. But what really saved him was the party's immediate retreat back inside the chamber. Head creased but otherwise intact, Jake extricated himself and breathed as deeply as a horse, ungluing his lungs from his kidneys. Then he crept across the room, resuming his post at the door.

"I like the idea of a silver bullet," he heard Burgoyne say inside. "It has panache."

Carleton proceeded to quiz the messenger on the situation at Ticonderoga and Albany. The man claimed there were ten thousand American troops at Ticonderoga, and perhaps four or five thousand more at Albany.

Both numbers were wild exaggerations. There weren't ten thousand American soldiers in all of New York. In fact, Schuyler would be lucky to muster 3,500 at Ticonderoga, including militia.

That's what the British got for spying, though.

"I'll have nine thousand men marching with me June seventeenth," Burgoyne boasted as the governor started to argue that perhaps his attack should be rethought in light of the rebels' strength. "We'll pick up many more on the way, once the colonists hear my proclamation. I'm not worried about the numbers, not at all."

Jake silently congratulated Burgoyne for having given him everything he'd come north for. He fixed his wig atop his head, repositioned his eye patch and prepared to take his leave.

"We will have no problem as long as Howe follows orders," Burgoyne said. "The message is critical. The entire success of the campaign depends on it. Well, the entire success of the campaign depends on me." The general permitted himself a polite laugh, apparently expecting the others to join. They did not.

"Take the bullet and go," he told the messenger. "Leave directly."

"I'd hoped for some sleep, sir. My horse is tired after the long journey."

"Get him a new horse," commanded Burgoyne with a snap of his fingers. "Every hour is critical. Howe must come north with his troops the moment I set off. Let's go, man; this is a war, you know, not a summer party."

The impatience of generals knows no national borders.

"Sir, I have rode without stopping from the Bull's Head Inn near Fort Hubbardton."

"What is that, the Bull's Head? A frontier dance hall? Do they dress up their cattle and parade them on stage?" Burgoyne drew titters from his aides.

"It is a tavern, sir," said Herstraw tightly, trying to preserve some of his dignity. "Fortunately, the owner is secretly loyal to the king. He is a distant relative of mine."

"We will remember him when we liberate the area," said Burgoyne. "Go on, march off. You must be in New York City before the week is out."

"Sir, traveling too quickly through the enemy lines attracts too much attention. It is better to seem nonchalant. And this—"

"Leave this instant, or I will court-martial you for insubordination!"

Jake had just enough time to step back into a shadow —there was no way he was going near that desk again— when the door opened and the messenger emerged.

He was not a happy man. Dressed plainly, in a nondescript brown coat and white britches, Herstraw walked briskly through the room and stormed into the hall. Jake caught his profile as he passed—a large nose was his most distinguishing feature.

The door to the chamber closed as the general and governor renewed their discussions. Jake added one more aspect to his disguise—the slightly piqued manner of a secretary called from the dance floor to do his duty —and proceeded to the stairwell.

"I believe the general wants to see you," he told the soldiers who'd just taken up stations there. They obediently went off to see their master, having no reason to question a man who had obviously just come from inside.

Jake paused briefly in front of a mirror at the head of the stairs to readjust his eye patch—and watch Herstraw reach the landing. He planned on making his acquaintance very shortly—he'd tackle him outside, kill him and destroy his message. Just let the Briton get a few yards ahead so he wouldn't suspect he was being followed, and it would be easier than any of the dancing he'd just done.

Meanwhile, Carleton was unsuccessful in convincing Burgoyne that he had overestimated the local Loyalist sympathies and underestimated the patriots. Whatever its ultimate effect on the American Cause, the failure of his argument had immediate consequences for Jake. Burgoyne stomped from the office with the governor at his heels, both men silent, though no doubt cursing each other with great vigor inside their heads. Carleton happened to look toward the stairs, which Jake was just starting to descend.

Despite the dim light, despite the disguise, despite his preoccupations, despite fortune, luck, and Providence, Carleton recognized him immediately.

"Stop that man!" he yelled as loudly and indignantly as any royal governor had yelled these past three years of rebellion. "Stop him!"

Stop him! The very phrase has a certain epic ring to it, a certain correctness; one wants to utter it, one wants to respond to it, one almost wants to be the subject of it. Great forces are set in motion with these simple words. Other cries are taken up, alarms spread. Hearts beat double and triple time. All hell breaks loose. Just the sort of thing to make your night.

Especially if you're a spy and the halter waits as a reward for your capture. Jake leapt to the bottom of the stairs and rushed down the hallway to the ballroom. Along the way he doffed his eye patch, most of the plasters, and his wig, in effect taking up a new disguise undisguised. Once at the entryway to the ballroom, he dodged through as politely as possible, smiling to the right, apologizing to the left, spinning and sliding as if he were being followed by no one more troubling than a dancer whose toe he had stepped on.

"Stop that man!" shouted Carleton again as he reached the ballroom.

"I'll get him, Governor!" answered Jake, leaping toward the back door.

He was three steps from the doorway when he saw the soldiers who'd been posted outside coming through, bayonet points first. Jake veered to the right, looking for a suitable detour.

He'd run out of doors, but there were plenty of windows. Grabbing a small chair from the side of the room, Jake threw it before him, knocking the small panes of the large window in a great crash. He then hurled himself through, covering his face with his arms and rolling to the pavement, quite possibly breaking half his bones in the process.

He had no time for an inventory. Carleton had not

given up his blasted shouting, and the alarm was spreading to the street and nearby environs. Jake stumbled forward to his feet, hoping for some sort of momentum to take him across the Parade Square to the Water Gate.

That would not have been a wise way to go, being that there were even more soldiers at that particular spot than any other in the city. As so often happens in such cases, however, Fortune provided for our hero, causing at that moment a large gray steed to rush across in front of him, right to left. Jake, never one to question the whims of a lady, leapt immediately to the horse's back.

Fortune is not without her little jokes, however. In this case, while providing Jake with the means of escaping his pursuer, she gave him two other difficulties to contend with. Number one—the horse was being ridden by a major of the British cavalry, who objected strenuously to an unpaid passenger. Number two—the horse was heading in the direction of the boatyard, where a troop of soldiers were encamped.

The British major was undoubtedly brave and strong, but Jake had the superior motivation—he garroted the fellow with a hastily rolled handkerchief and pulled strongly to one side; when the major resisted, Jake used his weight and a kick in the horse's flank to change their momentum. The major went tumbling overboard.

The second problem took longer to solve, partly because Jake, his head still swirling from his plunge through the window to the pavement, did not realize which way he was going. It was only when he saw several shadows looming in the dark, answering the general alarm, that he realized his mistake.

What does one say to an armed host when one's suddenly sprung into their midst, and people running down the road are shouting various variations of "Stop that man!"?

"Who's in charge here? Sound the alarm! Hurry, a spy has escaped!"

And so Jake quickly rallied his pursuit, mustering the men and sending them down the quay back toward the governor's palace, ready to shoot anything that looked vaguely American.

He, meanwhile, sought out something to get onto the St. Lawrence with. A small birch canoe presented itself at the end of the wharf; Jake dove from the horse into the craft, pushing off into the water in the same motion.

It would have been more convenient if the boat had paddles. Nonetheless, he was able to make decent progress by leaning over the sides and rowing with his arms; by the time they felt as if they would positively drop off, he was clear across the channel, and the confused search on the shore just an inconvenient buzz in the background.

Eleven

Wherein, an assignment is made which will have
desperate consequences for our story.

The commotion caused by Lieutenant Colonel Jake Gibbs's sudden appearance in Montreal took several hours to die down. The ball was disrupted and the entire city put on alert; the wharves were sealed off and patrols were sent in all directions around the island without waiting for the morning to dawn.

In the meantime, Marie escaped quietly to her friend's apartment. Her fellow French Canadians held her in high enough esteem that the British could not move against her without raising the ire of the populace; as long as she protested ignorance and kept to herself for a month or so, she knew she would escape with no more serious damage than the loss of her beau, Captain Clark. She was angry with Jake for having exposed her, yet at the same time worried greatly about his fate.

General Burgoyne, in his offhanded and pompous way, dismissed the rebel as inconsequential. "A mere spy will not have any effect on my plans," said Gentleman Johnny, whose reputation as an overconfident horse's body part had been proven years before to everyone's satisfaction except Lord North's, who as head of His Majesty's government had the only opinion that counted. "I have half a mind to write a letter to Washington himself, detailing my plans," Burgoyne told Carleton when the first patrols reported they could not find Jake. "Let these backwoodsmen try and stop me; I intend on dining in Schuyler's mansion in Albany before Christmas."

Some portion of the general's bluster was undoubtedly

mere show, however, as he gave orders for the invasion force to accelerate its preparations. He spent the rest of the night dictating commands for his troops, determined to launch the first phase of his attack within the week. If he had never counted on strategic surprise in the first place, still he pushed his men to seize the tactical initiative before the American army could fully mobilize against him.

Governor Carleton did not even pretend to take Jake Gibbs lightly. In fact, the governor could be forgiven if he interpreted Gibbs's reappearance in Canada as little less than a personal affront. The anger he felt could not be placed adequately into words. Nor was it satisfied by the prolonged pounding he treated his desktop to.

And so the meeting that took place in the governor's chambers around three A.M. should come as no surprise. Carleton sat at his desk, grim; the lateness of the hour wore deeply on his face, fatigue having ingrained lines on his cheeks and brow. Ordinarily a calm and even mild man, Carleton was quite beside himself with rage. His lone visitor stood a few feet away, waiting for his orders as the governor did his best to bring his emotions back under control so he could speak. Finally, he found his voice.

"I have sent nearly a hundred men, and Burgoyne, despite his bluster, has his own troops on alert. But he is a wily man, this Gibbs. Half the army could look for him, and he would find a way to sneak through their ranks."

The man across the room from the governor nodded. Carleton frowned, then continued, his tone still strained.

"He stole my wig, you know. He had the audacity to take my wig and escape after he'd given his word as a British gentleman not to leave house arrest. But of course he no longer considers himself a British gentleman. My favorite wig—I'd bought it from Gladders in London."

Though he knew well where Gladders was and even felt some sympathy for the governor—the affront to his honor by a man he'd treated as his son made the governor look foolish—Carleton's visitor did not speak. He merely shifted his legs slightly as his large blue eyes calmly searched his commander. These eyes were twice the size normally apportioned for such a face, and set deep into the skull, so that he had the appearance of a wild owl, recording everything, scanning for his prey.

Major Christopher Manley had performed many tasks for the governor over the past six months, though none had begun with an interview such as this. He was confident, however, that the end result would be entirely the same.

Manley had a trunk full of talents, but his physical appearance belied his skills and strength. He was well over six and a half feet tall, standing a good head and shoulders above most every other man in the army. His body weight was not similarly portioned; his arms and legs were as thin as the branches on a year-old birch tree, and a girl would blush to have a waist as thin as his. His height made him appear awkward when he walked or ran, though his long strides actually made him fleet and he'd learned to use the leverage inherent in his limbs to great advantage in a fight. He was another breed of man on a horse, so light and yet so sinewy and pliant that he seemed to blend with the animal; the pair became a different being all together.

But as far as the British army was concerned, Major Manley's most attractive trait was his willingness to do whatever his commander asked—no, not asked, but hinted. For the major was a member of His Majesty's Secret Department, an agent of the shadowy brigade assigned specifically to Governor Carleton to carry out whatever tasks were too delicate for other branches to handle. If he appeared awkward at rest—even standing erect he was an unlikely collection of limbs put together by a sculptor in jest—he was as fluid and efficient as a Caribbean hurricane once set in motion, and twice as deadly.

"Burgoyne may be right about the rebels," continued Carleton after a new round of pounding on the desk finally drained his anger. "They are quite sharp when they face old men as they did taking Ticonderoga, but put a real army together and they fall back, as they did last fall. Still, he is a fool for overestimating his own abilities and the loyalty of these people. The Canadians—I'm boring you, Major, am I not?"

"You never bore me, Governor."

Carleton smiled. He had that rare ability in a British commander to know flattery when he heard it—and to turn away from it.

"Jake Gibbs is a deadly fellow. He helped stir up the populace against me while he worked at my right hand, and he scouted the Canadian defenses most effectively."

"If his work at Quebec is any indication," said Manley dryly, "I should think you'd be happy to have him spying about."

"The Americans attacked out of desperation," answered Carleton, aware that his great victory two years before was due at least partly to luck. "No, Gibbs is quite something. I'd heard rumors that he was killed; obviously they were wishful thinking." Carleton rose from his desk and began pacing through the room. "He could have assassinated me tonight."

"I doubt that, sir."

"No, it's true. He could have. Burgoyne as well. He's quite capable of such treachery. All of these Americans are. Show them kindness, and this is how they repay you."

Manley nodded, understanding what was meant perfectly. For in such a way are orders for gruesome assassination given, veiled with words of what others might have done. It would be against the nature of things to kill a gentleman, but a treacherous snake who did not observe the proprieties of life—such a man who would target a better for assassination—such a fellow was not a gentleman, and might be disposed of without prejudice.

"I have no doubt he will escape the patrols," said Carleton. "He did so in Quebec, and that was in broad daylight. They will not be mounted long in any event, and will not follow with the discipline necessary even if they are lucky enough to catch a whiff of his trail."

"I would think a man like that would have to be followed wherever he went."

Carleton nodded. The reader will wonder at the delicacy of the British commanders, so careful to skirt the truth of what they were saying. But officially the Secret Department did not even exist, and it was imperative that certain forms be kept—for otherwise, how was a true British gentleman like Governor Carleton to sleep at night?

"You know this fellow Herstraw, the messenger from New York?" Carleton asked.

"No, sir."

There was the slightest bit of disdain in Manley's voice. Messengers were ordinarily not part of the department's ranks, and even those who ventured far through enemy lines such as Herstraw were looked down upon as mere errand boys, no matter how difficult their jobs might be.

"He seemed competent enough. To have come all the way from New York—it could not have been an easy journey."

"It is a long journey," allowed Manley.

The governor smiled at the grudging admission. "I assume that he will return to General Howe. Gibbs undoubtedly overheard us talking, and will be on his trail. I would not want him overtaken."

Manley nodded.

"If you have occasion to find Herstraw before Gibbs, you will see that he carries a coded coin as an identifier," said the governor. "Captain Clark is familiar with the path he will take; knowing it should allow you to track our Mr. Gibbs more easily. The hunter becoming the prey, as it were."

Manley nodded.

Carleton returned to his desk, standing over it for a moment. It is only fair to admit that he felt the slightest hesitation before sealing his order for Jake's death. Lurking in his soul was the shadow of the initial affection that had attracted him toward the able young man years before in London, the emotion of father toward son. If circumstances had been different, he would have proved an affectionate and powerful mentor.

But the governor had not achieved his position in life without mastering his emotions. He reached inside his waistband and produced the key to the bottom desk drawer. Without further ceremony he unlocked it, removing a long, narrow silver box. A second key was retrieved from his watch pocket, and the box was opened to reveal a dagger as slender in proportions as Manley's body. The tempered blade shone even in the study's dim light, and as the governor reached across to hand it to his minion, the red jewel at the end of the hilt glowed like a flame stolen from the fires of hell. And so was a mission of the Secret Department commissioned, the knife an identifier to any officer of sufficient rank and position to realize such a thing as the department existed. The blade was not, as some writers have suggested, a mark that assassination had been ordered—but then, the mistake is understandable, since so many of their missions had that as their only goal.

Carleton returned the silver box to the bottom drawer. Reaching deeper, he retrieved a small bottle of brandy and two silver snifters. He poured out two small portions —this personal addendum to the ceremony that authorized a mission was followed only by the governor, as far as Manley knew.

Should he succeed or should he fail, only the two men in this room would ever know of the assignment. Once sent on his way, Manley would let nothing stop him, not even a direct order from another British officer—save for a command from the king or Sir Henry Clay Bacon, who as the ranking officer of the branch in America, would be presumed to be acting on the king's behalf. But not even the king nor Bacon could be given details of the mission, and as the first was across the ocean and the second was several hundred miles away in New York, their intervention was more than unlikely.

Manley folded himself forward to take the silver cup, sealing Jake Gibbs's fate—and perhaps his own.

"To Jake Gibbs," said Carleton, raising his drink.

"Yes," smiled Manley. "To his good health."

Twelve

Wherein, Jake makes the timely acquaintance of a Black Minqua half-breed.

"*Monsieur*, impossible!"

"Certainly you can," said Jake. He had the cart's horse by the bit, and despite the animal's protests, had no intention of letting go until its owner agreed to take him south. "You just told me you're going that way."

"*Oui*," said the man, a French farmer traveling with his *charette*, or wagon, to a small town several miles south of Fort St. John. "But it is a long way and difficult, and I could not possibly carry a passenger."

"There's plenty of room. Your cart is empty."

"*Monsieur, s'il vous plaît.*"

Jake sighed and reached into his money purse for a guinea. He tossed it to the farmer, then let go of the horse and strode to the back of the cart to board. The farmer smiled and made a clicking noise to get the horse going, barely waiting for him to get in.

It had been a long night. After abandoning the canoe downriver, Jake had walked across several fields and through a small woods before finding a road. With only the hazy light of the moon to guide him, he had stumbled toward the Richelieu River, which lay fifteen or sixteen miles as the crow flies east from Montreal. Jake was hardly a crow, and though he walked as quickly as he could and took the main road as much as he dared, he did not get very far very fast. The area was swampy and not heavily populated; he couldn't even find a horse to steal along the way. As the sun came up he was still several miles from Chambly; dead tired, he considered the farmer's sudden appearance an act of God.

The farmer soon had his horse at near-gallop, despite the mud and rocks that made up the road. Jake propped his coat beneath his head and tried to sleep, but the ride was too bumpy and he was too alert with the sense of danger.

Soldiers were encamped all along the route; it seemed as if the entire population of England and Germany had come across the Atlantic to deal with the rebellious colonies. Having approached Montreal from the west, Jake had not fully appreciated the enemy's strength until now, when he was in the middle of it.

Fortunately, most of the sentries were either still sleeping or lackadaisical; word of the escaped American spy would not reach them for several hours. They let the farmer and his homemade cart pass without challenge.

Jake's original mission was to get south with his information about the planned invasion. But he now had a second goal—apprehending the British messenger. Intercepting the letter from Burgoyne would lessen the chances the offensive would succeed; Burgoyne had as much as said so.

The man was on his way to an inn near Fort Hubbardton, had a head start, and was on horseback. The only way to catch up was to find transportation on Lake Champlain, but that was not going to be an easy matter. As the battle he witnessed on the way north attested, the British already had control of much of the northern reaches of the waterway.

Perhaps he could find a very small boat farther south that would escape detection. Of some consolation was the fact that Herstraw—if he played the role of a poor farmer, as he told Burgoyne—would probably not go on the lake himself, though he would stick to the roads along it, where he could count on finding British assistance if needed. So at least Jake would have a strong notion of where to find him before Bull's Head.

Another complication was the fact that Jake had left nearly all his weapons back at Marie's homestead. The American still had his small pocketknife, but that couldn't be counted on for anything but popping a blister. And his only gun was the four-barreled Segallas—an impressive and efficient pocket pistol, but unfortunately of limited range and firepower.

It didn't matter—he would kill the British spy with his bare hands if he had to.

The farmer urged his horse onward with a never-ending cacophony of clicks, speaking some language only he and the horse understood. The animal moved faster and faster; perhaps the farmer was promising him more oats.

And then without warning they stopped dead on the road. Jake pitched forward in a tumble. Expecting the worst, he reached for his Segallas and peeked up over the side board.

He was astounded to see the roadway before them empty. Indeed, the front of the cart itself was empty. The farmer had left it and was running toward the side of the road.

The American watched with curiosity as the Frenchman went to a small collection of stones by the side of the road and proceeded to cross himself, kneel and bow his head. He stayed in front of the shrine—a crude cross about two feet tall stood beyond the stones—for a good five minutes before jumping up and returning to the cart on a dead run. The horse neighed, the Frenchman clicked, and they were once more on their way, flying south on the road for several more miles before the entire drama was once more repeated.

The third time was too much for Jake.

"We're never going to get anywhere if you keep stopping every few minutes to pray," he said. "Can't you just say amen or something and get on with it?"

The farmer explained, or rather didn't explain, in very quick French that it was a holy obligation to stop at a martyr's shrine and pray.

"Look," said Jake finally, a second crown in one hand and the Segallas in the other, "here's the deal. Another crown if you don't stop, two bullets if you do."

The man objected that his faith had been questioned, and launched into a vigorous defense of the holy fathers whose blood had consecrated this ground. It took every ounce of Jake's self-restraint not to shoot the man.

Eventually a compromise was reached—the farmer would say a prayer as he passed each shrine, and Jake would add two crowns to the price of passage.

He grumbled as he handed over the money, due in advance. But though it depleted his purse, the new arrangement considerably speeded his progress, and by midday they had reached the small settlement outside Fort Chambly, the British post east of Montreal on the Richelieu. It wasn't much of a fort as such things went, some tall blockhouses and stockades, but it was formidable enough given the terrain and his own circumstances. Jake's muddied finery drew stares in the tiny village west of the embattlements, and he realized that he would have to find more suitable clothing if he hoped to pass south without being detained and questioned.

The suit had cost Marie a good deal in Montreal, but even clean it would be next to worthless here, there being few balls to attend. Nor was it possible to just walk into a tailor shop and buy new clothes, ready-made. What he needed was a fellow of roughly the same height and build who could supply, ideally, a hunting shirt.

Someone, in fact, similar to the man they were just passing on the highway, walking in the opposite direction. His sullen manner announced him as a *coureur de bois,* a woods runner or frontiersman, a trapper; his toque with its tassel announced him as decidedly French. He was wearing a homemade hunting shirt, cut from a piece of deerskin and imperfectly tanned. Most of the fringe was missing from one sleeve and the right side had been badly singed—a more perfect garment could not have existed in all of Canada.

Jake hopped from the cart, telling the driver he would meet him on the road south of the fort.

Theoretically, Jake could just jump the trapper, pummel him and take his coat. But being as how he was a visitor in this land, with some indeterminate portion of the army already after him, he decided to take a cautious and considerably more honorable approach and offer to buy it. The shirt was worth no more than a crown, if that;

he'd give him two guineas for it, and throw in his own jacket besides. He had no particular relish for the hat, but would take it if necessary to sweeten the deal.

But to bargain with the man, he first had to reach him. The trapper walked with a great stride, and Jake trotted and then broke into a full run to catch up.

"Excuse me," he shouted as the man turned down a small path that had appeared invisible until he stepped on it. "I wonder if I could have a word."

The man made no sign of having heard him.

"Sir," said Jake, running up behind him. *"Monsieur, excusez-moi. Un moment, s'il vous plaît."*

The trapper answered by turning quickly—and flashing a knife.

"Que diable voulez-vous? Laissez-moi tranquille!" the man shouted. What the devil do you want? Leave me alone.

"Just a quick question," said Jake, stopping short.

"I hate the English and their questions!" said the man in French.

"I agree with you there."

Apparently, this was not quite the answer the man desired—he lunged forward with his knife.

The polite approach having failed, Jake dodged to the side and grabbed his assailant's outstretched arm. While his being the same size as Jake was essential for the business end of their transaction, it made negotiations difficult—the trapper's strength was similarly portioned, and it took a good amount of wrestling back and forth before the knife fell away.

This was far from the end of the conflict. The trapper managed to trip Jake and they fell together to the ground. Two kicks in his flanks and Jake rolled desperately away, only to find the man's hands firmly around his neck.

Choking, Jake grabbed his Segallas from his pocket and pounded the brute's temple with it. Somehow, the trapper realized that he was being shown leniency and let go; Jake rose shakily to his feet, coughing as he caught his breath.

"Your anger would be much better directed toward the

British, my friend," Jake told him in French. "I'm an American patriot."

"So?" The man answered in English.

"I want to make a deal for your coat. I need to travel south," said Jake. "And I'd prefer not to stand out with all these British soldiers about."

"I hate the damn British," said the man.

"As do I."

"They've cheated me of my meat. I was not even paid. All I have left is my canoe."

"Perhaps, if we were traveling in the same direction," said Jake, sensing the possibility of an arrangement, "we could establish a coalition to our mutual benefit. How much was the meat worth?"

"I don't need your money," said the trapper.

But those are the words one speaks only as a precursor to true deal-making. For a sum of three guineas and ten shillings, the trapper agreed to give him new clothes and take him south on the river and then the lake, all the way to American lines. Besides the coins, his motivation seemed to be some modicum of revenge against the soldiers.

Their negotiations concluded, the man's manner changed. Softened was not quite the word, but the conclusion of the bargain initiated something akin to friendship. Men who live in the woods have a certain code of business that differs greatly from that followed in the city. It is not merely a matter of honor, but of fellowship, to conclude a deal with someone, as if more than money or fur skins were at stake.

The trapper called himself Leal le Couguar, or the Cougar. Jake realized only gradually that *le couguar* was not a nickname but rather an acknowledgment of his blood lines. For Leal was not fully French but part Indian, a descendant of the Black Minquas who had once populated the north-central stretches of the province of New York. These Indians—called the Erie or cat nation by fellow Iroquoian speakers—had been devastated by war with the Five Nations prior to the arrival of whites in the province. Those who had not been killed or adopted by the victorious tribes were scattered widely, ghostly remnants of a once proud and thriving people.

His canoe and gear had been stowed a short distance away, along the bank of a creek that led to the river. Leal gave Jake a short woolen jacket and smock made of white kersey, along with some leggings that fell over his shoes; he lacked only the addition of a toque to appear quite a wildman. This was soon supplied, and together they put the dugout canoe into the water and set off.

They pulled onto a small bed of sand along the shoreline to spend the night. After helping gather wood for a fire, Jake felt compelled to apologize for the way in which they'd met. He admired the man's courage and decision to help him; he was impressed by his strength and knowledge of the woods.

Leal nodded but said nothing.

Dinner consisted of green berries, some hard bread, and fish they caught in a small pool near the stream bed. Capturing the fish was not an easy task. The two men worked as a team, Jake armed with a large rock and Leal leaning over with a long, arrowlike spear or harpoon, ready to pounce as soon as Jake let the rock fly. In theory, the blow was to stun the fish, making them easier to stab; the reality was that the splash and subsequent shock wave made them difficult to see and alerted others to stay clear. They managed to get only two before the light failed.

Leal insisted that his companion have the larger, though the adjective exaggerates its size. Jake compensated by taking less bread. He was famished, and it took all his willpower to eat the fish slowly, lest Leal offer him his own.

When they were done, Leal took out a pipe and a small bit of rope tobacco obviously obtained in trade from a soldier. Ordinarily, Jake did not smoke, but it would have been ill-mannered to refuse; he took a very short breath and even then fell to coughing.

The half-breed smiled, and took back the long, smooth pipe. "I bought this from a Dutchman," he said in English before falling silent again.

They were quiet a long time before Leal spoke again.

"My mother's mother was Erie, but I have some Delaware blood as well, two grandfathers back. The Delaware are the fathers of all in these lands, the ancient people. But there is no longer any respect for the grandfather tribe.

"Do you see the stars above? The children have gone there. They go after dancing the bear dance. On the fifth night of the winter ceremony, the old men sing their song, and wish for the same deliverance. Someday, I too will sing."

Leal fell silent again, smoking. Jake, greatly fatigued, leaned down to the sand and began nudging off to sleep. The fire was warm on his face, and the woods behind him sheltered him from the wind.

He woke to find a heavy blanket thrown over him. Leal was sitting silently by the canoe. The sun had been up for at least an hour.

"We must leave," said the trapper. "We are not far from St. Jean, and it would be better to pass early."

Jake nodded and took his station in the front of the canoe. His stomach was empty, and though the hollow sensation sharpened his senses, still he would have liked at least a biscuit to soften the gnawing.

With every stroke of the paddles, the river widened; they were approaching the start of the lake. The shoreline to their right began to open, and all at once, as if part of a staged pageant, the settlement appeared. There were hundreds of soldiers and workers here, a veritable armada being fitted out for the pending invasion of New York.

It was as if the Royal Navy had taken up its great Atlantic fleet, miniaturized it by two-thirds, and set it down at the tip of Lake Champlain. The *Inflexible*, a ship capable of carrying twenty guns, sat at the head of the line, tugging and pulling in the running water. Behind her, men worked feverishly to outfit and arm a much newer craft, the *Royal George*. She would be dwarfed in the Atlantic, but here her twelve-pound iron cannon would batter anything the Americans could put against her.

The squadron included three ships that last year had belonged to the Americans—the *Washington,* the *Lee,* and the *New Jersey.* Directly in front of the fort—the sloping works were much less impressive than the navy, if that was any consolation—was a square, odd-looking ketch called *Thunderer,* a floating artillery battery designed to help break the walls of Ticonderoga.

Jake amused himself by considering how quickly the ship would find the bottom with the assistance of a well-placed explosive charge. But he gave no real thought to undertaking sabotage; he had a more important job downstream.

They were paddling through an armed camp, the river choked with redcoats. The great confusion of the traffic served them well; they passed the fort without once being challenged, if one excepts the crude curses of a British sailor in a skiff who felt they'd cut him off.

A small patrol in a whaleboat rigged with a sail pulled alongside a few miles south. Leal answered their hail in Mahican first, and then a bit of Iroquois, before going to English and explaining, very haltingly, that they were headed south to Crown Point, sent by Burgoyne to serve as guides. Jake had his pocket pistol steadied on his knee under the hunting shirt, but it wasn't necessary; an entire regiment of patriots could pass here if only they uttered the magic word "Burgoyne."

Their easy passage and his speedy progress did not console Jake, who realized now that the intelligence he was returning with for Flanagan and Schuyler would bring little comfort. The Americans needed months and perhaps years to adequately prepare for such an invasion force. And even if it were met successfully, Howe's attack from Manhattan would threaten disaster.

The messenger had to be stopped. The war would be lost otherwise.

Jake spent the entire afternoon studying the roadway along the lake, trying to will his nemesis to appear—but even as strong a will as Jake's could not work miracles. Though Leal assured him that the highway was the only reliable road to Hubbardton, he began to fear Herstraw had found some other way south.

They took a brief lunch on a small island on the east, a hundred yards at most from the rocky shore. Their refreshment was hard bread only, washed down by the water of the lake. By early evening Jake was famished and exhausted, and almost didn't join his guide when Leal picked up his rifle and motioned him toward the woods. But of course he had to, not merely to help catch dinner, but to show he was not like the soft Englishmen Leal held in contempt.

The trapper had decided on rabbit for dinner, and it took him only a few minutes to find one; a single shot and the animal lay at their feet. Leal searched for a second rabbit, and was rewarded within a few minutes. As a bonus, they found a few edible mushrooms nearby.

The dinner was among the most delicious Jake had ever tasted, far better than any he had in Europe or Boston or even his home of Philadelphia. Once more he was given the biggest portion, but this time he felt no need to contain himself, Leal's being nearly as plump.

"You wonder why I hate the British," said Leal after they had finished.

"They cheated you at the fort."

"That is only a small part of it," said the Minqua. He retrieved his pipe and stoked it, puffing thoughtfully and handing it to Jake. Nearly a quarter of an hour passed before he spoke again.

"I have a wife," said the half-breed. "She was stolen by them last year, in an attack."

"The British took her?"

"The Mohawk. It is the same thing. These tribes are cowards without their white grandfathers to protect them."

Jake knew better than to argue with the overstatement.

"She had gone among the settlers to sell some of our furs when the town was attacked. I arrived too late." Here the stoic mask slipped ever so slightly before Leal continued. "If she had been white, she would have been killed. It would have been a mercy."

Jake nodded. In fact, invading tribes often adopted women and children—and in very special circumstances, men as well—treating them as one of their own. But from

Leal's perspective, his wife's soul had been stolen—and so, therefore, had his.

"I have tried to get the British to make them return her, but no officer will even speak to me. They call me a devil, and spit at me."

The man's voice was calm. He held his chest perfectly straight and his head so level an egg would not have rolled off his hat.

"Do you know where she is?"

"With the Mohawk, it is difficult to tell. I have searched settlements west of here and not found her. But women often travel with their men, as Meeko did with me."

Jake told Leal of the group he had come across on his way north some days before. He had to fight against every instinct inside not to volunteer to help the Minqua; a detour now would be catastrophic for the Cause.

Leal took the information without comment, and did not reproach Jake for not volunteering his help. Instead he placed another piece of tobacco in the pipe and smoked strongly for a few minutes more.

"She is Algonquin and does not speak your language, or even French. Meeko is the name of a magic squirrel with great powers," Leal said. "In battle, the squirrel could be tapped on the back, and two sons would appear from her, stronger than their mother, whose strength itself was enormous. The squirrels helped the great hero Pulowech, the Partridge, in the days of the ancestors' ancestors.

"Her namesake will help me find her, I'm sure."

Jake nodded. Leal silently took up his blanket and curled himself before the dying fire. Jake stayed awake awhile longer, wondering at the great sacrifices even the innocent were making in the name of Freedom.

The next day he woke earlier, only to find Leal waiting for him again. Jake took the front of the canoe and rowed strongly, once more without breakfast. Crown Point lay ahead, and beyond it, Ticonderoga; a surge of adrenaline powered his strokes.

Jake continued to scan the road along the lake, hoping

Herstraw would appear. They'd come south so quickly, Jake began to suspect he'd beat him. But Jake knew he could not afford to wait at Bull's Head for very long, if at all; General Schuyler must be alerted to the invasion plans immediately. Even so, if the messenger were missed there, it would be increasingly difficult to find him.

Once or twice Jake's heart leaped as he saw a party on the shore, heading south, but these turned out to be false alarms. Finally, near midday, he caught sight of several wagons on the eastward shore. As he signaled with his head for Leal to paddle closer, his spirits soared—there was his man. Truly, God wanted the Revolution to succeed.

Herstraw was dressed in the yeoman's garb he'd worn in Montreal; indeed, he looked as if he had neither changed nor stopped en route. He rode at the edge of the group; whether they were strangers or escorts was impossible to tell.

Jake motioned with his hand to Leal, indicating they should paddle ahead. But as he turned to check the lake ahead, his glance was forced back by surprise—the party on the shore was being led by a fancy carriage, upon whose bench sat his former companion, Claus van Clynne.

What trick was Fortune playing here? As this was the most dependable road heading south, Jake should not have been so surprised to find him here. Still, could this be only a coincidence?

If Providence was disposed to placing van Clynne so conveniently at Jake's disposal—well then, he must be taken advantage of.

Jake paddled with a sudden burst of energy. Once they had gained some distance and rounded a bend, he turned to Leal and told him that they must part here.

Jake detected the slightest disappointment on the stoic's face before he steered the boat onto a small beach. He slipped the money from the money belt he wore and tucked it beneath one of the bundled packages —he wanted no argument from the man because he'd left a few shillings more than they'd agreed upon. These were the last of his coins, indeed, of all his money, but he was now within a few hours of the American line. There his troubles could be paid by Schuyler himself.

Leal did not shake his hand; instead, he held out his knife, hilt first, the same knife he had tried to kill Jake with two days before.

"Take this and remember me," said Leal. "The bone is from the elk. It comes from far north, and once held a blade of stone. There is a story behind it."

Jake took the knife and reached for his pocket knife, all he had to give in return. But Leal had already pushed off from shore.

"I shall tell you the story when we meet again," said the half-breed. "Our fates are intertwined."

Thirteen

Wherein, Claus van Clynne, Esquire, makes known the depth of his feelings about potholes and patriotism.

Jake had barely enough time to tuck the knife into his belt, dust the sand from his pants, and scramble to the road before the party appeared. They were on the shore opposite Crown Point and Ticonderoga, roughly midway from both. The land hereabouts was owned by men friendly to the patriot cause. If it was not so arable as that on the western shore, still it had a certain smell about it, the scent of Freedom.

Or so Jake would later claim. For now, he put up his hand and saluted the party, immediately drawing the attention of two men in the lead wagon, who aimed their long Pennsylvania rifles in his direction as soon as they saw him.

"Good Squire van Clynne, we meet again," said Jake, ignoring them as he walked directly to the carriage where van Clynne was seated. The two-wheeled phaeton was by far the finest vehicle in the convoy; painted a shiny black, it would have looked more at home in London or Paris, and undoubtedly done better on their streets. It had immense wheels, and the seat was set so high passengers would have an easy time boarding from the roof of a house. Pulled by two horses, a driver not more than fourteen years old sat bareback on one of the animals to guide it. Van Clynne's own horse was tethered to the rear; though heavily burdened with packages, he seemed to step along quite lightly, no doubt glad to be relieved of his master's weight.

The Dutchman sat in the middle of the bench, arms

folded. Despite his large frame, he bounced sharply with each bump in the road. The frown on his face deepened when he saw Jake pull himself up on the empty horse beside the driver.

"Who are you?" demanded van Clynne.

Jake laughed. "You do remember me, sir. We rode together to Montreal not four days since."

"I have not been in Montreal," said van Clynne frostily.

"We rode together nonetheless. You don't mind my heading south with you, I trust?"

With everyone looking at him, van Clynne realized it was much easier to take on this passenger than to explain him. He nodded to the boy and told him to go ahead—directions that were not specifically necessary, since the lad had not stopped nor even glanced at his new passenger.

"I did not recognize you in that getup," said van Clynne as the party moved down the left fork of the roadway, heading away from the water. "You look like a French half-breed. You've done well to lose your hat, though the one you've replaced it with is hardly flattering."

"I was just growing fond of it," said Jake, pushing the toque back on his head. "How was your business?"

"I have no wish to engage in conversation with you, sir. Just because I let you ride with me does not mean that I have taken you to my bosom. Remember that I know your true affections," he added in a barely audible hiss.

"Business was that bad, was it?"

"The wood that grows north of here is damnable, completely rotted by insects. The bugs nest in the very seeds as they sprout. Yet they expect twice what the finest boards will fetch in Poughkeepsie. Damnation take them all, that is what I say. I plan to change professions as soon as I return home."

"You found no wood to buy?"

"I didn't say that."

"Arranged for no furs?"

"What is your point, sir?"

"I was just wondering what you would do if you left off being a businessman."

"I'll become an innkeeper," said van Clynne quickly and with so much dignity that Jake began to laugh. "And what's wrong with that?"

"Every innkeeper I know is a jolly fellow."

"And?"

"You are a trifle disagreeable today."

"I am in my best mood in weeks."

"You do drag the leg of the fox with your complaints," chided Jake. "In your mouth, the entire world has declined."

"I am a speaker of the truth, sir; if that's what you mean by a complaint, then it's not my fault the world has fallen down. Look at this road, for instance. There was a time when it would have been twice as wide, and if it bothered to have potholes, then it would have had potholes deep enough to hide Brazil in, not these shallow annoyances."

"Those were the days," said Jake, "when potholes were potholes."

Van Clynne grumbled at being made fun of, saying he would resolve to be quiet if that was the only way he might win respect. But it was against his nature to remain silent; before they had gone a few hundred yards he once more took up his commentary, remarking on the carriage's inadequate spring design.

After the silence of the past few days, Jake found himself almost enjoying the never-ending patter, more so because twisting on the horse to receive it gave him ready cover to observe his British friend.

The messenger was not an athletic-looking fellow, being of slight build. If anything, he looked a little pasty in the fresh air. But Jake realized appearances must be deceiving, since it took some stamina and not a small amount of courage to travel back and forth between New York City and Canada.

More important than his physical disposition, the messenger kept a pair of pistols at the front of his saddle. No doubt loaded and half cocked, they ruled out direct confrontation, at least for the moment. Jake realized too that he could not count on his fellow travelers for assistance. Save van Clynne, he had no idea who any of them were or what their allegiance might be. And even van Clynne had proved that he was not above helping a Tory for the right price.

Nonetheless, Jake was confident an opportunity to overcome Herstraw would soon present itself, and said nothing as the party proceeded. Several hours passed before they took a fork on a road with a sign for Pittsford, and Jake once more became conscious of his need to return quickly to Schuyler with the invasion plans. But his concerns were quieted by the appearance of a small building flying the wooden sign of a bull's head—the inn Herstraw had bragged of to Burgoyne.

"The wife knows her ale here," van Clynne confided. "You will see. Her husband's an old countryman from England, but she was taught by a German."

"Old countryman" was a way of saying that the man was an immigrant, far more likely than native-born to side with the tyrant. That and his distant relationship with Herstraw, as the messenger had mentioned in Canada, were more than enough to explain his allegiance—and put Jake on his guard.

Jake slipped his hand to his belt before getting off his horse. The elk-handled blade Leal had given him was ready—all he needed was an opportunity to slip up behind the man and escape.

But escape must be guaranteed. No one else knew the information he'd traveled from Montreal with.

Perhaps, as insurance, he should tell someone else.

"Are you going to stand there in the middle of the path all afternoon?" asked van Clynne, shaking the dust from his coat.

"Claus, let me ask you something. You're a patriot, are you not?"

"Just because I have not raised a fuss as you rode my horse, do not think that I am your friend."

"But you have often done things for the American cause. And you know General Schuyler. He's a Dutchman."

"What are you getting at?"

"Where did you get such a carriage?" said Jake loudly, giving up his try at recruiting van Clynne when he realized Herstraw was walking directly toward them.

"You have much to learn about the art of conversation," said van Clynne. "You can't flit from one topic to another and expect coherence."

"It is a fine carriage."

"I have a buyer for it in Rhinebeck, who has always told me to keep an eye out. Unless you'd like to meet his price. It would be just the thing to top off your hunting dress."

"I think not," said Jake as Herstraw passed into the building. "Tell me, do you know who that man is?"

The Dutchman shrugged. "These are all farmers burned out by the Indians," he said. "There has been some trouble north, and they have relatives farther south."

"They're all patriots like you, then?"

"I gave you fair warning, sir. Do not press your luck. Here boy, let me see to that," said the Dutchman, walking off after his carriage.

The ale was as good as van Clynne had predicted. Perhaps some of the taste came from the heritage of the tankard it was delivered in. The wooden vessel consisted of staves held together at the bottom by a copper ring. The top was tied with a flat reed, and the handle had an animal's head carved on it, though the cup was so old and worn it was impossible to tell what sort of animal was intended.

To Jake it didn't matter; his attention was focused entirely on Herstraw, seated across the room. The messenger had taken the precaution of hauling his holsters in with his saddlebag, as if overly fastidious about his possessions. A gun was not more than eight inches from his fingers at any moment while he ate.

When the keeper asked if he would have some lunch, Jake nodded absentmindedly. He soon realized he was shoveling food into his mouth with abandon, hardly aware of the birch trencher plate it came on. The stew, made of venison, corn, and carrots, was a sizable feast for one who'd had so little to eat over the past few days.

Jake sopped up the stew's juices with a large crust of yeast bread, the first soft loaf he'd had in more than a week. The bread and his pocketknife were his only utensils, but he cleared the old-fashioned plate within a few minutes and asked for seconds.

Van Clynne's description of the party seemed accurate, in the main. This was to be but a short diversion before they came back to the highway south, proceeding through Fort Edward south to Rhinebeck, which lay roughly parallel to Kingston on the other side of the river. Several of these people had relatives there. Their politics were not paraded, but they seemed at least sympathetic to the American cause, as would be expected from their destination. And they did not act as if they knew Herstraw as more than a fellow met on the road.

Could he count on them to help with an arrest? Van Clynne didn't trust him, Jake knew, and they would probably take their cue from him.

The American agent left his second plate of stew half finished as he contemplated a desperate plan—stay close to Herstraw as he left the inn, then knife him from behind outside. Jump on a waiting horse and ride straight for the fort.

But that would be pushing his luck recklessly. They were now within American lines and near several forts besides; it would be only a few miles before some militia group or army patrol would cross their path. He could then unmask himself, arrest Herstraw, and command escort to Schuyler. It would not cause much of a delay to wait until then.

Jake, constitutionally opposed to delay but seeing little other choice, worked his way around the room to a chair across from Herstraw to size up his quarry. In the meantime, another member of the party pulled over his own seat and began talking to the disguised British messenger.

Apparently Herstraw had lost his horse somewhere north, most likely by riding it too hard through the night. The animal he was on now belonged to the farmer. The men negotiated a deal—the farmer wouldn't sell this mare, but promised he could buy a suitable substitute from his brother in Rhinebeck. In the meantime, he was welcome to ride the one he'd been on—provided he paid the six shillings they'd agreed on. Herstraw counted out two shillings in advance to seal the arrangement.

The deal concluded, Jake leaned forward.

"Are you related to my good friend, George Herstraw?" he asked. "He owns land south of Bennington."

"I think not," said the man. "I come from the Herstraws near White Plains."

"Is that where you're going?"

Herstraw nodded reluctantly. "How did you know my name?"

"I overheard you talking before," lied Jake. "And I thought you looked a bit familiar."

The pair engaged in a short conversation, Jake explaining that he, too, was on his way south to see relatives. The exchange of falsehoods complete, the American looked up to see his friend van Clynne entering the inn. No doubt he'd been detained by some business deal, Jake suggested to Herstraw.

"The man would sell his mother's dishes if there were profit in it," he added.

"I wouldn't know."

"You're not familiar with Squire van Clynne?"

"I am a stranger here."

One of the farmers stood up and announced it was time to reform the convoy. The group rose and began filing toward the door, where the innkeeper stood with his palm upturned and his thick arm out, collecting payment for lunch and beer.

It was only then that Jake remembered he'd given up the last of his money. His repast was only an English shilling or the equivalent—a fair and inexpensive price, surely—but he was as likely to find a coin in his money belt as he was to find the treasure of Captain Kidd.

Herstraw chose not to hear Jake's request for aid, and so Jake turned to the only other man here he knew.

"Squire van Clynne," he said solicitously. "Good sir, lend me the price of dinner and I will repay you in Albany."

"Albany, what place is that?"

"Fort Orange," said Jake, remembering van Clynne's habit of calling everything by its old Dutch name.

"We are not going to Fort Orange," answered van Clynne. "It's on the opposite shore."

"I'm good for the shilling," said Jake. "Surely you know that."

"It seems to me that I do not know that," said van Clynne. "You had money in your possession before, and now have squandered it. Does that make you a good risk? I think not."

"Claus."

"What would I have for collateral?"

"Collateral? For a shilling?"

"Collateral, sir. I never consider a loan without first considering the collateral."

Jake dug through his pockets. "My pocketknife," he said. "It's a Barlow, and worth a pound or two at least."

"Hardly," said van Clynne, not even bothering to look it over. "Do you have a watch?"

"No," said Jake. "Here, take the knife."

"I'll set my own terms, if you please," said van Clynne. "Let me see your hunting knife."

"That's not for sale at any price," said Jake. "I've borrowed it from someone, and expect to return it."

"And you won't return my shilling, eh?"

"I am good for a shilling, damn it. This knife is worth considerably more."

"Give me your money belt."

"My money belt?"

"If your purse is empty, you've no need for it, have you?"

It was difficult to argue with such logic, especially as he feared Herstraw might decide to get a head start on the company and bolt down the road. Jake pulled the belt off and held it up before van Clynne—who would have a difficult time getting it around his thigh, let alone his belly.

"Thank you very much, sir." Van Clynne grabbed the belt and flipped the innkeeper a shilling.

Jake hurried out the door into the sunlight—and the outstretched arms of several members of the local militia.

"Jake Gibbs, I arrest you on charges of spying for His Majesty the King."

There was a note of reverence in the soldier's voice when he mentioned George III. Jake did not have time to point out how unseemly that was coming from a patriot, however, for a chain was immediately flung around his shoulders and he was tugged to the ground. His protest was cut off by a thick fist that slammed into the side of his head and knocked him unconscious.

Fourteen

*Wherein, Leal le Couguar is rejoined for a brief but
sorrowful interlude.*

Convinced that the information Jake had given him
about the band of Mohawks and British loyalists held the
key to his wife's whereabouts, the woodsman Leal le
Couguar set out to find them. The immense difficulties
involved in traversing the wild country between Lake
Champlain and the upper Mohawk Valley, not to mention the problem of confronting the group single-
handedly, did not trouble him. If anything, he felt a well-
ing confidence—the kidnappers had traveled far to elude
him, but the gods had brought him a messenger to point
him in their direction. For Leal interpreted Jake's sudden
appearance on the road as nothing less than divine intervention, and trusted now that his mission would end with
success.

When he reached the shore, he took stock of his gear
and found Jake's discarded suit jacket. Leal had never
seen such fine material sewed into a coat, and wondered
why his friend had left it.

Perhaps if Jake had explained himself fully, perhaps if
duty had not prevented him from telling Leal the full
nature of his mission, the trapper's logic might have
taken a different turn. For though Leal was superstitious,
still he was a generally practical man and did not ordinarily interpret everything he saw or heard as a supernatural sign. But as he pondered his friend's strength and
apparent wisdom, the ease with which they had talked
together and the bond that had so quickly developed between them, the temptation to conclude that Jake was a

personal embodiment of spirits Leal had heard about
since childhood grew stronger and stronger. Blame isola-
tion and loneliness as much as superstition; in any event,
Leal pulled on Jake's coat, content to wear it as a token
of good luck and friendship—and maybe an invocation of
supernatural powers.

If there were unworldly powers at work, they were not
beneficent. For Leal's arrival on shore and his contem-
plation of the jacket was observed by Major Christopher
Manley, the agent of the Secret Department assigned to
assassinate Jake.

Manley had spent the past two days following Jake's
trail. Though it had grown cold on the west shore of the
lake, the agent had no doubt he would come across the
American if he persevered. Ticonderoga must be his
eventual goal, as that was where the American forces
were headquartered.

Many miles north, the limp body of an old farmer lay
near an empty cart, attesting to the major's brutal manners. Before his neck had been snapped, the Frenchman
had told Manley to be on the lookout for a half-breed
trapper. The jacket Leal slipped on told him he had
found the right man.

The woodsman would be a more difficult interview
than the farmer—Manley took his pistol from his saddlebag, checked to make sure it was loaded, and then advanced on him.

Pistol is a misnomer. The gun he presented to the Minqua had the heft of a thick blunderbuss, specially adapted
for Manley's treacherous work. It contained nearly a
pound of different-sized balls, and its short barrel flared
in a way that guaranteed the shot would spread in a
deadly pattern. It was good only for close work—a man
standing directly in front of the pistol at twenty-five feet
had a favorable chance of being missed by most of the
rapidly spreading shot—but at close range it was more
effective than an 8-pound cannon.

"Good afternoon," said Manley, stepping out of the
trees at the top of the lake embankment just a few feet
from the half-breed. "I wonder if you could tell me how
you acquired your jacket. It's quite a handsome coat."

Leal feigned to not understand. He spoke a few words in Minqua to throw the stranger off.

"You use a dead tongue," responded Manley, as if he not only knew the words, but had been expecting them. "I will not stand out of your way, no matter how you express it."

"What is it you want?" responded Leal in English. He hoped his hard manner would hide his shock. Never had he come across a white man familiar with his words.

Manley smiled. "Perhaps I have been searching for the last remaining Minqua."

"I am not the last," said Leal. "But it is rare to find someone who knows of my people."

"We can talk of your legends later—where did you get that coat?"

"I bought it."

"Where is the man you bought it from?"

Leal did not answer. The man's extreme height, his thin arms and legs, the odd prominence of his eyes—Leal must be forgiven if he wondered for just a moment if another spirit had taken human form and stopped him in the woods.

His amazement cost him dearly, for in the few seconds that he contemplated the possibility unearthly spirits had involved him in their own drama, his attention lapsed. The assassin saw his opening and leapt forward to grab him by the neck, wrestling him to his knees with barely a struggle.

Just as Leal began to react, he felt the cold metal of Manley's pistol poke against the bottom of his chin.

"Did you leave him on the opposite shore?" Manley demanded, rocking the gun back and forth so its mouth sucked at Leal's flesh.

"Yes," said the trapper.

"Where is he headed?"

Suddenly Leal felt ashamed, as if he had betrayed his companion with his one-word answer. To his mind, he had faced a major test of courage and failed.

How hard are the ways of the woods; how difficult the code of survival. What a civilized man might interpret as simple prudence or, at worst, expedience, Leal saw as fatal disgrace. His only choice now was to attempt to recoup his honor by a show of strength—and desperate action. He twisted suddenly and threw his elbow into Manley's stomach, diving for the ground as the British agent's gun went off.

Two of the balls went through Leal's left leg, burning their way through the flesh and shattering his bones. The pain was surprisingly light, though when he tried to stand up he tumbled down immediately. He crawled forward, reaching toward his gear and the tomahawk that lay six inches away.

He was just extending his fingers toward it when Manley clamped down on his hand with a boot.

"I would have killed you anyway, Indian, but now I can take pleasure in doing so."

Leal looked upward—not in the direction of his tormentor, but toward the trees. In that last moment of his life, he caught sight of a small squirrel chattering in a branch. He realized in that second that Meeko his wife had been killed by her captors—a possibility he had never allowed himself to consider, though it had always been the most likely outcome of her trial. He realized, too, that he was on his way to meet her, in some happier existence. And so he smiled as Manley brought his knife blade down to slash the lifeblood from his throat.

The savage's grimace so haunted the British agent that he contemplated burying him, an honor he would ordinarily never accord an enemy. In the end he decided he hadn't the time, and contented his conscience by turning the body facedown on the ground. Then he took the trapper's canoe and pushed it out onto the water. It meant abandoning his horse, but the animal had been effectively lamed by his ride here anyway.

Why had his prey gone to the other side of the lake when Ticonderoga was only a few miles south of here? Manley reasoned that it must be because Jake was trying to intercept Herstraw. That meant there might still be a chance to catch him before he gave his superiors details of the pending invasion.

In truth, Manley agreed with Burgoyne that it did not

matter much if the Americans knew exactly what they were faced with. It might even help intimidate them—the forces they had chosen to oppose were overwhelming, and realizing that could only lead to despair. For they were, after all, facing the greatest army the world had ever known; no amount of foreknowledge could help in a wrestling match with a vastly superior opponent.

Manley's real goal was the elimination of Jake Gibbs. If he could accomplish that before the spy delivered his intelligence, so much the better. He pushed his long, slender arms to row harder, the anticipation of his enemy's demise a powerful and refreshing fuel.

Fifteen

Wherein, Jake is mistaken for a traitor, and suffers the consequences.

$\mathcal{J}$ake came to in the back of a wagon, jostling against the side board like so many pounds of wheat. Trussed in heavy chain and rope, he felt like a prize pig put up for a holiday feast.

"Who the hell is in charge here?" he shouted from the bottom of the wagon. When that brought no response, Jake added a few more curses and increased the volume of his complaint.

A Hindu hymn would have had more effect. The wagon crashed merrily along, either by design or chance finding the largest ruts in the road. The shocks were amplified by Jake's chains, and the coarse floorboards rubbed at the few parts of his body that were not covered by restraints.

It took several minutes, but he finally managed to leverage himself into an upright position against the side of the wagon. The scene would have been comical had he not been in the middle of it.

The entire countryside had joined in the capture of the supposed Tory spy. Closest to him was a ring of militia in the haphazard but universal dress of the American irregulars, their only sign of service a green sprig stuck in their caps. Each of these men clutched a rifle or musket, mostly in rude aim at his person.

Next around was a group of older men and boys. The few who didn't carry rifles had weapons such as pitchforks, though some made do with axes and an older gentleman carried a large if rusty sword.

The next ring belonged to the women. There were fewer rifles among this group, but several pistols; wooden staves made up the majority of arms, and at least one broom could be seen. Finally came the children and the dogs of the village, yelling and yapping and barking, no doubt confused as to whether they were going to a picnic or a prison. All told, one hundred souls were giving Jake an escort fit for the king he was accused of working for.

Despite their large numbers, they were making exquisite progress; Wood Creek, a tributary of Lake Champlain that would take them to Fort Ticonderoga, already lay in view.

"Good citizens," said Jake, "your patriotism cheers me. But you are making a dreadful mistake. My name is Lieutenant Colonel Jake Gibbs, and I am on a mission for General Schuyler."

This drew titters from the crowd.

"Good citizens, hear me!" Jake tried again, rallying his best speaking voice. "A British spy is getting away even while we amuse ourselves with this diversion."

"Damn traitor," said one of the men, "we ought to tar and feather him, then take him to the halter."

So much for a career as a politician.

"Who's in charge here?" Jake demanded.

"You'd best keep your mouth shut," said one of the militiamen. "Several of these folk have lost relatives to the war, and they would like nothing better than to take retribution. You're lucky we're taking you to the fort."

Jake fumed, but there was little he could do. Surely his identity would be cleared up at Ticonderoga.

There was one slight difficulty he would have to overcome, however. Jake's everyday coat had buttons pressed with the Masonic symbol used by members of the secret service to immediately identify one of their brethren; a high-ranking intelligence officer would recognize them immediately. But his coat was lying more than a hundred miles to the north, in Marie's bedroom.

The symbol was impressed on one other item that ordinarily he carried with him at all times—his money belt.

It is inaccurate to say that Jake cursed van Clynne a hundred times as he was transported from the wagon to a small, flat-bottomed boat on the creek. More likely the oaths numbered in the millions, though one or two thousand were saved for the militia officer in charge of this procession, and perhaps one thousand found their way to General Schuyler and his assistant Flanagan for having him march all the way to Canada and back in record time, only to let him be arrested by their own troops.

The commander of the guard who met the boat had to step back two full steps under the force of Jake's tongue-lashing.

"I demand to be released. I am an officer in General Greene's command and was in the middle of a vital mission for General Schuyler. Let me go or I'll have you trussed and stood on your head for six months."

Typical of the patriot army, the officer's retreat was no sign of surrender. He didn't even bother with an answer, much less a counterattack, turning instead and walking toward the guardhouse. Jake's legs were tied in a way that made it difficult to stand, let alone walk; he was pushed from the boat and fell flat on his face. Before he could even attempt to roll to his feet, he felt himself lifted and bodily carried to a jail cell.

The hours he spent in solitary confinement worked wonders for Jake's temper. Before being locked in, he had been merely livid, ferociously upset and greatly insulted at being mistaken for a Tory scum. Now his wrath had truly continental dimensions, erupting in volcanic waves that would have impressed even Achilles, whose own well-nursed grudge had destroyed the Trojans' hero Hector and launched Homer on the way to epic stardom.

Still, a man with a profession such as Jake's often finds himself in situations where great self-control is called for. He develops, therefore, a veritable arsenal of temper-saving devices and tricks, all designed to cool the hot vapors of passion and let reason prevail. Mental diversions, exercises, complete flights of fancy—Jake employed them all, and was in reasonable control when he was finally led, chained at hands and feet, to the building where he was to be examined. In fact, he found himself nearly philosophical.

"You've been most businesslike," he told the sergeant as he was led into the interrogation chamber. "I won't hold this against you when I'm released."

The door slamming behind them stifled the laughter of the guards. Jake found himself facing an officer in a worn blue uniform.

Scribe, change the word "examined" above to "tried." As in, court-martialed. As in, penalty—death by hanging if guilty.

And what other verdict is there?

"Of what am I accused?"

"You're a spy, plain and simple," said the officer in a tired voice. The room was windowless and dark, despite the efforts of a number of candles on the desk. "How do you plead?"

"Plead? This isn't a court. This isn't justice. This is what we're fighting against!"

Jake's comment was answered by a sharp blow from behind, delivered by a guard at a nod from the officer.

"The prisoner will answer in turn, only the question which the court directs."

"I demand to see General Schuyler."

Another blow, this one a bit harder to the top of the shoulder.

"I am in charge here," said the officer.

"You're not the commander of the fort," said Jake. "Where's the commander?"

Jake swirled and ducked to the side as the private aimed another blow.

"I'm warning you," said Jake. "General Washington's regulations specifically forbid you hitting a prisoner."

The officer waved at the guard, who took a step back toward the wall. "Obviously, they are issuing rules of army conduct to all Tory spies," he said in a weary voice.

"I am Lieutenant Colonel Jake Gibbs of the secret service. Assigned to General Greene's staff, on temporary duty to General Schuyler. I request that you contact the general immediately."

"Which one?"

"General Greene, actually. At this moment I wish I'd never heard of Schuyler."

"I see," said the officer, making a notation on a piece of paper before him. "Sure you don't want to try for Washington?"

"Excuse me, but whom do I have the pleasure of addressing?" asked Jake. His contempt was unconcealed.

"Captain Horace P. Andrews, General Gage's staff. I'm empowered to try all spies."

"Begging your pardon, but first of all, as I understand it, if there's going to be a trial, it should be a standard court-martial proceeding. That would require—"

"I have ten minutes for you. Do you want to fill it all with protests, or will you plead for mercy?"

"What possible evidence do you have against me?"

The captain flipped through the pile of papers and pulled out a piece of foolscap filled with writing in a tight, cramped hand. With some difficulty because of the lighting, he began reading it in a loud monotone, uninfluenced by Jake's groans.

" 'I, the honorable Claus van Clynne, Esquire, businessman, hearty patriot, member of the New York Militia Auxiliary Advisory Force, sworn enemy of the British Parliament and hater of all things English, do hereby solemnly swear and warrant that the information which I am about to give is the absolute truth as I know it, and that I am witness to the following particulars without prior prejudice and with no personal gain or offering.

" 'To wit, in the first part, that the party who goes by the name of "Jake Gibbs," lately apprehended at the Bull's Head Tavern by the local militia, which was alerted by my own self while I smartly snuck away on another pretense, did attempt to enlist and hire me to take him north past the legally constituted and patriotic armies of the state of New York and the Congress of these several provinces.

" 'Said Mr. Gibbs did also threaten me bodily and physically during the course of our contact, and on one occasion fired four bullets in my direction, which, due to my dexterous efforts and the grace of God, missed. Said Mr. Gibbs made numerous other shows of threat and strength, the effect of which were to put me in a general mood of fear and concern for my own safety.

" 'Notwithstanding this and at great personal risk to myself, but in the true spirit of patriotism, I did endeavor to lead said individual Mr. Gibbs to a place where he could be apprehended by duly authorized militia or Continental Army units or, failing that, where I myself, at great danger to my person, might overcome and control him unaided.

" 'Said Mr. Gibbs being continually on guard and always alert and several times stronger than I, plus having the convenience of a multibarreled weapon, the likes of which have scarcely been seen in such environs, if at all, my efforts to capture him were for naught.

" 'Through evil stratagem, he eluded my grasp, heading straight for the British lines and the succor of his traitorous companions.

" 'Finding myself already drawn deep into Canadian territory, and having originally been destined there within to conduct lawful and legal business as granted by the general of this department, the good and patriotic Philip Schuyler of Fort Orange, a fine gentleman who honors the memory of his Dutch ancestors, I continued upon my way, making arrangements in connection with various and sundry businesses, all legal and without prejudice to the government of the glorious province of New Amsterdam, free and sovereign by the grace of God and the efforts of man.

" 'Having completed this business, I returned south, intent on informing certain military acquaintances of mine of this matter. At that point I had not the full knowledge of the perfidy of this fellow, who, not content with being a coward and deserting his own native cause, instead returned with the intent of doing it far greater harm as a spy and saboteur, going so far as to sound out the loyalty of the first group of persons he threw in with, obviously with the intent of recruiting them as a legion for the British.

" 'Fortune put us back together, Providence intending that I serve as but a vessel for the State in his apprehension. I alerted the local militia at the first opportunity, and the arrest was made with dispatch.

" 'I commend you good sirs on your patriotism, and remain, yours sincerely in Liberty, Claus van Clynne.

" 'Postscript—he extorted a pound sterling, English currency, at gunpoint from me, and I should appreciate recompense, over and above whatever token reward is customary in such cases.' "

The captain put down the letter and looked at the prisoner with as much sympathy as the snake would have elicited from Adam after the Fall.

At the very beginning of the epistle, Jake's anger had flashed, but as it went on, he actually grew amused at the distortion of events. Not only was van Clynne's pen as prolix as his tongue, he had quite effectively made himself the hero of the tale by shifting a few minor details around. Jake wondered what he would have done with the entire story had he known it—no doubt the portly Dutchman would have arrived at Ticonderoga with King George himself in chains.

The humor of the situation was lost on the captain. Being ignorant of Jake's perspective, he believed van Clynne's account, with some slight allowances for exaggeration and his habit of referring to things by the old Dutch names.

"By returning to our lines, you have as good as admitted that you are a spy," said the officer, "and the punishment for that is hanging."

"I *am* a spy," said Jake. "For General Schuyler."

"You have no papers and no identification. I have the sworn testimony of a good American citizen against you."

"Now, does that letter sound believable?"

"The testimony is from a roving member of the Committee of Correspondence." The captain nodded at the guards. "Take him back to the cell."

"Wait a second. I demand to see General Schuyler."

"He'll see you on the scaffold," said the officer as Jake was pulled from the room. "After you're cut down."

"And another thing," managed Jake before his mouth was clamped shut by one of the guards, "I only borrowed a shilling."

Sixteen

*Wherein, our hero is forced to contemplate the prospects
of a very brief career on the gallows.*

*H*aving witnessed firsthand certain defects in the Continental Army's criminal justice system, Jake returned to his cell with a long list of recommendations for its improvement.

The prospects for implementing reform, however, did not appear particularly bright. While the sergeant kindly removed the gag covering his mouth when they arrived at the cell, his hands and legs remained shackled. The large door swung closed behind him and two guards took up positions outside it. His pockets had been emptied by the mob; there was neither weapon nor key in sight.

Jake told himself the trial had been a sham designed to intimidate him. But if so, why was there someone working in the courtyard outside the barred window, setting a beam over a small stage?

He was a good distance from panic, but he did allow himself to consider the irony of his situation. He wouldn't even be able to give a speech such as Nathan Hale had, when caught in New York. What could he say? I regret I have only one life to give, and it's being taken by the wrong side?

"Sergeant, who is the commanding officer of the fort? I must talk to him immediately. It's urgent."

"The sergeant's not here, traitor," hissed one of the guards.

"Well, listen to me, who is in charge of the fort? I have to talk to him about the enemy's plans. I have to reach Schuyler."

"I'll bet you'd like to talk strategy with him, you Tory scum," said the sentry, who pounded the door with the butt of his musket. "Now shut up in there."

A primed musket surely would have gone off if it had been slammed against the door so hard. That was a valuable piece of intelligence—they would not be able to fire if he made a break across the open courtyard.

Now all he had to do was shatter these agonizingly tight shackles, burst through these immensely thick walls, and make a desperate bolt for it.

"Sergeant, tell the captain that I have valuable information for him about the disposition of the enemy forces."

"I'm not a sergeant, you Tory," said the man, slamming the door again.

"Get the sergeant, then. Get any officer. I have intelligence, damn it."

"I doubt he'd believe you."

"Listen," said Jake, realizing what he would believe. "Tell him I want to make a full confession. Tell him I'll give him a full rundown of the British Army's dispositions."

If he failed to find someone who knew him or would take him to Schuyler, he'd just signed his own death warrant—the captain would now be justified in having him hanged. But every hour in the gaol increased the odds that Burgoyne's invasion would succeed and Herstraw would reach Howe; desperate times require desperate action.

He could hear whisperings outside the door, and then footsteps away. Jake folded his arms and waited. The sergeant soon arrived and the door was opened.

"The captain thought you would come around," said the man, motioning with his hands for Jake to follow him from the cell. "Decided to make a clean breast of it, eh?"

"When you're caught, you're caught," said Jake. He took a step forward and was tripped by the chain, wrenching his ankle horribly in the fall.

His pain was so severe the sergeant ordered the leg manacle removed. When Jake was helped to his feet, he seemed barely able to stand, and had to lean on the sergeant for support. The guards, full of themselves, as if they had played a role in breaking the prisoner down, began whistling and walking ahead, their chests puffing with their prize.

As the sergeant stepped through the doorway into the courtyard, Jake dragged his injured leg heavily. The distance between the guards and their prisoner lengthened.

Two bare scrapes across the courtyard and Jake's wandering eye caught sight of an unattended horse. In a flash his ankle magically healed—he smashed the sergeant alongside the head with his elbow and leaped toward the animal, intending to ride all the way to Albany if necessary, to find Schuyler and get him to rally the defenses against Burgoyne.

But escape was not to be so easily accomplished, for Jake found his path blocked unexpectedly by a figure looming from the darkness on horseback. A pistol was silhouetted against the moon.

"Stop or I will shoot you, and even in the dark I doubt I will miss."

Jake pulled up short, surprised not only by the shadow's sudden appearance, but by the fact that the voice accompanying it came from a woman.

"I must see General Schuyler," he managed to say just before the guards caught up with him and a hard smash from behind knocked him to the ground.

Someone ran up with a lantern. Jake came to in a half-lit fog, barely able to make out the forms before him.

"I must see Schuyler," he repeated.

"I think that can be arranged," said the soft, feminine voice before him.

The words brought his eyes into focus. He was staring at the most beautiful woman in all of New York and perhaps the entire North American continent, certainly at that moment, and most absolutely in the view of Lieutenant Colonel Jake Stewart Gibbs: Betsy Schuyler, the general's daughter, stood over him.

"You're goddamn lucky I decided to come north tonight. And goddamn lucky that my daughter accompanied me. If she hadn't been bringing her horses to the barn, those men would have killed you for escaping. What put such a thought in your head?"

And so Schuyler, in the manner of all great generals, had shifted the situation around to turn the blame on the subordinate before him. Jake, in the manner of all great subordinates, took it stiffly, with barely a frown, waiting for Schuyler to finish before pointing out, with all due respect—but not a farthing more—that not only had the general placed him in the situation, but the general's own officers had been ready to hang him.

"Captain Andrews has already explained that was merely a ruse," answered the general. "And besides, he is attached to Gage, not myself."

Jake decided this was as much satisfaction as he was likely to get, and devoted himself to giving the general his full impressions of the British situation, along with the knowledge of Burgoyne's intentions. Schuyler received the intelligence with the gravity it deserved, nodding appropriately and making sure his secretary took copious notes.

Jake's skills as a draftsman were put to the test penciling out what he had seen of troop dispositions and fortifications around St. Johns and Crown Point. He had an artistic bent, having briefly indulged in some drawing and painting lessons during his studies in England, and saw himself capable of at least attempting a style similar to Watteau, the French master whose great works dated from the beginning of the century. Watteau's handling of color and its nuances would be particularly apt here, producing an emotional effect that would rally his audience to repel the invaders.

But of course there was no time for such subtlety. Jake merely crayoned annotated diagrams showing the L of the breastworks around St. Johns with the relative location of the boats of the British flotilla. Still, there was a certain flair to the twists he gave the sails, and only a dull observer would miss the fact that the British flag was purposely placed upside down and at half-mast.

Artistic grandeur was not needed to show Schuyler the great dangers he faced. Burgoyne's forces were tremendous on their own, a full threat to Ticonderoga and Albany behind her. But have Howe come north, and clearly the Revolution was lost, and not just in Schuyler's home state. Control of the Hudson River would split the entire country in two, since there was no way of communicating north to south without crossing the river. With the sea blockade against Massachusetts growing in effectiveness, the great cause of Freedom would wither and die.

"We have only a few weeks at most to strengthen the northern defenses and prevent disaster," said Schuyler while he studied the map with Jake. "But even if I can hold off Burgoyne, Howe will strike me from behind. I can't fight both armies. Albany will have to be abandoned."

The general's forecast, dire as it was, reflected the unfortunate strategic realities of his position. Even if Washington decided to leave Philadelphia vulnerable and undertook an all-out effort to engage Howe in the Hudson Highlands, he was unlikely to stop him.

"We have to intercept the messenger," said Jake.

"Absolutely," the general grunted. There was a flash in his eyes. Undoubtedly he was thinking of the same thing that had just occurred to Jake.

"Perhaps we shouldn't stop him completely," said the general. "If his message were merely changed and then delivered, it might serve us better. If no answer arrives, Howe may send north for one or simply wait. But if Burgoyne told him, 'Fine, go where you want,' we'd be much better off. He'd pack his troops off for somewhere else."

"Too bad we can't send him back to England," said Jake, well aware that freeing Howe from a campaign up the Hudson would mean other complications.

"You have ten days to accomplish the mission—change the message or kill him if you can't. After that I will have to prepare for a withdrawal from Albany."

Jake nodded as the general rose from his desk and walked to the door, where he called to one of his aides. "Alert Captain Kalman's company that they'll be riding south in the morning. Kalman is one of my best men," he told Jake. "His troops will be more than an adequate escort."

"Begging your pardon, sir, but a company of soldiers will draw too much attention. I'm best off on my own."

"I'm confident of your abilities, Jake, but I'm reluctant to send you by yourself. It's too dangerous."

The general's concern for his welfare—as if he were sending him into a stormy night without an overcoat—was touching. Their short interview had done much to reverse the impression Jake had received when he'd called on Schuyler with his father on business before the war. It was almost as if Schuyler's experiences since then had ennobled him somehow.

Or maybe they were both just tired.

"I merely have to get into his things while he's sleeping. Sneaking into Burgoyne's ball under Carleton's nose was much more difficult."

"I wouldn't have approved that, either."

Jake smiled and shrugged. "If things go wrong, I can just shoot the bastard. I'll be behind our own lines, after all. It shouldn't be too hard enlisting help if I need it."

Besides, Jake knew one portly patriot who would be only too happy to help—once certain facts were explained to him in a logical, if forceful, manner.

It took considerably more persuasion, but Schuyler finally gave his consent for him to proceed alone. Being a general, however, he could not do so with a mere nod of the head. A grand and windy speech was called for, lauding Jake's sense of patriotism and duty, complimenting his bravery, inciting his courage. It was almost too much to bear.

"Do this as a lover of Freedom," Schuyler said as he hit his stride at the end. "Do this for your family and your country. You have the fate of our freedom in your hands."

"General, you will win the governor's race this year in a hare's trot with a speech such as that," said Jake.

Jake was not the only agent busy that evening. The man who had tracked him from Canada was in fact lurking but a few hundred yards away in the shadows of the fort, contemplating his next move.

After killing Leal, Manley had paddled his canoe

across the lake, where he found the road heading south. It took no great powers of deduction to realize Jake must have taken that path, nor was it very difficult for Manley to persuade the first traveler he came upon to give up his horse. The poor man thought the mere crown he offered in exchange for the animal much too cheap, but he gladly settled for less when Manley displayed his pistol. The traveler got down quickly, handed him the reins, and then made a dash for the woods.

He got three steps away before Manley's bullets took him in the back.

Once mounted, the British secret agent pushed the horse hard down the trail. But when the road forked, he went nearly a mile down the wrong path before realizing his mistake. Manley lost time inquiring about the Bull's Head; when he finally arrived, he was too late to do anything but observe the throng escorting Jake to prison.

He followed the mob as it carried Jake to justice. While part of him admired the poetic justice inherent in their mistake, Manley felt cheated at losing such a formidable quarry and resolved to cheat the hangman of his prize. Disguised as a citizen from the nearby town, he entered the fort on a flimsy pretense and was headed in the direction of Jake's jail cell when the American made his escape. The British major was thus privy to the discovery of Jake's true identity. He left the fort almost in a state of relief.

As Herstraw had intimated, the owner of the Bull's Head was a clandestine Tory. He did not understand the meaning of the ruby-hilted knife that Manley flicked into the table in front of him, but it certainly got his attention.

"We will need someone to gather information from the fort on the prisoner they took away," Manley said. "And then I need some men to help me ambush him."

"You're breaking him out?"

Manley smiled. "Something like that."

"My brother's daughter works as one of the cook's servants."

"Put her to work, then. I have no doubt he'll leave early in the morning; I want to know by what route."

"He'll leave?"

Manley didn't bother to enlighten the keeper. He considered all colonials, even Loyalists, little more than primitive simpletons.

"Get me some Madeira," he said. "And then some dinner. There's much to be done tonight."

The keeper didn't like being summarily ordered about by anyone, even a disguised British officer. He had fought in the French and Indian War, and was still in reasonably good shape. The fellow opposite him, with his odd-featured face and paper-thin physique, might be exceedingly tall but could not have matched his own weight.

But even as the first syllable of protest emerged from the keeper's mouth, he realized he had misjudged his guest. Manley's arm, acting against the table as a fulcrum, clamped tight on his neck and pulled him forward, holding him out of his chair.

"Killing rebels makes me thirsty," said Manley. "Bring me a drink now, before your own allegiance comes into question."

When he was released, the innkeeper ran for the pipe of Madeira he'd been saving for his daughter's wedding.

Seventeen

*Wherein, Jake's pursuit of Burgoyne's messenger is
sidetracked by diversions on Lake George.*

Sobered by the possibility that Albany would be abandoned—though Jake hoped the general's statement was
mere rhetoric like the more flowery portions of his
speech, designed to bolster his agent's resolve—the lieutenant colonel spent a fitful few hours in a cramped camp
cot, dreaming of Sarah and what would happen to her
family if they were forced to run for their lives. While he
slept, a new message for Howe was forged and reforged,
the counterfeiter trying to get the slants and loops of
Gentleman Johnny's hand right. Finally, it was decided to
just write the brief message in an ordinary hand, as if a
secretary had done it, and copy Burgoyne's signature as a
countersign at the bottom. Even so, it took several at-
tempts before the message could pass as genuine.

The silver bullet was more easily prepared—a round
ball with a three-quarter-inch diameter had been taken
from a Tory traitor some months before; polished, it was
ready to be pressed into service by the other side.

Polished, or covered with a bit of grease? Darkened, it
would be difficult to tell the difference between it and a
bullet for a Brown Bess, at least without picking it up.

Had the spy done that? There was no way of knowing
until Jake caught up with him; he would have to be supplied with grease and deal with the problem if it presented itself.

The silver ball, with an almost imperceptibly thin seam
around its equator, was deposited into a special pocket
stitched into the lieutenant colonel's waistband. This

waistband was part of a new suit of clothes General Schuyler provided. The plain black britches and brown coat were hardly the cutting edge in fashion, but they were versatile and unassuming. He even managed to find a new tricornered hat with an eagle-feathered cockade, so the spy wasn't completely bereft of dash.

Considerably more important were the three pistols said to have been manufactured some years before by a disciple of the noted Boston gunsmith John Kim. They were not much different from the standard officer's pistol perfected by the esteemed Barnett of London, whose work Jake had had occasion to appreciate in the past. No more than nineteen separate pieces accounted for each, if one took the lock mechanism as one. Jake could quickly strip them for inspection and cleaning, which he did upon receiving them. Each came with its own holster, so he could mount them on the horse as he pleased.

The half-breed's elk-boned knife and his own pocketknife were also returned by the militia, which had confiscated them upon his arrest. But his Segallas was missing.

The militia lieutenant swore that no member of his unit would have dared to steal the weapon; all were caught up in patriotism, he said, and would not have given the slightest thought to personal profit.

If what he said was correct, then Jake believed he had some hope of having the pistol returned to him, since he knew one man who would not think his patriotism conflicted with profit. In fact, Jake had several scores to settle with the good squire van Clynne.

The Dutchman was an odd sort of character, businessman enough to have shown him north for an exorbitant fee, patriot enough to turn him in once he thought Jake might truly do some harm. The American spy might even be tempted to applaud the Dutchman, on the grounds that he had acted according to what he thought was the good of the Cause.

Such a temptation would have been easily resisted. For the price of a laugh and a strong coffee at breakfast, Jake managed to convince Captain Andrews to give him the letter accusing him. Reading it renewed his harsher opinions quite readily.

"No hard feelings now," said Andrews, spooning a mountain of eggs into his mouth. "You know I wouldn't have actually had you hung."

"No hard feelings at all," said Jake, slapping his ersatz friend on the back so hard that the captain fell to the floor. "Of course you wouldn't have."

He reached down to help the good captain up. He helped him so well that the captain's momentum carried him across the room to the door, which he would have exited, had it been open.

"An officer should not allow prisoners to be beaten, no matter their allegiance," said Jake as he stepped over the captain's supine body and went to find his horse.

Schuyler had not only left orders for Jake to be supplied with the finest horse in the fort; he'd sent word to the small schooner that had taken him north on Lake George to await Jake's command. This brought with it an unexpected development—Betsy Schuyler was planning to travel from the fort to the family home at Saratoga via this same vessel.

Though confident he would be able to overtake the travelers as they rode at their leisurely pace down the Post Road to Rhinebeck, Jake was reluctant to delay his start for even a few minutes. Though she had saved his life—or at least helped him escape further imprisonment —the agent bristled when the fort's liaison officer told him that she would accompany him to the boat. But his fears about feminine delays were unfounded; she was already waiting for him at the fort entrance, sitting on a horse and flanked by two black militiamen.

"This is a pleasant surprise," said Jake. "I had not expected to enjoy such company so early in the morning."

"Your tongue is as handsome as your face," replied Betsy smartly, the slight touch of sarcasm completely disarmed by her smile. "Let us see if your horse is as good as father promised."

Jake took up the challenge and they began racing toward the boat. Though the others were not riding weak beasts, his proved by far the fastest; Jake reached the boat slip well ahead of them. There he found a premonition of complications to come.

The sloop that had carried General Schuyler north was gone; in its place was a smaller flat-bottomed craft, rigged with a single, undersized sail. The boat's master explained that the schooner had been called to the southern shore of the lake late yesterday on another mission. The ship had run into difficulty overnight because of the storm, which had been more violent here than at Ticonderoga. He, however, would be honored to take its place.

Something in the captain's quick tone made Jake suspicious, but there was no obvious reason not to take the man at his word. The party's four horses were put aboard with some difficulty, Jake's especially objecting to the rocking motion of the boat. Nonetheless, they were quickly under way, the captain and his boy supplementing the sail's propulsion with long, single-oared paddles. Betsy sat at the front under a jerry-rigged tent, shading her dark, hauntingly pretty eyes and counting the chestnut trees in the distance. Jake—one pistol folded under his arm, another in his belt—stood next to her, scanning the lake ahead.

Even in a moment of great tension, a woman's presence could perfume his dreariest mood with optimism. How much more buoyant were his spirits now, when the excitement of a new mission had his blood bubbling with the enthusiasm natural to all men of action. Betsy's long hair, flowing under her hat and across her back, unfettered save for a small bow, reminded Jake of an angel's wing, drifting back as it played the harp. And her shoulders spoke of strength rare among women bred in a city. In short, Jake felt himself falling under her spell.

But his mood fell back to earth as he realized the men accompanying her were not militia guards but two of the family's black slaves. Like most of the very wealthy families in New York, the Schuylers kept both blacks and whites as part of their "family." The two young men were descendants of a woman who had been with the family as a young girl; to Betsy they were like brothers—except that they could not go about nearly so freely.

Occasionally limited by indenture periods, sometimes "liberalized" by tenant farming arrangements, slavery of whites as well as blacks operated under a variety of disguises even in such an advanced province as New York. Jake's own mother had come to America as an indentured slave, a young Irish girl sold into service so the family could eat for a few weeks.

From one perspective, perhaps, the arrangement had worked out for her; she had been able to escape the bonds of poverty and, by bartering away personal dignity, had managed to rise above her station. Jake, her only son, could on a whim purchase twenty contracts such as the one that bound her.

But to Jake's mind, her slavery had killed her, shortening her life and robbing him of her comfort when he was only a young boy. Any overt sign of the institution stirred strong feelings.

Despite Betsy's great beauty, he kept his tongue in check, fearing it would begin to gush with his displeasure. She, on the other hand, was anxious to engage him in conversation, prodding him with comments on everything from the hardships of the war on women to the beauty of the day—it had rained around midnight, but the clouds had been burned away by a full sun.

Betsy asked how he had been promoted so fast; he gave a few short instances of his exploits in Boston and Quebec.

She asked if he had a true love.

"I have many loves," said Jake truthfully. "My country and my duty are foremost."

"My father would be pleased with that reply," she laughed, "but not I."

Jake replied with a stony silence.

Though slaves, Betsy's escorts bore themselves like the heroes they had been named for. Roland was a slight man, barely bigger than the woman he was escorting. Charlemagne was of the same size as Jake, though not quite as trim around the waist. Both black men went about their business quietly, exuding a kind of confidence that made it obvious why the general sent his daughter in their company.

Sailing south of Cook's Mountain, Jake watched with minimal interest as a long dugout canoe with four men in it passed northward. Its rear oarsman was considerably taller than the rest; lash a rope to his head and he might provide enough height to rig a small sail. But otherwise there was nothing of interest in the vessel, and Jake turned away.

Two minutes later he happened to look back and found the canoe trailing their wake. Immediately he leapt to conclusions.

"Get this thing moving," he barked, waving his guns as he ran to the back of the boat.

Jake was greeted by the sharp whistle of a musket ball fired from the canoe, now barely twenty yards away and closing fast. He fired in return, his bullet splashing against the hull of the small boat. A rifle went off behind him—Roland had fired—and the lead man in the canoe collapsed backward.

Jake aimed his second pistol and fired at the tall man. He missed again, but this time his bullet carried through the floor of the canoe, and the craft immediately began to list to one side.

As Jake ran to his horse and saddlebags to reload, he realized that the trailing canoe was not their only concern. Charlemagne fired a pistol and then collapsed, caught by a bullet fired by their own boat's captain. Next, two men appeared from the side—a second canoe had come up alongside and launched an assault.

Wasting no time to reload, Jake grabbed his last pistol and placed its ball square in the forehead of one of the boarders. But his defense ended a moment later when the captain grabbed Betsy and held a hatchet to her throat.

"I think you will surrender now," declared the captain as his fellow pirates clambered aboard. While one of the men trained a rifle on Roland, Charlemagne's limp body was roughly kicked off into the water.

"Careful, Colonel Gibbs," said a voice behind Jake as he stepped toward the man with the rifle, ready to spring. "Step back by the horses—I'm sure you wouldn't want our friend here to do anything to the pretty miss he has in his arms, would you? If I'm not mistaken, she's General Schuyler's daughter—I imagine the general will pay a considerable ransom, don't you?"

Jake turned and found himself face-to-mouth with a gun that looked as if it were a cross between a pistol and a swivel cannon. It had a horn for a barrel, and the weight of a blunderbuss. He didn't bother asking for a closer inspection, but felt sure he'd find twenty or thirty lead balls jammed down its throat.

Now where have we seen such a gun before? And where have we seen such a giant of a man, near seven feet tall if an inch, towering over the boat?

"We have not had the pleasure of meeting before," said Major Manley with mock grandeur, "though I must say, Colonel Gibbs, your reputation does precede you."

"Nothing bad, I trust."

"Oh, very, very bad," said Manley. "You disappoint me in the flesh. I had not thought I could look down on you so easily."

Jake's feelings of generosity had expanded in direct proportion to the weapon facing him, and he let his captor have his little joke.

"Kill him quickly and let's make shore," said the boat's commander. "They're liable to send out a search party at any moment."

"Why is it so many Americans are cowards?" Manley asked Jake. "Even the ones who are on our side. They're afraid of their own shadows."

"Perhaps it's the light they're afraid of."

"Oh, well put, fellow," chuckled Manley. "The light of truth and all that. We are not too pompous, are we?"

Betsy had fainted under her captor's grasp and was left to fall to the deck. Considering the commotion, everyone else aboard was acting with remarkable calm. The horses pulled at their restraints, annoyed by the smoke and noise, but their reins had been tied so tightly that they couldn't do more than whine and complain.

Jake leaned back against the ropes as the ship bucked. Leal's elk-handled knife was in his boot, too far away to be useful. Under such circumstances, delay was the best —and only—tactic.

"You're not simple pirates, then," he said, his tone as light and mocking as Manley's. "That's a relief."

"My assistants are, I daresay. Recruited with a few pieces of gold and a promise of amnesty, though of course they swear they have been loyal subjects all their lives. As for myself, I have some aspirations toward a large piece of land in England, so I doubt I would qualify as a pirate."

"How pleasant," said Jake, "to be touring America while you wait for your father to die back home."

"Just like a rebel, substituting sauce for substance," said Manley. "Where would you like me to shoot you, Colonel? In the head or the stomach?"

"Neither, to tell you the truth."

"Come on, Major, let's be done with it, eh?" said the boat's captain. "We're exposed here on the water. There are militia patrols passing by the east shore every half hour."

Manley's eyes flashed from blue to a deep purple. He spun quickly toward the captain. "I do not need you to tell me my business," he said. "You will do as I instruct, and be glad that I leave you alive."

"I'll thank you not to point your weapon at me," said the captain, a good deal of the bluster gone from his voice. "We are on the same side."

"Are we?"

The man nodded.

"Perhaps I'll follow your advice," Manley told him. "But should I shoot him, or slit his throat?"

As he spoke, he reached into his belt line and pulled out the thin knife Carleton had given him as an emblem of his office. He illustrated the second option by running the blade point along the surface of the captain's own throat.

"As you p-please," said the Tory, now absolutely spooked.

Manley turned to point his knife at Jake, a broad smile breaking on his lips. Just at the moment the grin reached its fullest, just at the point when his pleasure might truly be said to have peaked with anticipation, the corners of his mouth turned downward.

The change in his expression was due to the bullet that exploded through his back and into his gullet, fired by a pistol Betsy had secreted beneath the folds of her skirt. For she had fainted in form only—the general's daughter was quite a soldier herself.

The momentum of the bullet threw Manley's knife from his hand through the air toward Jake. In one motion he grabbed it and slashed the ropes that restrained the horses. They bolted on cue, knocking over his guards and sending the boat into a high tumult. Roland wrestled with the Tory pirate next to him and the two fell off into the water. Everyone else quickly followed as the vessel swamped.

Jake swam for the empty canoe and boarded it; he soon found Betsy and pulled her in. Roland, too, was rescued; he had a large gash on his side where a bullet had grazed him but was otherwise all right. None of the remaining kidnappers could be located, and Jake did not think it wise to dawdle looking for them. The American agent was well aware of the symbolism contained in the knife he'd used to help gain their freedom; he'd had his various tête-à-têtes with the British Secret Department before.

Jake paddled quickly if somewhat gingerly toward shore; each time he poked his oar into the water, he half expected to strike poor dead Charlemagne, floating uneasily in his grave.

The horses thrashed violently but beat the canoe to shore. Waiting for their masters, they shook themselves off as if they'd just gotten out of a pond after a summer romp.

Alerted by the gunshots, a handful of soldiers rushed to the shoreline to provide assistance. Jake, Betsy, and Roland were taken to a nearby house to dry off and gather their wits. Jake congratulated Betsy on her heroism, saying that her father should present her with a medal; she, in turn, praised both Jake and Roland, and mourned greatly the death of her friend Charlemagne. Her sentiments softened Jake's previous opinion; perhaps she was enlightened enough to regret the evil of slavery, if not courageous enough to correct it. In any event, he was moved by her emotion and eulogy of her slain retainer.

The lieutenant colonel accepted a mug of rum from the owner of the house and stood briefly in front of the fire to warm his britches. It was barely noon and already he'd had a full day; a good part of him wanted nothing better than to rest here until the next morning. But this small adventure had already delayed him more than he wished.

The fact that the Secret Department had sent one of its agents after him complicated things. Hopefully, the assassin had been assigned by Carleton. Hopefully, he worked alone and in complete secrecy, as the branch's procedures generally dictated. Hopefully, he had not had a chance to alert Herstraw.

So many hopes, so little certainty or time.

Jake still had the bullet, safe in its secret pocket. He also had Leal's knife. But he was once more without a gun, having lost all three Kim pistols to the lake. He borrowed a weapon from one of the militia officers, along with fresh powder and ball, promising that Schuyler would restore them.

His horse seemed to have enjoyed the morning—the beast gave a good whinny and stomped his feet, urging his rider to get going.

"But your clothes aren't even dry, and your hair is wet," said Betsy when Jake came back inside to take his leave. She had gotten out of her dress and was wrapped in a large quilt blanket. Somehow, the shapeless fabric was even more flattering than the beautifully brocaded garment she had worn this morning.

"I'll dry on the way," said Jake, who permitted himself one last diversion—he leaned forward and kissed her.

"Good luck," said Roland solemnly at the door.

"And to you," said Jake. "I hope you will be justly rewarded for your bravery with freedom."

Across the room, Betsy was nodding. So at least some good would come from this.

Eighteen

Wherein, Jake pursues the messenger and that eminent squire, Claus van Clynne, seeking to return to the latter all that is owed.

The ambush on the lake caused a delay in Jake's plans, not only because of the time involved in the incident itself, but because the loss of the boat meant he had to proceed by land, where it was more difficult to make up the lead Herstraw had obtained. Schuyler had given him ten days to accomplish his task, but in truth this amounted to something closer to eight, since he would need to leave time to return to Albany with word of his success.

The general's horse was a fine beast, with thick muscles and long legs, quick eyes and sharp movements. But the strongest animal needs food and rest, and this one was no exception. Every delay was a frustration. Though Jake stuck to the main roads, these were not so fine as to guarantee quick progress. Aside from the potholes, there were long swathes of mud left by the recent heavy rain.

By the end of the second day, Jake had only just reached the other side of the river from Albany, and had yet to spot his quarry or even hear definite word of him. He stopped in an inn and tried to catch some sleep—even his boundless energy required an occasional nap to be recharged—but the proximity to Albany turned his thoughts to Sarah and her family. After two hours of fitful stretching and wrestling with the covers, he rose and set out, doubling his efforts to catch up with the spy's party.

Jake soon adopted a desperate routine: He'd hop from his horse on a dead run as he pulled up to a house or inn, plunge inside and shout for the proprietor. In the shortest speech possible, he'd demand to know if a man answering the messenger's description had traveled through; then he'd ask about van Clynne, whom he realized would be a more memorable guest. If the answer were no—and for a while it seemed as if it would always be no—he'd rush back outside and resume his journey.

The approach lacked subtlety, but his inability to find any trace of Herstraw worried him a great deal. He feared that the messenger had changed his route and perhaps his tactics.

Finally, late in the afternoon, a startled innkeeper in Claverack told him that a party answering his description had passed through that morning, hoping to make Rhinebeck by nightfall. Jake thanked the man, threw a gold guinea down for his troubles and fled back to his horse.

With the next few miles of the journey passing uneventfully if quickly from Columbia to Dutchess County, the narrative will take a slight detour to address the matters of the patriotism of the countryside, as it bears not a little relevance to the attitude of the men passing through it. If, for instance, you are wondering why Jake rides with a loaded and cocked pistol in his hand as night comes on, here is the reason.

As a general rule, it is often posited that the strength of local support for the Revolution varies in direct proportion to the closeness of the British Army; that, in the case of the Hudson Valley, the closer one draws to the city of New York, the more support one finds for the so-called Royalist party. As is usual with generalities, this one is good enough from the distance, but on close inspection reveals particulars that render it meaningless. Dutchess County, midway up the valley between New York and Albany, was considerably less enamored of the patriot cause than geography would dictate. In the spring of 1775 a document called the Proclamation for Association—roughly an agreement to resist the tea tax and other obnoxious elements—was signed by 1,680 of the county's residents. Not a bad number, except when one considers that another 882 were against it. Across the river, Ulster voted 1,770 to 80 in favor of the measure.

While we have no wish to slander the good worthies of Dutchess, it is nonetheless necessary to point out that a sizable portion of the countryside had not been convinced by the intervening years to join the Cause. Many merchants refused to accept money issued by Congress as legal tender—an act tantamount to treason, and requiring some sort of response, as several speakers declared late that evening at an emergency meeting in Rhinebeck's Traphagen Tavern.

Other speakers—all men whose service as patriots could not be questioned—noted that the paper money had lately begun to depreciate sharply in value. Taking paper currency was thus becoming as much a test of personal fortitude and thrift as of politics. The greatest threat to the Revolution might not be British guns, they allowed, but rampant inflation.

Though Jake's polished tongue would undoubtedly have settled the matter firmly for the patriot side, he did not pause to enter the debate as he walked quickly though calmly through the house. He met the inn's owner —Traphagen himself—coming down the hall with a pitcher of beer in one hand and cider in the other. Pretending to be a friend, he asked after Herstraw, and found that the inn's only guest at the moment was a rather cantankerous Dutchman who had gone off to bed already, complaining about the sorry slide of village inns since the Dutch had lost their monopoly.

Imagine the joyful reunion when two friends, long separated by the travails and trials of war, are suddenly thrust together. Imagine the look one has, expecting that the other has met with an untimely and violent end. Imagine the utter relief and weeping, the shouts of deliverance, the unfettered glee.

Imagine all of that, and throw it far from your head.

"But how did you escape!?"

"Out of the bed, you bastard," shouted Jake. "You're just lucky there's no one else in the room, or you'd be apologizing for waking them."

"Now just a minute, sir," said van Clynne indignantly. "I am many things, but my parentage has never been in doubt."

"Up!"

Jake poked his pistol beneath the covers and tossed them aside, exposing the full length of van Clynne's bed shirt, a fussy red flannel affair.

"Surely we can discuss this," said the Dutchman. "To shoot a man in bed while he sleeps!"

"You're not sleeping," said Jake, leaning to put down the lamp he had carried with him—just in time to free his hand and grab the pocket pistol van Clynne swung up from behind his back.

"I've been looking for this," he said, snatching the Segallas triumphantly.

"I was holding it in protective custody," blustered van Clynne. "Several of the mob wanted to take it and sell it, but I wouldn't let them."

"I'll bet." Jake flipped a shilling onto the bed. "I'll ransom my money belt as well."

"Well, you're the first Tory I've met who pays his debts."

"I'm not a Tory. I'm an American agent of the secret service, assigned by His Excellency General Washington to the Northern Department for special duty."

"Whatever you say, sir. Whatever you say."

Jake reached inside his coat and took out a letter from Schuyler guaranteeing him free passage.

"That's nothing," said van Clynne, not even bothering to read it. "I've got a million letters. I'll sell you one from King George, if you like."

"And here is the deposition you wrote accusing me," said Jake, throwing it on his chest. "How would I have obtained it if they hadn't freed me?"

"Many a soldier can be bought during these desperate days, I'm ashamed to say."

"Where's my money belt?"

Van Clynne pointed to a bureau in the corner. Jake backed to it, keeping the Dutchman in aim. In truth, this was not very difficult, given the brightness of his flannel.

"Look at the back of the belt." Jake flung it at him.

Van Clynne's brow furled as he gazed at the symbol, which had been appropriated from the Free Masons. Unless one were admitted to the brotherhood, the stylized eye contained in the design was not easy to see. Its use by members of the secret service was more by way of convenience; they were, after all, members of their own even more select group. Nonetheless, its innate esoteric nature was enough to impress nearly anyone.

"That could be the stamping of your horse's shoe, for all I know," said van Clynne, flinging the money belt back. "The fact that you are a member of a college fraternity is hardly impressive, sir. Not at all."

"How do you think I escaped from the fort?"

"You're a brave and able man. I know that from your dealings with the renegades."

"Damn you—I'm on a mission for Schuyler. Ask me any question you want about him. Ask me to describe his house in Albany. It's Georgian, with a rail around the roof."

"If you're referring to his drafty barn south of Fort Orange, anyone could have that information. It's well known that the general has a house outside the city."

"The color of his daughter Betsy's eyes—brown."

"Her beauty is legendary, though how she sprang from him I could not say."

"Listen, van Clynne." Jake stepped across the room and put his gun to the Dutchman's throat. "Because of you, the man I was following—a real British spy—escaped. I want you to tell me where he is."

For a man with a loaded pistol pressing against his skin, van Clynne displayed a remarkable calmness. "Is it true that you are a spy?" he asked.

"Not a spy, an agent of the secret service under General Washington, assigned to General Greene and on temporary duty for General Schuyler."

"Even better," said the Dutchman, gently pushing the pistol aside and rising from his bed. "I admit I was wrong about your being a Tory. I can see from your bearing that you are a fine patriot."

"And?"

"Perhaps we should discuss this situation over a beer downstairs," said the Dutchman, stroking his beard. "I am, after all, a man of business."

* * *

He was indeed, but as van Clynne soon related, his no-
madic existence as a well-connected traveling broker was
the result of a series of reversals that had severely shaken
his family. While his story was, as one would expect from
even a brief acquaintance, filled with exaggeration, diversion, and a few outright misstatements, in the main it was
believable, and might be boiled down to the following:

During Dutch domination of the area, the van Clynnes
had been granted a large patent on the western shores of
the Hudson. But the coming of the British had put the
ownership in question. The choicest parts of the estate
had been usurped by a British merchant. With the con-
nivance of several powerful Dutchmen (it pained van
Clynne to admit this, but it was true; not even a Dutch
patroon could be trusted, especially where land was involved), the Englishman had robbed van Clynne's grandfather of his land. Ever since, the family had devoted its
resources toward getting back its birthright. The efforts
had succeeded only in landing the family deep in debt to
a dozen solicitors, both in America and England. Bills
had lately begun arriving from the Netherlands. Though
his business dealings made healthy profits, still van
Clynne could not get far enough ahead to satisfy all his
creditors, let alone pay for new court costs.

"What exactly do you want me to do about it?" said
Jake, fighting back a yawn. By now they had the taproom
all to themselves, save for a poor young lad who served
them beer and napped, though not necessarily in that
order.

"If you really do know General Washington, then you
can help get my land back," suggested van Clynne.

"I don't know about that."

"The family is all Tory! They've fled."

"Why don't you appeal to the local magistrates?"

Van Clynne made a frightful spitting sound. "Half of
them are descended from the thieves who robbed my
family. But a letter from your friend, General Washington—"

"I didn't call the general my friend. He is my commander. Our commander."

"If I'm truly as vital to your plan as you said," smiled

van Clynne, "you'll be happy to help. Indeed, I would be most valuable to the patriot Cause. I flatter myself when I say I am a man of many talents."

"You flatter yourself, indeed."

The Dutchman launched into a few minutes of extended hyperbole concerning his great love of Freedom and the like. Jake finally cut him off.

"I will put in a word for you, but I can't make any promises."

"Deal," said the Dutchman, sticking out his hand and shaking. "Our friend has traveled on to Fishkill to stay with some acquaintances, then leaves in the morning bound for White Plains via the pass in the mountains south of the village. I know a quick way to the town. As I've concluded my sale of the coach, I'm free to take you there first thing in the morning."

"We're leaving now," said Jake.

"Now? It's past ten. And it's dark."

"It usually is at this hour."

"We can't travel at night. The highways are filled with all sorts of robbers and Indians."

"We'll go by water, then."

"Actually, I think the rumors of danger on the roads are quite overblown," said van Clynne.

Nineteen

Wherein, a slight diversion of the tale is made, for reason of celebrating the patriotic village of Fishkill, and rescuing its cows.

If there is a town in upper New York that has done its yeoman's duty in the War of Independence, it is tiny Fishkill. After the British took Long Island and New York City in 1776, they followed those conquests with a battle for White Plains farther north. This was a bloody and dangerous fight for the patriot Cause, all the more so because it followed such serious losses. But victory turned the tide of the war. General Howe—the same general with whom Jake is presently preoccupied—had to retreat to New York City to consolidate his gains and lick his wounds as the fall began slowly turning to winter.

The Americans likewise had wounds to lick, and a great many of them were healed in Fishkill, a small village some forty or so miles north of where the battle had taken place. The entire hamlet became a hospital, with sundry buildings, tents, and even the roadway used as operating theaters and recovery rooms. The air reeked with the smell of hard-won Freedom and Liberty, the cries of suffering echoing between the hills and across the creek that marked the town.

The same campaign that caused the fall of New York and the blood at White Plains sent the state congress fleeing northward, briefly landing at White Plains and then, on August 29, 1776, to Fishkill. The village gave not one, but two of its churches to the congress, beginning with Trinity on the east side of the Post Road. This was not so great a sacrifice as might be expected, for Trinity here as elsewhere meant "English," which in turn meant

"Tory," and any sympathizer in the neighborhood by now had either fled or gotten very good at holding his breath.

It did not take long for the politicians to be driven down the street by a second invading horde—a flock of birds entered through the glassless windows and took up residence, punctuating the proceedings with loud cries and other comments on the quality of debate. The congress adjourned westward down the road to the Dutch Reformed Church, which not only had the benefit of glass, but also happened to be across from one of the finest pubs in the state.

The village lasted as state capital for only a short while, the representatives soon hearing of better quarters and even better taverns farther north at Poughkeepsie and then Kingston; nonetheless, its contributions to the Cause will be long remembered.

Alas, upon their arrival in the center of town several hours before dawn, Jake was in no position to celebrate the village's history. Despite his eagerness to help, van Clynne's knowledge of Herstraw's whereabouts had not proven as precise as promised. It was not that the Dutchman couldn't locate the house where the messenger was staying. On the contrary; he located the house in three different places, and could offer no method of telling which might be the genuine article. Jake's plan to sneak inside and switch the messages while the man slept was thus dealt a temporary setback. And as it would soon be light anyway, he decided his only course was to wait until a better opportunity presented itself.

They could at least be reasonably sure the messenger would take the pass south through the Highlands over the Post Road. The only other way to White Plains was to first travel northeast to Wiccopee, a highly unlikely route for anyone to take. Or so Jake, who with every passing minute became more and more aware of Schuyler's deadline and the possibility Albany would be lost, consoled himself.

The Episcopal graveyard had a good vantage of the highway, and Jake suggested they take turns napping there until morning. Van Clynne stated in the most absolute terms that he would sooner step foot in a British counting house. His fear of cemeteries was nearly as great as his phobia of water. He cited superstition after superstition against it, and implied he would stand straight up in the middle of the road all night rather than sleep in a graveyard.

"Then you take the first watch," said Jake, tying his horse to a stake and taking his blanket among the stones. "Wake me in an hour, or if he passes."

For Jake, a cemetery was not a place of horror but one of succor; if it was haunted, undoubtedly the spirits would be friendly toward such a righteous cause as Freedom. So what was to worry?

"Plenty to worry about," grumbled van Clynne, sitting against a tree at the very edge of the yard. "There are many people I wouldn't like to meet dead, I'll tell you. It's only the fear of death while they're alive that keeps them in line. Remove that, and there's no telling what they might be capable of."

"People treat you the way you treat them," said Jake. "If you didn't try and swindle everyone during life—"

"I'm not a swindler, sir. I'm a businessman."

"My family has been in business itself for many years, and I've never seen anyone as contentious as you."

"What do you sell?" asked van Clynne, interested as much in having someone keep him company in this dreary place as in finding out Jake's history.

"The story I told of my family business going north was true. My father started with his brother importing drugs to America. That's still our main business, though more in spirit than dollars."

"Ha! And you call me a swindler. It's no wonder you have such a cheery view of the world," said van Clynne. "You're born to be an optimist, promising that things will get better if only you drink a cure."

"I need no more than an hour's nap. Wake me then, and you can have the rest of the night."

"I can't sleep in a graveyard."

"Fine. Wake me at dawn."

Van Clynne continued his complaints as Jake drifted off. The Dutchman grumbled about the price he had obtained for his fancy carriage, which he now saw was at

least five crowns too low. He grumbled about the
weather, despite it being as fine as any spring in the past
twenty years. He even grumbled about the fact that the
gravestones were not laid in perfect lines. He grumbled
so much that he soon fell into a contented snore.

Contented but loud. It woke Jake directly.

The patriot spy was both annoyed and amused to see
the Dutchman curled between two headstones, his arm
lopped over one as if consoling a lover. Fortunately,
Jake's half-hour snooze had been enough to restore his
alertness, and he decided he'd watch the road himself the
rest of the night. There'd be time enough to sleep when
this job was done.

He had sat at his gravestone for about a quarter hour
when he saw a strange sight emerge from the pre-morn-
ing darkness. A half-dozen cows were being paraded by a
fellow up the road. Most remarkable of all, their progress
was entirely silent.

Jake soon realized why—the animals' feet had been
clothed in thick, matted boots. He went and woke van
Clynne, wondering what sort of illness had infected the
local citizenry or their animals.

"It's not sickness at all," explained the Dutchman in
between hushed grievances at being roused from a beautiful dream of his family's former estate. "The man must
be one of the cattle thieves who's been ravaging the valley. Between speculators and these villains, cow bone has
become more dear than a lion's whiskers."

Van Clynne exaggerated, but not as much as usual. He
also insisted that, no matter how pressing their other mission, this thief must be apprehended—half of those cows
surely belonged to good Dutch families and were intended for the nearby Continental Army barracks.

Even though it was highly unlikely he'd be traveling
this early, Jake was loath to divert his attention from
Herstraw. Van Clynne ceased to argue and began
shadowing the cattle thief himself. Reluctantly, Jake
tagged along, vowing to turn back the moment the silent
parade of cows took a detour that made it impossible to
see the highway.

Fortunately, his vow was never put to the test. The thief herded the animals into a yard before a barn only a few hundred yards from the churchyard and very close to the road. As van Clynne ran off to alert the local sheriff, Jake snuck down to keep an eye on the thief.

A confederate was waiting with a lantern at the door, and together the two men congratulated themselves on finding so many fine beasts.

"I'll get them ready inside," said the confederate. "You stand guard and wait for Cardington."

"We've got only an hour if we're to be out of here when the sun dawns," said the thief who had led the parade.

"Just watch outside while I do my business."

A small stream ran a few yards from the edge of the building. Jake climbed down the embankment and returned with a handful of smooth pebbles. It took a few tosses against the side of the barn for the thief to realize the light noises were not coming from within. He picked up a musket and went to investigate.

A quick punch across the face dispatched him to Sleep's bedchamber. Jake appropriated the fellow's belt and trussed him with it. Then he returned to the front to wait for the sheriff and van Clynne to return.

And there they would undoubtedly have found him, had he not heard a wagon approaching down the highway at high speed. Jake, assuming it was Herstraw, cursed his luck and ducked back around the side of the barn. He was just about to run back for his horse, still tethered in the churchyard, when the vehicle pulled to a stop in front of the barn. A man dressed in a butcher's smock left the reins and ran to the door.

"It's me, Cardington!" yelled the man. "Open the door, Bulfinch. Quickly!"

"Where's Griffith?" asked the man inside, opening up.

"Damned if I know."

"Can't be trusted to do anything. We'll dock half his share," said the thief, hurrying the man and wagon inside.

Having gotten himself involved, Jake was reluctant to let the thieves succeed in butchering the animals before van Clynne and the sheriff arrived. He decided to chance a quick sneak into the barn so he could catch the butchers before they quite got red-handed. Providence, after all, must have placed him in the churchyard at the moment the villain passed for a reason.

The door was locked against a frontal assault. The only other opening that presented itself was a loft window on the second floor. Getting to it required several running jumps—noisy running jumps at that, though the sound of the animals inside drowned them out.

In order to make the final leap, Jake had to leave the guard's musket outside, and thus had only a single pistol in his belt, and his knives, when he climbed into the loft. He had, at least, plenty of cover to work with, as the entire interior light was supplied by a pair of lanterns on the ground floor.

The two butchers were preparing their first victim as Jake crept to the edge of the balcony. But before he could map an attack, there was a loud knock on the door, and the sheriff ordered the men inside to cease and desist.

"We'll give him a bit of a surprise," said Bulfinch, dropping the ax he had taken to slaughter the cow. He picked up a gun from the wagon as the lights were doused.

Feeling his way along the railing, Jake discovered a rope hanging off the ledge. He whisked it up as the two thieves prepared their ambush.

"Come on in, Sheriff," called Bulfinch. "The door's open."

The sheriff was not the fool the thieves took him for, using a long stick to prod open the door. He ducked as it swung back and two guns fired in rapid succession.

Ducking was wise but unnecessary, for the shots had been fired at Jake's prodding. His encouragement, actually, was accomplished by the heels of his boots—he swung from the rafters into both men the moment the door creaked open and gave him enough light to see. Archangel Michael did not look so bold when he swung down with the heavenly hosts, nor was Satan as surprised as the two cattle thieves, who collapsed backward in a

heap and were easily apprehended by the sheriff, Lars
Skinner.

Jake and van Clynne took an early breakfast with Lars's
thankful wife, Willa, who happened to own one of the
purloined cows. Her hospitality was all the more welcome as her house was located just southeast of the highway fork, which meant that no matter where Herstraw
had stayed, he would have to pass by.

Her apple pie was also among the best Jake had ever
tasted.

"An old Dutch recipe," whispered van Clynne as the
woman went to the stove for more coffee. "I tell you,
Dutch housewives are the best."

"What are you saying behind my back, Claus van
Clynne?" demanded the woman, returning.

"A compliment, surely," said van Clynne.

"As a matter of fact, I have a crow to pick with you,"
said Mrs. Skinner.

The squire put up his hand, but it did not stem the
attack. Besides being the sheriff, Mr. Skinner and his wife
made some pewter items, which van Clynne occasionally
endeavored to sell for them. In Dutch—and very sharp
Dutch at that—Mrs. Skinner lambasted him for having
been slow to pay for his last consignment, which she had
subsequently learned had sold in half the time van
Clynne had intimated.

An exaggeration, he said.

Hardly, retorted Mrs. Skinner, citing her evidence.

Amused, Jake concentrated on his pie. Apples were
heaped nearly eight inches tall between the thick crusts.
A trace of maple sugar sweetened each bite. And even
though it would have been very expensive, Jake swore
there was a hint of cinnamon inside.

As the argument continued, the Dutchman gradually
shifted into his cajoling mode, assuring the housewife
that there had been no delay, and that if there had been a
delay, a pause of a few days one way or another was
never a problem when friends were involved, and above
all, it was simply a misunderstanding.

Mrs. Skinner folded her arms and suggested that perhaps the sheriff would have another opinion when he returned home. Van Clynne quickly adopted a new gambit.

"Alas, we have urgent business on the road," he said. "But before I leave, I would like to purchase a bottle of your elixir."

"I never sell that! I give it to friends for free."

"Well, I thought from the way you were carrying on—"

"You should be ashamed of yourself, Claus van Clynne. Implying that we are less than friends. My great-grandparents came to America with your great-grandparents."

Van Clynne put on a contrite look—and winked at Jake as Mrs. Skinner disappeared into the back. She returned presently with a small, milky-white-colored bottle. Van Clynne immediately began singing her praises.

"You do not often find women such as Willa Skinner!" he declared. "Even the wilden trek to her door."

"We haven't had Indians on this land for ten years," said the housewife. "And if I saw one, I'd shoot him."

"My friend is an apothecary," van Clynne told her. He spoke in a stage whisper Jake was obviously supposed to overhear. "Let us see if perhaps we can work an arrangement that will make you rich."

The freckles on her face turned white with the suggestion. "Oh no, no, my cures are never for sale. This is not a cure, only an aid," she told Jake. "My grandmother passed down the recipe. An educated man will think it superstition."

"It is just the thing for indigestion," said van Clynne, tapping his belly. "And I'm an expert on the subject." He turned to Jake. "I tell you, sir, you could make a fortune by selling this. A Dutchwoman's cure, call it."

The timely passing of their quarry on the road cut off further debate. Jake motioned to van Clynne, who immediately rose from the table, hiking his breeches.

William Herstraw was riding his large black mare quite lazily, though Jake noted that he had one of his flintlock pistols slung in a harness in front of his right leg; undoubtedly its holster was loose enough to swivel upward easily.

Herstraw, too far to see more than shadows inside the house, gave a generic nod from his saddle but kept going.

"Let him get a little ahead," said Jake. "And then we can catch up."

Mrs. Skinner looked first to Jake and then to van Clynne for an explanation.

"A certain business deal that has to be perfected," said van Clynne.

"The man has the look of a Tory," said the housewife. "He should be shot straightaway."

"Let's go," said Jake.

"If I find you are doing business with turncoats," Mrs. Skinner called out behind them, "I will apply the tar bath myself."

Jake and van Clynne had gone only a few yards on the road—and around a curve that hid the house from view —when the Dutchman stopped and took the bottle of stomach cure from his pocket.

"You feel sick?"

"No, I'm pouring this into the dust."

"Why?"

"It's rot and poison," said van Clynne. "I wouldn't feed it to a dog. The woman is a shrill at business, and her potions are the only way to get on her good side."

"Speaking ill of a Dutch housewife?"

"They are great at everything," said van Clynne, "except cures. Especially those they claim to have gotten from their grandmothers." He turned his nose and kicked the horse as he upturned the medicine, which splattered across the ground. "Her ale—now that is another story completely."

Twenty

*Wherein, the plan to exchange bullets meets with
unexpected reversals.*

Jake's plan was relatively simple—change the bullets
when Herstraw wasn't looking. Everything else was just a
matter of logistics.

But logistics are critical in war. Jake still hadn't seen
the other bullet; he did not yet know if Herstraw had
covered it with grease or some other disguise, nor where
he kept it. A certain amount of delicacy and patience
were now required, as well as diversion. Herstraw would
naturally be suspicious of a man arrested as a spy and
then released.

Jake would have to protest his innocence in such a way
that convinced Herstraw he was indeed guilty but had
succeeded in fooling the Americans. Assuming he was
like the rest of his brethren, the British officer would
think the American authorities naturally deficient, and
would thus be inclined to believe any example of their
incompetence, as long as the example could be given sub-
tly.

"It will be best if I do the talking," Jake told van
Clynne as they drew close. "You know nothing, except
that I came upon you along the road as we're doing to
him. Remember, let me do the talking."

"I shall be my natural, reticent self," declared van
Clynne.

Which of course was like King George III declaring
himself a democrat.

"Look who I found!" shouted van Clynne as they drew
near Herstraw. "Our good friend the traitor!"

Jake consoled himself with the thought that, should he find it necessary to shoot Herstraw, it was quite likely that van Clynne would find himself in the cross fire.

"I'm sure I don't want to associate with a Tory spy," said Herstraw haughtily.

"Come sir, I think I'm as good a judge of character as any man," said Jake.

"And what do you mean by that?"

"Simply that we are both traveling in the same direction." Jake gently signaled his horse to move ahead. Now was a dangerous moment—the British messenger could easily swing up his gun and shoot him in the back of the head.

But the moment passed, and Jake soon heard Herstraw's horse trotting alongside.

He turned to see the pistol pointed squarely at his face.

"I don't trust you, Tory," said Herstraw.

Jake softly pulled back on his reins.

"Let's approach this calmly," suggested van Clynne. "I'm sure the traitor has a good explanation."

"Perhaps he will give it to St. Peter, then," said Herstraw, cocking his weapon.

"I will tell you what I told them at Fort Ticonderoga," Jake said in a steady voice. He was most impressed by Herstraw's act—had he not seen him leaving Carleton's office, he might almost believe he was a real patriot. "My brother, who lived in Canada, was killed during an Indian attack this past fall. By the time word of this reached me, it was January and the roads were impassable. I traveled to Montreal to ascertain whether the stories I had heard were true, and now I have the unfortunate task of relaying the information to our mother."

"Why didn't you say this when we spoke in the tavern, then? Or to the soldiers when you were arrested?"

"I wouldn't think of burdening a stranger with my troubles," said Jake. He knew from experience that his stiff and formal tone made his lie all the more believable to British ears. "As for the soldiers, had they not acted so hastily, I would readily have explained. I have a note from the militia's commanding officer exonerating me, if you care to see it."

"That won't be necessary," said Herstraw coldly. He lowered his weapon.

Good thing, too, since Jake had no such letter. He told the story so convincingly, however, that even van Clynne seemed moved, and had trouble answering when Herstraw asked why he was traveling south.

"Business," said the Dutchman finally. "Always business. If there's a shilling to be made—"

"And how are you going to make this shilling?"

"Yes," put in Jake, "that is what I would like to know."

"I have a consignment for certain pewter pieces," said van Clynne smoothly. "And I am going to White Plains to see a man there about selling them."

Herstraw frowned, but pressed no further. He could not object too strenuously to their joining him without risking their own suspicions, dangerous to do so far behind enemy lines. Travelers who met on the road were expected to journey together, for protection as well as fellowship. And undoubtedly he regarded Jake as a Tory deserter riding to New York City. As such, Herstraw would think he might be useful in an emergency.

"You don't mind that we ride with you?" Jake asked innocently, rubbing it in.

"I do mind, indeed."

"Now, now, be more congenial to your fellow travelers," said van Clynne. "You never know when you may need a friend. We may meet up with shady fellows along the way."

"I already have."

"He's going to White Plains, as we are," van Clynne told Jake. "He has a brother there who owes him money, and he's going to collect it. A fool's mission, if you ask me. Never lend money to a relative; the best that can happen is they will forget to pay you back."

Jake ignored the Dutchman. "I recall you telling me your relatives lived there," he told Herstraw. "Did you buy that farmer's horse in Rhinebeck?"

"Twenty pounds," answered van Clynne. "Can you imagine?"

"A good buy," answered Jake, trying to signal with his eyes that van Clynne should shut up.

"Oh no. If I were arranging it, believe me, I could have gotten it for half. Yes, it's a fine horse, but mares are always worth less."

A small patrol from the garrison that commanded the pass in the hills below the village stopped them and briefly asked their business. The soldiers were quickly satisfied and the travelers resumed their journey. Jake let Herstraw accelerate at first, gaining a bit of a lead, then prodded his mount to catch up. The horse seemed glad—the animal was positively a wonder, made to run very fast and undoubtedly for days on end. It did not like to proceed at anything less than full gallop, and was constantly urging its master on.

Surveying the British messenger, Jake concluded that the silver bullet was probably sitting in the bottom of the hunting bag Herstraw had slung over his shoulder. It would be a simple matter to wait for an unguarded moment, take the bag and exchange the bullet. All he had to do now was wait.

And wait and wait, as Herstraw neither stopped nor dropped his guard while they rode south at a moderate pace. Van Clynne filled the time by haranguing them with a theory that the water in this area made for a very good ale, if boiled and then allowed to sit overnight in a tin tub.

"You're wondering why tin, no doubt?" said van Clynne.

"I'm not wondering about anything," said Herstraw. "Except how to survive your prattle."

"Tut tut," said van Clynne generously, proceeding to explain the relation of "flavor noddles" in the otherwise pure water and the magnetism of the metal vessel.

The land here was in American hands, being still many miles north of the British lines at New York City, but that hardly made it safe from attack. Their superiority on water gave the British a mobility that was difficult to combat.

The Americans had undertaken a massive defensive measure to block off the Hudson River to British ships, stretching a large chain across the Hudson at a bend just north of Peekskill. An assaulting army would have not only the chain to contend with, but a series of forts and artillery batteries that would make the narrows treacherous going.

Nonetheless, Jake's tactical eye saw many gaps in the defenses. And while the fact that no patrol challenged them on the road southeast of Peekskill meant their cover stories wouldn't be put to a test, it also meant that British spies and rangers would have an easy time getting in and out of the area.

Peekskill had, in fact, been attacked twice this past year, once in February and again in March; both assaults had done real damage. The British had occupied the village during the last raid, and there were some who said the redcoats' retreat was due to whim, not fear. The HMS *Dependence* was lurking offshore somewhere, and farther south, Dobbs Ferry was an effective British stronghold.

One thing Jake had to admit, the British messenger had gall as well as courage. He was living up to his boast to Burgoyne, traveling right through the heart of patriot country. Jake watched him carefully, half expecting a sudden bolt toward Dobbs Ferry for a rendezvous.

"You're always brooding sir, just staring into space," van Clynne said to Herstraw as they rode. "Why are you so moody?"

"I'm not," he said, his response so gloomy that it contradicted itself.

But Jake realized the man wasn't staring into space; instead, he was examining the defenses. Now here was a messenger with ambition—he would have a full report for General Howe once he arrived in New York. No wonder he went toward White Plains instead of seeking a safer route along the river.

Jake's apothecary studies had taught him about the root of a certain tree that could induce amnesia. Such a potion would come in handy now—he could slip it into Herstraw's drink and wipe out his knowledge of the American defenses.

Of course, there was no way to get the root cure here, as it grew only on a small island south of the Cape of Good Hope in Africa. But thinking of it led Jake to settle on a potion that would help him accomplish his more immediate and important aim of switching bullets—sleeping powder. He could mix a particularly potent version from some simple ingredients, assuming he could find an apothecary shop along the way, as well as a reason to go into it.

A feigned stomachache was just the thing. He began moaning straight away, and as they passed through a small village, excused himself to find a cure. His most difficult task was convincing van Clynne to continue on without him. A series of clandestine hand signals did not work, nor did a hissed warning have much positive effect. Finally, he had to beat the Dutchman's horse away, ordering him in a threatening whisper to catch up to Herstraw and not let him out of sight.

The apothecary bought supplies through the Gibbs family firm, charging twice the recommended markup—which itself was nearly ten times his purchase price. The result of all of this free enterprise was that Jake paid forty dollars for some powders that cost, at most, thirty cents at their source. The purchase greatly depleted his supply of paper money; the man noticed Jake's annoyed countenance when he announced the price, and he told Jake to be glad he still took Continental money.

At least the man was selling unadulterated medicines, and seemed to know his trade, Jake noted, for he warned against inadvertently mixing the potions, which ostensibly were for ptomaine poisoning, warts, and hay fever, along with a potion that occasionally cured love sickness. "If they meet each other, even for an instant, you'll fall dead asleep," said the druggist.

Jake nodded solemnly, saving his smile for outside. The smile remained on his face for more than a mile down the road, until he came suddenly to a fork. Signs on both branches claimed each the best way to White Plains.

But here van Clynne proved his resourcefulness as well as his usefulness. He had pitched his pocketknife, easily identified by the inscribed initials, on the side of the proper road. Jake scooped it up and soon rejoined them.

Herstraw seemed almost relieved to see him—the Dutchman now had someone else to talk at. Which he

did, practically nonstop, through lunch and for the rest of
the day. All the while, Herstraw kept his bag right at his
chest, and Jake could find no opportunity to inspect it.

The sun was already gliding toward the trees and they
were still north of White Plains, despite their steady pace.
This was not a good area to travel through during dusk,
let alone at night. On the one hand, it was unsurpassed in
beauty, running through the foothills that rose from the
Hudson. A hundred-plus years of colonization had not
succeeded in erasing its wild nature; the trio passed under the watchful eyes of a hawk, heard the cries of a lone
owl, and even saw a herd of deer run through the nearby
forest.

But Nature's wildness brought out something evil in
the men who lived here. A traveler sticking to the main
road during daylight was safe enough, but venture along
some secondary route and you were ten times as likely to
meet a bandit as a friend. The war had done more than
scramble allegiances; it had weakened codes of conscience and morality, making outlaws of men who just a
few years ago would have been working at forges or
farms. Some were driven to banditry by necessity, their
lands having been burnt or their places of business destroyed, but there were many with less mitigating circumstances.

The three travelers readied their weapons in case they
were attacked. Jake was careful to keep the ruby-hilted
knife under his jacket—while Herstraw might not know
its special significance, Jake didn't want to test him.

They were not quite to Young's Corners when Herstraw decided he could go no farther, and pulled off at a
large "ordinary" or inn along the road. Jake and van
Clynne allowed themselves to be guided by his movements; though he sneered, the upper-class English gentleman in him expected nothing less.

A figure at the edge of the road nodded in their direction as they stopped. Herstraw, as charming as ever, ignored the man's greeting. Van Clynne made up for his
companion's deficit in manners by strolling over for a
chat that began with a complaint about how darkness was
no longer as dark as it once was.

Following Herstraw inside, Jake watched the care with which he placed the hunting sack next to his chair and hooked its strap around the leg. He might just as well have pasted a sign around it, saying the bullet was there. The American took a seat nearby, waiting to pounce as soon as Herstraw left the room.

"Strange fellow," complained van Clynne, entering the room presently. "Claimed to have business! No time to talk."

"What a surprise," said Jake.

"At least he agreed with me about the lack of shine in the stars."

It was a long-accepted if unwritten law that the inns throughout New York must come equipped with a pretty young woman to soothe travelers' woes. This inn proved the rule unfortunately by being an exception—to call the woman who waited on them in the great room around the small fire unattractive was to call a mountain lion a house cat. The parts of her narrow figure seemed ill-acquainted with each other. The main distinguishing mark of her face was a nose that could have been aligned properly only by being broken in three places. She'd suffered the pox as a child; the disease had left scars the size of large coins in the corners of her eyes. Her teeth were ragged, with one missing toward either side.

How then to explain van Clynne's rising color when he saw her? Or the fact that, when she offered to soothe his feet in some salts, he became so flustered he seemed close to fainting?

"Is she not the most beautiful thing you've ever seen?" van Clynne whispered as she left the room to fetch a basin.

Jake wiped the top of his lip, partly in amazement, mostly to keep from laughing out loud. "Is she Dutch?"

"Who cares?"

Van Clynne sat back in his seat, eyes watering as the maid—a guess, but surely no proof is needed on that account—undid the thick buckles on his shoes and reached up to his calf to unfurl his stockings. The water in the basin literally hissed when he put his foot in.

The woman, with a gentle smile that would have scared a full flock of grizzled vultures, told van Clynne that he could call her Jane. She began rubbing his toes with a cloth, caressing each stubby little piglet as if it were a newborn fresh from its mother.

Herstraw, meanwhile, had procured himself a rum and taken out a small pipe for a smoke. He sat stiffly upright in the Windsor-style chair, his eyes seemingly unfocused but undoubtedly examining everything in the room. The heavy beams absorbed what little light the fire and a few candles on the wall gave off; the low-ceilinged room was nearly as dark as a dungeon.

The inn's only other patrons were a pair of older gentlemen in the corner bent over a checkerboard. They pushed their pieces forward with quick, sharp moves in rapid succession, as if playing out a game they had gone through many times before.

The innkeeper, a jolly bald-headed fellow by the name of Prisco, made the rounds with a pitcher of malt beer, glancing to make sure all cups were filled. He raised an eyebrow when he saw the girl working over van Clynne's feet.

"My niece," he said to Jake, inspecting his mug. "She seems to have taken a shine to your friend."

"It appears mutual."

The man winked at him. "I was recently made a justice of the peace, so a union could be quickly arranged."

"You'd have to take that up with Claus."

"And where are you bound, sir?" asked the keeper.

"Down the road a bit." Jake overemphasized his discomfort for Herstraw's benefit. "I have some family business to attend to. A dead brother, killed by the Indians in the north."

"Sorry to hear," said Prisco. "These are dangerous days."

"They are indeed."

Jake sat back with some satisfaction. In a few hours he would make the exchange and set off for Albany. Once there, a few sips of wine with the general—and a few long draughts with Sarah—would be an ample reward for his troubles. He might even get a chance to sleep for more than a half hour.

The innkeeper went over to the checker players, silently filling their mugs before disappearing into the back room. Jake watched with some astonishment as well as amusement as van Clynne leaned up and whispered something to the girl, who blushed in response.

He could not imagine what the Dutchman might have said. But then, he didn't have much time to consider the possibilities, for at that moment the room was invaded by a knot of Continental soldiers in powder-blue uniforms.

Invaded was not too strong a word. The men, armed with Pennsylvania long rifles and pistols, plunged in with weapons loaded and ready, flailing them around as if they expected at any moment a troop of redcoats to burst from the fireplace. They shouted conflicting commands—don't move, hands up, you're all under arrest, stay where you are, against the wall. Their commanding officer trailed in behind them, sword in hand.

Jake did not know every officer in the American army, of course, but he had some reasonable expectation of knowing a few this close to New York City, more so since some of the local detachments had been under the command of General Benedict Arnold not too long before. But this man and his ill-fitting bag wig were strangers.

That was perhaps just as well. Realizing he was once again about to be arrested, Jake cursed to himself but resolved to go quietly, preserving his secret identity until he was outside.

Nonetheless, he was disappointed that van Clynne—who else could it be?—had not believed him and sold him out, which undoubtedly had been the true purpose of his brief conversation outside. Jake was surprised at his own misjudging of character—he had truly believed van Clynne was sincere when he said he would help him.

With great restraint, he stayed mute in his chair, noting that Herstraw did likewise. Even the two old men took the interruption calmly—until one of the soldiers made the mistake of overturning the game board with his rifle barrel.

The man who'd been winning came within an inch of

strangling the soldier before being restrained. The other remained sitting, though his passionless expression had changed to a great smile.

Van Clynne reacted to the commotion with casual aplomb, falling from the chair with a start. One of the soldiers' weapons discharged, which brought the innkeeper running into the room with his pitcher of beer. It was not until the keeper's wife appeared with a rolling pin in her hand and a very stern expression on her face that the scene quieted.

There were two soldiers for every civilian in the room. They took up positions and trained their weapons as the major straightened his uniform and strode before the fireplace. Jake rose slowly from his chair, stepping over van Clynne to approach the major.

"Sir—" started Jake, but the major put up his hand to silence him.

"You there," he said to Herstraw. "What's your name?"

Herstraw identified himself, and was told to empty his coat pockets. He laid the contents on the table—a handkerchief, a small penknife, and a coin. The officer inspected each item carefully, pausing over the last. He then announced that Herstraw was under arrest as a spy for "His Majesty the King."

"You can't arrest him," protested van Clynne from the floor.

Jake silenced him with a stiff kick in the side. Herstraw, with the look of a man who knows the jig is up, began walking with the soldiers out the door. The innkeeper briefly started to protest, but the soldier pushed him back in the doorway. Jake, desiring a closer look at the major's face in case he might still recognize him, grabbed his arm and asked why Herstraw was being arrested.

"He's a known spy," said the officer. "And unless you want to go and hang with him, you'll sit back down and shut up."

Had he not seen Herstraw's bag sitting on the floor,

Jake might have volunteered to accompany him to jail. As it was, he didn't move away quickly enough—a soldier caught him in the stomach with a rifle butt, sending him quickly into the chair.

Twenty-one

Wherein, the good squire van Clynne reveals that he is in love with sweet Jane, and she, a true patriot, volunteers for service in the American Cause.

Still trying to catch his breath from the unexpected blow to the stomach, Jake reached over the chair railing and picked Herstraw's bag up off the floor. With the exception of van Clynne, still rolling on the floor where he'd fallen, the others had gone to the door to watch the Continentals carry off their prisoner. Jake was thus free to rifle through the messenger's possessions without being labeled a thief.

He was already working on the problem of reuniting the messenger with his bag and the bullet when he made an unfortunate discovery—there was nothing in the bag except tobacco.

After feeling through the brown leaves to make sure they did not somehow hide the bullet, Jake flung them into the fireplace, sending a thick, pungent perfume through the room. He searched the empty bag once more for good measure and secret pockets, then flung it, too, into the flames.

It wasn't difficult to track the soldiers and their prisoner. They moved down the road guided by torches, and marched without particular haste. Jake's progress was aided by the fact that van Clynne remained back in the inn, protesting that he had been injured greatly by both the fall and Jake's boot. The Dutchman said he couldn't possibly think of moving for at least an hour or two, during which time he would follow what surely would have been a physician's best advice—drain several large helpings of ale, and receive comforting attention from sweet Jane.

The reader will be left to imagine that burgeoning love scene while the narrative turns to Jake's pursuit of the British spy and his American captors. Neither the main road nor the side road where the soldiers turned was populated by more than a few squirrels and some sleeping rabbits, but there was a small schoolhouse located just before a bend in the road leading to a small bridge over the creek. A church had been across the street, but having been destroyed some years before by fire, its congregation had built a new structure in a more convenient location closer to town. The ruins provided a perfect cover for Jake to watch the soldiers as they locked Herstraw in the school and then posted guard—two men in the front, one in the rear. The remaining men, along with the major, proceeded on down the road, whether toward a camp or to look for more traitors, Jake could not tell.

Herstraw's capture had been a remarkable piece of work, one that could only be ascribed to the workings of John Jay's committee against conspiracies. Jake had heard that the committee had sources in every tavern and general store north of New York, but to apprehend the messenger mere minutes after he stopped at Prisco's— surely the committee must employ the services of a soothsayer. Knowing to look for the identifier or token (obviously the coin) that would show the British that the messenger was authentic was also a clever piece of intelligence. Jake told himself he would have to congratulate Jay the next time he saw him.

Well, not exactly, since the arrest happened to be directly against American interests. And while Jake knew Jay well enough, he was likely to have a problem convincing the local militia major to arrange a fake escape without some letter from him. He had only six days left of Schuyler's deadline; it could take at least that long to find Jay, whose official duties took him all through the valley.

On the other hand, three men amounted to an almost pitifully small defense, and Jake decided it would be most expedient to proceed on his own. He soon found himself

back at the tavern, asking Prisco where the old outhouse
had been located.

"The old outhouse?"

Some will jump to the wrong conclusions regarding
Jake's next actions, which involved his taking a shovel
and a lantern to the site and mucking around in the dirt.
But in actual fact, he was working on sound scientific
principles. Jake was seeking saltpeter, a critical ingredient of the explosive powder he needed to turn disabling
sleep powder into a proper slumber bomb.

The black gunpowder in his saddlebag already contained about seventy-five percent of the nitrate-rich ingredient; he needed a bit more to make sure the sleeping
substance would disperse quickly and as evenly as possible. Ideally, Jake would have used a much finer exploding
powder and constructed the bomb casing with a half shell
of wood instead of newspaper, but one made do on the
battlefield.

His laboratory was the inn's kitchen, where the innkeeper, his wife, niece, and the two old gentlemen stood
in the doorway, ready to run if something went wrong.
Van Clynne, in his typically close-mouthed way, had in-
formed them of the entire nature of the mission during
Jake's absence. He justified this leak on the grounds that
the innkeeper's wife was Dutch; their loyalties therefore
were beyond question.

Considerably more reassuring was Prisco's revelation
that he served on the local committee of correspondence.
He presented some letters and a small wax seal as further
evidence; Jake ignored the letters and nodded at the
stamp, even though he had no idea what it might really
signify. The fact that he was a justice of the peace meant
that at least his neighbors trusted him, and Jake would
have to do the same.

"Did you recognize the soldiers?" Jake asked as he
worked. "Are they from the garrison at White Plains?"

"No sir, though I'd daresay there are so many troops
coming and going from the towns around here that I
wouldn't know them all. They're not the militia, I'll tell
you that."

"I could see from their uniforms. They're brand new."

Jake turned the image of the man who hit him back through his mind's eye. Not only was the material fresh but his coat buttons were very fine and shiny; that was rare in patriot camps. Perhaps Washington had finally prevailed upon Congress to appropriate proper sums for the army's support.

While the others took Jake's warning about the volatility of his bomb's ingredients to heart, van Clynne stood directly in front of him at the table. The fact that the Dutchman had no idea how the contraption worked did not keep him from offering advice.

"I would put more gunpowder in."

"Why would you do that?"

"For a bigger explosion."

"A bigger explosion would throw the ingredients all over the place," said Jake, sorely tempted to toss a little of the sleeping dust in van Clynne's direction to make sure it worked properly. "And it might cause more damage than I wish. The trick is to have them mix at the proper moment, but not completely scatter. Trust me, I've been making these things since I was ten."

When finished, the bomb was about the size of a small fruit pie, with a crude fuse soaked with the potassium nitrate. It wasn't particularly elegant, and was considerably more clumsy than the small exploding balls he'd used as a lad on his mother's cat, but it would work well enough.

As long as they could find a convenient way to get it in front of the guards. It was too awkward to throw from any distance.

"Dress it up as an apple pie," van Clynne suggested, "and present it to them on a silver platter."

"Actually, if we put it in a picnic basket and left it in front of them, it might work. But we'd need to divert their attention somehow."

"Simple," said van Clynne, reaching to a side table where the innkeeper's pitcher of beer was sitting, "all we need is a beautiful damsel to bring it to them."

"And where are we going to get one?"

"Well, we have one ready made—Jane is not only

beautiful, but brave and of fine Dutch stock, as I predicted."

Jake's breath caught in his chest.

The woman was no doubt most kind and sweet and
generous. He would grant without argument that she had
the courage of a dozen lions. Undoubtedly she had a full
bushel of other fine assets. But Jake, not merely an expert on female beauty but a rather liberal partaker of it,
could find no way of conceding that she had even a shred
of this quality, which was so critical to their plan.

How to say that, though? He was too much a gentleman to insult a lady. Certainly, there was no way to
comment directly on her physical charms or lack thereof
without directly violating the most sacred rules of conduct.

"But . . ."

"But what?" van Clynne inquired.

"Well," said Jake. "I'm not sure."

"True, in the dark it will be difficult to appreciate the
extent of her beauty," allowed the Dutchman. "But what
man would not go weak-kneed as soon as he saw her,
even in the shadows? And that would give her the time to
leave the basket and then run off, wouldn't it?"

"It will be very dark," Jake conceded. He glanced over
in Jane's direction, hoping to see that she had fainted
with fright at the prospect.

"If things are as you said, sir, I will gladly help. I would
willingly risk my life for the sake of our country's liberty."
She stepped forward and rolled up her sleeves in deter-
mination, as if the job were in the bucket of water at her
feet.

The bucket of water at her feet—she didn't see it, and
tumbled forward across the room. As quick as a bee darting into a ripe tulip, van Clynne caught her in midair. He
held her for just a moment in a pose at once tender and
exceedingly comical; Jake didn't know whether to laugh
or cry.

What arguments could he suggest? What impediments
to true love admit?

Hell, if the guards ran from fright, that would work,
too.

"Let's go, then," he said. "Before they decide to hang our friend."

Van Clynne was stationed in the old church ruins with two muskets borrowed from the innkeeper, Jake's pistol and the Segallas. If the bomb failed to go off, he would raise enough of a ruckus to make it seem as if an entire regiment of Loyalist rangers were coming up the road. Van Clynne was not to hurt anyone, however—these were patriots, after all.

Jake, meanwhile, would sneak up on the soldier in the rear of the building, grabbing him from behind and administering a handful of sleeping powder when the bomb went off. Besides a reserve of the powder in his snuffbox, his only weapons were the knife tucked in his boot and the other strapped in his coat; he was counting on the youth's inexperience to make him an easy target.

A patch of brambles covered the last thirty yards from the woods to the rear of the building. It was slow work getting through them, and Jake was only two-thirds of the way when he heard a commotion from the front. Something had gone wrong—Jane was not supposed to arrive for at least five more minutes.

He dove through the brambles, but it was too late to grab the soldier. The Continental didn't even hear Jake's curses—he ran to the front of the building and was immediately cut down by gunfire.

This wasn't van Clynne, either—a squad of redcoats had seized control of the jail and nearby road. Having made short work of the guards, they brought up a wagon. Jake watched from behind the building as Herstraw was taken and placed in the back.

He ducked into the brambles and snuck back down the road as two British soldiers did a quick sweep behind the building. Finding nothing, they joined the others marching double-time down the road.

Who had alerted them? And wasn't it odd that the wagon had come from the direction the patriots had taken earlier, the same direction they were now going in?

Jake, extremely good at geometry, did not like the way the angles added up on this rectangle. He slipped quietly back up the road, grabbing Jane as she was walking toward the building.

"I heard the gunshots," she said. "What's going on?"

Signaling for her to keep quiet, he led her around to the ruins of the church, where they met van Clynne, who'd displayed eminent good sense in remaining hidden throughout the brouhaha.

"Now that you're here, we can take these insolent—"

"Sssshhhhh!" Jake insisted. They crouched behind the stones of the foundation, waiting silently. In less than a minute a horse and rider rode up, went past the school-house about a hundred yards, and then returned.

"All clear!" called the man on horseback.

Jake had to put his hand out to keep van Clynne from rising. "He's not talking to us."

"Who then?"

The question was answered by the bodies of the dead soldiers, rising from the dust as if Judgment Day had come.

"Hurry now," said the man on horseback to these newly created ghosts. He threw a bundle down from his mount, and the men quickly exchanged their blue coats for red.

Jake had to clamp his hand back over van Clynne's mouth to stifle a curse. It was now clear how the Americans had known where to find the British messenger, and what identifier to look for—they weren't Americans.

"The man on the horse was the fellow who didn't have time to talk to me outside the inn," said van Clynne when the men had gone.

"He's the baker in town," added Jane. "He's been stopping by the inn every night for the past three days. I must tell my uncle that he's a traitor. They'll tar and feather the damn bastard."

"Sweet Jane," protested van Clynne, "such words should not touch your lips."

"You can't move against him now, or they may realize we know about their operation," Jake warned. "You'll have to wait until he gives himself away somehow."

"We'll watch the bastard," said Jane. "And then we'll crush him."

"Now, now, sweet Jane," said van Clynne, patting her arm gently. "You really should control your emotions. Such words should never come from so beautiful a mouth as yours."

"The British killed my parents. I hate all Tories."

"Just so, just so. But a sweet thing like you—no hate should come from your lips. No vile words. Why, just speaking those syllables has turned the air around you rancid."

"Damn," said Jake, jumping up and grabbing the picnic basket. "That's the fuse on the sleeping bomb!"

Twenty-two

Wherein, the chase is joined, with much excitement and not a little sleeping.

Jake caught the smoldering cord just as the nascent flame reached for the fuse and its black powder charge. His fingers were singed, but otherwise he was uninjured.

Such could not be said of van Clynne or Jane. The pair bore no physical wounds, but the blows they had lately suffered were deeper than any inflicted by a 24-pounder. Cupid had loaded his muzzle with heart-shaped grape-shot, and scored bull's-eyes on both. The results were horrible to see—moon-shaped irises wide open in the starlight, slack jaws, knees quivering and threatening to buckle. Such a bad case of love sickness had not been seen on the American continent since Pocahontas saved Captain Smith from being the guest of honor at a settlers' roast.

While unexpected, this development was not without potential benefits—Jake suggested that, van Clynne having kept his side of the bargain, he was now free to pursue other matters.

"I wouldn't dream of leaving you until our mission is accomplished," protested the Dutchman as they returned to the inn for their horses. "You can't overpower these redcoats by yourself."

"I don't intend on overpowering them," answered Jake, who wasn't quite sure yet what he did intend, but was confident he would think of something.

"I know every Dutch man and woman from here to the tip of Long Island. I'm related to half of them, and the other half are as good as relatives."

"You didn't know Jane."

"On the contrary, it turns out I met her late mother's father at a pig auction several years ago."

Don't touch it, Jake told himself. Don't touch it.

"Getting my land back has become even more important to me now," added van Clynne, gently touching Jane's arm. "I intend to settle down and raise a family of my own—if I can find the right woman."

Jane's glow lit the night.

"Have anyone in mind?" Jake asked sarcastically.

"Don't pry, sir. Decency and good manners prevent me from broaching certain subjects until time runs its course. There is a particular Dutch way of doing things, and you will find that it is much more in balance than your English or American way. The woman a Dutchman courts is a gentle, angelic thing, unblemished; he must work his way toward her slowly. The process is long but vastly rewarding."

As van Clynne finished his impromptu ode to Dutch love, he squeezed Jane's elbow. She responded by giving him a friendly if forceful swat on his rear. This took him by surprise, and he emitted a sound not unlike a cow's hiccup.

It seemed to Jake that Jane might be neither as angelic or unschooled as van Clynne supposed, but he let that pass. He conceded that the Dutchman might be useful—if and only if van Clynne followed his directions explicitly. The squire must fight against his natural tendency, however commendable in other circumstances, to move to the fore. He must do exactly as he was told. And he must do it quietly.

Van Clynne naturally agreed completely. In short time they had rounded up their horses and their things, setting out up the lane the redcoats had taken.

"My guess is that they've taken this road to avoid White Plains," said Jake. "With luck we'll catch up to them before the Bronx River."

Their luck was even better than that. A mile and a half south of the schoolhouse, Jake caught sight of a torch. After tying their horses to a tree, the two patriots crept through the nearby field and saw a redcoat guard snoozing by the side of the road. He was easily avoided in the dark, and they snuck through the field to see what he was guarding.

It turned out to be a temporary camp just inside a small copse at the edge of a cornfield. The guards here were considerably more alert than the man back at the road—four were continually circling the encampment.

Judging from the number of tents and all that had gone before, there could be as many as twenty lobster-coated soldiers in the camp. They were undoubtedly grenadiers, probably handpicked; while Jake harbored no great admiration of the English army's skills, still it would be difficult taking them on head-to-head. And even if he could, say, sneak into their camp and plant his sleeping bomb—he'd furnished it with a new fuse—a direct attack would serve little purpose. To accomplish his mission, he had to somehow trade bullets with the British messenger without Herstraw getting suspicious. The bullet was probably secreted somewhere on his person—perhaps in a secret flap in his breeches, just like Jake's. Any switch would require a delicate operation.

Not if he took his pants off to sleep, van Clynne suggested. They'd be lying at the foot of his bedroll or on a small stool. It would be child's play to sneak into the tent, find the secret pocket, switch the bullets and get away.

A little powder on the man's nose, and the search could be conducted at leisure.

"Just what I was thinking," said Jake. "Make sure the horses are ready when I return—it shouldn't be more than an hour."

"You're going into the camp without me?"

"You tramp through the woods like a drunken bear."

"I'll create a diversion," said van Clynne.

"That's not necessary. They're all sleeping. It's just the guards I have to get past."

"A diversion would be just the thing. Where is your sleeping bomb?"

"Listen, Claus—if you move one inch from here while I'm gone, I'll have you hanged. And I'll make sure you never get your property back, or marry your Jane."

"That's a nasty threat, sir."
"See that you remember it."

Not wanting to be overburdened, Jake took only his
Segallas pocket pistol, the elk-handled knife and the assassin's, plus the sleeping powder in his snuffbox. And
the fake silver bullet, of course.

The guards' circuit of the camp was done in pairs, with
each team moving roughly parallel to each other. He was
able to find a spot in their patrol where a small clump of
woods covered the camp side from the approaching
team. The only complication was the freshly planted
cornfield that lay between him and the trees; he would be
exposed as he ran across nearly thirty yards of ankle-high
plants before reaching cover. He let the patrols pass
twice, getting his timing down, before making his dash.

Ten feet from the woods, a tree trunk lay hidden in the
shadows. Jake never saw it; he was upended and shot
across the ground, landing with a dull thud. The soldiers
who had just passed turned around immediately and began approaching, guns at the ready.

Jake lay prone, the Segallas clutched in his right hand.
He'd been lucky, frankly, that it hadn't gone off.

The soldiers stepped through the sprouting corn, calling to the other patrol. Was it dark enough for them to
miss him? Their feeble challenges indicated they weren't
quite sure what they had heard—Jake prayed for a rac-
coon to cross their paths.

The other patrol approached from the right, answering
the calls of the first. Jake could not move without making
it easier for them to see him, yet if he stayed here, he
would surely be found.

He was just considering which direction might be the
safest when the air was rent by a strange, drunken song
from the roadway.

Van Clynne!

"My love's an angel, an angel's my love!" he sang in a
voice that would have pierced the wax in Odysseus's
men's ears.

But Jake could not have wished for a more melodious
or welcome sound. The soldiers immediately turned

toward it, demanding that the singer show himself and leave off that awful screeching.

"Is it a wounded cat?" Jake heard one redcoat ask as he ran by, not five feet from his head.

He scrambled to his feet before the men reached the road. The British base was silent, its inhabitants undoubtedly fatigued by their exploits earlier in the evening. For isn't it true that tyrants must expend great energy pretending to be free men, while those who are truly free go about their business without a breath of exertion?

Leaving such weighty philosophical considerations to the narrator, Jake went from tent to tent, searching for his man. Continentals in camp often pack six or eight men into small canvas rectangles such as these, but here the British soldiers were living practically like officers, with only two to a tent. That made his task all the more difficult, giving him twelve places in all to search. His inspection was aided by a glowing ember at the end of a long stick he snatched from a doused fire; he used it to light a candle he found along the way, holding the flame ever so briefly upward before dousing it. The system was hardly efficient, but at least it gave him enough light to see.

The law of averages states that, for any given tent, Jake had a one out of twelve chance of finding his quarry. As he worked his way through the camp, his odds gradually improved, so that any gambler would increase his bet with each new tent. Such a man would have hit the jackpot at tent five.

Naturally, the problem with playing the odds is that they work both ways. One gets lucky on one side and unlucky on the other. What, for instance, are the odds of an explosion going off just after Jake crawled into the tent, an explosion loud enough to wake Herstraw?

Whatever the odds, it happened. Herstraw, alone in the tent, bolted upright with the noise. Jake had just time to duck beneath his camp bed. He smothered both the candle and ember with his body; this was one time a warm feeling in his chest was less than comforting.

Herstraw shouted, "What?" and then followed with

some incomprehensible mutterings, still on the border between rest and waking.

A lullaby would have been just the thing to send the messenger back to Sleep's bosom; regrettably, Jake had neglected to take choir while at Oxford. The sleeping powder would do the job just as efficiently, but as he reached for the snuffbox, Herstraw's grumbles grew to coherent shouting.

"What? Fire? What's going on?"

Lying on his stomach, his chest smoldering, his face pressed into the dust—Jake decided it was best not to offer an answer.

"Where are my britches?" cursed Herstraw. "Where's my coat? What the hell is burning? Damn it. Where are my boots?" Herstraw fumbled around and found them, pulled one on and then cursed louder than before. "Damn bullet. Damn Burgoyne. Damn all generals!"

Herstraw pulled the bullet from the boot.

Thus was solved the mystery of its location. The round ball glinted in the darkness, indicating it remained in its natural metallic state and would be easily exchanged.

Not at the moment, though—Herstraw dropped it back down his shoe after his foot was inserted and ran from the tent.

Now it was the American's turn to curse. He rolled from under the camp bed, made sure the fire on his coat and shirt was out, and then crept to the tent entrance. Outside, the British were mustering their senses, trying to discover where the explosion had come from, deciding that their search should include a quick inspection of the camp.

Jake had only just the time to fling himself onto the bed before a soldier with a lamp came inside the tent. Jake pulled a blanket over himself with one hand and fumbled for the Segallas with the other.

"Get up, get up," said a redcoat, kicking at his feet. "Come on. The captain is forming search parties!"

"Oh," mumbled Jake, his hand shielding his face from the light—and detection. "Coming."

Fortunately, that was enough to satisfy the redcoat.

But the patriot had no time to congratulate himself on

this slight indication that his luck had once again returned. This phase of his mission was both clearly over
and clearly a failure; it was time for him to practice that
famous military maneuver, hasty retreat.

He pushed up the bottom of the canvas tent side opposite the entrance and rolled into the brush. The redcoats
were still in great confusion, running back and forth in
the dark. This made it somewhat easier for Jake to proceed through the woods, back toward the field where he
had left van Clynne.

He knew that the loud explosion must have come from
his sleeping bomb pie. Obviously he had used too much
gunpowder and packed the paper too tightly, since it was
meant to be nearly silent.

It was also meant to be nonlethal. The volume of the
blast tended to be in direct proportion to its explosive
power; from the sound of it, there would be no living
survivors within a dozen yards or more.

Jake was surprised at the hint of actual remorse he felt
about the possibility of losing his erstwhile ally and assistant. But his foreboding did not adequately prepare him
for the sight he came upon as he reached the edge of the
woods near the road. Four redcoats lay head to toe in a
perfect line, each sleeping like a baby. At the head of this
line lay the good squire van Clynne, whose snores we
have already established as being at least as bad as his
singing.

He proved impossible to wake. Jake considered
whether it might just be best to leave him there, but the
Dutchman knew too much about his mission now to be
discarded. And—dare we suggest it?—the American spy
was becoming just slightly attached to the grumbling
Dutch merchant.

Never suggest it, for Jake would deny it strenuously,
citing instead his duty as an officer and gentleman not to
leave a fellow soldier on the field of battle, whether
wounded, dead, or sleeping. He took off his singed coat
and shirt, leaving them on the ground next to van
Clynne's body. Then he removed the Dutchman's shoes
—an event that proved as much a test of strength as
anything that followed.

Relieving one of the redcoats of a flint and striker, he set his shirt once again on fire, then picked up van Clynne and began running down the road.

"Running" might not be wholly accurate. "Waddling" would give a better description of their escape. Jake had considerable strength, but van Clynne had a more considerable waist, and these qualities worked against each other. By the time Jake was fifty yards away, "dragged" might provide a better picture than "carried." Perhaps the word "rolled" might also be used.

But literary precision was sacrificed for speed. Jake and his somnolent companion proceeded through the woods at the best pace he could muster, until finally reaching their horses.

Twenty-three

Wherein, a new plan is concocted hard on the heels of a debate regarding the nature of Dutch ingenuity.

"You cannot deny, sir, that my intervention played a crucial role in the operation."

"I was just about to grab the bullet when you set the bomb off. If it weren't for you, I'd be on my way back to Albany by now."

"The explosion was a result of a faulty mechanism for which I clearly cannot be blamed. You were the author of the weapon. I offered my advice, but you declined it. 'An expedition has but one chief,' I believe you said."

"Why did you light the damn bomb?"

"I lit it to cover every contingency."

"I thought maybe the redcoats set it off in retaliation for your singing."

"Part of a well-designed plan, sir. As was your appearance. Perfectly on cue."

"I see. You planned that."

"I knew you would arrive and spirit me away, yes. Now, your decision to make the scene appear as if I had spontaneously combusted—brilliant, sir, truly inspirational. I begin to wonder if you have some Dutch blood in you."

Jake pulled back on his reins, stopping his horse. "Why is it that you attribute every good quality you come across to the Dutch, and every bad quality to some other nationality?"

"I simply speak the truth. It is well known that the Dutch are a superior breed of people."

By now it was well past noon. They had spent the early hours before dawn in the barn of a tradesman whose house was a half mile south of the redcoat camp. Van Clynne had vouched for the man upon rising—it should not take much to guess that he was Dutch—and they approached him for breakfast. After satisfying their hunger and borrowing a pair of shoes for van Clynne and a shirt for Jake, they returned to their quarry, shadowing their movements south.

The problem wasn't finding the British troop—apparently unperturbed by the occasional patrols the Americans sent through this no man's land, the redcoats marched loudly along the road. The difficulty was coming up with some plan to change the bullets without Herstraw catching on. Jake began to worry that he would have to admit failure and simply assassinate the devil.

Which itself would not be an easy task.

"The Dutch are the most advanced race in learning," van Clynne proclaimed as Jake pushed his horse up a hillock to check on the troop's progress. "The world has not seen the like of our technological achievements since the days of the Chinese. I would have told you of the design for a spring-loaded fuse, had you expressed the slightest interest."

A pair of British soldiers were proceeding as the vanguard. Behind them, the main body with Herstraw and the other officers was just pulling off the road to rest. The foot soldiers were burdened with heavy packs and made slow progress. They were still some twenty-five miles from Manhattan; if they continued at this pace, they would not make the city until nightfall, if by then.

"Such a bomb can even be constructed with an instantaneous fuse, working on impact," continued van Clynne, prodding his poor horse in Jake's footsteps. The animal strained under the added burden of gravity, but was a patient beast, not complaining despite the boot heels in its side.

"What are you muttering about?"

"Noach Vromme, a fine Dutch inventor whom you should meet. He lives in the woods near Skenesboro. Took a wife from the Mohawk—scientists are eccentric, you know. So, there they are, camping again," he added, spotting the British soldiers for the first time. "They have the stamina of chipmunks."

Jake shook the reins and his horse carried him away from the road. Van Clynne's mount struggled to catch up as they continued south, aiming to get ahead of the lead element on the highway.

"So what is our plan?" asked van Clynne when they returned to the road. "Another sleeping bomb for the entire regiment?"

"That's hardly a regiment," said Jake. "But I think not. I have only a few grains left in my snuffbox."

"Poison their water, perhaps?"

"Killing them would defeat our purpose," said Jake. "Besides, I don't have any poison."

"Surely we can rally a few militiamen in the vicinity and waylay them before they cross King's Bridge."

Inspiration works in very mysterious ways. The Greeks had invented the muses as its agent, picturing loosely dressed nymphs whispering in artists' ears. As an attempt to explain creativity, it had its flaws—what poet would bother writing with a partially clad woman in the room? More likely, inspiration worked as a thunderbolt thrown by . . .

A fat Dutchman with a big mouth?

"Of course," said Jake, snapping his fingers. "I've been going about this the wrong way. Howe doesn't know Herstraw and isn't expecting him. It would be a simple matter for you to go in his place."

"Excuse me, sir, but I believe the effects of last night's sleeping drug have lingered in my brain. Did you say, for me to go in his place?"

"Who else?"

"Well you, of course," protested van Clynne. "You are well versed in these matters, while I am just a lowly assistant and amateur."

"You're Dutch, though. The Dutch have a natural superiority in all matters."

Jake had never met Howe himself, but there were more than enough officers in his retinue, to say nothing of the city, who knew him under other guises. It would strain credibility for him to try and pass himself off now as a messenger. But van Clynne was perfect.

"All you have to do is give him the bullet, doff your hat and be off. You say you work for Burgoyne, and his adjunct will never be the wiser."

"What if he gives me another assignment?"

"Even better. You take it straight to me, and we'll give it to Schuyler."

"This is a most precarious plan, sir. What happens when the real agent shows up?"

"I'll arrange for an accident to greet him in New York. That will take a little doing, but it won't be as hard as sneaking into their camp again. All I need is a marksman or two, or perhaps some thugs on the street." Jake considered his options. "I shall have to call on one of the Culpers to help me."

"Why can't this Culper fellow carry the message?"

"What do you know about Culper?"

"Nothing, sir, nothing."

"Forget the name. It means nothing to you."

"It would mean even less if we could forget this plan."

"Listen, Claus." Jake's voice had the iron in it that only a deep love of Liberty could inspire. "You said you wanted to help me so you could get your property back. You claim to hate the British and believe in Freedom."

"All true. Very true."

Jake brought his horse around and was now facing van Clynne. "Do this for your land, Claus."

"I want to make sure I'll survive to enjoy it. It's one thing to confuse these rogues, but the British commander-in-chief . . ."

Jake, well aware of Howe's reputation as somewhat less than astute except when the battle was directly before him, began to laugh. "Oh don't worry," he said. "You'll have him debating the merits of beer over Madeira within a minute or two."

"There is no debate over which one is better," said the Dutchman with great solemnity.

Jake knew it would be better if van Clynne met the general before Herstraw met his accident. Partly this was a matter of logistics; the troop had now passed into very secure British territory north of King's Bridge, where a surprise attack would be well-guarded against. Fort Independence—the name had not prevented it from falling into British hands—lay to their west, and the redcoats and Loyalists here were constantly on guard against attack, having successfully fended off an American raid several months before. An ambush would be infinitely easier on Manhattan island, where the troops would not be as alert, and where some or all of the patrol might fall away.

Delaying his assault would also guarantee that, if Herstraw somehow escaped, in the worst case Howe would be presented with two messages completely at odds with one another. Past experience showed that the inclination in such cases was always to give the first more weight.

But how to guarantee that Herstraw was delayed sufficiently to finish second in this race?

"Too bad we can't get them to detour to my friend Roelff's," suggested van Clynne. "I'm sure he could arrange to detain them—perhaps a little of your powder in their ale would do the trick."

"Where is it?"

"North of Morrisania on the Harlem Creek," said the Dutchman, using the Dutch name for the narrow portion of the upper East or Salt River. "There's a small patch of calm water untouched by the riptides, and there Roelff has his inn and a small ferry besides. He does a very nice business. And," van Clynne winked at him, "he has a daughter you would like."

Having seen firsthand what van Clynne considered beautiful, Jake's mind could not have stood the strain of contemplating what the young girl might be like. Fortunately, it was spared that labor by the more pressing problems.

"This Roelff would help us?"

"Of course, he's Dutch. And with a few crowns on the side, one's patriotism is easily enforced. Besides, the British look for excuses to stay there—the daughter is exceedingly fair. The soldiers make camp in the yard outside while the officers stay inside. It is their usual arrangement."

"How do we get them there?"

"I cannot be expected to shoulder this entire operation myself. You must supply some initiative yourself. We are, after all, equal partners."

"Equal partners?"

"Just so, sir, just so."

The reader can conclude on his or her own how the conversation proceeded, quite possibly suggesting the various arguments that were raised and points made. In actual fact, Squire van Clynne carried these out singlehandedly, or single-tongued, if there is such an expression. Jake's attention was turned to other things, namely the two British soldiers who appeared practically from nowhere and demanded to see their rights of passage.

These papers were calmly produced. The soldiers reviewed them, though it was obvious to Jake that in fact neither man knew quite how to read. The pair were poor conscripts taken from some north country tavern in England during a drunken stew. They'd be eminent candidates for desertion—but now was not the time to convert them.

"Do you want me to help you with that?" he offered congenially, slipping from his horse and going to the soldiers to turn the paper in its proper direction.

"How do we know you wouldn't read the wrong thing?" said one of the men gruffly. He poked his bayoneted musket in Jake's direction, but the American put his hand gently on the barrel and turned it away.

"Because I'm a loyal subject of King George, just as you are," said Jake, reaching into his jacket. "Care for a pinch of snuff?"

"Never touch the stuff," said the soldier.

"Well, I will, sir, and thank you for it," said the other man, cheerfully handing back the papers.

Jake held out the silver snuffbox.

"Very nice," said the man, taking it and opening it carefully.

"You must be a gentleman or something, eh?" said the other soldier.

"Or something. What's this? Your friend seems sleepy."

Jake grabbed the box from the man's hand just as he collapsed to the ground.

"Jesus. Tom, Tom, get up, damn it, before the corporal comes. What'd you do to him, mister?"

"Me?" Jake flailed his hands, warding off blame. "What could I have done? I was talking to you."

"And he—Jesus, I'm—"

Falling asleep, too, as Jake's innocent protests had shaken the powder into the man's face.

As a matter of fact, Jake felt as if he could use a good strong cup of coffee right about now. But first things first.

"I was about to suggest your magic dust might be appropriate," said van Clynne.

"Grab their guns, then help me get their clothes off."

"What for?"

"If you were as inventive as you claim, you'd already know."

"You're not going to suggest that I wear a redcoat uniform!" protested van Clynne. "My father will turn over in his grave!"

If they had had time to sew these two uniforms together, Jake would surely have suggested that. In the actual event, however, it was he who donned the private's coat. Van Clynne fulfilled the other part of his plan, which was to hide in the woods with the weapons and create a commotion at Jake's signal. For Jake had concocted a stratagem that would have made the great Elizabethan playwrights proud—the Americans were once more attacking Fort Independence and the nearby bridges.

Illusion is mostly a matter of timing. Two men can appear to be two hundred or even two thousand, if the circumstances are right. Jake dashed down the road in his stolen uniform, happening upon the two British privates who formed their troop's advance party. He shouted and screamed, his horse wheeling, dust flying.

"Take cover," he screamed. "The damn patriots are

attacking King's Bridge disguised as Indians! Dyckman's is already cut off!"

The two soldiers shouldered their weapons, but were not sufficiently impressed by Jake's warning. Their attitude began to change, however, when he wheeled and fired off his pistol—only to be answered by two shots from the woods.

The soldiers dropped to their knees and fired back down the road. Jake slipped quickly from his horse, holding it by its tether.

"Where are your troops, where are your troops?" he demanded as the soldiers tried to reload in the dust.

"Down the road," said one of the men, ducking as the rebels in the woods fired again.

"How many?"

"Twenty. We are escorting a messenger to New York."

"Twenty, is that all? There are two thousand damn rebels down from Connecticut, half of them with Pennsylvania rifles!"

At this the British soldiers nearly lost their weapons as they dropped to the dirt. Ever since the British column marching back from Lexington had been picked off by snipers from the woods, any patriot with a rifle and a halfway decent hunting coat was assumed to be both a marksman and superhuman, able to shoot around trees and at vast distances.

Jake found it necessary to join them as a new volley sounded, a bullet whizzing uncomfortably close to his head.

"Take him by another route!" Jake warned the men as he struggled to reload his pistol. "Double back to the intersection a half mile east and then head south to a Dutch path in the hills. There is a ferry owned by a man named Roelff. He is a Royalist and dependable. All the officers know him. The path on the other side leads to the Bouwerie Road."

Jake steadied his horse as another bullet whizzed past. Van Clynne's part in the play was proving a little too realistic for comfort.

"Go quickly. I'll try and hold them off." He took aim and fired at the imagined rebel horde. His fellow redcoats were marveling at his bravery, undoubtedly impressed that a man who was dressed as a foot soldier spoke like an officer—and was mounted, to boot.

Their desire to linger in the vicinity, much less to ask questions regarding Jake's own circumstances, were quickly dispatched by a bomb that exploded a few yards away with a great whoosh. Careful examination of the weapon and its trajectory would have shown that it was formerly a powder horn, that it had been very crudely constructed in a manner producing much spark but little damage, and that its trajectory originated not from the rebel position but from Jake's own hand. However, in the smoke and dust, careful examination was not a viable option. The soldiers ran for their lives back toward their troop, shouting the alarm.

Twenty-four

Wherein, the name of Manhattan is fully explicated, as are several new complications in the plot.

Jake thought it prudent to shadow the task force's movements for a distance, occasionally sounding muffled alarms and firing a few guns to make sure they proceeded in the proper direction. Fortunately, van Clynne's estimation of Roelff's loyalties proved correct, though the cost threatened to become a sticking point when the man said he would only take "real" money, real in this case being coins. Jake, having only American paper money left, managed to persuade van Clynne to advance the sum and even, after many threats, veiled and unveiled, to cease off haggling. The whole procedure consumed a large portion of time, and they were just running down the small path at the rear of the inn to take possession of Roelff's flat-bottom skiff when the patrol's advance guard made an appearance at the front door.

The waters were too rough to chance having their horses swim with them. But Roelff's pole-driven skiff barely fit both animals, and it was nearly as difficult to persuade them to come aboard in the waning light as it had been to get van Clynne to part with his money. Finally the small party pushed off, Jake levering the pole with all his might. Van Clynne put an equal amount of exertion into holding his eyes closed.

"Hallo there!" called one of the redcoats, arriving at the slip.

Jake, who'd doffed his redcoat uniform and was back in brown breeches and white shirt, waved at the man, pretending to misunderstand his order to return.

Van Clynne's horse had the same sentiments toward the water as its master. Once it sensed the shore nearby, it bolted from the small craft with such force that the boat overturned.

"I'm drowning, I'm drowning!" screamed van Clynne in the water.

"Stand up," said Jake, busy grabbing their things from the water. Fortunately, he had taken the precaution of placing his knives, gun, powder, and bullets in the water-tight bladder inside his saddlebag. But everything else, including Jake himself, was soaked.

"I was testing your reflexes," protested van Clynne as he waded ashore.

"Do you need help?" called one of the soldiers.

Jake shook his head, but then pointed at the bottom of the boat. "A rock has come through," he shouted, pushing the long craft ashore.

"It looks all right from here," shouted the soldier.

"No, look," replied Jake, picking up a boulder from the riverbed. He smashed it through the boat's bottom. "See what I mean?"

"I will never, ever, go back upon the water. Never!" Van Clynne's teeth staccatoed a death march. "Noah himself could grab me by both legs and I would not yield."

"Isn't that Noah up ahead?"

"Your jests are not appreciated, sir. Not appreciated at all. What's more, they are not funny. Perhaps you should try some other target for your little comedies."

"Claus, you're taking things much too seriously," said Jake. He'd wrung his clothes out as best he could, but they were still damp. "Relax now. Tell me about Bouwerie Village."

"I will not, sir; there is nothing to tell."

Van Clynne's face turned white and he began hyperventilating. Jake feared a heart attack.

Not at all. The good squire was merely about to sneeze.

The resulting explosion trumpeted through the hills with the force of an 18-pounder, scattering birds and small animals in its wake. Not even the famed proboscis of Antony van Corlear, Henry Hudson's trumpeter for whom Anthony's Nose farther north is named, could have made such a stupendous honk. This sneeze was followed in rapid succession by two smaller ones. Smaller only in proportion to the first; by themselves they were most impressive, and had Jake not witnessed their predecessor, he would have run for cover.

"God bless you."

"And now I have a cold, and it will be on me all summer. Infernal water."

"I'm surprised you're not bragging about Manhattan," said Jake, trying to put his companion in the more optimistic frame their success required by changing the subject. "I've heard its purchase described as the greatest land deal of the century. And it was executed by a Dutchman."

"Minuit was a phony and a crook. He didn't even deal with the proper Indians."

"You're speaking ill of a Dutchman? This is a new development."

"You should check your facts before you taunt me, sir. Your Mr. Minuit was born on the Rhine in Wesel. That is a far pace from Amsterdam, I do believe."

"Wasn't he was working for the Dutch West India Company?"

"I could work for the emperor of China. Would that give me slanted eyes?"

"Maybe."

"Speak seriously, sir. Minuit went on to establish New Sweden. Do you think a Dutchman would ever be involved in such ridiculousness?"

"Why is it ridiculous?"

"Baths at every house! Baths in the middle of winter! If that is not the most foolish race on earth, I am sadly mistaken."

We will leave the Dutch squire and his wet prejudices briefly to address another injustice, this one leveled against those of van Clynne's own heritage and, by extension, all who have ever lived on Manhattan island. It concerns the name of the place itself. Now it will be observed that "Manhattan" is an unusual name, one with little precedent in Europe, Asia, or Africa. The thoughtful reader will therefore conclude that it must have originated in America herself, most likely with the original inhabitants. In that, the reader will be largely correct, as the name appears to be an emendation of an Indian word that sounded, to European ears, as "Mana-ha-ta."

So far, no harm done. But an English writer—nothing less could be expected from such a quarter—early put out the rumor that the original meant "orgy," and so dressed this up with wild explanations—midnight sojourns with men, women, and goats the mildest—that the word soon went around that Manhattan was Sodom on the Hudson, a place worthy of a heavenly thunderbolt.

This jealousy dates from the time when the settlement at the base of the island was called New Amsterdam, and the official language Dutch, not English. But the English's subsequent possession did little to quash the rumor, and throughout the Old World and a great deal of the New, the rumors grow like ragweed. New York is supposed to be the center of wickedness, with not only orgies, but men literally flying hither and thither at a moment's notice, propelled by the devil underground. It is supposed to be a place where women paint their faces as if they were men, and walk about with pantaloons beneath their dresses, while their husbands communicate through secret stones with their wizardly fellows all across town.

Nothing could be further from the truth. The city Jake and van Clynne were now rapidly approaching was one of the finest in America, with wide, paved streets and a massive skyline three or four stories high. The city's progressiveness was shown not only by its pavement stones—few if any places in Europe could boast as many paved roads —but by the lamps hanging from its posts.

These had been lit a full hour or more as Jake and van Clynne passed the British artillery encampment above Dove Tavern on the road from King's Bridge. General Howe's headquarters in the Beekman Mansion lay ahead, overlooking Turtle Bay.

The bay was near America's most ignominious defeat the previous fall—but it would be too depressing for our heroes to recall that event at present.

Jake paused just before the path that ran to the mansion's front door. He could not see the soldiers who were guarding it, though he knew they would be there.

"Now just give him the bullet and be gone," said Jake.

"You're not coming in with me?"

"I told you, there's too much chance someone who knows me will see me and ask questions. Besides, it'll only take you a minute. If there are any generals with Howe, bow to them and quickly take your leave."

"I'd sooner kneel to a milk cow."

"Don't do anything to insult them. Act like they're your superiors." Jake ignored the Dutchman's frown. "Give the bullet only to Howe. And if you meet a general named Bacon—run, do not walk, out of the house."

"Who is he?"

"Howe's intelligence chief and the head of their Secret Department in America. A very nasty breed. Their people tried to kill me on Lake George."

"What!"

"Relax. The assassin was probably assigned by Carleton. Bacon doesn't know me."

"How can you be sure?"

"One more thing, Claus—if they ask for your signifier, tell them you were robbed along the way."

"My signifier?"

"The messengers carry tokens for identification. Herstraw has a coin, so I assume they're all using something similar."

"What type of coin?"

"I didn't get a good look at it. It doesn't matter; yours would probably be different."

"Why didn't you tell me any of this before?"

"It's nothing. Just say you were robbed. The bullet's your identification."

Not exactly, though the guards who accompanied van Clynne to the door were impressed by the clipped doubloon he managed to dredge from his stocking at their lieutenant's third request. The Dutchman whizzed it so quickly beneath the man's nose when he asked for his sign that it might have seemed like a flash of light—but of course one would expect the squire to be deft with his cash.

Alas, the general was not at his headquarters. According to the lieutenant, he was attending to business at Fort George, and would probably be found in a house on Pearl Street across the way.

Van Clynne expressed sincere regret that he could not leave his message with the lieutenant. He also declined his offer of an escort, and rejoined Jake at the edge of the roadway.

"It'll be easier there," said Jake, starting down the road. "Most likely he has some appointment with his mistress, Mrs. Loring. The guards will be well-liquored in that case, and I doubt they'll ask for an identifier."

"You may save your assurances for another fool," said van Clynne. "I have found a Spanish coin that will serve my purpose. Really, I wish you would see to all of the contingencies the next time you involve me in a plot. I am used to maintaining certain standards."

Jake let van Clynne complain until they reached the point at which Queen Street meets Hanover Square, very close to their destination.

"Your orders are specific," he reminded the Dutchman. "No one but General Howe himself. If he's here for the reason I suspect, he'll be in a poor mood and anxious to return to his lover. Remember that he issued a similar order to have Herstraw see Burgoyne personally, so stand your ground."

"A Dutchman always stands his ground. Just remember that you're to help me get mine back at the conclusion of this adventure."

Van Clynne dismounted and walked forward along Pearl Street. A detachment of foot soldiers from the Thirty-fifth Regiment stood at the end, on special duty guarding Howe's temporary headquarters. These redcoats were more brown-colored than red, due to the inferior dye used in their jackets' manufacture—a matter which van Clynne implied could be easily remedied for the right price.

"Move along, thief," said their sergeant indignantly.

His honor besmirched, van Clynne demanded to see the general immediately.

"Which general is that?"

"General Howe," retorted the squire, "unless he has gone and gotten himself sacked, as generals are so often in the habit of doing."

"And who are you?"

"You don't recognize me?"

"Recognize you?"

Van Clynne gave out a harrumph that attracted the attention of half the sows running wild in the nearby street.

"I will have you know, Sergeant, that I have just now come down from Canada on a mission from General Burgoyne—another one who's always changing posts— and have express orders to deliver a bullet to General Howe."

At this, the soldiers jumped to attention, their bayonets in a threatening position.

"This bullet, you fools. It has a message."

"I'll take that," offered the sergeant, but van Clynne was too quick for him; the bullet disappeared up his sleeve.

"I'll not give the message to anyone but the man assigned to receive it," said the Dutchman, "and you're not he."

"Let us see your token then, if you're a messenger," countered the sergeant.

Van Clynne produced his coin, waving it quickly in front of the sergeant's face. His hand was intercepted on its way back to his pocket—apparently the man had a bit of Dutch blood in him.

"We haven't used coins such as this since we abandoned Boston."

"They're all we use in Canada these days," said van Clynne, grabbing it back. "We have confused the rebels by reverting to the old style."

The sergeant was not impressed. "Give me your message or I'll slap you in chains."

"My orders are quite specific," answered van Clynne, producing a paper from his pocket.

"This paper is blank," said the sergeant.

"To you. It's written in invisible ink, in the contingency that I should fall into the hands of the enemy. We're not fools in the messengers' corps, you know."

"Fie!"

"I've heard of such things," one of the guards told his sergeant. "You hold it up to the fire and writing appears."

"If you hold this up to the fire, it'll burn," said van Clynne. "It needs to be treated with a special liquid, and then the message appears for only a brief second."

The sergeant was momentarily befuddled, and held the paper up to see if he could see anything.

"You may do your duty as you see fit," van Clynne said as he snatched back the paper, "as long as General Howe knows that it was you who prevented me from seeing him."

The sergeant, as suspicious as he was, was no match for van Clynne at the game of bluff. The Dutchman turned on his heel and took but a short step away before the sergeant reached out and touched his shoulder. The soldier's manner turned cajoling and pleasant, cooperative to a fault.

"I'd be happy to take you to see the general myself, sir," said the sergeant, "but he's spending the night in the harbor aboard his brother Admiral Howe's flagship. Business of a, shall we say, personal nature? Orders are that he's not to be disturbed by anyone tonight, not even the king."

"Aboard ship? In the water?"

"It's a most convenient place for a boat."

"Well," said van Clynne, reconsidering his position, "I suppose this can wait. It's just a little message; nothing important. I'll take it to him when he returns."

"Hold on, sir," said the sergeant, his touch now a firm grip arresting van Clynne's rapid retreat. "We're not expecting him on land tomorrow. I will have two of my men guard you until you row out to the general in the morning."

"Oh, that won't be necessary," said van Clynne. "Not necessary at all. I can quite take care of myself."

"I insist," said the sergeant, signaling two men over with his head. "There are still many rebel scum in this city. They may be lurking close by even now."

Van Clynne took a quick look around. He knew Jake was in the shadows somewhere, but the patriot was conducting his lurking in a most discreet manner, leaving van Clynne to improvise on his own.

"Thank you for your hospitality, Sergeant. Perhaps your men will accompany me to a tavern for a light supper. Have they eaten already?"

"We had our dinners at two, sir," said the soldier nearest him, "but have been starving ever since."

"Well then, come on," said van Clynne. "If there's one thing I know about, it's food. And you, Sergeant?"

"I regret that I have duty here. But Robert and Horace will take care of you."

"Horace. Is that a Dutch name by chance?"

"No, sir," replied the soldier as they started down the street together.

"Too bad, lad, too bad."

Jake watched the procession pass him from a distance of about half a block. He had not been close enough to overhear the conversation, but it seemed obvious enough what had transpired—van Clynne had been apprehended and was on his way to be interrogated at the guardhouse. He cursed himself for letting the poor Dutchman play a role he would have been much better suited for. He could easily have fobbed off some story for anyone who might have recognized him, or thought he recognized him. Hadn't he recently bluffed his way past all of Montreal? His caution had only made the situation several times as precarious.

Jake was just wondering if he dared slip away and get assistance from some local allies when the soldiers and their charge made a sudden detour into a public house. This breech of duty provided a perfect opportunity, if he could act quickly. Jake trotted up behind, paused at the door to collect his breath, and then plunged inside.

Into an impromptu gathering of General Sir Henry "Black Clay" Bacon's intelligence staff, hosted by the notorious general himself.

Twenty-five

Wherein, an old acquaintanceship is renewed, though not happily.

The mention of the continent's head of the Secret Department reminds us that several days and many pages have passed since the villain Christopher Manley was left for dead in Lake George. The reader will recall that the British major was last seen with a rather ugly red spot on his belly, the product of a bullet fired by none other than Betsy Schuyler, who proved as brave as she is beautiful, and whose fine qualities will undoubtedly be sung throughout these states ere the war is over.

We lost track of the major in the tumult of the waves as the small boat went down. It would have been natural to assume that the major drowned; indeed, it was undoubtedly a firm hope.

But consider: Had Jake suffered a similar wound on a mission, would we have been as likely to conclude that he easily gave up the ghost? Would not our hero find a way to overcome his injuries and pursue his man? Would the mere puncturing of his stomach—as painful and inconvenient as such a wound necessarily is—end his career?

Manley's extended physique played a critical role in his survival. Had he been of ordinary height, the bullet that entered the right quarter of his back would have doubtless pierced his kidney, proving quite fatal. Alternatively, had his internal organs been as elongated as his body, the wound would have severed his lung with the same effect. But Manley's extra-long body was filled with organs of only average size, spaced out by extra helpings of mucus and membrane. Thus the bullet merely nicked through a portion of his small intestine, releasing a great deal of blood but not his soul.

Which is not to say he wasn't in severe pain as he struggled to find the surface of the lake. Here again, his long arms and legs helped him, providing a natural buoyancy that brought him to the surface. He caught sight of Jake swimming for the canoe and waited until the American reached it; then he took a huge gulp of air and submerged, avoiding Jake's scan of the waters. By the time he resurfaced, the Americans were paddling for shore.

Manley's struggle to reach the rocks opposite was monumental; were the author of different sympathies, it might be described in heroic detail as an inspiration for all who would follow in the swine's boot steps. Suffice to say that Manley made shore and was rescued by his compatriots, taken to the home of a Loyalist, and nursed to health.

Not nursed so much as bandaged, for the British agent was determined more than ever to accomplish his mission. Manley had served the Secret Department in France and Spain, and never once had he failed; he wasn't about to let some colonial outwit him. Nor was his arrogance tempered by any new appreciation of the rebel's abilities; he considered Jake's escape a mere product of luck, aided by the dastardly expedient of a pistol kept up a woman's skirt.

The possibilities of such a double entendre amused him as he traveled south by horseback, attempting to pick up Jake's trail. He rode as quickly as he could despite his wounds; a flask of rum that he sipped from every hour was his only concession to the nagging pain.

In fact, Manley increased his discomfort by chewing constantly on leaves of a certain South American tree whose properties allowed him to go without sleep. The plant—natives use the word "coca" to describe it—grows in the Portuguese jungles of Brazil. It has nearly magical properties to provide energy and ward off sleep; members of the Secret Department had discovered them nearly a hundred years before while infiltrating the Portuguese court, and often made use of them in special circumstances. But there was a heavy price to pay for the increased alertness the leaves provided—the juices were extremely caustic, churning even a healthy stomach. Manley's injured organs were in such a state that every few hours he found it necessary to dismount and vomit. The blood disgorged in the fluids would have been enough to make a lesser man faint.

The British agent succeeded in tracking Jake to Rhine-beck, where Traphagen remembered seeing him in the company of a Dutchman a day or so before. His boy had overheard them talking about Fishkill; Manley went there and after several hours finally found the housewife who'd given them breakfast. It was fortunate that the British major was wounded and in a hurry, for under ordinary circumstances he would have thought nothing of killing his informants as payment for their cooperation. Instead he posed cleverly as an agent for General Schuyler, winning their confidence and even assistance. Twice he was able to trade horses, exchanging a beaten beast for a fresh mount.

It would be happy to report that Justice Prisco, our good innkeeper so recently met, saw through this ruse and managed to send Manley in the wrong direction. Alas, Major Manley had not achieved his position in the Secret Department by influence alone, and was able to weave such a convincing tale that the judge was easily taken in. Manley accounted for his wounds by saying he'd been shot by Tory bandits; he told the keeper and his wife that he must find his old friend Jake to recall him for an important mission to Canada. Prisco told him Jake was on the trail of a notorious British spy, who'd apparently been rescued by the British Army earlier that evening.

Sweet Jane alone was suspicious—the visitor made no mention of her new sweetheart, Claus van Clynne, a man whom she understood would be vital to any secret operation in the state, if not the country. Asked the direction Jake and van Clynne had taken, she wove a confusing verbal map that sent him toward Connecticut until he realized that he'd been hoodwinked. Cursing and heaving, he struggled to find his way back in the dark.

Twenty-six

Wherein, Jake chats with Sir Black Clay, and ends the hideous torturing of his companion van Clynne.

Even the most astute follower of the Revolution will be excused if General Bacon's name is not immediately familiar beyond the brief mention a few pages earlier. General Sir Henry Clay Bacon—"Black Clay" is a nickname affixed only by his enemies—plays a crucial role as an adviser for General Howe, yet he has always managed to stay carefully in the background. His official responsibilities as director of intelligence for General Howe's army naturally encourage a low profile.

Bacon is also the continent's ranking member of the Secret Department, and as such, answerable directly to the king—not to civilian authorities, not even to Howe himself. The general is as discreet about this half of his identity as the department itself, and unlike other British officers, does not make a habit of bragging about the smallest of his achievements.

He also possesses an innate shyness, proceeding from the circumstances of his birth. For the general is said to be an illegitimate son of King George II, produced in his dotage during a liaison with a courtesan. There are wild rumors of his being stolen from his mother as a young boy and raised by another family whose last name he adopted, but we have not time to go into such stories with Jake standing momentarily tongue-tied on the threshold across from Bacon.

One other fact of his birth, and indeed a major contributor to his most prominent physical feature, should be mentioned briefly before returning to our tale. The general was born with the caul or birthing sheath upon his face. While in many circumstances this is seen as a sign of good fortune, it was the opposite in Bacon, for it imparted a strange congenital disease. The general's face had been slowly eroding since birth. Starting from a slight red mark on his forehead, fully one-third of his face now appeared consumed by a deep, corrosive disease—the black clay of his nickname.

Jake saw the mark and immediately knew whom he was facing. But before he could retreat, a strong arm clamped him around his shoulder. He was dragged forward into the room, much in the manner a bear might invite a friend for dinner.

"Well, if it isn't our good friend Dr. Jake, the only man in all of the colonies whose headache powders can actually effect a cure," said the bear, known to his friends as Major Elmore Harris. "Come in and sit down, my good man. Gentlemen, make room. General, I'd like to present a good Royalist and possibly the best doctor the colonies have produced, Jake Gibbs."

The sincerity of Major Harris's praise was exceeded only by the amount of rum on his breath. Jake had given the major a bottle of headache powders the last time they met. He had also managed to steal some papers relating to the disposition of British troops on the island and the neighboring Jerseys. The circumstances under which the papers were taken should have left little doubt as to who their purloiner was, but the major's manner as yet betrayed no ill will. Jake could only play along, letting himself be dragged to the table, smiling and bowing as he was introduced all around.

General Bacon sat at the end, with a proper border of space around him, befitting his rank. He acknowledged the introduction with the slightest nod of his head.

Did these officers suspect Jake's true profession? If so, they gave no indication as the conversation progressed. After the unedited praise of his headache cure, the major went on to other matters, such as what Jake had been doing with himself these past few months.

"Searching for new cures," he answered, trying to think of the reply whose details were least likely to be challenged. "I have spent some time among the voodoo peoples on the Caribbean islands. You've heard of them?"

The response was unanimously negative.

"They come from Africa and have a curious approach to nature," Jake said, sensing the coast was clear. "I have lately traveled north into the wilderness in search of some of their ingredients. My ambition is for an oil that will speed the mending time of bones."

"But doctor, why would you want that?" asked one of the officers. "Then you would have less time to try your medicines, and receive considerably less profit by selling them."

They had a good laugh at the general practice of apothecaries, which they understood Jake to be despite his using the title of doctor. In England there was a strict difference between the two, and a good deal of snobbery existed against druggists—provided, of course, you weren't sick at the moment.

"I have attended the University of Edinburgh," Jake said stiffly, seeing a chance to escape gracefully by naming the world's most advanced medical college. "I resent the implication."

He rose.

"Don't be too sensitive, my good fellow," said Major Harris. "It was only a joke."

"Thank you, but I have other business here."

"I had a question for you," said Harris, whose grip on his arm suddenly tightened.

"We can discuss it another time, in different company."

"The doctor is right to be insulted," said Bacon. At his first word, even the people at the far end of the room stopped speaking. "There is much to be gained from studying other peoples. I myself am interested in the voodoos."

"That's gratifying to hear, General," replied Jake. The two men's eyes met in the grim light of the tavern. Each instantly had a sense of the other—though Jake hoped the general's was not as deep as his own.

"I would be interested in discussing them with you,"

continued Bacon. "Unlike some of our other officers, I have better ways to spend my days than whoring among the rabble."

His men looked down at the table.

"I would like very much to talk with you sometime," said Jake, bowing—and in the process loosening Harris's grip. "But it will have to be another time. I was on my way to see a patient here."

"In the tavern?" asked Harris.

"There are benefits to consulting in such a place," said Jake, taking a step back. "The patient tends to be more at ease."

"I would like to ask you about certain papers," whispered the major, "which are no longer in my possession."

"What type of papers?" asked Jake in a loud voice.

Harris's face suddenly turned red. He could not say in front of this company, certainly not in front of the general, without volunteering himself for a court-martial. But the matter being opened, it needed a satisfactory closing.

"Oh, the copies of the *Gazette*," said the patriot. "But I thought you wouldn't mind. They had that excellent article making fun of Washington—I've already sent them to my father and sister. Those are the papers you mean, aren't they?" Jake added. The look of innocent puzzlement he expressed would have fooled the king.

It took only a half look around the table to convince the major that, yes, that was precisely what he was talking about.

"You will call for dinner Sunday," Bacon commanded. "Promptly at one."

"Thank you, sir; I will be there." Jake gave a little salute with his head—a bit too much flourish, but such gestures were never wasted on knights. "In the meantime, gentlemen, let me warn you that an epidemic of a newly discovered strain of the flu, 'Greene Disease,' we doctors call it, is expected this spring. I should recommend a good dose of mercury to get your systems in order before it strikes."

Having prescribed poison for them all, Jake effected an escape, ducking from the front room into the hallway.

As he reached the threshold, a loud screech emanated from upstairs.

A cow being harpooned made a more harmonious sound. Jake's first reaction was to cover his ears; his second was to listen more carefully. It did not sound like it came from van Clynne, but in truth it did not sound like it came from any human being.

Had Jake stumbled onto one of Bacon's notorious torture chambers?

Any consideration for his own safety vanished as he leaped up the stairs, determined to rescue his friend. By the time he reached the top of the first flight, the cries had become low moans of pain. He realized they were coming from a closed room on the next floor up, just off the railed landing. Two leaps and he made the top of the steps. Another stride and he was halfway to the door. With the next he had his pistol in hand.

Jake flung open the door, leaping to the middle of the threshold to confront the damnable British.

One of whom had passed out at the table, the other of whom was producing those hideous sounds by moaning loudly into a large bowl filled with beer.

"It's about time you showed up," said van Clynne, rising from the table. "I was beginning to think I was going to have to find you myself."

"What happened here?"

"The English simply cannot hold their liquor." Van Clynne reached back and took a last gulp from his tankard.

It took several blocks for van Clynne to detail his encounter with the sergeant. Night had now progressed far on her path; the stars twinkled above the dusty glow of the streetlamps and the moon attempted to peek through the clouds.

"It seems General Howe is not content with amusing himself with the mistress Sultana," van Clynne said, relating what the soldiers had told him once they'd started drinking. The reference was to one of Mrs. Loring's less vulgar nicknames. "He went out to the ship for a rendezvous with a certain Miss Elva Pierce this evening, and awaits a Miss Melanie Pinkleton tomorrow. Apparently, he can't decide if he likes blondes or redheads."

How did van Clynne know the hair color of Mrs. Loring's new rivals?

"Because, sir, I know both families. The Pierces are of no account, being English, but Pinkleton—I daresay the girl bounced on my knee once or twice as a child. Her father was a good Dutchman, God rest his soul, but you see what comes from marrying a Scotch woman?"

"Red hair."

"And much worse."

"Would she recognize you?"

"Claus van Clynne is not a man easily forgotten."

"The guards expect you in the morning to deliver the bullet?" Jake asked.

"I'll not go on the ocean if my life depends on it," said van Clynne. "Not this evening, not in the morning, not ever. We're better off trying our luck at Roelff's. I know a handy way from King's Bridge."

Jake weighed the options. Howe being aboard ship would make escape a difficult contingency, especially since the mistress would complicate things. And the Dutchman's remarkable cunning in disposing of his two guards this evening might not be so well received among the British as it was with Jake.

"Are you sure the officers will stay in the inn, and not in the camp?"

"It is all they ever do. I don't understand the attraction myself, but apparently they are enamored of Roelff's daughter."

"All right. Assuming Roelff has convinced them to stay, you'll arrange with him to be placed in the same room with Herstraw. You go in ahead of him so he can't block the door against us. After he falls asleep, you let me in and I'll exchange bullets."

"Why must I take the harder assignment? Why don't you?"

"We'll take our horses near the opposite shore," said Jake, ignoring the question. "I know a place we can tie them north of the British armory, and get a rowboat besides."

"A rowboat!"

"We can't risk going back by King's Bridge. It's too far north, and besides, they'll be suspicious of any night traveler, especially if word has gotten out about the sham battle we fought this afternoon."

"I would rather reconsider this entire operation from the point of view of dry land," said van Clynne.

Twenty-seven

Wherein, it is discovered that where there is smoke there is not necessarily fire.

For about half the distance across the East River, the trip was idyllic. A nearly full moon hung in the sky, shadowed occasionally by clouds but throwing ample light for Jake to steer by. The stars stood ready to offer navigational assistance. The only sound besides the measured rowing was the howl of a wolf somewhere in the distance.

And the gentle trickle of water lapping against a piece of wood.

Unfortunately, the wood in question was part of the interior floorboard of the boat. The leak did not become apparent until they were midstream, but thereafter it progressed with such speed that by the time they were twenty yards from shore they were more in the water than in the boat.

Remembering his experience coming in the other direction, van Clynne stood as the water approached his lap, figuring he had only to stand and walk out of this predicament. Unfortunately, rivers are rarely symmetrical.

"Help!" shouted the squire as he sank beneath the waves.

Jake threw his shoes to shore and dove into the river just as the boat gave up all pretense of floating. The icy grip of the river closed quickly around his chest. The water tasted bitter as well as cold. It splashed into his eyes, stinging and making it hard to see.

Van Clynne was gurgling and splashing somewhere

nearby. Jake stroked in the direction of the sounds, but found nothing.

Suddenly, he realized he wasn't hearing anything anymore. Wiping his eyes, Jake looked around and around, scanning the surface. He could make out the shadows of the nearby shore—but no van Clynne.

Desperate now, Jake tucked his upper body into the river and dove straight down, extending his arms in a vain hope to snag his drowning companion. Still nothing.

He had to come up for another breath of air. Once again he scanned the surface, saw not even a hint of his companion, then pressed back below. He swam in a broad, desperate circle, fighting against the current.

Lungs bursting, Jake started to kick for the surface when his foot struck something soft and mushy. He bent down and snagged a piece of thick cloth—van Clynne's jacket.

Fortunately, van Clynne was still in it.

He pulled him to the east shore and dragged him onto land. The Dutchman's body was cold and he didn't appear to be breathing. Jake turned him onto his stomach —no small feat in itself—and began pumping rhythmically, hoping to restore him to life.

It was nearly a minute before the Dutchman began coughing. Soon, however, he was exhaling both water and oaths, uttering curses in Dutch, English, and a language all his own. Teeth chattering, he finally righted himself, and they proceeded to Roelff's inn.

Given its strategic location, the inn was not a large one, consisting of two rooms downstairs, several smaller ones above, and a kitchen in the basement. Jake and van Clynne found the British messenger Herstraw and the officers of his escort in the second room of the first floor, sitting around the fire.

"Well, look who's here," said Jake cuttingly as they entered the great room. "Our friend the violent patriot."

Van Clynne's teeth were chattering too strongly to join in the greeting. Roelff, surprised to see them but utterly discreet, fetched blankets and immediately stoked the fire. Jake took a flagon of rum in hand and pulled up his

chair near the Englishmen, refreshing the cups of all but
Herstraw, who was drinking cider.

"It turns out that our destination was similar after all,"
Jake said to Herstraw, eliciting only a grunt in response.
"Are you going to introduce me to your friends, or will I
have to make my own acquaintance?"

Herstraw shrugged. Jake immediately proclaimed how
happy he was to see "fine English gentlemen" after having spent the past few days among the "insulting colonials."

"We have just been chased into the water by the rebel
rabble," he lied. "They ambushed us near King's Bridge,
and the only way we could get away was to dive into the
river. I thought poor Claus was going to drown."

Van Clynne shivered on cue. Color had not yet returned to his cheeks, and his beard was pasted to his neck
like a drowned rat's tail.

"And what is your business here?" demanded Herstraw. "What happened to the mother in White Plains?"

"My mother lives in New York," said Jake. "I did not
think it wise to admit that in the revolutionists' country.
My friend here, Squire van Clynne, does much business
behind the lines, and advised me wisely."

Van Clynne coughed vaguely in agreement.

Herstraw snorted in derision as Jake congratulated
him on having played the role of a rebel so convincingly.

"I had my suspicions, but at the end you fooled me. It
has been a troublesome journey," added Jake. "Really,
who do these damn rebels think they are? Give me five
minutes in a locked room with Washington, and I tell
you, this war will be over."

"I shouldn't underestimate Washington," suggested
the lieutenant to his right. He had a vaguely Scottish
accent. "He served with us during the French and Indian
War."

"You don't look old enough to have been there," said
Jake, topping off the man's cup.

"My father served under Braddock. Washington was a
man of great ability, I can tell you. There are certain
skills of leadership that cannot be underestimated."

"Not one of the rebels can match even our worst private," said the captain. He was the same man who had posed as a patriot major at Prisco's. Jake feigned not to recognize him, and the captain didn't bother announcing himself. "Most of the American commanders are foreign has-beens. Imagine, taking Lee in—that's a sure sign of insanity, if not incompetence."

Jake readily agreed—the capture of American Major General Charles Lee by the British the year before still ranked as the single most important patriot victory in the war.

"What do you think, Herstraw?" he asked. "I suppose that you are an authority on such matters."

"Why is that?"

"You seemed to be an authority on everything, the last time we spoke."

Herstraw took that as the veiled insult it was, and scowled.

"Major Herstraw is just completing an important mission," said the friendly lieutenant. He held out his cup for a refill. "He's seen General Burgoyne, and is now on his way to meet General Howe."

"Really!" said Jake, instantly adopting the starstruck Tory role. "I should like to meet both gentlemen."

Herstraw said nothing. His eyes cast a withering stare through the room, and someone less bold than Jake might have ended the conversation.

"What is General Howe like?"

"I don't know."

Herstraw stood; Jake watched as he walked toward the other side of the room, near the outside door. But he wasn't leaving, merely calling to the innkeeper for a refill.

"The general is a very refined man, with very strong opinions. He is an excellent tactician," said the lieutenant.

"He often plays the fool," said the captain. "He is always looking for an excuse to delay an attack. I don't care who hears me say it—we should have beaten Washington by now, and it's the commander's fault. If he didn't spend his time whoring and drinking, we'd all be better off."

That bit of blasphemy—common enough among the

general's officer corps—sent the room into a momentary silence.

"What about this General Bacon?" asked van Clynne, starting now to come to himself. "Is he a fool as well?"

"What do you know of General Bacon?" demanded Herstraw.

"One hears things, here and there," tutted van Clynne.

Herstraw sat back in his seat. "Black Clay and his men be damned. They hold themselves above us all, regardless of their rank."

"We do not talk of his work," the captain told van Clynne. "I'm surprised that you know of him."

"He's famous among Loyalists who want to see a firmer hand applied to the rabble," explained Jake, who wished van Clynne hadn't mentioned him at all. "Otherwise we know little of him. What does he do?"

"You ask so many questions," teased the lieutenant, "we might take you for a rebel spy."

Jake laughed. "That would be quite ironic, since I was taken for a British one near Ticonderoga. They even detained me in a prison cell. I thought my days on earth were over."

"Believe me, son, if they had truly thought you were a spy, they would have hanged you straight out," said the captain. "Many Royalists have been mistreated at their hands. Fortunately, this nonsense will be ended soon."

Jake tilted his head, all ears for details on how that would come about, but the captain's attention was drawn to young Miss Roelff, who entered the room with two pitchers to refresh the men's drinks.

Now here was a Dutch beauty. Her long hair was precisely curled on each side of her rosy face. Her bosom was ample and not too modestly covered by the top of her dress, while her waist was narrow, the dress sliding from her hips like a graceful bell made from the petals of a flower. No wonder the British took any excuse to stop here.

"I wonder, Captain," said Jake when she had left, "how the rebels can be strong enough to attack us at King's Bridge."

"Don't be impertinent," warned Herstraw.

"No, it is a valid question," allowed the captain, who was starting to feel expansive, thanks to the rum. "Even a weak foe will make use of darkness and temporarily superior numbers to strike momentarily at a weak spot. You will see in the morning that the rebels have been defeated, run off without a single loss of a British soldier."

"I hope so," said Jake, sounding sincere.

The conversation turned to lighter matters, and by some inevitable but untraceable process, came to be dominated by van Clynne.

"Do you know how many pigs there are in New York?" said the Dutchman, complaining about the city's hodgepodge development. "They outnumber the people. And why? Because the English have no sense of order. They let things go willy-nilly, unlike the Dutch. When this was New Amsterdam, believe me, not a tulip row was misplaced."

"Are you getting tired?" interrupted Jake, seeking to put van Clynne's mind back on the plan, which called for him to make his way to bed. "You look like you're getting tired."

"Not in the least."

"I'm tired," said the British captain. "It's time to get to sleep. I'll just check on the men."

"I'll go with you," said Herstraw, rising. They were joined by the lieutenant, who walked behind the two men a bit like a younger brother tagging along after school.

"I think I'll get a breath of fresh air before I turn in," said Jake, stretching his arms as he rose—and making some desperate gestures to van Clynne in an effort to get him to arrange things with Roelff.

The Dutchman's memory was not faulty, just highly selective. He could easily recite the names of ninety percent of the Dutch inhabitants of New York City and the northern counties. He could tell you which of them owed him money, the terms, and when it was expected to be paid back.

He could not do nearly so well, however, with the amounts he owed to them, at least not voluntarily. Likewise, when it came to a plan he did not particularly endorse, his knowledge of its details tended to fade.

Roelff's upstairs rooms being relatively small, they were all equipped with only one bed. Now, van Clynne was a seasoned traveler, and very much used to sharing his bed, with or without the convenience of a bed board to separate him from the fellow next to him. But he had always managed to avoid crawling beneath the covers with a British soldier. There was something in his constitution that found it naturally abhorrent; between his displeasure and the recent bath—let us say his mind lapsed.

Unaware of these moral objections, Jake stretched in front of the house, made as if he were yawning, and then quietly snuck through the bushes, listening as the officers talked about the two Loyalists they had just met.

They had accepted his story to a point; Herstraw believed "the tall colonist was a definite coward, obviously running away from the rebel draft with a story weaker than his stomach." In his opinion, "The fat one is some sort of roving thief; best keep your valuables well-guarded tonight."

If the king knew he was wasting British blood on such as these, Herstraw added, he would quickly recall his troops.

Having assured themselves all was in order and the guard strong, the Englishmen returned to the inn and went up to bed. Jake allowed them a five-minute head start, then went inside himself, deciding there might be enough time for an interview with Miss Roelff before the way was clear to proceed to the final step of his mission.

To say he was surprised to find van Clynne in the main room would be to state the obvious. To say that Herstraw had been placed in his own room by the landlord, and that the door was subsequently discovered to be barricaded, would be equally wasteful. To describe what tortures Jake imagined as suitable punishment for his erstwhile accomplice would undoubtedly break all rules of taste and propriety.

Thus, we skip ahead to Jake's plan to rouse the British messenger from his bed and his room by setting the building on fire.

"You can't do that," protested van Clynne. "Poor Roelff will be ruined."

"You should have thought of that before you failed to carry out your part of the plan."

"The swim in the river made me forget the plan, sir; that is a very different thing from being derelict."

"I didn't think a Dutchman was capable of such a character flaw as forgetfulness."

Jake was not, in fact, going to burn the house down, but merely make it look as if it were on fire. After alerting the innkeeper and getting him to remove his family to a safe distance (Roelff was a most obliging fellow, even condescending to accept the last of Jake's paper money in payment for his acquiescence), Jake took a bucket of embers upstairs. He'd already gathered some leaves and pans, and now set off a series of improvised smudge pots. The hallway quickly filled with smoke.

"Fire!" he yelled, banging first on the lieutenant and captain's door. "Fire!"

The officers, who didn't have to go through the bother of removing a barricade to get out, emerged and ran down the stairs. Herstraw took much longer, coughing from the thick smoke when he finally came out, both boots in his hand.

Jake, lying in wait with his mouth covered by a water-soaked rag, would have preferred that he left them in the room but had realized he wasn't likely to be that lucky. The patriot had taken up a post near the door just in case of this contingency, and tripped Herstraw immediately, sending him flying across the hallway into van Clynne, who had the duplicate bullet in his hand.

Caught off balance, the Dutchman staggered backward and then fell to the floor, as did the boot and its bullet. There was considerable and commendable confusion as Jake fanned the smoke toward the tumble of men and yelled at them to seek safety. The situation was compounded as the lieutenant returned to the house armed with two buckets of water, which he promptly unloaded on Herstraw and van Clynne.

"Goddamn it, you fool!" growled Herstraw, struggling to his feet. "Give me my boots!"

"They're right here," said van Clynne, groping for the bullet.

To describe what happened next, we have first to suspend this scene and turn the clock back a few short hours, joining a horse and rider on the road to Connecticut. The horse is worn almost to death, but the rider pushes on all the harder, ignoring his own pain and wounds.

The rider is Major Manley; having just realized he has gone off in the wrong direction, he is retracing his steps, inquiring after Jake at every house along the road. Finally he sees it would be more profitable to ask after Herstraw and his British escort. His horse gives way, there are various and sundry other difficulties—with no wish to make this villain seem more heroic than necessary, we join him outside Roelff's, where he meets the soldiers assigned to accompany Herstraw. They are oblivious to the "fire" just now being lit, grumbling that they have to sleep in tents while their officers push aside soft goose feathers and ogle the proprietor's daughter.

"Six of you, come with me," commanded Manley in such a presumptive tone that the men did not even think to question him. He led them straight to the house, where the alarms were just breaking out. Assuming that his quarry was somehow involved, the assassin rushed inside and up the stairs—and straight into van Clynne, tripping over the prostrate squire as he grabbed for the bullet.

The shouts, the alarms, the smoke—greater confusion had not reigned since a mouse snuck into the queen's birthday celebration. Guns were fired over van Clynne's head; Jake shouted and fired back. People flew through the air like witches, and there was all manner of running and disorder. It was a miracle that the Dutchman was able to pluck the two silver balls from the floor where they'd rolled together and toss one into Herstraw's boot as the messenger grabbed it and ran outside. If luck did not clear van Clynne's path, then the patron saint of portly Dutchmen surely did.

Jake's timely fling of a smudge pot into Manley's face may also have helped, as the British secret agent's long body provided an effective barrier to the soldiers rushing behind him. They sprawled across the hall as if felled by one of those double-chained balls ship captains use to take down an opponent's rigging.

"I've found you at last," gasped Manley.

"Just in time," said Jake, falling upon him. "I still owe you something from the lake."

Everything else happening in that cramped hall melted away as the two men locked their bodies in a desperate duel. Though Manley had spent much energy arriving here, he was far from weak, and managed the first serious blow, flicking Jake off his back. He jumped to his feet and kicked at him, landing a sharp blow to his ribs.

Jake bounced up, dodged another kick, then aimed a punch at Manley's chest. The force of his blow was dulled when the Englishman turned at the last moment. The pair exchanged a few glancing shots, then momentarily fell back against the opposing walls to catch their breaths and clear their eyes in the thick haze of smoke.

Never had Jake fought a man so much taller than himself. His limbs were narrow and yet he had remarkable strength, whipping his punches back and forth as if he were cracking a bull's tail. Jake threw himself forward, fighting off the pummeling to grab Manley around the torso. He shoved his knee upward; Manley moaned as he fell back. But the British agent surprised Jake with a roundhouse right as he surged forward again, and the American fell off to the side.

Not even the coca leaves Manley chewed could match the fury in Jake's muscles as he called on his body's reserves to deliver him from this English demon. Liberty herself aimed Jake's fist as he threw it, cracking Manley's head back against the wall. Manley brought his arm around and punched Jake's neck, but as he tried to slide away, Jake struck with the dagger he'd caught in midair on the lake. The red ruby in the hilt end seemed to glow as the sharp blade found its way into the villain's heart.

Three times he plunged into the vast chest, waiting until he felt the death rattle reverberating through the long body as it slipped to the ground. He withdrew the knife and saw his enemy's last glance, a bewildered, angry look that foretold several centuries of restlessness for his now homeless soul.

Jake had no time to ponder Manley's future as a ghost. He stepped back through the tumult of bodies sailing around him, then plunged down the steps, escaping outside.

Twenty-eight

Wherein, a small but critical error is discovered, leading to yet another change in plans.

Given the reverses of the past twenty-four hours, Jake felt somewhat relieved to make the edge of the woods without pursuit. He felt even better when he heard a familiar grumbling up ahead in a clearing.

Van Clynne had smashed his foot upon a log and was implying that Heaven had placed it specifically in his path. The squire's mood lifted upon seeing Jake, whom he'd feared had been killed or at least captured by the untimely arrival of the British.

"Thank God you're all right," said the squire, clapping him on the back and forgetting all about his injured toe.

"Thank God for you, too," said Jake. "You were a wonder in there, Claus. I really must admit I couldn't have pulled this off without you. Wait until General Washington hears this story."

Ordinarily, van Clynne would bask in the glow of such praise. In fact, it is hard to imagine otherwise, given the squire's hopes for the restoration of his property.

But the Dutchman was a great student of odds. And though the average bystander would have computed the chances of his getting the right bullet into Herstraw's boot at fifty-fifty, he knew that certain other laws came into play at a moment of crisis. Call it van Clynne's law—the shoe will always be on the wrong foot when catastrophe strikes.

"The wrong bullet!" exclaimed Jake.

"Perhaps I am wrong," said van Clynne. "You open the bullet and read the message."

But of course he was correct. And none of Jake's curses—nor van Clynne's—could change that.

The troops had moved their tents to the front of Roelff's property and doubled their guard. The windows were ablaze with light; no doubt van Clynne's friend was now earning the extra money he'd been slipped by denying any knowledge of the rebels.

Much to his chagrin, van Clynne agreed with Jake that there was only one course open: return to New York City and carry out the exchange aboard Howe's ship, while Jake arranged a reception for Herstraw in the city.

The prospect of crossing the water did not thrill the Dutchman, and he was silent the entire journey through the woods south of Roelff's and down the road to Morrisania. They had hopes of finding a boat there they might borrow.

The phony patriot raid had not only delayed Herstraw and his company, it had placed the entire countryside on high alert. Jake and van Clynne nearly ran into a pair of German soldiers, who were fortunately too angry at some slight from their sergeant to pay more than passing attention to the shadows diving for cover by the roadside.

When the mercenaries had passed, van Clynne gathered his bearings and led Jake through two yards and a path down to the rocky shore. A canoe was tethered a short distance away. Alas, the path there was treacherous and wet; the Dutchman soon slipped and only just managed to keep himself from crashing into the sharp stones.

The Dutchman's fear of water had not abated, and so he may be excused for closing his eyes as he crawled forward on the rocks and groped for the vessel.

They were quickly opened by a series of excited commands, in German, to give up and get out of the boat. As van Clynne dove in, Jake leaped from the lane into the canoe, a bullet whizzing by his head and plunking into the water not three feet away.

The other German was, fortunately, a worse shot, and Jake took advantage of the few seconds they needed to reload by paddling out into the current. All subsequent bullets whizzed harmlessly into the night, as long as you don't count the one that struck van Clynne flat in the chest.

The musket ball is a curious projectile. Much of its potential force is lost in the gases that escape around it in the smooth bore of the barrel. Still, it retains a considerable amount of oomph; while not particularly accurate at one hundred yards—or ten, for that matter—it can still blow a nice size hole in one's chest.

Or in van Clynne's.

The Dutchman went straight over when hit, plopping with such force that the canoe bounced wildly on the waves, nearly causing them to swamp.

The plight of his friend gave Jake new vigor, and he soon made shore beneath the jagged heights of Harlem. It was difficult to haul the canoe up with van Clynne prostrate inside. Nevertheless, he managed; after securing it, he leaned back in the boat, wondering what he could do for the dead man.

"You can help me up."

"Claus, you're alive."

"My purse seems to have saved me," said the squire, reaching inside his clothes and coming out with a large leather bag filled with paper and coins—and one half-squashed lead ball. "Now if this had been a Dutch bullet . . ."

With Jake and van Clynne busy gathering their horses, tied a half mile away, now might be an appropriate time to sketch out the general environs of Manhattan island for readers unfamiliar with it. Trust that we will return to our heroes before anything of note occurs.

The northern portions of the island are wooded and hilly, not much different from Morrisania and East Chester across the shore. The Post Road—alternatively called the Road to King's Bridge—runs south from the northeastern corner a ways, then takes a sharp turn to find the center of the island, a kind of noose at the base of the long neck of Manhattan. Fort George and Fort Washington, not to mention a large Hessian encampment in the middle, cut the head off.

A battalion of ghosts haunt the grounds below the star-shaped walls of Fort Washington on the west side of the island. The fort had been the scene less than a year before of the patriots' greatest loss in the war, a terrible and needless strategic blunder.

After Howe had taken the city with a strike from the East River, General Washington retreated and held the Harlem Heights, a strong ridge about halfway across Manhattan. Following a brief but fierce and victorious battle, General Washington once more thought it prudent to retreat, taking up positions in White Plains and the Jerseys.

And leaving behind a contingent at Fort Washington. These battlements consisted of redoubts on a position that commanded the battery above Jeffrey's Hook. Among those who declared they could be held was Jake's mentor Nathanael Greene, who had come from a sickbed to assist Washington in the final stages of New York's defense.

Combined with Fort Lee directly across the river and the assistance of some purposely sunken vessels between them, the Americans sought to block British shipping north. But the British had already shown that the river defenses were no more than a passing nuisance to their boats, and given both the strength and disposition of the English, trying to hold the makeshift fort was a fools' mission.

Unfortunately, those who perished in its defense were brave soldiers, not fools; among the dead were many members of Lieutenant Colonel Thomas Knowlton's Rangers. Those who weren't killed were captured; for all but the officers this was mostly worse than death.

Knowlton himself had been killed earlier during the action at Harlem Heights; in fact, Jake could see the spot as the dawning sun began extending its rays through the trees. Though never assigned to the colonel's troop, he had always considered him a role model. His loss cost the patriots dearly.

But enough sadness. Jake and van Clynne pushed south quickly, hoping to gain as much time for their operations as possible. As they passed James Delancey's farm on the outskirts of the city proper, Jake held out his hand

for van Clynne to slow down; they trotted onto Grand
Street at an almost leisurely pace.

"Hungry?" Jake asked van Clynne.

"Famished," said the Dutchman. "But is it wise to venture onto the seas with a full stomach?"

"You're only going into the harbor."

"Is not the harbor an arm of the sea?"

"I think you need a tall mug of ale, despite the early
hour," said Jake.

"Rum," answered the Dutchman. "Strong rum."

After showing van Clynne inside a small inn where he
was on good terms with the proprietor, Jake ran across
the street to the shop of a purveyor whose name will be
recorded here as William Bebeef. Bebeef was a man valuable to those whose politics coincided with Jake's, doing
good service by them. He was, unfortunately, suspected
by the British of being a member of the Sons of Liberty,
but as of yet he was free to come and go without apprehension. A large part of the reason for this was his fame
as a supplier of various apothecary potions—and a few
formulas that went beyond the usual cures for measles
and love sickness.

Bebeef's encyclopedic knowledge of medicines and
chemistry went far beyond Jake's own, and the agent had
some hope the old man could conjure a temporary cure
for van Clynne's water phobia. But Bebeef was not in the
shop; as a precaution, he'd taken to staying nights with
his sister in Brooklyn. The lad he'd left in charge—woken
with a discreet shake of his cot—was a mere apprentice
who had hardly progressed beyond simple cures for dog
distemper. Jake did not have any time to spend cobbling
together concoctions himself, much less send for Bebeef.
By way of compensation, he borrowed a package the
chemist stored against contingencies, figuring his own
might prove more urgent.

The bundle was a special type of bomb shaped like a
miniature keg, bound of a very light fire wood. A short
fuse ran off each end and was twisted above the middle;
there was the space of perhaps three seconds between
lighting and ignition of the explosive.

The powder at the center of the weapon was packed

very tightly and shaped into an odd series of curlicues, held in place by starch-stiffened paper baffles, which, Bebeef had explained to the boy, acted like a magnifying lens, except that they worked on sound, not light. The effect of his meticulous engineering was to produce an explosion so loud that it could literally stun anyone within fifty feet into a temporary state of shock. Jake had seen one of these "noise kegs" stop the advance of a British column up Long Island last fall. While awkward to use, it was just the thing to cool a hot pursuit. Jake placed the bomb in his saddlebag, intending to reserve it for their escape from the city this afternoon, and then went inside the inn to retrieve his companion.

The Dutchman was on the point of ordering a piece of pie to go with his rum.

"I thought you weren't hungry," said Jake.

"The good woman tells me the pie here is made according to an ancient Dutch recipe, and it would be a shame to pass it by."

"Take it with you then," said Jake. "We have to go."

The Dutchman grumbled, but otherwise offered no protest as Jake called for a bill. "I was thinking," he said, tugging Jake's sleeve. "Perhaps I should take some of that sleeping powder with me, in case I have trouble aboard ship."

"I have no more," said Jake, "and there isn't time to prepare any. Besides, if you're caught with it, Howe will realize something's up."

"Only after he wakes."

"The operation depends on his never suspecting a thing. Here," said Jake, reaching into the scabbard at his belt and producing the assassin's knife. "Carry this with you."

"That skinny thing?" Van Clynne pushed the dagger aside on the table. "I have my own knife, thank you."

"It's not just a knife. You see this?" Jake pointed at the ruby.

"I rather doubt the general will be bribed by such a bauble."

"The knife is used only by members of the British Secret Department. The fact that you have it will signify to

Howe that you're a special agent. It will make him trust you."

"Really?" Van Clynne picked the knife up and examined it carefully. "The Secret Department?"

Jake nodded solemnly. Van Clynne turned the weapon over in his hand.

"Will they believe a Dutchman is part of their army?"

"I don't see why not," said Jake quickly, trying to boost his companion's morale. In truth, the higher ranking officers might. He hoped van Clynne wouldn't have to put it to the test. "The British are not very given to asking questions where the department is concerned," he added truthfully. "Generally, their agents have only one mission —to kill someone. They've assassinated princes all over Europe. Supposedly, they've even killed a pope or two."

"And who should I say I'm supposed to kill?"

"You don't say under any circumstances. If you do, they'll have to kill you."

The reader will be left to imagine the conversation as it proceeded, with van Clynne continuing to question the contingencies and Jake continuing to assure him that it would not matter. The discussion continued in hushed tones as they rode amid early rising British soldiers and local residents to Pearl Street, where the boat to take van Clynne to Howe would be waiting.

The masts of the British Navy, along with the various commercial vessels in port, formed a hedgerow across the front of Brooklyn Heights. Admiral Lord Richard Howe's flagship the *Eagle*, where his brother General Sir William Howe was staying, was a good distance out, near Staten Island. It was a heady, proud ship of the line, and while far from the biggest in the British fleet, nonetheless it was a leviathan here.

Van Clynne tried not to look at any part of the water, not even the seafront before them as they approached the port. Instead he conjured the vision of his pleasantly landlocked homestead. He could see himself staring up at the long gabled roof, admiring the smart windows, the small roof over the door. All he had to do was close his eyes, get across the water, and give Howe his bullet.

"Oh my God!" said van Clynne suddenly. "I don't have the bullet."

"I've got it right here," said Jake. "Relax."

The admonition was answered by a sharp smack across the back that sent Jake flying into the dust. It had not come from van Clynne—the sergeant of the guard and three of his minions stood before the portly Dutchman.

Twenty-nine

Wherein, van Clynne overcomes his fear of water in a
most unconventional but expedient manner.

"**W**here are the two men I sent to escort you last night?" the sergeant demanded of van Clynne.

"What do you mean, knocking my friend down?" responded the Dutchman. "And where did you come from?"

"We have been standing right here the whole time. You would have seen us if not for your incessant jabbering. Your friend would do well to stay out of our way," he added. "Or perhaps we will find some use for him."

"You can be sure that I will make a full report of this to General Howe," said van Clynne.

"Never mind that. What did you do to my men?"

"Your men," replied the squire with consternation equal to the sergeant's, "can't hold their liquor. They took me to a tavern and proceeded to make a spectacle of themselves. I had come to expect more from the British Army. It had been said, in fact, that the men of your regiment were considerably more accomplished at whoring than the army as a whole." Van Clynne touched the point of the sergeant's sword gingerly, then pushed it away. "The next time you post an honor guard, I would expect the chosen men to be of a higher caliber. If they want to guard me, then they had better keep up with me in all departments."

The sergeant's face, which had started so haughty and self-assured, began to melt into a slippery mass of confusion. With van Clynne in control, Jake's presence was only an unnecessary complication; he was best off slipping away.

Except that the bullet had flown from his hand before van Clynne could grab it. Now where was it?

On hands and knees Jake scoured the ground in search of the ball as van Clynne continued to harangue the sergeant. The Dutchman had a special quality about him when he really got going. Here was a man who might sell London Bridge back to the king.

Ah, but could he sell it to Miss Pinkleton, who must be the redheaded girl at the very far end of the block? What other young woman would be dressed so smartly this early in the day, and walking here besides? The sergeant —and the nearby whaleboat—had obviously been waiting for her, not van Clynne.

Jake saw the girl with one eye; with the other he spotted the bullet in the dust. He scooped it up and jumped to his feet.

"Now that I see you're in good hands," he told van Clynne, "I'll be taking my leave. General Bacon is expecting me." He reached into his pocket and took out a blank paper; as he handed it to van Clynne he passed the bullet along with it. "You'll give General Howe my note?"

"Oh, yes," said van Clynne.

"Let me see that," said the sergeant, grabbing at the paper.

The bullet rolled from van Clynne's palm down his jacket sleeve well before he let go of the paper. The sergeant opened the scrap furiously—only to discover it was blank.

"Naturally," said Jake. "You don't think I'm going to risk something like that falling into rebel hands. They're all around us, even here."

There was a definite magic ink craze in the colonies, the sergeant concluded; next he would find one used for a shopping list. But there was nothing to do but give it to van Clynne.

"Row him out to the general. I'm sure he'll find him a comfortable companion."

"I'm not leaving this spot without an apology," said

van Clynne. "My friend was knocked down and I was treated most rudely. I deserve an apology, and possibly restitution."

"Don't push your luck," said the sergeant.

Though van Clynne's sense of dignity had little need for prodding, he continued to protest as part of a delaying tactic initiated by certain frantic hand signals and gestures Jake made as he ran off down the street.

The secret agent, careful to block Miss Pinkleton's view of the confrontation, doffed his hat with a sweeping gesture as she approached. Red curls flowed from beneath her bonnet, and her light purple dress flared in a satiny glow from her hips. She might be sixteen. Certainly she had not wielded her fan often, as he could tell from the awkward way she unfolded it and tried to flutter it before her face.

"Miss Melanie Pinkleton?"

"Yes," she replied in a bashful voice.

"Allow me to introduce myself," said Jake as he straightened. "I am Jake Gibbs, on special assignment to General Howe."

"Oh," said the young woman. "Pleased to meet you."

Jake stood closer, speaking in confidential tones. He was more than a foot taller than she was; her body was so slight he could easily have tucked her under an arm and carried her away.

But these operations required a certain delicacy, with Howe's guards only a half block away.

"The general has asked me to speak with you confidentially."

"I'm on my way to see him now."

"Here, quickly, come this way with me," Jake said, tugging her arm in the direction of a side street.

"I'm not going anywhere with you."

"Please," said Jake, smiling with all of his might. "You would not wish to present a scene on ship, would you?"

A look came over her face, the dark threatening cloud that spoils a perfect summer afternoon. "It's her, isn't it? Mrs. Loring."

Jake nodded solemnly. Miss Melanie Pinkleton suddenly appeared close to tears.

"He told me he was going to break it off with her," she said, her voice breaking.

"Come with me, Melanie," said Jake, gently wrapping his arm around her shoulder. "Let us talk for a bit in private. I know a fine tavern nearby, run by a friend of mine, a certain Paul Smith."

"He's a rebel!"

"Well," said Jake, "we wouldn't want to hold that against him, would we?"

Undoubtedly, a philosopher of the four humors basic to human life would be able to explain van Clynne's fear of the ocean as an imbalance relating to the overabundance of liquid in his person; like naturally repels like, and thus he seeks to avoid it at all cost. Van Clynne's own theory related to a childhood memory—he had been dropped into a large barrel of water as a child and held down for several minutes, and ever since worried about being drowned.

The squire is a man of business and not science, and thus will be forgiven for mistaking the origin of his fear. The relevance here, however, is that once in the rowboat, he could think of nothing but that event, and as a result, his knees began shaking so badly the sergeant charged with rowing him to Howe demanded to know what the problem was.

"Yer gonna shake us right into the water, laddie. Get a grip on yer knees."

Van Clynne nodded weakly and pulled them together with his hands.

"First time out in a boat?"

Van Clynne shook his head. With even this gentle motion his stomach threatened evasive maneuvers.

"First time with a Scotsman, I daresay," ventured the sergeant. "Yer in good hands, laddie—never lost one yet."

Van Clynne gave him a brief, weak smile, his eyes still locked on the floorboards. The wood, though wet, allowed him at least a vague fantasy that he was on the solid ground of an old tavern.

"Have ya ever seen a bonnet as smart as this one?" offered the Scotsman, trying to divert van Clynne's attention. He was referring to his headgear, one of the most distinctive marks of his unit, the 42nd Royal Highland Regiment of Foot, aka the Black Watch. A round, overgrown beanie with a plaid band and a large, fuzzy crown that shot up above the wearer's head, it looked as if an exotic, blue-skinned animal had encamped on his head.

The oarsman's idea of stealing the Dutchman's attention from the sea was a good one, and might have worked especially well in this case, given van Clynne's strong feelings on the subject of hats. Unfortunately, his question had the effect of drawing van Clynne's eyes to his head—and the vast blue ocean behind it.

In no more than a second, the squire's view changed from sea green ocean to dark, blank space. Van Clynne had fainted.

"In short, miss, the general is a rogue." Jake pushed her coffee cup aside—for some reason, Paul Smith's inn was always out of tea—and leaned across the table to take her hands. "Your affections are wasted on him."

"But he is so handsome and . . ."

Her voice trailed off.

"And you love him?"

She started crying again. Jake took a new handkerchief and pressed it gently on her cheeks.

Now the reader will undoubtedly protest that Jake Gibbs calling another man a rogue was but the latest chapter in the famous history of pot and kettle. But Jake is not without his moral codes, and he is not being completely hypocritical here, given the girl's tender age. Besides, he has a much larger purpose in mind.

"I wonder if this whole episode is not the story of our country in a nutshell," said Jake, helping her dry her tears. "The British beguile us, take what they want, and leave us for someone else."

The girl, gaining control of herself, looked at him coldly. "You're a rebel, aren't you?"

"A patriot, perhaps, not a rebel, miss," he said, smiling. "But what I've told you about the general is true enough. He has a wife at home, you know, and many mistresses. Mrs. Loring is just the most infamous."

"We've sworn allegiance to the king."

"Does that mean we should let the British treat us as chattel? Should we be subservient to their foulest desires? Don't we owe allegiance to ourselves first?"

"You speak well, sir. I fear you're merely trying to take advantage of me, like the general."

Jake rose to go. "Not at all. But if you're more interested in love than politics, you might find Smith's lad there of some interest. And about your own age."

Miss Melanie frowned, but Jake noted that she not only stayed seated as he walked toward the door, but motioned to the boy that her cup was in need of refilling.

"God, he's a plump one."

"I don't see why we're fighting for these Tories. They're living off the fat of the land, and we barely get a lime every other week."

"Sharp now, don't drop him. Watch it!"

Van Clynne plunged unceremoniously to the deck of the flagship. The seamen undid the ropes they had used to hoist him, leaving him sprawled like a beached octopus.

The fall to the deck caused a slight concussion and headache; it also raised certain voices in van Clynne's head, most prominent among them those of his father and grandfather, who told him to get off his duff and get on with the business of winning back the family estate.

Van Clynne was helped to his feet by a member of the general's guard. The soldier escorted him to the quarterdeck of the *Eagle*, where Howe sat on a couch under a red-striped tarpaulin before the captain's quarters. He looked for all the world as if he were enjoying breakfast on his country estate, having just come in from the hunt. A soldier stood behind him as a waiter; two guards were a few yards back. Otherwise the quarterdeck was empty. The ship itself had only a bare skeleton crew aboard.

Many people have had their criticisms of General

Howe, but no one has ever claimed he was not a gentleman of the highest order. After his visitor was announced as an important messenger from the Canadian provinces, Howe raised his hand and with a sweeping invitation asked van Clynne if he had "supped."

"No, sir," said the Dutchman, still not recovered from his journey. "It is a bit early in the morning for dinner."

"Well, join me anyway," said the general. "My officers are seeing to their troops, and my brother is off on an inspection. I do not like to eat alone. I am awaiting a visitor, but you can keep me company until then."

"Miss Pinkleton has been delayed," said van Clynne unwisely. The general's face clouded as the Dutchman fished for an alibi. "There was some sort of commotion at the shore. I heard several women fighting, I believe."

"Damn. It was Mrs. Loring, wasn't it? They saw each other, did they?"

Van Clynne shrugged.

"Well, come sit with me. Damn. Women will be my ruin."

"I agree with that, sir. Most heartily. Men are always too generous in their affections, and it leads us to vulnerability."

Jake's instructions had been simple and direct—get aboard, give Howe the bullet, and come back to New York as quickly as possible. But several things occurred to van Clynne at the moment. First, that this might be an opportunity to gain valuable intelligence from the general about his battle plans, information that General Washington would cherish so deeply the return of his land would be beyond question. Second, Jake had no legal authority over him. Third, even if he were still feeling a bit seasick, that was no reason not to eat something.

And last but not least, anything he could do to delay the torture of another water crossing was well worth the effort or risk.

So he sat down to dine with General Howe, and with the first whiff of food felt his stomach undertake a remarkable recovery. Indeed, the plate had lain on the table no more than half a minute before van Clynne allowed as how perhaps he was feeling a bit hungry after all. The general smiled, and instructed his man to bring another helping. The food was rabbit, skillfully cooked in what the general claimed was a French style, slowly roasted on a spit.

"It is excellent, Your Generalship, but I must protest its appellation. Good Dutch housewives have been preparing rabbit this way for a hundred years or more."

"Is that so?"

"Yes, and a bit of wild parsley, I dare say, would add more flavor."

Howe was pleased by the fact that he was eating in a style that owed its origin not to a cowardly if formidable enemy, but one that had been defeated more than a hundred years before. His mood grew steadily expansive, aided by several draughts of what he called his "morning Madeira." Within half an hour he had forgotten his disappointing new mistress completely.

Van Clynne, too, began to feel more and more in command of the situation. It would not be an exaggeration to say that he envisioned himself as being in a position to change the course of the war, not merely with the message he was delivering, but with his sharp business sense. For what else is war but a negotiation brought to its extreme? And who was this man sitting across from him but the head negotiator for the other side, at least in this section of the continent? A man strongly partial to the American side, according to all reports.

Two eminent men of business, sitting down to lunch— untold fortunes had been made this way.

Who among us has not been carried away by such grand visions? Especially when the wine is good and flowing so freely?

"Is this not the best wine you've tasted in the colonies?" Howe demanded as they paused, waiting for their chocolate.

"Begging your pardon, sir, but wine is wine. The Portuguese are experts at it, but it is just a fashion. Now ale— ale is all together an art."

"Ale? That's a commoner's drink."

"On the contrary. It has been blessed by kings, even in your great country. Why, it came from the Egyptians themselves—I have it on good authority that their pyramidic-shaped temples were actually brew houses."

"Indeed," said Howe. He was not used to finding underlings so knowledgeable or agreeable.

"Do you have any aboard?"

"Pyramids?"

"Good British ale, General," said van Clynne, bumping up Howe's patriotism. "This drink the Portuguese make—well, it will do for breakfast, I suppose, but I have always wondered what the English could do if they decided to be grape growers. Then we would have wine. You have only to taste British ale and you understand perfection. But I wonder if the Portuguese hold back with the wine they ship out of their country. I tell you, sir, I don't fully trust them. They are very warlike."

"Warlike?"

"Naturally aggressive. I wonder if they aren't using some of their islands as a base for spying on England. I have often thought of how they might be defeated in a war. I would much like to hear your famous tactical skills applied to such a problem."

"A flanking assault, of course," said Howe, his voice assuming the strong tone of a man born to lead troops to battle—not to mention draw vast squiggles and arrows on oversized maps. "Sailor, a cask of the best ale on deck immediately! And find out where our chocolate is."

Thirty

*Wherein, Jake arranges a reception for the British
messenger Herstraw.*

*W*hatever the state of Revolutionary fervor in New
York City prior to its invasion, its capture by the British
greatly amplified the presence of Tories there. By now
the city had become a safe haven for all manner of Loyalists. In direct proportion it became inhospitable to true
patriots. But this did not mean that there were none left
among its citizens. On the contrary. Many of the vast
population, especially the lower rungs of working people,
stood by Liberty's flame, though they'd taken the precaution of hiding it beneath a bushel. And there were still
Sons of Liberty about, as well as a good number of regu-
lar spies—one of whom Jake was on his way to contact.

The meeting place will surprise many students of New
York's politics, for it was nowhere else than the coffeehouse of James Rivington. This is the same Rivington
who publishes the *Gazette,* that hideous newspaper that
has given vent to the most evil mutterings against the
Cause of Freedom imaginable.

So how, then, to explain that Rivington's was the headquarters for one of General Washington's most accomplished spies, Culper Junior? How to explain that this
Culper Junior—as he remains under cover, we will use
only his code name—worked for Rivington and, by some
accounts, owned half the coffee shop with him? Was it
merely a perfect cover? Was Rivington, a notoriously
loudmouthed British apologist, a double agent? Or a
fool?

Jake wasn't sure. He knew only that Culper Junior was

completely loyal to the Cause. Beyond that, the coffeehouse was a perfect place to set up shop as a spy; not only was it the preferred place for Royalists to gather and discuss business, but nearly every British officer in the city of any importance spent some part of his day there. Any child with half a wit could gather a full dossier simply by wandering among the tables.

Culper Junior was neither a child nor someone possessing only half a wit. He noticed Jake at the door amid the early morning crowd immediately, and arranged to have one of his lads present him with a note directly: "Next to the Coffeehouse Bridge. Five minutes."

The Coffeehouse Bridge is not a bridge at all, but rather a long wooden platform running down Wall Street for about a block between Dock and Queen streets. Ordinarily it is used for auctions; the reader might envision it as a stage set in the middle of an area convenient for commerce, and not be far wrong.

Exactly five minutes after he had taken up his station, Jake was met by the small boy who had handed him the note in Rivington's. "Met" was not quite precise; this was a clever lad, who took the precaution of approaching Jake with mock nonchalance. Suddenly darting toward him, he tugged at Jake's shirt as if stealing something, and ran away. Jake marveled at the ruse—there was nothing in his shirt to steal, of course—and charged through the traffic with mock abandon.

The boy was quite fast, and his sudden bursts left Jake winded by the time they reached the alley where his appointment would be kept. The lad stopped short and pointed to a door. Jake smiled, patted him on the head and tossed him two pence as he opened it.

With this much preparation to keep them from being detected, Jake felt his confidence growing that this difficult business would be quickly concluded. Imagine his surprise and chagrin, therefore, when he was met inside the door by a German jaeger and his bayonet point.

Jake was not weaponless; besides the pocket pistol, he had his large officer's pistol in the side of his belt. But it was not primed, and in any event, by the time he retrieved it the Hessian would have stitched a decorative five-cornered star pattern on his chest. Discretion, therefore, was called for—Jake smiled, held his hands out as a sign of error and no harm done. His mind worked desperately for the few German words he knew; "mistake" must be among them, but for the moment the only one he could recall with any certainty was *bier*, obviously inappropriate.

The mercenary held his position but did not advance. Jake reached back for the door latch and realized that either it had changed shape and location or another soldier with his bayonet extended was standing behind him. Slowly and as calmly as possible he took a step to the side, offering a sign of surrender with his hands. He still had his forged British warrants and identity papers; surely he could work this out given time.

Granted, time was not one of his most plentiful commodities. He consoled himself by noting that at least van Clynne would be halfway back from the ship by now.

"The trick is in the malt," van Clynne said, swirling his mug around and then holding the cup toward the general. "You see the toasted color? That is all flavor, sir. All flavor, I assure you."

The general studied the liquid, then took a sip. He swished it around his mouth as van Clynne had demonstrated, rolling his tongue first to one side then the other before swallowing.

"I never understood that there was so much science to drinking beer," said Howe.

"It is a great, deliberate science," said van Clynne, signaling to the sailor to refill their glasses. "What's more, it is an art."

"You don't have to be anywhere in particular?"

"General, I am completely at your disposal."

"Very good," said Howe, reaching for his mug, "very good. You shall join my officers in a small discussion. You can tell us what you've seen of the Neutral Ground and its defenses. Clinton in particular—an antidote to his pomposity would be very welcome, I dare say."

"With pleasure, sir; with pleasure."

* * *

Jake had backed himself completely to the wall. There were now four Hessians guarding him. The men wore green and red uniforms, and would have been identified by Jake as members of the Hesse-Cassel Field Jaeger Corps, a crack unit composed primarily of hunters and riflemen who had much the same reputation for toughness and accuracy in shooting as the frontier elements of the Pennsylvania militia.

Except for one small detail, which loomed large in the well-trained eye of the patriot agent: They had bayonets.

The bayonet is a most deadly and efficient weapon; theoreticians of warfare claim with much validity that it, not the bullet, is the true vanquisher on the battlefield. But the bayonet was not typically fixed to a rifle, which was the jaegers' weapon of choice. Nor were these rifles —the knives had their stems slotted into standard-issue British Brown Bess muskets.

Riflemen with muskets?

This lack of syntactical symmetry might mean many things, not least among them that the British had decided to handicap their most effective units with weapons ill-suited to their tactics.

Or perhaps not. The side door promptly opened to reveal Culper Junior, smiling and laughing. The rest of the company quickly joined in.

Sons of Liberty in disguise.

"How do you like our Germans?" said Culper, clapping Jake on the back.

"They've got the wrong guns."

"Still, they fooled you." Culper's amusement quickly passed when he saw that Jake wasn't laughing. "I'm sorry for the trouble, but we have to take many precautions these days. There are Tory informers everywhere."

"I need your help intercepting a messenger," said Jake. "He's on his way to General Howe."

"Howe is on his brother's flagship in the harbor."

"Exactly." A look passed between them indicating there was considerably more to the story, but that it would not be made explicit. "Can I borrow your German troop? We have to move quickly."

"They're at your disposal," said Culper. "As is my lieutenant, Mark Daltoons."

Herstraw and his escort had passed the eight-mile stone south of Day's Tavern on the King's Bridge Road down to the city by the time one of Culper's boys—the same who had led Jake to his "trap"—spotted them. That left precious little time to arrange the diversion at McGowan's Pass, less than a mile away.

It had been at McGowan's Pass the previous September that a stout group of American patriots held off Clinton's advance guard, keeping them at bay while Washington and Putnam regrouped at the Harlem Heights above. The action here this afternoon was considerably less severe, but just as hotly contested—the British messenger and his escort, along with some sentries routinely posted to the area, found themselves suddenly under heavy bombardment.

The first egg hit Herstraw square in the forehead. Just as he opened his mouth to protest, it was filled with a putrid, year-old apple—half bitten, incidentally, by one of the attacking troops, none of whom was over ten years old.

Three dozen young lads held the woods above the ravine, raining all manner of vegetable debris on the helpless redcoats. A brilliantly coordinated hammer and anvil movement had left the troop trapped in the defile. Just as the first egg was lobbed, the hammer was launched—a large cart of manure was dumped over the side of the hill behind the troop, cutting off retreat. And then the anvil: at the head of the column, two large and odoriferous carcasses of former cows were deposited on signal from a trapezelike device in the trees.

The assault being made by children, the British troops found themselves frustrated to the extreme. They dared not fire, for fear of hitting one of the urchins and causing a major incident; yet they could not advance in the face of what was a rather ferocious stream of rancid fruit and vegetables, together with some rocks and miscellaneous debris.

They formed a defensive perimeter as best they could,

and once their assailants' ammunition ran low, dispatched a party to rout out the young rebels. The boys led these on a merry chase, avoiding capture yet staying close enough to entice the soldiers onward. In this way, the messenger was delayed nearly an hour until close to one P.M., and his guard force much depleted.

Herstraw was heard to complain as they marched south that never had he witnessed such a poor state of affairs as that experienced over the past few days. The colonials were harassing the whole countryside. Common thieves, such as the scoundrels who stole all of Roelff's plate and silver before trying to set the inn on fire the night before, ran rampant. Children were able to make fools of a company of handpicked grenadiers. Perhaps, said Herstraw, the British were not preordained to win this war as he had earlier believed.

This brought strenuous objection from the captain, and the two officers were still arguing when they were met in the road by a small group of Hessians up from the harbor. Had it not been for this disagreement, the captain might not have left Herstraw; like most other British soldiers, he had no respect for the Germans, though their army was as professional as his. But his orders were only to conduct the messenger into the city, and here they were standing at the intersection of Broad and George streets, well within the precincts of the north ward. If the truth be told, Herstraw had been quite a pain the whole way; the captain was only too glad to be rid of him. With no other ceremony, he promptly turned his men around and marched northwards to reassemble his force.

Herstraw was impressed that Howe had sent out another guard, even if it was composed of foreigners. The only English speaker was a young man of thin build who hardly looked old enough to shave. Nonetheless, the young man wore the markings of a sergeant; if the promotion was due to his exploits on the battlefield instead of experience, well, so much the better. The fact that the sergeant was on horseback also did not arouse suspicion, but their path through the city—down Wall and then over Queen, heading away from the fort—did.

"The general has set up an auxiliary headquarters,"

explained the sergeant. He had an apologetic tone in his voice. "It has to do, well, you know of Mrs. Loring, I assume."

Herstraw showed great restraint in not asking any further questions, and the sergeant displayed equal discretion in not volunteering further information. In fact, such discretion might be thought unparalleled—provided, of course, that the man were truly what he claimed he was. But if such were the case, he would never have conducted Herstraw to Nicoll's mansion, which had been temporarily appropriated by the Sons of Liberty under Jake's direction a half hour before.

Nicoll was a Tory who had fled the city some months before the British invasion and hadn't yet found the chance to return. The house had a good view of the east ward and the harbor. The officers from one of the guard companies who occupied it had just so happened to be called out on special assignment a few moments before Jake's arrival.

Well, perhaps this wasn't entirely a coincidence, since they had been called out to look specifically for Mr. Gibbs, who was now suspected of having been involved in the firing of New York the previous fall. At least that was what the warrant claimed. Considering that the warrant also described Mr. Gibbs as being five-foot-two, with black hair and brown eyes and well past his prime, perhaps the warrant should not be fully believed.

In any event, the front room of the mansion was now under the control of a lieutenant and his aide. (The lieutenant bore a remarkable resemblance to Culper Junior's own chief lieutenant, Mark Daltoons, and the aide, if not for the mustache, looked somewhat like the real Jake Gibbs.) Herstraw was marched before them and presented by the sergeant, who snapped to attention with all the ceremony of a guard presiding at Buckingham Palace.

"Very good, Sergeant, that will do," said the lieutenant as his aide inconspicuously took up a position behind the messenger. "Mr. William Herstraw, I presume. Do you have identification?"

Herstraw took out his coin and handed it toward the lieutenant, who waved it to his aide. The assistant

plucked the coin from the messenger's hand and slid it
into his pocket.

"I am given to understand you have a message for the
general," said the lieutenant. His accent made him sound
as if he had come from Westminster not a week before—
a remarkable achievement for Daltoons, who had never
been farther east than Brooklyn.

The elaborate fiction he and Jake had constructed here
was aimed not at retrieving the bullet—that could be
done as soon as Daltoons leaned forward, pressing the
lever attached to the pistol wired beneath the desk. The
Sons hoped to follow Herstraw through the city after he
made his delivery, thereby gathering hints about the British messenger network. Jake had let himself be persuaded on this point by Culper Junior, but in truth had
some doubts about whether Herstraw would agree to
hand over the bullet without a struggle.

"My orders are to see the general in person," said the
messenger.

"I'm afraid that won't be possible," answered the lieutenant. "That is against procedure."

"Nonetheless, those are my orders. I'll wait until he's
undisposed, if that's the problem."

"That would be a very long time," said the mus-
tachioed aide, who had his pocket pistol loaded out of
sight up his sleeve.

"General Burgoyne gave the order to me directly, and
I am honor bound to carry it out," said Herstraw, turning
to face the aide. "Excuse me, but have we met?"

"I don't believe so."

"Why do you wear a mustache?"

The aide—we all know it's Jake, don't we?—feigned
embarrassment before answering.

"It's to hide a scar I received. My upper lip was cut at
Lexington."

"Lexington? Whom did you serve under?"

"I was serving under the lieutenant here."

"Impossible. His unit was not in Boston at the time."
Herstraw rose and took a step back as recognition
flooded into his eyes. "I know you!"

Thirty-one

Wherein, Jake finds himself pursued through the streets of New York.

It's nice to be recognized, but only if recognition brings with it some token of esteem or affection. The only thing displayed by the spy was a pistol, which he promptly leveled at Jake's chest. This gained him a temporary advantage, allowing him to ease back toward the door.

His retreat removed him from the aim of Daltoons's rigged pistol. But neither Jake nor Daltoons was too concerned, since the sergeant and his Hessians were standing outside the door, prepared for this contingency. In fact, as Herstraw reached for the door handle, Daltoons dove to the floor, out of the line of fire—the ersatz Hessians had orders to shoot if the door was opened without a signal from Jake.

The maneuver was premature. The contingent of British officers roused from the building earlier had chosen this moment to return with a company of their men. Angry at having been sent on an apparent wild goose chase, the officers were surprised to see their posts taken up by Hessians, and more surprised still when one of them shot at them. A general cry and alarm went up, a shout, a shot, a great number of alarms—Chaos, the great, disorganized goddess of riot and confusion, had arrived on the scene.

And not a moment too soon. Jake leapt forward, throwing his body into Herstraw's as the British messenger ducked in the doorway. Herstraw's bullet missed him as they crashed to the floor. Jake lost his pocket pistol in the tumble and had to settle for a few hard strokes with his fist against Herstraw's chin. The British messenger responded with a surprisingly robust chop to Jake's kidneys, followed by an even more painful smash with his knee to the American's stomach.

Jake rolled away. Herstraw made the mistake of interpreting his retreat as surrender, rising to his knees and grabbing for the Segallas. But as his fingers touched the handle of the small gun, his insides suddenly burned with an intense, unquenchable fire. Jake's elk-handled knife sliced through the tender flap of skin just under the edge of his rib cage and danced through his arteries and organs in a grim minuet of death, draining his strength. In the next moment it drained his life as well—Jake reached forward and perforated Herstraw's throat, blood spilling across the floor in a vicious spurt.

Daltoons, meanwhile, jumped to his feet and secured the door against the maelstrom outside. Jake took his Segallas back from the dead man, grabbed the silver bullet from Herstraw's boot and followed Daltoons to the window.

The gunfire outside the room suddenly stopped, and the two men dove through the glass just as the British soldiers crashed in the door.

Aboard Howe's flagship, van Clynne and the general had conceded that, as a rule, the hops added to British beer left something to be desired. Wilder breeds would bring more exotic flavors, van Clynne maintained, and the general could find little to argue with there. In fact, the general was starting to show signs that he would find little to argue with anywhere today. His normally reticent tongue had been loosened by the large meal and the equally plentiful drink, and he had begun to find his guest, at first invited solely for the purpose of offering him some company on an otherwise dull morning before his staff meeting, stimulating and interesting. Though Dutch, this van Clynne displayed a pleasing etiquette that complemented his wide-ranging knowledge. He seemed well-acquainted with even the most minute piece of history connected with the province, Dutch especially. He also appreciated the vast difficulties the general had with the administration of his task.

The colonists were a strange bunch, both men agreed. Here the general and his brother Lord Richard had shown great leniency, all the patience of overindulgent fathers, and yet their many entreaties had been scorned. "I show mercy in the Jerseys," said Howe, "and I am repaid with Trenton! Imagine, attacking on Christmas Day!"

"Scandalous," agreed his guest.

Howe had rarely seen such a facile grasp of the facts and situation, nor felt such a sympathy with a man he had just met. In short, van Clynne was just the sort he wished to have on his staff as a civilian assistant, and the general was getting around to asking if he would consider such a position when he realized, somewhat to his chagrin, that he had yet to receive the message van Clynne had come to deliver.

"Well, Sir William, yes, it is time to get down to business indeed," said van Clynne, who in fact felt that another hour of talk and he would have this entire Revolution wrapped with a bow. "I have spent this past several days in hurried flight from Montreal, ordered to meet you by General Burgoyne himself."

At the mention of the rival general, Howe's entire mood changed. "Gentleman Johnny," he spat, using the name as a sailor might a curse. "He's nothing but a playwright."

"And a bad one at that."

"It is a sad reflection on our state that such a man has been promoted to a position of power," admitted Howe. "I myself only took the post as commander in America because I saw it as my solemn duty. Like many others, I hesitated to fight such a war against our brothers. You know that I have always had the greatest sympathy for Americans."

"Who could blame you?"

"But our hesitation allows men like Burgoyne to march through. Gentleman Johnny, indeed."

"He wears ridiculous hats," said van Clynne, laying on the worst insult he could think of.

* * *

Jake found himself in the street, holding the stolen silver bullet in one hand and the bloody knife he had used to kill Herstraw in the other. The soldiers in the building began yelling and loading their guns; Jake took advantage of the short respite to run like hell.

As usual in Revolutionary campaigns, the British were slow to pursue. They had mustered all of their men for a frontal assault, and took their time regrouping. Daltoons tossed Jake a pistol and then ducked down an alley to the right; Jake decided they would do better by splitting up, and ran straight ahead. Along the way, he dropped the redcoat jacket and other parts of the uniform, hoping to look like a civilian; he also wiped the blood-soaked knife and slipped it inside his boot, not wanting it to incriminate him if he managed to pass into the crowd on the street.

Unfortunately, there was no crowd to pass into. The soldiers made their appearance a block behind him and began their chase in earnest. They had their bayonets fixed and gleaming, and ran with the abandon of lions chasing the Christians in ancient Rome. Still, Jake might have escaped except for the untimely arrival of a group of cavalry from the west.

New York City being a garrison town, one British unit or another was always within rock-throwing distance. This troop, in fact, was within half that mark—as they began to comply with their fellows' cries for assistance, Jake scooped a stone from the pavement and let it fly directly in the face of the lead man. It hit not him but his horse, which was the next best thing. The animal reeled, alarming and confusing its mates; Jake had just enough time to dive into a building on his right.

This admirably handy edifice was owned by one Madame Terese Lucia DeCose. Madame was a French dressmaker who had arrived ten years before from the banks of the Seine, armed only with a long needle and some sharp ideas of fashion. Like many immigrants, she saw America as a ripe opportunity for advancement and a fresh start. With only occasional backsliding into her old profession—in Paris, Madame DeCose was what was known as a courtesan—she had achieved her American dream. Her shop was patronized by a small but monied group of New York women, a handful of whom happened to be there this afternoon to listen to madame discourse on the latest trends in brocades.

Jake saluted them most politely as he dashed through the front room with its displays. Faced with a choice at the end of the hall, he went left into a room that happened to have a window opening onto an alley. It also had a patron in a very advanced stage of undress, as she was getting ready for a fitting of a new stay and gown.

Under normal circumstances, Jake would have found some way to console her exposed embarrassment at being found naked. The fact that she was only nineteen, of extremely graceful shape and with very fair—and natural—blond hair would have made it a most difficult chore, but Jake would have borne this penance somehow, managing a cheerful, brave face.

But these were not normal circumstances, and Jake had to leave this delicate task to the British, following hard behind. The woman's screams had the effect of not only directing the soldiers to Jake's escape route, but hurrying them along. He was barely out the window when they burst through the door. One of the men fired a gun, and its bullet whizzed past him as he fled up the alley.

An alley closed off on one end by the approaching cavalry, and on the other by a brick wall.

The wall belonged to an older building, which had suffered much from the elements; with a leap, Jake found a good enough handhold to boost himself to a second floor ledge, and from there to the roof. This was nearly fatal; he slipped on the tiling and nearly tumbled back to the ground. Momentum, fortunately, had given him just enough impetus to move in a diagonal across the roof, and Jake managed to fall against a chimney and propel himself in a ricochet straight onto the gable of an adjoining building.

The crash rattled his teeth and not a few of his bones, but his unexpected course—and the damsel in distress—had thrown off the pursuit. Jake now had a small space to escape in. Without waiting to catch his breath, he scrambled up the roof and over the side, sliding toward the corner, where he hoped to find a rain spout that would provide a handhold to climb down. His luck was with him and he began to rapidly descend—only to run out of spout considerably short of the ground. He had to jump nearly twenty feet.

At first it was not obvious that the sharp pain in his knee was anything other than a temporary complaint. Jake hobbled a few steps toward the road, more concerned about the sounds of redcoats rallying than the grinding of his leg bones together. In fact, when he met a wagon at the end of the alley, he didn't even bother pausing before levering himself over it.

He did more than pause on the other side, however—he collapsed in a heap as his leg gave way. It was only with the greatest exertion of energy—and a few close musket balls—that Jake managed to stand and pull himself aboard a horse tied to a nearby post. He yanked the leather stays loose and the animal obliged his deepest wishes by fleeing up the street.

Thirty-two

Wherein, Jake's injuries are discovered to be acute, and van Clynne concludes his negotiations.

New Yorkers are a funny lot. They have no greater or lesser esteem for the rule of law than citizens elsewhere; they are not, as one writer (undoubtedly a Tory) has charged, "a sorry class of criminals intent on knifing as many of their fellows as they meet before bedtime." But they are a particularly focused people, and when on a mission connected with business, can be quite single-minded about achieving it. Thus they tend to ignore things that, in retrospect, strike outsiders as impossible to ignore.

The shouts of the redcoats chasing Jake, for instance. No vast flood of citizens came to the soldiers' assistance, no vigilante Tories sprung up to seize Jake's horse and hand him over to the authorities. The soldiers were naturally disappointed. But this was the entire experience of the British in the New World. They felt that all they would have to do was show up, shout a bit, and the Revolutionaries would be nabbed before they could turn the corner down William Street.

Such was the gist of Howe's complaints that very moment aboard ship in the harbor. He was quite unaware of what was going on in the city, of course, but he would not have been too terribly surprised.

Van Clynne was quite aware that he had stretched out his visit considerably longer than necessary, and notwithstanding the difficulty of his return across the water, was now anxious to leave. But his mention of Canada had provoked the general into telling the sad tale of his

brother George's death at Ticonderoga during the
French and Indian War. He seemed almost on the verge
of becoming weepy. This was no way for a general of
Howe's station to act; the entire scene was becoming unseemly.

"Buck up, man, buck up," said van Clynne. Much to
his surprise, and the general's, he slapped Howe across
the face.

This brought Howe to his senses, not necessarily a wise
thing to do.

"I could have you tied to the anchor and dragged
across the harbor for that."

"I was only trying to say, Sir William, that you are
forgetting your assets."

"I'm not forgetting anything, you fool. I command the
entire British Army; what do you command?"

"Myself, occasionally." Brave words, though van
Clynne was trembling inside. Nonetheless, he had
learned long ago in business negotiations that, once you
have someone's attention, you must proceed quickly or
risk total failure. "This bullet contains a message from
General Burgoyne. I was instructed to deliver it personally to you, General. Here it is, and now I will be on my
way."

"You will stay a moment," said the general in a voice
that did not invite disobedience. Howe called to one of
his guards to supply a pocketknife; the silver bullet was
soon opened and its message unfolded.

"What does he mean, telling me not to come north?
Who does he think he is, giving me an order? Not
needed, indeed. We'll see about that."

As long as he was on the horse, Jake's leg only hurt. Pain
was not exactly a stranger to the patriot, and he was as
bothered by it as most of us are annoyed by a mosquito
bite.

The great crowd of traffic he rode into had the advantage of slowing the British, but it also slowed him, and
when Jake and his horse approached the end of Spring
Street, he saw that his way was blocked off by a set of
wagons. Unable to urge the strange horse through, Jake

decided he would do better on foot. He theorized that he would be able to slip into the crowd unnoticed, and thence find a place to hide. But airy theory came to earth with a sharp rip from ankle to knee as soon as he hit the ground—his leg was more damaged than he thought.

Jake's blood ran from his head, and as he stumbled forward through the crowd what little balance he had was lost. He bashed into the side of a small farmer's wagon, ricocheted into two or three people and then landed in the dirt. With a great exertion of will and muscle, he flailed forward, crawling and groping, but got no farther than a sturgeon might if plucked from the nearby river.

He was still crawling when he came head first into a large leather boot. Grasping on the leg to boost himself up, he felt himself lifted by a pair of hands from behind. Too late he realized that the hands were attached to a body clad in red.

Howe stormed back and forth across the deck, his florid face swollen to twice its former size, or so it seemed. The star he wore on his coat as a sign of his rank and duty glowed hot with wrath; at every moment it threatened to launch itself into space.

If it did, and if it could be guided, surely it would seek out Howe's rival general many miles north in Canada. The message van Clynne had carried was so tactlessly worded that Howe's interpretation of it as an insolent order was quite understandable. Under ordinary circumstances, the merest mention of the name "Burgoyne" invited displeasure. Howe, with some justification, felt that Gentleman Johnny had spent much time in Boston lolling at headquarters and claiming credit while he himself was out risking his neck at the head of the troops. There was also a political element to this jealousy. Both men had been parliamentarians, but Burgoyne was generally conceded the flashier figure; Howe, if he had gone into the Commons for anything but to help his military standing, would never have gotten further than a splinter-stuck back bencher.

Years of insults reared up as his temper was released. The masts shook with it; the deck began to wobble. The

Norse god Thor, had he achieved half this effect with his thunderbolts, would have been well proud of himself.

Van Clynne stood calmly through it. He had experienced much worse trying to cut half a crown off the price of a load of beaver pelts.

"I have been planning a Philadelphia campaign," said Howe when he caught enough control of himself to form his thoughts into complete sentences. "I had been planning to seize all of the colonials' capitals and then negotiate in a civilized manner. But this—he aims to make me look the coward. Don't bother coming north to Albany! He's saying that he will beat the rebels single-handedly. The arse."

"Begging your pardon, sir," said van Clynne gently, "and while I agree with your opinion of the general, is it not he who is the coward here?"

"How's that?"

"Well, the note does not say he is attacking Albany. On the contrary, it says nothing to that effect at all."

"And how do you know?"

"You've read it three times to me, Sir William, and I would have to be either a dunce or deaf not to know it by heart now. 'You're not needed; don't bother coming north. Yours, General Burgoyne.'"

"Is it not the most insubordinate piece of piss you've ever heard?"

"It is indeed, but if I may be so bold, that is all it says." Van Clynne paused, firmly in control. How many contracts had he dissected with similar rhetorical skills? How many agreements with the Indians had he navigated? To him, this message, with only ten words including the signature, was a trifle. "The general does not say he is coming south, does not say he intends to attack at all. Most likely, given his reputation, he means to stay in Canada. He will fill his time with delays and ballroom dances. Remember how late in the year he and Carleton attacked last year."

"Carleton is a good man. He is a bulldog as a general."

"Yes, but he has been sacked by Lord Germain and is returning to Britain. Without Carleton as his prod, how far will Burgoyne get this year? Ticonderoga? He will dawdle away his early advantages and then, at the first sign of snow, pull back."

Howe, himself no fan of the continent's winters, began mulling this.

"If he were intending to attack," continued van Clynne, "he would surely have said."

"Not if he were worried that the message would fall into rebel hands."

"Impossible!" declared van Clynne, his voice rising. "He knew I was the messenger. Besides, the patriot lines are like a sieve."

"Patriot?"

"Excuse me, General; I go among them so much on my missions I fall to using their own terms. I meant to say, the dastardly scum cowards."

"And when he doesn't attack, he'll blame his short-comings on me—saying that I was the reason he failed."

"But you have his note," said van Clynne, closing the transaction. "And of course you shall have my testimony."

"Yes, yes. You're a good man, van Cloud."

This was one time the Dutchman was content to have his name misunderstood. He gave the general a salute, stepped back to bow, and turned to leave.

"Stay awhile and we shall talk," said Howe. "I may have a position for you in my civilian cabinet."

"I can't, sir, truly. I'm flattered, but I have pressing business north. I am under Burgoyne's command, after all."

"I had forgotten, given the way you speak of him."

"Well, we have no choice as to who we serve when duty calls," said van Clynne, echoing the argument Howe had earlier made on why he reluctantly took the commission to fight in America.

Howe was just about to say that he might be able to do something about a transfer when he was interrupted by the arrival of a lieutenant of the city guard. The breathless man rushed upon the deck and ran to the general so quickly the marines nearby jumped up in defense.

"A rebel horde has broken into the city!" the man exclaimed. "All of New York is in revolt!"

"Damn. You see the troubles I have," Howe told van Clynne. The general took three long strides to the side of the ship. In that small space, his physical bearing underwent a mighty transition; van Clynne recognized at once how he had come to command the army. His belly—smaller than the Dutchman's, but by any other measure large—tucked up and in, his chest bolted forward, his chin jutted like an advance scout clearing the woods. Ajax had not looked so regal.

"My boat, quickly, and send for two companies of marines," he shouted. "We will land directly in the harbor and rally the defenses."

Howe turned to van Clynne. "You're best off staying here, until we have this matter under control. For your own safety."

"But I—"

"It's an order. The wrong rebel might see you in my company, and endanger your future missions."

It took van Clynne only one look into the huge swells lapping at the hull to convince him there was no sense arguing. He could stay aboard until the riot quieted—and the waves slowed.

Or darkness came on, when he wouldn't see them.

Thirty-three

Wherein, Jake is confronted with the British version of justice.

*J*ake's attempt to punch the British sergeant who was pulling him to his feet was thwarted by another soldier from the rear. Numerous hands were now clamped upon him, and he was thrust back to the ground. A crowd began to gather; if they had been slow to help the redcoats, they made up for it with threats against Jake now. He was blamed for everything from the burning of New York to the introduction of smallpox, and the pitch of the by-standers soon reached such proportions that the soldiers were as much protecting him as preventing his escape. Indeed, escape would now have been difficult, as his legs and arms were clamped in chains.

A succession of officers arrived to take charge of the scene, a lieutenant relieving the sergeant, a captain the lieutenant, a major the captain. They got as far as a colonel before they felt satisfied that there was sufficient authority to take him to the fort.

It was not immediately clear what would become of him there, or at least it was not clear to Jake. He had said nothing the entire time, and they had said nothing to him; he had not been searched, except for weapons. The bullet he had snatched from Herstraw remained at the toe of his boot.

Jake was prepared to trade his life for the surety that the patriot plot remained undiscovered. But he couldn't simply drop the bullet on the street; even if he could get it from his boot unseen, the fact that it was made of silver guaranteed that it would be quickly noticed. The best solution was to drop it into the river. Getting there, however, was a major problem. He couldn't just ask to be taken out for a boat ride.

Or could he?

"Now that you've calmed yourself," declared Jake when his captors paused some distance from the crowd, "I demand to be taken to General Howe."

"You're in no position to demand anything," said the colonel. His eyes were set so deeply in his face that Jake wouldn't have been surprised to learn he labored each night with a vise to drive them farther into his skull. "We caught you in the act of sedition."

"I'm on a mission from General Burgoyne. I demand to see Sir William Howe personally."

"Oh you are, are ya?" The speaker was a bulky sergeant who emerged from the knot of redcoats around him. His dress and in particular his hat immediately set him off as a member of the Scottish Black Watch. "There seems to be a run on such fellows today."

"Explain yourself," directed the colonel.

"I took one of 'em out there myself this noon. A peculiar fat fellow. Dutch. Never saw such a bad case of sea shivers in all my time—fellow fainted before we were off the pier."

"I don't know about any of that," said Jake over the snickers. "Just take me to Howe."

The colonel held a brief conference with the other officers, and it was decided the prisoner should be presented to the general, who could sort this out for himself. He was thus led to a whaleboat for the voyage.

Jake's idea had been to sit by the side of the boat, sneak the bullet out and drop it overboard. He would then be free to deliver a verbal message that echoed the one van Clynne had delivered.

If he ran into anyone who already knew him—or rather, thought they knew him—he would have to explain how he'd come to be in Canada, much less join General Burgoyne's command. But that tale could be easily invented. In the worst case, he could simply leap overboard and sink to the bottom of the river, dragged down by his manacles and leg irons, taking his secrets to a watery grave. This was just the brave sort of thing that spies and secret agents are forever doing to encourage Posterity to write their names large in the history books, inspiring generations of schoolboys and picking up the tourist trade.

Lest you think our hero incurably romantic, note that he was much more inclined toward staying alive and living a quiet old age. But his prospects steadily dimmed as he was tightly bundled for the voyage with thick strips of woolen cloth torn from a blanket, chained to an anchor and placed between four men in the large boat. Hercules himself could not have broken free, no matter how heroic his mood.

Jake had one consolation. Considerable time had transpired since he and van Clynne had parted ways. As he had outlined the plan, van Clynne's mission aboard ship should have lasted no more than five minutes. He interpreted van Clynne's aversion both to water and the English as reinforcing those instructions; the Dutchman was not one to linger in disagreeable circumstances, let alone dangerous ones. The fact that a sergeant ashore reported having transported him earlier in the day added to Jake's ease. He concluded that his compatriot's phase of the mission had gone well—we will avoid the descriptive "swimmingly" as being in dubious taste. In Jake's opinion, van Clynne must be halfway to Albany now.

So consider his surprise when, upon being hauled aboard the *Eagle*, he looked around the deck for a place to dispose of his bullet and found Claus van Clynne instead.

His mind did not concede immediately what his eyes showed it. No, it took an eternity for these organs to agree that the rotund man walking toward him was indeed his erstwhile assistant. There was much blinking in the meantime. There was also much internal cursing.

"Jake, it's about time you got here," said van Clynne, clapping him on the shoulder. "What's with the chains? Was it the only way to get you into the boat? You've got to overcome that fear of water, man; there's nothing to it."

Jake tried through certain small head and eye movements to warn van Clynne away.

"You know the prisoner?" demanded one of the officers.

"Know him? He's my fellow agent."

The guards took great interest in that.

"We have been trying to intercept a traitor named Herstraw," said van Clynne. "We've followed him all the way from Quebec."

"He told us nothing of that," said one of the officers. The soldiers who did not have their guns drawn on Jake trained them on van Clynne.

"Of course not. The Sons of Liberty have disguised themselves as His Majesty's subjects, and lurk everywhere. Did you capture this Herstraw fellow?"

Van Clynne looked directly at Jake. They were now committed on this path, and Jake knew he would doom not only himself and van Clynne but the entire mission by trying to change it.

"He escaped, but I killed one of his men." Jake displayed a look of disgust that would have soured the milk in a cow. "These buffoons crashed in on me just as I caught him. They were so inept, I thought at first they must be rebels themselves."

A general commotion ensued, with the various members of Jake's guard protesting that they had only been doing their duty and why did he run and how did they even know his story was true?

The argument had not progressed very far when Howe returned to the ship. Though relieved by the fact that the rumors of a rebel riot in the city were unfounded, the commander was nonetheless in a foul mood—not only had his day been disrupted, but a quick visit to Mrs. Loring's house had found her not at home.

Jake and van Clynne soon found themselves at the apex of a large semicircle, delivering their story to the general and his audience. Van Clynne, of course, was constitutionally unable to deliver any speech briefly. His entire recitation of his trip from Montreal (where of course he hadn't actually been) to Ticonderoga (another place he had not burdened with his presence) took nearly a half hour, not counting all the diversions and stops along the way. In brief, his story was this:

Burgoyne had charged him with bringing the message to Howe, and after much difficulty, he had. Jake, as loyal an assistant as God ever made, though naturally he might have been even better had he been born Dutch, accompanied him south. En route, a man named Herstraw had tried to get into their good graces by traveling with them. Thanks to a hazily if much explained stratagem, they were able to deduce that he was a rebel agent working to apprehend them. The pair kept their guard up so that he was forced to accompany them all the way until the city. Thereupon they decided to split their forces—Jake would endeavor to lead the man astray, pretending to have the bullet, and van Clynne would go aboard and deliver his message. Back on shore they would unite, break up the Sons of Liberty spy ring, and expose the traitorous snakes, much to the joy of all England.

While van Clynne spoke, Jake tried with various signals to ask if he had shown Howe the ruby-hilted knife. But van Clynne ignored or could not correctly interpret his pantomime, and merely increased the volume at which he expounded his tale.

There were more holes in the story than a fisherman's net. Why, for instance, had van Clynne neglected to mention the plot once he was aboard with the general?

"Well, Sir William, that is an excellent question, and points up my own inferior nature. Frankly, I was overawed by your august personage. As you know, your hospitality so overwhelmed me when I first came aboard that I fully forgot my mission and became engrossed in your learnéd disputation."

"And how did this Herstraw realize that you were a messenger?" demanded the general, not in the least swayed by van Clynne's flattery.

"A good question, Sir William, one that I will defer to my assistant, as he is more familiar with that portion of the case."

"Because, General, Major William Herstraw was enrolled as an officer in your messenger service, and thus gained access to the comings and goings of all messengers."

Jake's excuse was perfect, but he could not have angered Howe more had he accused the general of trying to steal the queen's handkerchief. To a man, the British officers on deck held their breath as their leader's fury simmered.

"The same man was assigned to deliver your last message to Burgoyne," Jake said quickly. "He was clearly a double agent, and saw van Clynne get his assignment."

The general shouted for the staff officer in charge of dispatches. The man came running from another part of the ship; asked if a Major Herstraw worked for him, he responded affirmatively.

"Did you know he was a rebel?" demanded the general.

The officer began a vigorous defense, saying that Herstraw was among the best of his men.

"Why do you think he was able to get through such hostile territory so quickly?" Jake asked.

"What proof do you have?" the staff officer countered.

"If you'll unbind my hands, I can give you the message he intended to trade for the real one. The coward handed over the silver bullet when he saw I had him cornered, and confessed it all before his escape. Apparently the rebels have laid a trap and wish you to attack north."

The guards loosened his binds enough to allow Jake to reach inside his boot and retrieve the bullet.

The two notes from Burgoyne were quickly compared. Obviously, one was a forgery. But which one? The note that van Clynne handed over had purportedly been written by a secretary, with the general merely countersigning. The other was a full, if brief, letter in what seemed to be the general's hand.

"This signature is certainly his," said Howe, examining van Clynne's message. "But this letter you say is a forgery seems to be in the same hand."

"Does it make sense, General, that such a man as Gentleman Johnny would stoop to write an entire letter himself?" asked van Clynne.

"No, it doesn't," said Howe, crumpling the note in his

hand. "Nor does this sound like the braggart, begging for assistance." He threw the letter overboard.

Jake barely kept himself from breaking into a smile. Finally, he thought, his mission was at an end.

Not quite.

"But we have no positive proof of your identity either," said the general. "Take them to prison."

"I have the coin that all messengers carry," said Jake. "Burgoyne gave it to the squire, and he gave it to me in case I was captured."

The captain of the messages inspected the token. It was, of course, authentic, having come from Herstraw himself.

"But he could have taken it from our man as easily as he stole this bullet."

"True," said the general. "It seems to me they're a little too clever, especially this Dutchman—take them away and call my officers to conference."

"The knife," hissed Jake.

The knife?

"Ah yes," remembered van Clynne, producing the weapon from inside his coat.

The soldiers surrounding Howe did not know the significance of the weapon, and jumped to their commander's protection. A short scuffle ensued as van Clynne attempted to peacefully hand over the blade and the soldiers fought not to receive it.

"Bring me the knife," said Howe, who of course did understand its significance. He eyed it—or more accurately, the man who had produced it—suspiciously. "Why did you not show me this before?"

"Well, sir, I, uh, didn't. Considering my orders."

Howe pursed his lips. The agent was quite right not to speak of his mission or his identity. On the other hand, he could not think of a more unlikely member of the Secret Department.

"How did you come by this—and why would someone of your station be asked to deliver a message?"

"I can say nothing, except that I am a Dutch cousin, as it were, on borrowed assignment."

Such was the mystery connected with the branch that

Howe was not sure whether or not van Clynne might actually be telling the truth. He was about to send for the one man who might have some hint—General Bacon—when Bacon's boat pulled up alongside the *Eagle*, unbeckoned.

"Another nest of vipers crushed," said the intelligence chief preemptively as he walked onto the quarterdeck to report to Howe. A flock of subordinate officers traipsed at his heels, careful to keep several paces back. "My men apprehended several Sons of Liberty in German uniforms. Dr. Gibbs—what are you doing here?"

"It's a long story, General, but the short of it is, I have been mistaken as a Whig."

"You know him?" asked Howe.

"We're to have dinner Sunday," said Bacon, "to discuss certain aspects of the voodoo. Your name came up earlier today, Gibbs, in connection with a plot by these rebels. Have you gotten involved with them?"

"A good question," said Howe, pulling the general aside. Bacon's men gathered around him, listening to the discussion. Their backs were between Jake and the two generals, effectively screening them from view.

The nature of the Secret Department meant that only a handful of agents were known to Bacon, and at any given moment there were bound to be a few operating in his theater whom he had no authority over or knowledge of. A man assigned to Carleton or Burgoyne could easily be a stranger to him.

But this Dutchman?

"The doctor, perhaps," said Bacon. "I sense something about him that stands out. On the other hand, we used foreign agents in Spain for the prince's assassination."

The two generals punctuated their debate by stealing glances at the pair of prisoners. Though he couldn't overhear, Jake knew precisely what the problem must be—who would believe van Clynne as a secret agent?

And yet, wasn't that the most powerful argument in his favor?

Howe called one of the ship's officers over to join the conference. In the meantime, Bacon took a knot of men aside and dispatched several back to the city, whether on this or other business, there was no way for Jake to tell.

Once more the debate was rejoined, this time continuing for nearly a quarter of an hour—a comparatively short time for a British command conference, as anyone familiar with Howe's notorious delays attacking New York will realize. Finally, the remaining subordinates parted and the two generals emerged nodding. They directed their attention toward Jake, not van Clynne. Which was fine with all concerned.

"You're a doctor?" Howe asked.

"I'm not admitted in London," said Jake, "but I attended Edinburgh."

"My officers say he has the best headache remedy in the colonies," said Bacon. "But of this profession as a messenger I'm completely unaware."

"It's not a profession, Sir Henry. I met Squire van Clynne while on a trip to obtain rattlesnake venom from the Indians near Canada. We fell in as fellow travelers, and when he needed assistance, I rendered it. I had not realized he was in service of the Crown. I assumed that, since he was Dutch—"

"Careful," said van Clynne, warming to his role. "Remember your oath."

"What oath is that?" said Bacon, his birthmark glowing.

"I have taken an oath not to reveal his oath, which itself is based on a prior oath of my own," said van Clynne. "Kill me for it, if it is your pleasure."

"It may well be a pleasure," said Bacon, turning back to Jake. "You have been north before."

"Many times, Sir Henry. My travels take me far and wide."

"Behind rebel lines."

"I have sworn allegiance to the king, and will do so at any time or place the general prescribes. I have lost my land for it. I am not a traitor, sir. Science requires me to travel. My headache cure, for example." Jake turned to Howe, who had a skeptical look on his face. "Unfortunately, my latest duties detained me from obtaining the ingredients necessary for my potion, General, but I will gladly supply you with a complimentary bottle from my next batch. It would be most beneficial to me, actually, to have your endorsement."

It would be fitting, would it not, if the matter of Jake's identity could be settled by some headache powder? After all, the Americans were the biggest headache Howe and all of Britain could ever have, and the expedient of using a cure for a much smaller one to escape would be but poetic justice. Unfortunately, neither Howe nor Bacon was much on poetry. When they retreated a ways on deck to discuss the matter once again, Jake would not have bet a farthing that Shakespeare entered the discussion.

This new conference was cut short by the arrival of a fresh contingent of guards who ushered a small group of prisoners aboard. The men were chained and in very poor condition, with welts and bruises covering their bodies. Dragged and pushed forward, the poor wretches were too beaten even to groan with pain.

"These are the Sons of Liberty we found in the city," said the lieutenant in charge of the detachment. "Their ring leader is that one."

He pointed to a man in a plain brown coat, just now being led over the side. He had been spared the humiliation of a beating; his clothes were so fresh they appeared new, and while his face had been smudged with grease or dirt, he bore himself with an almost aristocratic manner, if such can be said of a man in chains.

"What have you to say for yourself?" Howe demanded of the prisoner.

"Long live Liberty!"

A sharp cuff on the ears knocked him to the deck near Jake's feet.

Jake wanted to help him, but doing so would only seal his own fate. Instead he took a step back and kicked at him. Jake's legs were still manacled, and he was able to make his miss look more than convincing—he slipped as if he'd forgotten his binds, so that the thing he did completely against his instincts appeared the most natural action of all, a loyal British subject trying to kick away treason's snake.

The soldiers laughed as Jake tumbled backward onto the deck.

"You bastard," said the Liberty man. "I know who you are. You helped launch the plot against us."

"Who is he?" demanded Howe.

"Jake Gibbs," said the prisoner. "As notorious a Tory as any in the countryside."

The Son of Liberty spit on Jake as his guards restrained him. The huge, venomous piece of spittle burned his face.

A look passed between them at that second. Everyone else in the party, even van Clynne, would swear it was hate; Jake recognized it as the solemn torch of Freedom.

"Unchain him," Howe said to the guards around Jake. "Then take these prisoners ashore and hold them on charges of treason."

No apology was offered, and Jake didn't care to make an issue of it. He asked only for a cloth to bind his knee; that done, he tested it and found it reasonably sound. He was mildly surprised to find his pocket pistol and Leal's knife, surrendered during his capture, returned to him.

Van Clynne, meanwhile, was preparing to leave the ship. He practiced keeping his eyes closed as he walked toward the railing.

"Aren't you forgetting something?" Bacon asked.

"Of course," said van Clynne, sweeping down in a graceful gesture. "Thank you for dinner, Your Honor," he said to Howe.

"Your weapon," suggested Bacon.

Jake noted the glimmer in the general's eye, and felt his hope of escape sinking to the bottom of the harbor.

"I was afraid you'd come to relieve me of my duty," said van Clynne so smoothly that even Jake was impressed. The Dutchman put forward his hand bashfully. "I feared you had orders from the king to, er, countermand me, as it were."

"For whom is the knife intended?"

Van Clynne met the question with his usual bluster—which naturally was the proper response. Bacon gave back the knife with a stern warning that he would be watching for the Dutchman—and expected Jake to be prompt for dinner. The pair was soon back on the water, being rowed into New York, the end of their mission in sight.

Thirty-four

Wherein, some general facts and opinions regarding the Sons of Liberty are expressed, and Duty requires a new mission.

When in 1765 England imposed the Stamp Act, laying a tax on virtually every document necessary to American life, from newspapers and journals to deeds and custom manifests, the colonies rose en masse against it. But while many commentators date the activities of the various organizations now known as the Sons of Liberty from that year, it should be noted that the Sons were active by 1745 at the latest in New York. They were an effective and innovative group that prior to the open declaration of hostilities was, contrary to British propaganda, a most moderate influence on the populace.

Many instances serve to prove this argument. There was, for example, the matter of Cadwallader Colden in New York, the lieutenant governor who had armed and reinforced Fort George after the people made their opposition to the stamps known. He intended they would take these ignoble swatches whether they liked them or not, and seemed ready to go about slaughtering anyone who opposed him.

The Sons responded by stuffing an effigy of Colden onto a carriage and parading it to the fort. This was quite a show, with hundreds of seamen as well as local citizens attending. To a man, the British inside feared a horrible slaughter—and not of the citizens opposing them. But the Sons, taking a temperate view, led the crowd to content itself with merely burning the effigy.

They also sacked the mansion of the fort commander, Major James, a disagreeable sort who clearly deserved it.

The stamps were henceforth abandoned, and peace restored without the loss of a single person on either side. Clearly, the Sons have suffered great libels from their oppressors' pens.

Once the redcoats occupied New York, many of the more notorious members of the group had to flee for their lives to the countryside. Those who remained found it necessary to hide their loyalties. This did not end the organization's operations in the city, but did make it very difficult, even for those familiar with the group at its highest levels, to identify exactly who was and who was not a member.

It was for this reason that Jake did not know the man who had saved him, even though he had often had occasion to call on the group for assistance. He had no doubt, however, that the man who saved him had been acting on Culper Junior's orders. As he told van Clynne when they clambered onto the wharf, his gratitude was boundless. The Liberty boy had risked death to save them. It was just this kind of selfless activity that would guarantee the country's future.

"I quite agree," said van Clynne, his legs still wobbly from the journey. "I know of a place just north of King's Bridge where we might purchase some food and drink at a fair price. It is run by an old Dutch friend of mine whose sympathies are quite with the patriots, though he has stayed in the neighborhood due to his health."

"Fine, we'll eat there tonight. First we have to retrieve our horses and my bomb. Then I've got to find a wagon."

"Tonight?"

"We've got to rescue our friend," explained Jake, leading the way back toward the stable where he'd boarded the horses. "They'll be taking him to jail on shore before they hang him. I'll have a plan cobbled together in no time."

The only plan van Clynne wanted to hear was one to escape the city. Directly.

Van Clynne pointed out that Jake was under orders to return to Albany, that there would be great consternation if he failed to meet Schuyler's time limit, etc., etc.

Jake never answered. There was no possibility he could

be swayed. His sense of duty and honor, his obligation and his gratitude, combined in such a way that he would have swum against Gibraltar had the Liberty man's rescue depended on it.

It might be said that the Dutchman admired his companion's resolve and character, realizing that he could call upon them if he were in a similar situation. Nevertheless, it would have been very much against van Clynne's nature to simply shut up. Thus, he was still arguing when Jake finally found the four-wheeled wagon he wanted. That the wagon was accompanied by a driver was not critical, since the narrow lane in front of the storehouse where it was parked was temporarily deserted. Jake snuck up behind the man and knocked him unconscious in a trice.

Wanting to keep his accounts even, the American agent tucked a few of van Clynne's continentals—at three percent interest—into the man's shirt.

"He'll have a tough time explaining those if he's a Tory," said van Clynne.

"Truly a shame," answered Jake, taking up the reins and leading the horse and wagon forward.

They stopped three blocks away at a small but crowded store. Van Clynne stayed with the wagon, grumbling about the difficulty of finding a good parking spot in the overcrowded city.

"Still talking to yourself, Claus?" asked Jake when he returned a few minutes later.

"The city was never like this under the Dutch," van Clynne claimed.

"The traffic will be lighter near the jail," said Jake, taking a jug of pitch he'd just bought and pouring it into the back of the wagon.

"What are you doing?" exclaimed van Clynne as Jake placed a candle in the middle of the sticky black puddle.

"Just get going—make a left at the end of the block and drive north. Hurry."

The British inevitably took the same path from the docks to the jail; Jake had scouted it several times previously. That preliminary work proved handy now; they crossed town in the space of five minutes and found an alleyway along the narrow street two blocks from the prison's portals.

While van Clynne drove, Jake turned the wagon into a mobile fire bomb. His plan was a simple one—van Clynne would light the candle, then drive the burning coach across the roadway, blocking the street. Jake would launch his noise keg from the rear, temporarily paralyzing the British guards.

"And not us?"

"You should be far enough away, if you stay with the wagon."

"While it's on fire?"

"You're afraid of fire as well as water?"

"I'm afraid of dying prematurely."

"Here, stop this candle wax in your ears. The concussion can shatter your eardrums."

"So we'll leave the man we're rescuing deaf?"

"Just temporarily," said Jake, jumping down. "Remember to light the wick back here before you pull into the road. It will take a few seconds to flare up, and I want the flames impressive enough to catch their full attention before I launch my bomb. Don't forget to cut the horse's reins, and when the bomb goes off, grab our men and run up that alleyway. I'll take care of any guards who are still standing."

"Perhaps it would have been better to steal a coach instead of this wagon," said van Clynne. "A man with strong legs could bolt over this, even if it is on fire."

"If he's unconscious, these salts will revive him," said Jake, handing van Clynne a small potion bottle he had purchased at the store. "Be careful with it—under normal circumstances it's used as a rat poison."

"But—"

"Just don't let him drink any," said Jake, untying their horses from the back of the wagon. He secured them to a side post and then quickly worked some wax into their ears as a precaution against injuring them.

"I'll meet you three blocks north by the church," said Jake. "I know a place where we can stay until it's dark. With luck, the commotion will bring a few of our friends forward, so escape won't be difficult."

"Perhaps we should enlist them beforehand," suggested van Clynne. "In my opinion—"

"I can't hear your opinion," said Jake, stopping his ears. "Wait until the first man passes Kiefer's there, then pull out. Put your ear stops in!"

Van Clynne's complaints continued, but Jake was oblivious to them—why hadn't he thought of this simple expedient days ago?

As he trotted down the street to take up his position, he saw shutters were being shut on the street above—the procession of prisoners was nearing.

This was a poor street, and before the British invasion, many of the folk here had supported the Revolution. Trapped by the quick occupation, they had learned to keep to themselves, especially during the almost daily marches to the gaol. By the time the patrol and its five prisoners appeared at the head of the block, there was no one on the street.

Except for Jake, who took up a spot in a doorway about ten yards from the alley where van Clynne was waiting. A few strikes of his flint and he had the small candle in his hand lit; his only other chore now was to wait.

The candle was necessary to light the bomb, whose fuse was too short and quick-burning to let it be set in advance. Jake could not rely on flint to ignite the fuse at the last moment; he needed his hands free. He set the candle down on the ledge of a small window that looked into the doorway; the effect was much like lighting a votive at the altar of the cathedral in Paris.

"Why are you putting a candle on my window, mister?"

Jake turned around and saw a young girl, five or six years old, tugging inquisitively at his leg. He had to take the wax from one of his ears to hear her.

"You don't want to burn down my house, do you, sir?"

The prisoners, with their redcoat guards behind, were dragging themselves forward not twenty yards behind her.

Jake could have ignored the small girl, trusting that Fate would keep her out of harm's way once the small riot he planned began. But there was something in him that could not ignore a child wandering innocently toward danger. He took the wax from both his ears and stopped it in hers, then quickly picked her up in his arms and pushed at the latch on the top of the split door, intending to shut her inside.

The latch would not give way. He had to step back and kick at it, not once but twice, and then finally place all his weight behind the thrust before sending the top flying inward.

"Stay inside, sweetheart," he told her, forgetting she could not hear him. "The patriots are fighting for Liberty today!"

Have you ever heard such overwrought words? "The patriots are fighting for Liberty today!" With a very large exclamation point at that. In the middle of a fight, when his own safety hung in the balance. At any moment he might be discovered. At any moment he might be killed.

"The patriots are fighting for Liberty today!"

Corny? But whose fault is that, if that was the reality? Does not everything noble sound, under some circumstance stripped of its context, overwrought?

Such words build revolutions and legends. They inspire minds and warm hearts in the cold reality of the trenches, keeping blistered feet trudging along the line toward the most distant goals.

"The patriots are fighting for Liberty today!"

Jake jumped back out into the street, right behind the rear guard, just as van Clynne pulled his chariot across the road in all its fiery glory. Jake leaned back and lit the bomb as the troops and their prisoners began shouting in alarm and confusion.

The explosion, loud to begin with, was amplified by the closeness of the buildings to the street. The shock waves were such that the ground trembled and people ten blocks away thought the world surely had come to an end. No glass within a hundred yards remained intact, and two-thirds of the British guard fell over like bugs catching a whiff of Dr. Pete's Miraculous Fly Powder. The rest were dazed, groping for their weapons as well as their senses, and had been rendered suddenly deaf.

As was Jake.

At least he had been expecting the blast. He shook his head a few times and ran forward, pistol in hand. The disposition of the force was not immediately clear in the smoke and dust, and he moved cautiously, still getting his bearings as he hopped over the prostrate bodies of the fallen guards.

Van Clynne, meanwhile, had been thrown from the wagon by the concussion. Spitting out a mouthful of dirt, he rose and grabbed his musket, standing in the center of a silent street.

More than most men, the squire lived in a universe of noises—a good portion of them his own making—and for a brief moment he was as dazed as anyone else on the block. But the heat of the nearby fire quickly brought him back to rights; he unpacked the melting wax from his ears and was once more himself.

There were shouts on the next block over, and someone was calling "Fire!" The smoldering pitch and dry timbers of the wagon combined to produce a flow of dark smoke and flames. The poor horse that drove the wagon had been knocked unconscious, and van Clynne had to step gingerly between its legs as he looked for the prisoner he was to rescue. Before he reached him, he found the four other men lying chained together in a heap on the ground, so close to the burning wagon that they were hot to the touch. Fearing the men would combust, van Clynne tried for a moment to rouse them; when that failed, he reached for the potion bottle.

Bottle, as in glass—it had been shattered by the squire's fall.

Cursing, van Clynne doffed his coat, thinking to wave the sodden corner under the stunned men's noses. But in order to do so, he had to put down his gun—which left him awkwardly unarmed when he looked up again and found a British sergeant measuring his sword against his belly.

Van Clynne smiled and, following his first instinct, tried to talk his way out of the situation.

Whether that would have worked under other circumstances or not, it certainly could not here—the sergeant had been rendered deaf by the blast. Fortunately, he'd also been knocked a little dull. Van Clynne tossed his jacket into the man's face and the sergeant stumbled backward, dropping his sword.

The sharp scent of the rat poison in van Clynne's pocket worked as well as Jake had predicted; after no more than two steps the man had full control of his senses. Fortunately, by then van Clynne had full control of the sword and began tattooing his insignia on the man's chest. He disposed of him with a swipe so hard the sword broke at its hilt.

"Damn inferior British metal," grumbled van Clynne, scooping up his coat and gun as he returned to the prisoners. "How can they claim to rule the world, when they can't even find a decent ore deposit?"

At the other end of the confusion, Jake came upon two soldiers who had survived the blast with some shadow of consciousness. He fired into the chest of one of the redcoats, who was holding his bayonet forward in a stunned, senseless pose. He grabbed the barrel of the gun as the man collapsed to the ground, mortally wounded; then he swung it around for a bayonet duel with another soldier. The sharp knives and metal barrels crashed against each other with heavy clicks and bangs, but both Jake and the soldier were oblivious to the cacophony.

The soldier was shorter than Jake, but he was stocky and strong; the American's quick victory owed more to the lingering effects of the blast than physical superiority.

Two other redcoats were rushing forward in what looked to Jake as an attempt to kill the prisoners where they lay. He ran the first through the back with the bloody bayonet. Caught by surprise, the man jerked to his right so quickly that the musket flew out of Jake's hands. The soldier's own weapon, propelled by his death spasms, caught Jake flat in the chest; it was fortunate indeed that he had been close enough to be struck by the barrel and not the blade, for the blow might well have chopped him in half.

Jake, surprised and with his injured knee hurting again, fell to the dirt on his back. The dying man lunged forward, trying with his last gasp to cut Jake's throat with the knife at the tip of his weapon.

A sudden burst of energy propelled Jake's elbow into the ground and levered him out of the way. The soldier fell into his place, destined never to rise until Gabriel sounds his final trumpet.

With a cringe of pain Jake stumbled to his feet. He found it easier to hop than walk, and took two steps, looking for van Clynne and the Liberty man who had saved his life. The smoke from the fire and dust from the battle combined to turn the roadway almost as black as the night, but there was no mistaking what he saw next— a bright officer's sword, pointed directly at his nose.

Thirty-five

Wherein, our hero finds himself at sword point, and discovers other disagreeable facts relating to his situation.

Jake stepped back gingerly, the pain in his knee momentarily vanquished by the officer's sword. He had his pocket pistol hidden beneath his shirt, but the man gave him no opportunity to grab for it, keeping his blade at Jake's face as he retreated backward. Theirs was a slow, steady procession, a study in precision greatly in contrast to the pandemonium nearby. The officer was grinning, obviously confident that he had the advantage. Possibly he hoped to take Jake alive, for otherwise he should have pressed his advantage with considerably more vigor. He could at least have slashed a few times in front of Jake's face to increase his fear. Instead he moved forward with the steady pace of the grim reaper, intent on his duty and confident he would eventually have his man.

A strategy presented itself to Jake as he felt the wall of the building behind him. A candle tossed in someone's face has the effect of drawing his attention away from everything else. Jake could then whisk his gun out and fire at leisure.

The officer followed him as he edged along the building. He had not yet called on Jake to surrender, and as Jake backed up he realized why. The officer's eyes were crossed in psychotic wrath; the blast had knocked some part of his psyche loose, and he meant to back Jake against the wall and slowly, gradually, run him through the face with his sword. He would make the American an example of what happened to traitors to the Crown.

Jake fully intended to be a model for others, but with a

much different outcome. He reached the window where the candle was, put out his hand—and came up empty.

It wasn't there.

Jake took his eye off the officer for the briefest of moments, a mindless reaction at losing the item he most sought. But inattention at certain moments is nearly always fatal.

So it would have been in this case, had not the officer been hit squarely in the head by a round ball made of lead, approximately three-quarters of an inch in diameter. The bullet left a vast splatter of red and a look of puzzlement on the man's face as he fell to the ground.

"The patriots are winning," said a fair, slim-waisted woman in her mid-twenties standing in the open door with a musket in her arms. The little girl Jake had helped inside earlier peeked from behind her dress.

Jake was still suffering temporary deafness, but there are certain thoughts so profound they can break through any disability. He kissed her cheek gently in gratitude, then grabbed the officer's sword and rushed back to the prisoners and wagon.

Given the circumstances, the kiss was a long delay, and though Jake did not berate himself for it, van Clynne certainly might had he seen it. In the event, however, the Dutchman was much too busy trying to rouse the chained prisoners by rubbing their faces with his antidote-drenched coat. He managed to revive one, but the potion had lost its potency, and he soon realized that his only hope of saving them was to drag them down the street, away from the fire and confusion.

By now the nearby citizens were rallying to the situation. It is true that the crowd was far from unanimous in its support of the patriots, and it will be duly recorded somewhere that a few Royalists ran to aid the soldiers. But van Clynne found his efforts to haul the prisoners to safety assisted by three or four strong lads, one of whom was already yelling the way to a smithy. He let them take charge of the men and turned back to find the fifth Liberty man, the one who had saved their lives aboard ship.

He found him lying on the ground, still dazed. Van Clynne hoisted the man on his back—it was easy enough, if you thought of the man as a pipe of beer—and was just scanning the street for an escape route when Jake came up running.

Hopping, actually, since the pain in his knee was acute. Even so, an escape in the general confusion was child's play. Their horses quickly recovered, they started up the street as everyone's attention was drawn to one of the shops which suddenly erupted in flame. A few loud explosions indicated that perhaps its owner had not been the good Loyalist his neighbors thought.

The smell of burnt gunpowder was still fresh in Jake's nostrils fifteen minutes later, when he and van Clynne paused on their hasty retreat from the city. They had commandeered another wagon—this one free for the taking, its driver apparently giving his full attention to the fire. The rescued Liberty man slept soundly in the back as van Clynne drove its two horses and Jake rode along behind with van Clynne's. Jake's hearing had returned, providing some compensation for his other aches and injuries. The Dutchman was as worn as he, and with night already well on its way, both wanted nothing more than to find some field where they could sleep.

This was not the place to do so, however. They had to get north of the island as quickly as possible, before a thorough search could be mounted for the escapee.

As van Clynne steadfastly refused to go anywhere near the water, the best course was a quick run north across King's Bridge. They would need papers, however, to pass the sentries there. Jake knew a man nearby whom he could call on in need, Edward O'Connor, a farmer well-connected with the patriot network in both the city and Bouwerie. While he was loath to expose anyone else to risk today, Jake decided he must contact the man and see if he could facilitate their escape.

He also hoped the farmer could care for his liberated prisoner. The Liberty man's reaction to the noise keg was extreme, and Jake worried that he had been permanently harmed. The man was still unconscious, and Jake feared his bumpy wagon ride was complicating his injuries.

"O'Connor's farm is just on the other side of this hill,"

Jake told van Clynne. "Pull the wagon behind those trees there and wait while I go and see what sort of reinforcements I can get."

"The only reinforcement I need," said the Dutchman in a grumpy voice, "is a good mug of ale and a feather bed."

"We'll stop at Prisco's tavern," promised Jake. "I'm sure you'll find a warm reception there."

Van Clynne garumphed in reply—but it was a gentle garumph, as his responses went.

O'Connor told Jake that passing out of the city over either of the northern bridges would be extremely dangerous, even with the proper papers, as a general alert had been sounded because of the earlier riot and reports of rebel activity. It would be much easier to escape by boat to the opposite shore and then north through East Chester. In fact, he could send word to his brother and have the boat waiting when they arrived. A second dispatch was made for a doctor, and O'Connor ordered his daughter to prepare a bed in the barn loft while he went back with Jake to fetch his fallen comrade.

"These trees or those?" O'Connor asked as they descended the hill to the road where Jake had left van Clynne.

"These," said Jake, leading the way.

To the wrong trees.

But the wagon was not behind the other clump, either. "You sure it was here?"

"Positive," responded Jake, but after a few minutes of searching he had to admit that he was not sure of anything anymore. He and O'Connor ventured across the field to a spot that presented yet another excellent hiding place, shielded not only from the road but from their approach.

There they found the wagon. And van Clynne, with his hands tied behind his back and his mouth gagged.

O'Connor put his lamp down next to him and undid his knots and gag, but before the Dutchman could say anything, Jake felt a sharp poke in the back.

"We've been waiting for you to return, Mr. Gibbs,"

said the Liberty man. "I almost believed that you had abandoned your friend. Such a sad statement that would have been on rebel morals. Get over there where I can see you."

Jake extended his hands slowly. "What is this?"

"Generals Bacon and Howe felt your story just slightly too convenient, so they launched a plot to catch you out. General Bacon felt that, if in fact you were a spy, you would have a great sense of honor and feel obliged to rescue the man who helped win your freedom. I was dubious, I admit, but the general proved correct. He is an unfailing judge of character."

"Undoubtedly," said Jake.

"I was coming out to the ship with the prisoners when his aides stopped me on the water and told me to prepare the ruse. I'm afraid we had to beat the rebels quite a bit more than usual to make sure they were in no position to give me away."

"Clever," remarked Jake sarcastically.

"I was afraid you might have remembered me from the tavern the other night. Fortunately, your attention was distracted that evening. Or perhaps my American accent put you off. To adopt an accent—she is nothing, eh?" The last phrase was spoken in a tortured English that seemed to spring from a Frenchman.

"You were undoubtedly in the shadows, where all scoundrels belong," Jake answered.

"Call me Captain Lewis," said the man with mock generosity. "General Bacon has accorded you a great honor, Mr. Gibbs. He says that I need not kill you immediately. He hopes to keep his dinner appointment, after all."

"He's taken to cannibalism, has he?"

"You—" Lewis ignored Jake and pointed to O'Connor. "Retie the knots on my fat Dutch friend there. The gag first. The man never shuts up."

"I don't think we'll do that," said Jake. "You've only got one gun, and there are three of us."

"I have two guns," said Lewis, throwing back his coat to reveal a second pistol. "And the sword besides. Really, I don't expect much trouble. A fat Dutchman! To think the generals actually thought he might be a member of the Secret Department! A bad joke, surely."

Jake stepped slowly to the side, lengthening the distance between himself and his compatriots. Even if the others were unarmed, Lewis would have a difficult time preventing them from escaping in the dark. They had only to kick over the lantern to get away.

Jake, on the other hand, would be shot unless he could think of something quickly.

"General Howe seemed persuaded by the authenticity of the Dutchman's message," continued the officer, no more than six feet away. "But it's not the first thing he's been wrong about since he came to America."

"Snuff the light and throw the bomb!" shouted Jake, diving to the ground. "Throw the bomb!"

There was, of course, no bomb, and it was not much of a diversion—just enough to momentarily confuse Lewis as he fired. Jake rolled on his side and then immediately jumped to his feet. With the long day's last shot of adrenaline, he managed to find his opponent's neck with his fist. But his blow was as weak as the flip of a trout's forefin—Lewis's bullet had caught him in the shoulder, sapping his strength.

The British officer reached for his second pistol but could not grab it before Jake hit him again, this time with his good hand. The punch knocked Lewis backward and sent the second pistol to the ground, unfired. He regained his balance and took a sharp swing at Jake, knocking him to the right. He fell on him, and the pair rolled together, scraping and pulling.

Van Clynne and O'Connor hastened to help, the farmer grabbing a thick wooden staff from the side of the road while van Clynne intended to rely on his fists. But the light was too dim and the antagonists too tangled for either man to find a suitable target.

Lewis kicked Jake in the ribs, loosening his grip. Reaching down to his boot, he grabbed a dagger and slashed at the American, determined that no matter what else happened, he would have his man dead.

Jake rolled backward down the slight incline, dodging Lewis as he lunged. He, too, reached for his boot—and came up with the elk-handled knife Leal had given him. Lewis fell upon him and the two blades sang a metallic song of death.

What poet could miss writing such a finale, with the savage's knife extracting revenge against the brutes who killed him? But Fate's rhymes are more complicated than a sonnet's—with one bold swipe, Lewis knocked the weapon from Jake's hand. The British agent wheeled back for a final blow.

A smash from O'Connor's stick provided a temporary respite, knocking Lewis sideways and allowing Jake to scramble to his feet and grab Lewis's fallen knife. Lewis, not seriously hurt, picked up the other blade, and the two men were again handily matched. They circled each other, looking for an opening.

Van Clynne approached the tumult with the caution of a cat sizing up his prey. He waited until Lewis was a mere arm's length away, then leapt forward to grab him around the neck, trusting that Jake would spring forward and provide the coup de grace.

Unfortunately, O'Connor had a similar strategy in mind, attacking from the other side with his stick, which he wielded like a battering ram. Lewis was too accomplished a fighter to be taken by either man, and somersaulted away at the last moment, leaving them to fall against each other. O'Connor's stave hit van Clynne square in the forehead, and the good squire fell senseless to the ground, pinning the farmer beneath him.

While Lewis found his feet, Jake beat a temporary retreat to his horse, grabbing his pistol from the holster.

"If you're such a brave fellow, you won't need a gun," said Lewis behind him. "A gentleman would keep this on an even footing."

Not three minutes before, this same British agent was preparing to plug Jake's vitals with his own bullet. Now he'd suddenly adopted the pose of an honorable gentleman, calling for a fair fight.

"All right," said Jake. He rested the hand of his injured arm in his shirt at his waist and tossed away the pistol.

The instant he did so, a wide smile broke on Lewis's

face, and the pernicious British agent pulled a loaded gun from behind his cloak. His sprawl had taken him across the spot where it lay on the ground.

"Too bad I'm not a gentleman," gushed Lewis, lifting his weapon to fire.

He got it no more than halfway before the two small balls from Jake's beloved Segallas struck him square in the face, putting out both eyes and hastening him to Lucifer's cavernous fires below.

"Too bad indeed," said Jake. "I might have left the pocket pistol in my belt if I thought you were."

Thirty-six

Wherein, our adventure finds its conclusion, though the story is far from over.

$\mathcal{J}$ake freed O'Connor by rolling the unconscious van Clynne off him, but then hastily signaled to the farmer not to revive his friend. The passage across the East River would be considerably easier if the good squire was left in his present dormant state. Besides, the Dutchman had earned a good night's snooze.

Jake found himself somewhat pressed, between his bruises and bandages, to lift the large, snoring squire into the craft he found waiting for him at the river. But he was assisted on this score by several local Sons of Liberty, to whom he was much obliged. He was thankful, also, for their plan of depositing Lewis's body in the ruins of the city house destroyed by an explosion. It was to be discovered amid the charred remains of the other "prisoners"; the generals would hopefully believe that he perished in the unfortunate fire. Other contingencies would be taken to otherwise assure Howe that his messenger and his message had been authentic, including false reports of where Jake and van Clynne had spent the night.

Even if Howe came to doubt the message was real, his famous inclination toward hesitation would at least gain the Continental Army more time to prepare a defense. It was not beyond the realm of possibility to imagine Sir William staying put in New York forever. He was a fine general once he was gotten to the battlefield; he was an excellent man for making plans as well. But the two parts of him did not fit so together; he was forever worrying about preserving his strength, keeping England's manhood alive, and indeed, may have been a bit soft on the rebels besides. All he had said to van Clynne, after all, had been said in earnest.

The reader familiar with the events of our great war so far will realize that nothing remains in stasis forever. But Howe's next action lies beyond the small scope we have set ourselves here.

Jake, too, would inevitably find himself in a new adventure. His profession demanded it, and he contemplated what shape it might take as he and the unconscious van Clynne were rowed across the river, where a pair of fresh horses waited their arrival. The wound in his shoulder had been cleaned and no longer hurt. His knee had been wrapped; though stiff, he could manage a half run. All things considered, the agent was in reasonable shape for the journey back to Schuyler.

The general would undoubtedly brag that he never actually considered abandoning Albany—and would turn and silently thank God that Jake had managed to return before the plans were put into action.

As the boat reached the shore, Jake shook van Clynne to wake him. The Dutchman continued to slumber. Finally, loath to leave him behind but unable to wait any longer, Jake ordered the squire refreshed with a bucket of river water.

"What happened?" demanded van Clynne. "How did we get on the damn ocean again?"

"I grew tired of your snores," said Jake. "Come on, if you're coming. We have many miles to cover tonight. I want to cross to American lines before dawn."

"I'll have you know, sir, that I was not snoring," said van Clynne indignantly as he got out of the boat. "A Dutchman is constitutionally unable to snore. It is an impossibility."

"Just as you're unable to complain."

"Just so, just so."

Van Clynne's snores were to become a source of some annoyance in the days ahead, leading Jake to try several stratagems before finally succeeding in putting an end to them. The remedy he used involved a certain herb much valued by the Indians and found along the way—but perhaps the reader will find it more fully described in the next book.

An Historical Note

I have reviewed the story as told in the old manuscript and find the surrounding history, at least, plausible. The sources on whether and when Howe was ever supposed to come north to assist Burgoyne are mixed, with arguments continuing to this day. Howe seems to have written a letter to Carleton in April of 1777—similar to the message Herstraw is said to deliver—indicating no northern assault was planned.

Despite the distance and the presence of a large number of hostile citizens between the British in Canada and New York City, communication was necessary and carried on by different messengers traveling in disguise, roughly in the manner the original author outlines. The subterfuge of a silver bullet was used not only during the Revolution, but the French and Indian conflict as well. Indeed, one hears so much about silver bullets that one begins to wonder if not all the supplies of that precious metal were used exclusively in their manufacture.

I relied on so many sources in checking the accuracy of this book and the others to follow in the series that it would be impossible to cite them all, or even a fair portion. The same could be said of the people who have helped me along the way. There is literally an army of librarians, reenactors, local historians, and raconteurs who have assisted me at every turn, many not even aware of my detective work. The kindness of these people is almost unfathomable. For instance, I turned up unannounced one night at the Blodgett Memorial Library in

Fishkill, looking for some information to verify the claims made in the chapter where Jake stops there. For the next three hours Toni Houston pulled out books and sources, maps and pamphlets for me, filling me with a wide range of information about things I hadn't even known I wanted to find out. Her response was typical, and I single her out as an example of the thousands of people I came across who are helping keep our country's heritage and spirit alive by sharing it selflessly with others.

I should also thank my agents, Jake Elwell and George Wieser of Wieser & Wieser, and my editor, Pete Wolverton, of St. Martin's, for their help along the way.

One last thing: You quickly find out once you start reading accounts from the Revolutionary days that it's best to take everything with a large grain of salt. It would probably be wise to follow that same spirit here.

—J.D.

THE FIRST FRONTIER SERIES
by Mike Roarke

At the dawn of the 18th century, while the French and English are locked in a battle for the northeast territory, the ancient Indian tribes begin a savage brother-against-brother conflict—forced to take sides in the white man's war—pushed into an era of great heroism and greater loss. In the tradition of *The Last of the Mohicans*, *The First Frontier Series* is a stunningly realistic adventure saga set on America's earliest battleground. Follow Sam Watley and his son Thad in their struggle to survive in a bold new land.

THUNDER IN THE EAST (Book #1)
_____ 95192-2 $4.50 U.S./$5.50 Can.

SILENT DRUMS (Book #2)
_____ 95224-4 $4.99 U.S./$5.99 Can.

SHADOWS ON THE LONGHOUSE (Book #3)
_____ 95322-4 $4.99 U.S./$5.99 Can.

BLOOD RIVER (Book #4)
_____ 95420-4 $4.99 U.S./$5.99 Can.